THE MAGIC TOUCH

Still, something about London got past the icy detachment he'd carefully built up over the years, to strike at the very heart of him. Adam leaned in to steal a kiss, checking the impulse to stare down into that heart-shaped face and those pretty dark-lashed eyes. Her lips, soft and inviting, opened as she gasped in surprise, unable to resist, or rather, not wanting to make the effort. He pressed his advantage, cradling the back of her head in the heart of his hand as he brought her body hard against his.

"No," she said in a half growl, half moan. "No." But she didn't push away, didn't resist, and her response was every bit as hungry as his. She was unstrung, but she wasn't passive. Tangling the fingers of one hand in his hair, she backed him against the wall by the window, sliding the palm of the other over his shoulder and chest, seeking out buttons and popping them through their holes like a ruddy magician. There was no denying that the lady had a magic touch, and his reaction was instantaneous.

<u>BOOK YOUR PLACE ON OUR WEBSITE</u> AND MAKE THE <u>READING CONNECTION!</u>

We've created a customized website just for our very special readers, where you can get the inside scoop on everything that's going on with Zebra, Pinnacle and Kensington books.

When you come online, you'll have the exciting opportunity to:

- View covers of upcoming books
- Read sample chapters
- Learn about our future publishing schedule (listed by publication month *and author*)
- Find out when your favorite authors will be visiting a city near you
- Search for and order backlist books from our online catalog
- Check out author bios and background information
- Send e-mail to your favorite authors
- Meet the Kensington staff online
- Join us in weekly chats with authors, readers and other guests
- Get writing guidelines
- AND MUCH MORE!

**Visit our website at
http://www.kensingtonbooks.com**

SHAKEN
AND
STIRRED

Sue McKay

ZEBRA BOOKS
Kensington Publishing Corp.
http://www.kensingtonbooks.com

ZEBRA BOOKS are published by

Kensington Publishing Corp.
850 Third Avenue
New York, NY 10022

All Kensington titles, imprints and distributed lines are available at special quantity discounts for bulk purchases for sales promotion, premiums, fund-raising, educational or institutional use.

Special book excerpts or customized printings can also be created to fit specific needs. For details, write or phone the office of the Kensington Special Sales Manager: Kensington Publishing Corp., 850 Third Avenue, New York, NY 10022. Attn. Special Sales Department. Phone: 1-800-221-2647.

Zebra and the Z logo Reg. U.S. Pat. & TM Off.

First Printing: February 2004
10 9 8 7 6 5 4 3 2 1

Printed in the United States of America

Chapter One

At precisely 11:47 on the Eve of St. Sylvester, the last day of the old year, the Llewellyn clan's newest spy came in from the cold. All of Vienna was steeped in celebration, and the snow-rimed streets, festive with holiday lights, were as crowded as the lobbies of the upscale hotels. To London Llewellyn, this unplanned stopover in Vienna was a mixed blessing. If not for a weird quirk of fate, she would have been stateside by now, fighting the New Year's Eve traffic on the Beltway instead of begging a night's lodging with her older brother, Benji, in a foreign country on the craziest night of the year.

It had started on the tarmac at Prague International Airport when a crazy with a box cutter, who thought he was the Messiah, had provided the preflight entertainment. During her nine months abroad, London had come to appreciate the laid-back Euro lifestyle. But laid-back, live-and-let-live wasn't her first choice when some headcase high on holy narcissism and methamphetamine was threatening to take down the flight crew, starting with the flight attendants.

London had just finished an assignment and was

headed stateside for a quick debriefing and a long, much-deserved vacation. For twenty minutes, she'd been eyeing the refreshment cart. Queen of the white-knuckle fliers, she was fantasizing about a neat Irish whiskey or three when Jesus rocketed from his seat at the rear of the aircraft, grabbing the flight attendant and threatening to slit her throat if his demands were not met immediately.

London groaned just thinking about it. She'd been living undercover as a military attaché while observing and gathering information, and in all that time she hadn't come close to being made even once until the fiasco on the plane.

Who would have thought that subduing one wack job with her infamous please-God-just-kill-me-now scrotum-twist hold would have merited a celebratory dinner and brass band? And the more modest her protests, the more insistent the Czech Republic officials became. Finally, to prevent growing concerns from turning to outright suspicion, she had surrendered, allowing herself to be properly thanked for her heroism, key to the city and all.

Who knew that the flight attendant would turn out to be the niece of a top-ranking general . . . the same general she'd stolen documents from the previous week?

If the incident on the flight hadn't been bad enough, she'd missed her train on the U-Bahn, Austria's underground subway system, arriving late. She just hoped Benji hadn't decided to paint Vienna red without her. Her shoes were too tight, and her feet were killing her.

London put her bag down at the front desk, sending the bellhop her best touch-it-and-die glare, and groaned at the cramp in the small of her back. She had just enough euros to take the subway back to the airport, and she wasn't tipping some flunky to do something she was perfectly capable of handling herself, even if she did feel like hammered dog shit. "*Herr* Stuyvesant's room, please?"

The desk clerk, a pale-haired, washed-out version of John Cleese, looked her up and down, and London swore she saw his lip curl below his pencil-thin mustache. "The Prince Wilhelm is a respectable establishment, *Fräulein*. We do not allow solicitation." Before entering the lobby, London would have doubted it was possible to speak *Hochdeutsch*, High German, with a pronounced and watery lisp. Somehow, he managed it, sounding like a transvestite with a chronic sinus condition.

London set her jaw. She'd spent half a week's wages on her little black dress and Italian leather pumps, the same pumps that were a half size too small and had cut off all circulation to her toes twenty minutes ago. The dress was a knockoff of a Christian Dior, her hair was damp and straggling from her topknot, and she didn't appreciate this glorified gofer casting slurs on her morality. "Do I look like a prostitute to you?"

His raised brow was answer enough.

London's temper did a slow simmer. "Look, Adolf, it's already been a bear of a day. Save the lip and give me the damned room number. *Herr* Stuyvesant is expecting me."

It wasn't quite a lie. She'd spoken with Benji after the incident in Prague, and she'd hinted that she might delay her return to the States by a day or two. Of course, she hadn't told him that she'd be dropping by, but what were a few surprises between siblings? She was the only baby sister he had, and she had no doubt that he'd be delighted to see her . . . as delighted as one Llewellyn could be when subjected to the company of another.

Not that they weren't a close family.

They were very close.

In fact, maybe they were a little too close—keeping in touch, keeping tabs on one another, continually stoking the fires of their competitiveness. Psychologists called it sibling rivalry, but London and Benji had honed their one-upmanship to an art form.

Benji, older by four years, had been London's idol for as long as she could remember, but she would have died before telling him that. She couldn't recall a time when she hadn't looked up to him. Benji . . . the golden child, the chosen one.

Benji had followed their father, Patrick, into the Agency, just as Patrick had followed his father. "The Company" was a Llewellyn family tradition, and it only seemed natural that London, the only female in a pack of hard-nosed Irish-American males, follow suit and pursue a career with the Agency. She could have gone the way of the DS&T, DI, or DA. But the Directorate of Science and Technology was full of geeks, the Directorate of Intelligence were glorified paper pushers, and she wasn't sneaky or underhanded enough to work in the Directorate of Administration.

Besides, the Directorate of Operations was her best chance for action, adventure, career advancement. The DO was where her grandfather had begun his career, at the beginning of the Cold War, where her father had distinguished himself in Laos, where Benji was making his mark—the only place for a true red-blooded Llewellyn male . . . or female.

Benji had welcomed London into the fold, fresh from training and green as new spring grass, by letting it leak at the Christmas party that London had gone through a sex-change operation during her first year of college. He'd driven it home by repeatedly calling her Lance, then whispering profound-sounding apologies for his slips.

It had taken her three weeks and a photocopy of her birth certificate to convince her coworkers that she wasn't—nor had she ever been—a transsexual, and a few homophobes in the DA still gave her the fish-eye when she was around. The memory didn't soothe the ragged edges of her frayed temper any more than did the knowledge that she'd never quite managed to pay him back for that one. "The room number?" she said pointedly, "Or must I make a scene?"

"Three-thirty-three," he said in carefully enunciated English, turning to an elderly Swiss couple, dismissing London.

"Danke," London said, "asshole."

She got to the elevator as the doors were closing, but managed to jam her carry-on through the opening and, when they opened again, wedged herself between a fat man who reeked of fried onions, and a frizzed blonde with spike heels and a slim black cigar. The blonde eyed the massive run in London's black stockings, then turned her head and blew a stream of blue smoke at the ceiling. The fat man shifted his weight from one small foot to the other, scratching the left cheek of his woolen-clad ass, bumping against London.

London sent him a glare, and he muttered and moved half an inch. "You sure as hell better be staying in tonight, Benji. If you're out with the guys while I'm marching through hell, I am *so* gonna be pissed."

Herr Maximilian Schinze was a Cold War relic with a shattered right kneecap and a pronounced hitch in his stiff-backed stride. Gossip among the hotel staff put the old gentleman as an East Berliner who'd profited mightily in the black market in the days before the borders opened. A few speculated slyly that *Herr* Schinze was funneling a portion of his vast wealth to right-wing politicians with a decided neo-Nazi slant. Coldly polite, rigidly formal, Max had become something of a fixture at the Prince Wilhelm in the two weeks since he'd checked in, marching around the hallways and riding the elevator, nodding to the staff on his way to and from his twice-daily walk past St. Stephan's Cathedral.

In room 350, with the door secured, the curtains drawn, and Max's gray wig and mustache on the dresser, thirty-nine-year-old Adam De Wulf slipped on the short-tailed black jacket worn by the hotel staff, slipping the lock pick into the inside breast pocket, then checking his watch.

Thirteen minutes before midnight.

Max had been the perfect cover, his persona and his background carefully and meticulously constructed down to the minutest detail. The old gent had been more than useful. He'd been so crotchety, so bloody real, that he'd raised more hackles than eyebrows. Disguised as Max, he'd cased the hotel's layout, timed the elevators, observed the staff. He knew precisely the amount of time it took to get from the third floor to the lobby and from the lobby to the roof, and every possible escape route in between. He knew which doors were routinely kept locked and which were left carelessly open, which of the hotel staff indulged a bit too freely in their lunchtime lager and which ones were staunchly sober . . . Every eventuality was planned for, and all he had to do was wait.

Josephine Brille, a thirty-first cousin of the queen and a respected member of the London Orchid Society, occupied a suite at the opposite end of the hallway. Lady Brille had arrived day before yesterday just as his sources had indicated, along with crates and boxes, heat lamps, humidifiers, and an ox named Willhelm, whose dual purpose was to curl Lady Josephine's toes and guard the orchid entrusted to her care by the Society until its presentation.

The transmitter crackled, and Willhelm groaned directly into Adam's ear. Lady Josephine cackled wickedly, "What a wondrous, unique specimen you are. Why, I can hardly wait to see your stamen."

"Poor bloke," Adam murmured. "Got your ruddy hands full with that one. Not only does the old gal like to bend the elbow, the lady's libido's on overdrive."

"Lady Josephine . . ." Willhelm pleaded. "There's no time. They'll be waiting for you."

The lady giggled, rolling her tongue in an exaggerated purr. "My motor's running, my little stud-muffin! I say we let them wait!"

"But the Society—"

"You make me feel quite rejected," Josephine complained. "I thought you fancied me."

"I do," Willhelm assured her. "I do, and we shall have the whole night ahead of us. But first, the presentation."

"Oh, very well. You will escort the Lady down?"

"Most certainly," Willhelm assured her. "At the stroke of midnight, precisely as planned."

Adam unlocked the door and cracked it just enough to see the elevator doors close on an elderly woman swathed from head to foot in royal purple, then checked his watch again. The elevators were ancient, and from the third floor it took two minutes and forty-five seconds to reach the lobby. At two minutes, forty-six seconds, Adam picked up the phone. "Room three-ten, please." He waited as the connection was made, straightening his collar and cuffs. "Mr. Willhelm Helsfinger? Dis is de front desk. I haf some very bad news.

Lady Brille collapsed as she vas coming out of de elevator. Ve called de *Krankenwagen*, but she is asking for you. Can you come right avay, please?"

"Dear God. Yes, yes. I be right down." There was a loud click as Willhelm hung up the phone and dashed to the elevator. The doors were closed, and he slammed his palm against the button several times in his impatience. The doors opened; Willhelm got on; the doors closed. Adam removed the earpiece from his ear and went into the hallway. He grabbed a covered tray off the cart sitting in the hallway and shouldered it. He rapped softly on Lady Brille's door and, when there was no answer, discreetly picked the lock and slipped silently inside.

Lady Brille's suite consisted of two boudoirs, connected to and sharing a sitting room. Willhelm's quarters were impeccably kept, but Lady Josephine's were strewn with discarded clothing, abandoned hangers, lipstick-stained hand towels, and several pairs of fur-trimmed mule slippers in various gaudy brocades. Adam barely spared the mess more than a glance before opting for the sitting room. In an alcove, perched on a spindle-legged table and lit by a spotlight from above, was the beauty that had lured him halfway around the world . . . the Lady of the Night, a fabled black orchid so rare, so extraordinarily lovely, that it took his breath away.

Adam lifted the gold planter, itself worth a small fortune, and felt a strange catch in his throat. "Julia's passion. You're about to come full circle."

In a few seconds, he was in the hallway, headed back to Max's room. By his calculations, Willhelm had found Lady Brille by now and discovered that the report of her collapse had been a ruse. One or the other, perhaps both, would be headed back upstairs at this very moment to assure themselves that all was well—which, of course, it wasn't.

He had just enough time to secure the Lady in Max's false-bottomed luggage and return to his crotchety alter ego before they started screaming theft. Then he had only to hire a car and make a timely departure. Miles Müller, a friend from the old days, was waiting for him in Salzburg with his company jet.

The plan was simple: get the goods and get out—out of Austrian airspace, off the Continent.

And all he needed was a few more seconds.

Lady Brille's suite was 310; Max's, 350, the opposite end of the hallway, conveniently near a window and a fire escape.

Adam's pulse picked up a notch.

Three-thirty . . .

Blimey, he was wired.

He hadn't experienced an adrenaline rush this acute in three years. His senses of sight and hearing, seemed magnified by three. Details leaped out at him that he would have missed otherwise.

The door to 333 was open a crack.

The elevator dinged a floor below; then the soft whir of the lift resumed.

Three-thirty-one . . .

Three-thirty-two . . .

Another melodic *ding* and the doors to the car opened, only it was the elevator in front of, not behind him. Willhelm backed out and started to swing around as the second lift arrived and a fat man in a dingy black worsted suit got off, followed by a shapely young redhead. Adam took the doorknob to 333 in his hand, stepping inside the room and into the middle of a nightmare.

The darkness was backlit by the brilliant flash of fireworks for the space of a second or two, then plunged into blackness again. The roar of a crowd sounded from the streets below. A brief second of startling clarity, a figure frozen in the harsh blue-white glare, a featureless face and staring eyes, black gloved hands, pistol and silencer. Sprawled on the bed was something dark and motionless . . . a long shadow, three-dimensional, a tall man with dark hair.

Adam saw it all with freeze-frame clarity and the same surreal flash-dark-flash of a photographer's strobe. The shooter dropping into a defensive crouch, eyes narrowing behind the cover of the mask as he spun, gripping the gun with both hands and leveling it at Adam's heart.

Every sacrifice Adam had made to be here flashed behind his eyes in that instant: all the planning, the preparations, the risk, the squandered payoff. His breath squeezed from his lungs, the air hissing through his clenched teeth. He could see the shooter's finger tense over the trigger, and the skin at his nape crawled with anticipation.

Separated by the length of a body, they were too close for Adam to exit, too close for him to avoid the bullet. He heard voices in the hallway outside—Lady Brille's and a young woman's . . . an American woman—and wondered what would become of Julia after.

Who would care for her when he was gone?

The doorknob turned, and the door opened, a shaft of light arcing across the royal blue carpet. A halo of red-gold surrounded her spiky topknot for the space of a breath, and then the door closed.

Adam heard the hiss of startled breath escape the shooter, and dropped the Lady of the Night onto the bed at the corpse's feet, lunging for the weapon. The shooter was stocky, a few inches shorter than Adam and with a

shorter reach, but strong, and panic and the will to survive more than made up for the disadvantage of Adam's
greater height. He gripped the bloke's wrist with both
hands as they went around and around, each caught in
the macabre life-or-death dance.

Meanwhile, Red paused just inside the doorway, as if
unsure whether she was coming or going. "Benji?" she
said, her voice soft, suspicious. "Look, bro, it's been a
bitch of a day, and I'm not in the mood for your sadistic
little mind games . . ." She fumbled for and found the
light switch. The light kicked on; the shooter swore,
kicking Adam's right shin, trampling his instep in a desperate attempt to break free.

Red, frozen in shock by the bed, slowly sank to her
knees. "Mother Mary, full of Grace . . . No . . . oh, God,
please, no!"

The young man's assailant squeezed off a shot, the
bullet striking the wall above her head. "Don't just sit
there!" Adam shouted. "Get out of here!"

Her green eyes, smudged beneath with black mascara, wide with disbelief, remained fixed on the corpse.
Another round fired, this time into the ceiling. Plaster
dust rained down on her little black dress.

On the floor above, a woman screamed hysterically, a
shrill wail that went on and on.

Adam kneed his opponent in the groin, then smashed
his fist into the masked chin. The blow stunned the
shooter. He shook his head, his grip loosened, and
Adam hit him again.

He staggered back, recouping enough to shove Adam.
The pistol went flying, landing on the bed beside the
corpse, and as Adam found his feet again, the assailant
made a break for the window, shattering glass and landing on the fire escape, where he rolled and came onto
the balls of his feet, agile as a cat.

There was a click-click-click sound, like low automatic-weapon fire, as he rode the fire escape to the first floor. And then there was quiet, except for the sounds of commotion outside in the hall, and the cheers from the distant crowd.

Adam was still attempting to catch his breath when he turned back to Red and went still.

Those green eyes with their spiky black lashes were huge above the barrel of the silenced 9mm automatic. Between the angel of death and Adam, the Lady of the Night lay on the bed where he'd dropped her.

"Step away from the window." Her voice was ragged, strangely hollow, and he was suddenly certain her duress had everything to do with the dead man on the bed—a dead man to whom she bore more than a passing resemblance. Same dark auburn hair, same green eyes, same smattering of freckles just visible above the weapon—a weapon that gave Adam a good case of the willies.

"Damned if I'm not a bit weary of looking down the barrel of that thing. What say you put it aside and let me get about my business?"

London's shock was wearing off; her mind was registering details.

He was an Australian, his accent faint but unmistakable.

Six feet one, 185 pounds—a little more, a little less.

Dark hair with just a hint of curl, square jaw, and the bluest eyes she'd ever seen. Like the Mediterranean on a cloudless day.

She swallowed hard. "You aren't going anywhere."

The elevator bell rang. Male voices and footsteps were coming closer, muffled by the plush carpeting. He shot a glance at the door, then met her gaze again. "It's easy enough to understand why you've got your feathers ruffled, but I had no part in your friend there being belly-up."

"Pardon my skepticism, but you're here, and Benji's . . ." She couldn't seem to force the word and recoiled from it, focusing all her energies on him. She wasn't stupid, and she wasn't gullible, and her finger itched to squeeze the trigger.

"None of which has a damn thing to do with me." He lowered his head slightly, looking from under his brows—a George Clooney move if ever she saw one. It screamed a devilish, sensual charm that would have had a devastating effect on London if she hadn't been so numb. He spread his hands, keeping them carefully at his side, and took a step closer. "The Lady and I ducked in here to avoid the crowd. Had I known I'd be interrupting a murder, I would have found a nice, cozy broom closet somewhere."

Another step closer.

London's finger tightened over the trigger. "You like to live dangerously," she said. "One more step, and you won't be living at all."

"C'mon, Red. Be a good girl and put down the gun. I didn't come here looking for trouble. I just want the Lady, that's all."

"The lady? What lady?"

His gaze lowered to the ugly-looking specimen lying on the carpet. It had come out of its gilded pot and lay there, a tangle of spider-leg roots and a fluted dark flower. "I've gone to a lot of trouble to find her. A lot of expense. Just let me take her, and we'll both disappear."

"At the very least, you're a witness to the murder of an American citizen and an employee of the United States government," she told him, "and I'm still not convinced you aren't somehow involved. Someone has to

answer for this; someone has to pay for what happened
to Benj—"

He snorted. "Someone has to pay, and you don't give
a damn who it is. All you want is a scapegoat, and anyone with a fucking pulse will do in a pinch, is that
right?"

London shrugged. He might be telling the truth. His
anger seemed real enough. But she wasn't willing to
take the chance and let him go. Like it or not, he was all
she had, and she wasn't about to let him get away. "I'll
let the authorities sort out the details. If you're innocent,
as you claim, you have nothing to worry about."

"I never said I was innocent. I said I had no part in
your fella's murder." His expression changed subtly,
hardening, growing more intense. His blue eyes seemed
to burn with an inner fire, and London could only wonder at the cause. "I'd rather not bother with the *Kripo*, if
it's all the same to you. I like to keep a low profile . . .
It's my MO." A breath of a pause. "The orchid?"

"Not a chance."

"If you intended to kill me, you would have done it by
now." He started to reach for the orchid; London
squeezed off a shot, the bullet spent in the carpeted
floor an inch from his hand.

Like a woodcutter startled by a tigress in the bush, he
froze. Their gazes locked—his clear, blue, magnetic;
London's glassy with emotion. "Don't make me kill
you," she said, her finger unsteady on the trigger.

The doorknob turned.

He glanced at the orchid, his expression heavy with
regret, then made his decision and took a step back, and
another. "Stop, damn you!"

The door burst open; simultaneously, he broke for the
window, diving through the shattered glass and onto the

fire escape. *"Die Waffe, junge Dame! Gesetz hinunter die Waffe!"*

"Er erhält weg!" London snarled. "Quickly! For Christ's sake, he's getting away!"

"Gesetz hinunter die Waffe!" The guard had assumed a shooter's stance, his weapon gripped in both hands, his face a furious red above the sights: he trained on London. *"Die Waffe!"*

All the tension drained from London, leaving her empty, a brittle husk so fragile, she feared that if anyone touched her, she might shatter into a million pieces. Obeying the guard, she opened her hands and let the weapon fall to the carpet. It landed beside the strange-looking orchid. . . .

A brisk night wind whistled through the broken window, the pale striped curtains billowing on the icy blast, then flattening again. The dark rectangle between the panels was empty.

London's thief had made his escape. "I'm an attaché with the United States military," London said, unable to suppress the hollowness in her voice. "I want to speak to someone from the American embassy."

She didn't even wince when they handcuffed her. Odd, she thought. She didn't feel anything at all, besides a keen sense of disappointment that Benji's killer had gotten away.

Chapter Two

"You know, people are starting to talk. You're here before everyone else in the morning; you don't leave till"—he stopped and glanced at his watch—"nine-fifty-three. If you keep this up, you're going to get a reputation for not having a social life."

London glanced up from the stack of files on her desk. "That's because I don't have a social life."

She tried to smile to soften the statement but couldn't summon the emotion, and it felt more like a grimace. The effort didn't help her cause or erase the look of concern on Wyeth Pinchot's boyish face. He came into the cubicle and perched on the edge of her desk, casually thumbing through the stack of paperwork there: every scrap of information she had been able to lay hands on concerning Benji and the operations in Austria, and several odd publications on orchids. "London—"

"I know what you're about to say, so do us both a favor and save it."

"The Agency is looking into Ben's death. We're going to do everything humanly possible to find the person or persons responsible. We have a team in Austria right now, Halman and Shumacher—"

"Halman and Shumacher couldn't find their own grandmothers if they were pointed out to them."

"Halman and Shumacher are two of the best men we have in the field. If anything has been overlooked, they'll find it."

"All right," London said, putting up a hand to stall anything else he might add. "But what about the witness? Are they going to find him, too? Or isn't that on your list of priorities?"

He sighed like a man who was weary of the same tired old argument, but his voice never lost that patient tone that London found so patronizing. "London, we've been over this a thousand times . . ."

It pissed London off. The way he was speaking to her, like a parent to a child crying for some exorbitant toy they couldn't afford, the way they handled the investigation— as if the end result was a foregone conclusion, something she had to accept, like it or not. Yet, if he thought for a moment that she would let it go before she was completely satisfied, then he'd vastly underestimated her capacity for hardheaded tenacity. "And we'll go over it a thousand more. Until you finally hear me. Someone else was in Benji's room when I got there. A man . . ."

He held up his hands to stop her. "Six foot one, one hundred eighty pounds, Australian accent, dark hair, blue eyes, and a strong jaw. I know, I know, and except for the height and weight, you're describing Mel Gibson. Look, I want to help; we all do. Ben was like a brother to me. No one wants to nail the guy that took him out more than I do, but this isn't the way to do it."

"He was more than just a brother to me, Wyeth. He was all the family I had left." She knuckled her cheekbone with a fist, a sharp wave of embarrassment washing over her at how emotional and ragged she sounded, how small and on edge. "God, that sounded so pathetic." Maybe he was right. Maybe she was obsessed, and maybe that obsession wasn't healthy. He wanted her to stop, to drop the crusade she had started forty-five minutes after Benji was buried, and there was only one problem with that. She wasn't sure she *could* stop. Wyeth wasn't living her nightmares. He didn't miss Benji as she missed him, he didn't have to quietly suffer the emptiness in Patrick's eyes, and he didn't see the thief's hard face every night in his dreams.

Wyeth laid a hand on her shoulder. "I know, kiddo. But I'm worried about you. I want you to think about taking a little time off."

London snorted. "Time off? To do what?"

"I don't know; go down to the shore for a week or two. You must have a string bikini tucked away in your closet somewhere."

London shook her head at the absurd turn the conversation had taken. "Wyeth, it's February. The wind off the water's enough to freeze an Eskimo."

"I hear Nassau's nice," he said, "or go visit your mom's sister. I'm sure she'd be glad to see you."

"I love Aunt Helen, but she's exhausting, and Surrey's too far."

"Maybe not. Distance is exactly what you need," he insisted, the sage, foster brother. "Distance, distraction. A chance to catch your breath."

"I breathe just fine, thank you." It was deep in the blackest part of night that she woke, choking with grief, trembling with anticipation, certain he'd been there in the room while she was sleeping, unable to catch her breath. She couldn't seem to get him out of her thoughts.

But Wyeth couldn't know that.

No one could.

She needed her job now, more than ever. She needed access to the spider web of communication, contacts, agents, spies, government officials, foreign and domestic . . . Someone somewhere knew something about the thief, about Benji's murder, and it was only a matter of time until she could ferret it out.

Despite what Wyeth thought.

She was going to find the witness.

He was going to help her. It was as simple as that.

"I'm serious, Meg," Wyeth said. "The deputy director was asking after you. I'm not the only one who's noticed the hours you're keeping."

Meg. He was the only one besides her father and Benji who had ever called her that. A gentle reminder that he was the big-brother figure in her life now that Benji was gone. Why did that rankle?

Because no one could ever take Benji's place. Because it was just unfair, unthinkable, unjust. Because Benj should be here, with his outrageous sense of humor and his overachiever status. He should be here to rub it in when he made some major coup at the DO, to play his infuriatingly ridiculous practical jokes, to buy Patrick the Unsatisfiable the perfect birthday gift, and to provide a much needed buffer between the old man and his difficult youngest child during the holidays.

Because he should have been here, damn it, and he wasn't, and it made her angry and sick inside and wanting to hurt someone the way his loss hurt her. And because there was no one in her life to help ease that pain. No one she could turn to for understanding.

"Subtle, Wyeth. Real subtle." But she got the point: *Be careful, London, or you'll find yourself on a nice, long enforced vacation.* The deputy director of Operations could do it, and all it would take was a word in the right ear.

"You're running yourself into the ground. Look, I know how hard it's been on you, and I wouldn't say this if I didn't feel I had to, but maybe you should see someone."

"You want me to see the Agency shrink?"

"All I'm saying is that talking it over with someone might make you feel better."

"Talking it over isn't going to bring Benji back, Wyeth. And the only thing that will help me feel better is if I can find the scumbag responsible for taking him away."

He let go of her, jamming his fists into the pockets of his trousers and hunching his shoulders against the loss they shared.

She'd lost a brother; Wyeth had lost a friend and colleague.

London felt the sting of guilt. "I'm sorry. I didn't mean to take it out on you. Just don't ask me to see Dr. Dread. If she gets her hands on a Llewellyn, she'll want to do a case study on genetic neurosis in Irish-American families."

He smiled, and the tension shattered, but an underlying sadness lay like a thin pall of acrid smoke between them. "Okay, okay! You win—for now. But I want you to think seriously about that vacation. You could stand to have a little fun, and it would relieve my mind to know you were baking on a beach somewhere instead of burning the midnight oil in a windowless cubicle."

"I'll think about it."

The promise was halfhearted but enough to satisfy him, at least for the moment. He got to his feet. "I'm going to hold you to it. Don't make me talk to Patrick about you."

SHAKEN AND STIRRED 25

"Like he'd give a flying—" London said. "Sorry. You didn't need to hear that."

He cocked a hip, bracing a palm against the door frame, a good-looking guy in his mid-thirties. Blond hair, complexion that ran toward ruddy good health, the kind of guy who turned women's heads—and might have turned London's if he hadn't been Benji's best friend and a royal pain in her ass all through her adolescence. "You're too hard on him. You're also too damn much alike. It's the reason you can't get along. C'mon. It's late. Let me drive you home."

"My car's in the parking garage, so I'll pass. But thanks, anyway." She put up a hand to still his objection. "I'll be out of here in a few minutes."

"Promise?"

"Promise." He gave her a last searching look, then went out. London let out the breath she'd been holding, and stacked the files she'd been going over, stowing them in her briefcase. Wyeth worked directly under the deputy director of Operations as part of HUMINT, Human Source Intelligence, and could question her actions here at the center, but he couldn't tell her what to do in her time off.

Her apartment was on the outskirts of Almira, a town of about five thousand, located about twenty minutes from D.C. She made the drive on automatic pilot. Wyeth was right about one thing: She was walking the edge. There were times when she felt as fragile as spun glass, when the wrong word, the wrong look, would shatter her and send her spiraling out of control. It was something she didn't like to look at too closely. She hated the idea that she was anything less than hellishly competent.

Weakness was the enemy.

Vulnerability wasn't an option.

Llewellyns didn't have backbone. They had steel, at least according to Patrick.

Funny, but driving alone through the bleak winter night, the headlights of her 1980 Porsche reflecting in greasy pools on the wet pavement, she had no sense of that steeliness, no inner strength to fall back on . . . just a truckload of stress, a shitload of frustration.

The duplex was dark when she arrived. She'd forgotten to leave the light on, and some teenage punk had shot out the street light a week ago. Juggling briefcase, Chinese takeout, and keys, she found her way onto the porch and fumbled with the lock. Colonel Sanders, her short-tailed tabby, wasn't immediately underfoot, cause enough for suspicion without the weird sensation that she wasn't alone in the apartment.

The skin on the back of her neck crawled, a creeping sensation that came with the awareness that someone was there, possibly waiting to strike—someone whose eyes would have adjusted to the darkness and who could see her perfectly well, watch her every movement while she saw only shadows.

Sucking in a bracing breath, London reached for the light switch, fully prepared to drop her late dinner and come up swinging.

"What kind of self-respecting spook keeps a key under the mat?" Her father's voice came out of the shadows, as dryly critical as ever.

"The kind who locks herself out on occasion. It's a good neighborhood, and thanks to the cop who lives next door, I haven't had to worry about break-ins . . . until now, that is. Dad, what are you doing here in the dark?"

London hit the switch, and Patrick Braeden Llewellyn blinked. She put down her packages. Colonel Sanders was sprawled on the back of the sofa, his hind paws draped over the cushions, his tail switching angrily. The cat hated Patrick. "Some watch cat you are," London said, scratching the tabby's broad head.

Patrick snorted. "The least you could do is get yourself a good watchdog. A woman alone? Anything could happen."

"I like living alone. I like my independence. Besides, I can take care of myself," London said, hating herself for rising to the bait, for feeling the need to justify and defend her own actions, her lifestyle choices.

"Like Ben took care of himself?"

London sighed wearily. "God, please don't drag Benj into this."

"It was carelessness that cost Ben his life, Meg. There's a hard lesson in that, if you're not too damned arrogant to see it. To admit—"

"Admit what?" She'd been christened London Margaret by an English mother whose marriage was on the rocks, and who had thought it a fitting revenge on Patrick, a third-generation Irish-American whose first loyalty had been to The Company as opposed to wife and children. Ella had admitted years later that when Patrick had returned home from an overseas assignment and was confronted by a daughter named London, he'd looked as if she'd just cut off his testicles with a carving knife.

The joke, however, had been on London. Patrick called her Margaret, Maggie, and Meg, but she had never heard him speak her given name, not once in twenty-eight years. "Admit what, Dad? That Benji died because he didn't live up to the Llewellyn family standard? Or that I failed him, and that's why he's gone? That maybe if I'd been there just a few minutes sooner—"

"I never said that," he barked back at her, then took

the silver flask from his pocket, twisted off the lid, and
drank.

He didn't have to say it.

He didn't need to speak the words.

She thought them constantly.

If she hadn't busted the wannabe Messiah's balls on
the plane, if she hadn't been detained in Prague, if she'd
gotten to the hotel five minutes earlier . . . if she'd
avoided arguing with the desk clerk, maybe she could
have prevented it, maybe she could have saved Benji,
maybe . . . maybe . . . if, if, *if* . . .

Like the slow drip of a Chinese water torture, the
doubts, London's fears of inadequacy, her pain of loss
and overwhelming regret wore away at her confidence,
eroded her spirit, threatened to consume her. "Is that
what you were doing sitting here in the dark? Drinking?"

The question was purely rhetorical. She knew the
truth of it without asking. He'd felt the odd urge to con-
nect with his offspring, but Benji was gone. She was all
he had left, and he coped with his disappointment by
anesthetizing himself with whiskey.

For a second, she held her breath, hoping that just
once in her life he would forget that he was such a hard-
ass and soften. *I came to see my daughter. Because I
love you, and I need for you to know that. We'll get
through this, Meg, you and me, together*. It was a nice
fantasy, but it didn't happen. Patrick had never known
softness. He didn't know how to give it, he wouldn't accept it, and she was a fool to expect it from him.

"Wyeth called."

"Jesus, not now."

"Watch your language, Margaret. No daughter of
mine—"

"You know what? It's my fucking house, and if I want

to curse at the top of my lungs, that's what I'll do." She forced herself to stop, immediately filled with regret over the outburst, not exactly sure how to mend what was broken between them. They pushed each other's buttons. They always had. "Look, it's late, I'm worn out, and I have work to do. Could we please postpone this argument? I just want to get this General Taos in my stomach before the sauce congeals and it's rendered inedible. You're welcome to join me, if you want, but I won't discuss my job, or Benji, or that prick Wyeth Pinchot, who I intend to kill first thing tomorrow morning."

"Don't joke about it," Patrick said. "It's disrespectful. Wyeth is like part of the family. Have you ever considered that maybe he knows what's best for you?"

"And I don't?" She really didn't want to play this game, but it was so ingrained into their relationship that she couldn't seem to help it. Twenty-eight years old, and the moment Patrick opened his mouth, she instantly reverted to a rebellious troubled teen.

"Wyeth has a good head on his shoulders, and you would be wise to listen to him."

Damned bulldog persistence. It pushed London closer to the edge on which she'd been balancing for weeks, then shoved her completely over into total rashness. "Wyeth Pinchot would be wise to keep his big mouth shut and his nose out of my business! He may get off on the big-brother act, but it's the last goddamned thing I need right now! In case the two of you have forgotten, I had a big brother, and he's gone! Nobody, no matter how sane, smart, or rational, is going to take his place!"

She may as well have slapped him. The force of that accusation hit him square in the heart and pushed him back a step. "And I had a son," he said quietly, coldly. "But it appears now that I have nothing."

"Yeah?" London said, choking the word past the tight constriction of her throat. "Well, I guess that makes two of us. Good night, Dad."

She stood in the middle of the living room as he took up his hat and trench coat and went back into the night. Only when she was certain he was truly gone did she turn the dead bolt, then lean against the door, eyes closed as she gathered her strength.

At least now they both knew where they stood.

From bad to worse was a concept London understood. It wasn't in her nature to be a pessimist, but she'd observed that life tended to repeat cycles of troughs and waves. Her mother had decided to put the final blow to a miserable marriage when London was twelve, and though being forced to choose between the father she idolized and the mother she loved had been torment, it had only been the downward slope. The deepest part of the trough had come when her mother had been diagnosed with a brain stem malignancy.

The fast-moving cancer had rendered the separation moot, but burying her mother two months later had been the real black moment, as far as London was concerned. She'd never stopped missing Ella, even though months and years later life had started its inevitable upswing again. High school, graduation from Georgetown U with an advanced degree in criminology, and her acceptance into the Agency had been the high points.

There had been a few semiserious relationships along the way, Benji to keep her on her toes and to keep life interesting, and a job she loved.

Then, in a hotel room in Austria, she'd topped the crest of the wave and begun her swift downward plunge. Everything since had been a major downer.

When she arrived at the center the morning after Patrick's ill-fated visit, with a massive migraine beating in time with the rhythm of her heart, and eyes so blood-shot from lack of sleep that she had to wear her Ray-Bans indoors, she immediately sensed the bottom of the trough, and knew she wasn't going to like it.

John Yannick from Administration said good morning to her.

Yannick, who couldn't spare her a glance most days, who looked down on the DO's case officers as hot dogs, cowboys, and worse. And a case officer who also happened to be a woman . . . well, that was definitely a double whammy as far as Mr. Tight-assed Conservative was concerned.

London stared after him, eyes narrowed behind her shades. Yannick tried to do the young-man-with-cool-spiky-hair thing, but he didn't have enough hair to pull it off, and he came off as a balding guy with a bad case of bed-head. "Where's Vidal Sassoon when you need him?" London muttered, turning the corner, past the glass cages, heading to the cubicle she shared with Fred Johnson.

Johnson was the perfect incarnation of Everyman, except for the fact that he looked nothing like Harrison Ford. He had a small brick ranch in the burbs with a backyard barbecue, and a wife who chaired the local auxiliary. His kids were in college, and *normal* happened to be Johnson's middle name.

Johnson was out of the cubicle when London walked in. She'd just dumped her briefcase on the floor beside the desk and put down her Starbucks cup when Cidney Blankenship stopped by the desk. Cid was a platinum blond ex-marine, a body-builder in her spare time, and she had a keen sense of style. "Ooo, hey! Love the boots," she said. "Where'd you get 'em?"

"Target," London muttered into her coffee. It was a morning for muttering. Anything requiring more oomph and her head would explode.

Cid chewed on a hangnail. She was a compulsive biter and had little more than a slim half-moon beyond the cuticle. "Target. Cute name. I like paramilitary. Is that a Metro boutique?"

"It's a chain that caters to the fatally frugal."

Cid blinked.

London sighed, giving in. "You know, discount?"

"Oh." With a slow dawning comprehension came more confusion; then she waved it off. "Hey, before I forget, the DDO wants to see you in his office ASAP. Only ASAP in this case doesn't really mean ASAP. He's in a meeting till ten, so take your time."

"Thanks, Cid. I needed that." After her conversation with Wyeth last night, and her confrontation with the old man afterward, she had a very bad feeling about what was coming, and even a double espresso was not going to be sufficient to sustain her.

Twenty minutes later, she waited impatiently in the DDO's outer office. The deputy director's assistant/secretary shot her a curious glance now and then as London absently scanned the DDO's memento wall's collection of photographs. The DDO in a former life as a lawyer, then a judge. Black-and-whites of him with various dignitaries, of his wife, children, and two half-grown Brittany spaniels. While the family was smiling for the camera, the one dog had buried his nose in the other dog's ass. There were plaques and a miniature version of the Agency seal. "Be sure and have a look at the blowup on the far wall," the assistant advised. "It's a particularly good shot of the former president and first lady."

London moved to the enlargement. It was a shot of a reception in the Rose Garden at the White House, and the guest list had been stellar: Henry Kissinger, and Barbara Walters, Tony Blair and a few notables in the entertainment industry, among a crowd of dignitaries and political movers and shakers . . . But it was a shady figure standing just behind the DDO's right shoulder that caught and riveted London's attention—a tall, well-built man dressed in a dark blue suit. A man with a painfully familiar face . . . a face she saw regularly in her nightmares.

There was no mistaking him.

The square, sculpted jaw, prominent cheekbones hollowed slightly beneath, dark, curly hair. His expression was hard and impassive as he leaned forward to catch something the DDO said.

London's heart fluttered crazily and then began to race. His deep-blue eyes were hidden behind the stereotypical expensive shades favored by government types, but the dark glasses didn't conceal his identity, and she would have known that face anywhere. "Oh, my God. It's you."

The assistant glanced up. "I beg your pardon? Did you say something?"

"Yes, actually. The photograph," London asked. "Are you familiar with it?"

"Somewhat, yes."

"The man the director is talking to. His face is familiar, but I can't quite put a name to it."

"I can't help you there, but he would have been one of ours. Only staff flanks the DO and the DDO. Civilians wouldn't have the chance to get that close."

"Of course," London replied. "I knew that." And she had confirmed it. "Could you tell me when this was taken?"

"Ninety-nine, I believe. Yes . . . October."

"Three years." London took a long look at the thief's

face and then put fingertips to her temple. "Could you give the DDO my profound apologies? I'm afraid that I'm not feeling too well, and I think I should go."

The assistant sputtered at the idea of anyone running out on an appointment with her superior, but London ignored her, closing the door, leaning against it.

She'd have to rethink being furious at Wyeth for butting in where he didn't precisely belong. By having her called in here, he'd just done her the favor of a lifetime.

Back in her borrowed cubicle, London gripped a pencil till it snapped, staring at nothing, seeing that handsome face behind the expensive shades.

He was a spook.

A fellow spook, she amended. And as such, he might be quite difficult to deal with. The type that usually signed on for the clandestine service were adventurous.

Thrill-seekers.

Guys who loved living on the edge. And all were secretive—some to the point of near-paranoia. Just locating him might well prove a challenge, but it was one she was eager to face, determined to live up to. "No way are you gonna slip past me," London murmured. She picked up the phone and dialed Cid's extension.

"Personnel, Blankenship. How may I help you?"

"Cid, it's London. I need to confer with you on something. Are you free for lunch?"

Cid had been with the Agency for five years, at Langley for two, and she knew her way around. The boy-cut platinum do and stylish clothing were deceptive, as was the fact that subtlety went whizzing right over her head.

As far as London was concerned, there was smart, and then there was *smart*. EQ and IQ were two very different things.

Cid's IQ ranged in the high 160s, topped off by a photographic memory. It was that talent for memorizing details that London was interested in, and she didn't give a damn that Cid became completely stymied by a stubborn knot in her shoestrings.

At lunch Cid had a salad with no dressing and a sirloin that had barely kissed the grill. London opted for a burger and fries, then didn't touch them. She couldn't seem to summon any appetite. "God, how can you eat that stuff?"

Cid cut into the steak, and red juices ran. "Protein is a bodybuilder's best friend. It builds muscle."

London wrinkled her nose. "I have all the muscle I need in my .38, thank you, and I find it a little unnerving when my meal moos at me."

"So what did you need?" Cid asked. "You mentioned personnel records. That's my area of expertise."

"I'm looking for someone."

"A specific someone? Or someone in a general sense?"

She gave Cid the physical rundown. "He's got to be with the DDO, or was. That much testosterone, it isn't likely to be anything else. Besides, he's got that air about him. An edge. Everything about him screams hard-ass male, only with a latent larcenous streak."

Cid got a dreamy look in her blue eyes and practically purred. "I dated a klepto once. Birthdays and Christmas were really interesting. How about it, Lon, hon? If we find him, will you introduce me?"

"Run the records for the last four years for me, will you? And see if anything comes up?"

"Will do. So, like when do you need this stuff?"

"Does yesterday sound good to you?"

Chapter Three

For two days and nights, London followed the paper trail on Adam De Wulf, employing every resource at her disposal, calling in favors—and it hadn't gotten her very far. She knew that De Wulf was an American citizen, despite the fact that he'd been raised in Perth, by virtue of having been born on U.S. soil to an American mother and an Aussie father. She knew that he'd returned to the states at the age of fifteen, after the deaths of his parents in a plane crash. He had an uncle, Jeremy Roberts, living in Cincinnati with two rottweilers, and a frazzled cat named Fluffy. Jeremy had an ex-wife who hated his guts and, by association, hated Adam. London knew that De Wulf had attended Ohio State U and earned a bachelor's in communications, which led him straight to the NSA . . . but eavesdropping had been too tame to satisfy him, and within two years he'd been accepted into the CIA.

His qualifications were impressive. He had a knack for mimicry and was multilingual, including but not limited to Yiddish, Turkish, Arabic, and Spanish. A wizard with a lock pick and computer codes, De Wulf understood the ins and outs of the technical side of the intelligence business. He could install surveillance equipment or make minor repairs, but it was his chameleonlike ability to alter his appearance that had made him so valuable. Described by one colleague as "a master of disguise" in a tone that brimmed with barely concealed envy, De Wulf had worked on assignment in Istanbul, Israel, Cairo, and Guatemala, and during his fourteen years with the agency, he'd achieved near-legendary status.

London scrawled the word *legend* on the pad in front of her, then editorialized beside it, *big hairy deal*. Hugging the phone to her left ear, she sighed, listening to Cid drone on. "Is that all you have for me?" she asked when Cid paused. "So the guy's a legend. So he's accomplished. He's also a second-story man, and I still haven't a clue how to find him."

"Look, we're talking major spook here," Cid said. "Chris Watkins described him as a loner, which is saying something, coming from him. Chris doesn't own a friend and couldn't buy one. So, *loner* in this case means *secretive*. You may be setting yourself up for a major disappointment."

"Don't even try to discourage me," London snapped.

"Hey, don't take my head off. All I'm saying is that I know his type, and he'll be impossible to locate if he doesn't want to be found." A moment's pause. "Look, Lon. What d'ya say we knock off early and hit Club Wild One? The sushi's great, and it just so happens it's karaoke night. The distraction'll be good for you. Besides, you know what they say: All work and no play means no sex and too long a life span."

"Mmm. I hear you." Perfectly noncommittal. She wasn't about to admit to anyone that she hadn't been laid since Christmas before last. The guys she'd met in the past eighteen months had either been Agency and mostly married, or so boring that she couldn't summon the enthusiasm for a second date, let alone a sexual encounter of the very intimate kind. Cid just didn't seem that picky. Wyeth stopped in the doorway at that moment. "Listen, can I get back to you on that? Something's come up."

"Karaoke . . . think about it."

London put the receiver back in its cradle. She still wasn't happy with Wyeth. His well-intentioned interference had earned her a major ass-chewing by the deputy director, albeit in fatherly tones, and if that weren't bad enough, he'd discussed her with Patrick. She was still smarting from that one and not ready to forgive him. The look on his face, however, was enough to rechannel her thoughts and allow her to put past grievances aside, at least for the moment. "This is about Benji's case, isn't it? They found something."

Wyeth laid a hand on Fred Johnson's shoulder. London had shared a cubicle with Johnson since her return from Vienna. "Get some coffee or something."

"No, thanks, Pinchot, I'm fine. Besides, I'm in the middle of something here."

Wyeth shook his head at the older man's propensity for denseness. "Then take a walk, will you? I need a word with London, alone."

London waited with ill-disguised impatience as Johnson got up and walked out. "Cut the cloak-and-dagger, and just spill it."

"It's not good, Meg." Then, at her pointed glare, he caved. "I don't know how to tell you this, but some evidence has surfaced."

"Evidence? Evidence as to who the bastard was that murdered my brother?"

"Not exactly—"

"Damn it, Wyeth!"

"I can't explain it, but it looks like Ben may have been involved in something illegal."

"Illegal? Benj? You've got to be kidding! Oh, my God. You're not kidding." She got up and moved down the aisle to the door, closing it, turning back to face him. "What exactly are you talking about here, Wyeth? Unpaid parking tickets? Benji wasn't known as Mr. Strait-laced for nothing."

"It's a lot more serious than that. We're talking espionage."

London snorted. "Well, duh." Wyeth just looked at her, his expression grim. "Oh, Jesus. You're serious . . . and you're insane. Benji would never switch sides. Not in a million years."

"Do you think I want to believe it?"

"I don't know what you want." London took two furious steps toward the desk and stopped herself. Her temper, worn thin by weeks of sleep deprivation and stress, was fraying like a rope come undone, strand by strand, bit by bit. She wouldn't accept what he was insinuating: that Benji, the brother she had worshiped, competed with, loved for the good man he'd been, had betrayed the Llewellyn family code by betraying his country, selling it out. "No." Her voice sounded hard and flat, but there was an edge of steel in it, a warning for Wyeth to back off.

"Meg—"

"No!"

"We found evidence: documents, passports, substantiated eyewitness accounts, and large bank deposits over the past nine months. It looks like he'd been working with a right-wing faction while he was stationed in Vienna. They've been gaining ground; there's a lot of anti-American sentiment over there, and word is that they were buying classified documents from one of our case officers."

"But not Benji," she insisted. "Benji blew his bank balance on an SUV last year. He made a nice down payment, but he wasn't exactly rolling in it, either."

"There were four deposits in the amount of twenty-five thousand dollars each, made in two-month intervals. You and I both know what officers make. When you put it all together, it's damning, Meg. Even you can't deny that. Look, you know how I felt about Ben. He was more than a friend. He was family, and I'd rather take this on myself than to lay it on him—or you. The findings aren't official yet—maybe something will come to light to disprove the accusations—"

"If the findings aren't official, then why are you telling me this?"

"Because I don't want you—or Patrick—to hear it from some fucking bureaucrat. I owe Ben that much."

This couldn't be happening. Not Benji. It wasn't possible. *Anyone but Benj.* He was wrong about it, and he of all people should realize how fucking wrong he was. Sick and desperate, holding on to her control with a grip that was rapidly slipping, she wished he'd take her cue and leave.

Wyeth continued to push. "Someone has to tell Patrick, Meg."

"You leave Dad out of this."

"He has a right to know. If you like, I could—"

"Will you butt the hell out! This is my family, not yours." The reminder stung, and his pain showed in the tightening of his mouth. His parents had died when he was eleven. Raised by an elderly aunt, with no siblings of his own, he'd been deliriously happy to be considered "part of the Llewellyn clan" because of his friendship with Benj. In fact, he'd reveled in it. London stared at him, her eyes empty and her chest so full of pain that she couldn't summon the strength to apologize. It took every ounce of will she had just to keep from losing it completely.

"I was trying to help, that's all."

"I know," London said, "but it's not your place to tell Patrick. I'll handle it."

His fists clenched at his sides. "You know, I used to envy Ben. He had it all: good grades, first-rate education . . . an old man who genuinely cared about him. And you." He laughed, but there was little humor in it, and the effort fell like so many pebbles tossed into the air and landing in deep snow. "Pathetic, I know, but even with all of this . . . I still do."

"I'm warning, you, Wyeth. You stay away from Patrick."

The muscles around Wyeth's mouth quivered and flexed, as if he wanted to add something and struggled to hold back. A pleading glance, and he left the cubicle. A second passed, and another, and London cleared the surface of her borrowed desk with a furious sweep of her arm. Papers, pens, paper clips flew, scattering over the floor. Her half-finished cup of coffee left a milky puddle by Johnson's chair leg. Footfalls approached, then abruptly halted.

London glanced up through a curtain of red hair. Her high-slung ponytail had come undone, and as always, the straight, shoulder-length do fell forward into her face. "What are you looking at?"

"Nothing. Nothing at all." Johnson hesitated in the hallway for a half beat. "If anyone wants me, I'll be at the water cooler. I'm beginning to feel at home down there." Turning, he marched off, his number twelves slapping solemnly against the highly polished linoleum. London sank into her chair and buried her face in her hands. As quickly as it had risen, her fury evaporated, leaving nothing but cold gray ash.

London left the center at 4:45 that afternoon. It was the first time since her return from Austria that she hadn't stayed late, and her walk to the parking garage was like an out-of-body experience. Colleagues who usually couldn't manage a nod went out of their way to speak to her, and those who were normally cordial were having trouble making eye contact. Still stinging from her meeting with Wyeth, London assumed the worst and wondered if the rumor mill had already seized upon the investigation's suspicions that one of their own had rolled over for an enemy state.

Cid's Humvee was parked next to the Porsche. "You headed straight home?"

London didn't bother to answer.

"If you change your mind about karaoke, give me a call."

London climbed into the Porsche and sat for a moment in the cold, watching her breath plume in the frigid air. Her dad always said that Virginia had a special kind of cold. There was something about the wind coming off big water that cut to the bones. Normally, London would have agreed with Patrick's assessment. Tonight, she didn't feel anything but a crushing sense of dread for what she was about to do.

She found him in Quincy's Bar on Grant Street, a dimly lit place with a thriving roach population and bad lighting. Another man sat drinking at the other end of the bar. Now and then, he glanced Patrick's way, and there was something in his shaded, closed expression that signaled he was "government"—code word for CIA. Patrick had a draft in front of him, and a cigar between his fingers that streamed a thin trail of smoke to the ceiling. There was an old episode of *Get Smart* on the television. Patrick glared at Agent Ninety-nine. "And this is supposed to be funny? What's funny about a shoe phone?"

"Stupid shit," the guy at the other end of the bar muttered into his beer. "I once knew a Czech agent who concealed a lock pick in the foreskin of his pecker. 'Course, he had a dick like a goddamned donkey. Shoe phones? Shit! That's nothin'."

"Hey, jackass, watch your mouth down there. There's a lady present."

The offender looked glum. "Yeah, yeah. Sorry."

"Dad, for Christ's sake. I know what a dick is. It's no big deal." The bartender walked over. London managed a weak smile. "Hi, Quincy. How's Stella?"

"Big as a barrel."

"Another baby?"

He shook his head. "Nah. It's those damned tortilla chips. She's got some sort of food fetish or somethin'. Listen, London, what can I get you?"

"Whiskey, neat, and make it a double. And while you're at it, set Dad up, too."

Patrick digested this with a sidelong glance in her direction, then turned his attention back to the greenish flicker of the television set. "You come here to apologize?"

London watched Quincy pour two whiskeys. She'd never been graceful at knocking them back, but this time, her thoughts on Benji and her eyes on her father who watched her, she took the double at a gulp, her only reaction a watering of her eyes and a slight gasp as she grabbed some air. "Chip off the old block, Pat," Quincy said with a wink, then walked to the end of the bar to exchange a few jokes with his other customer.

"So?" Patrick said.

"Dad, we need to talk."

"You pregnant?" he asked bluntly, taking a drag from the inch-long stump that had been a cigar, then crushing it in the ashtray.

London sighed. "I haven't had a date in six months."

"Takes nine, as I recall."

She gave him a level look. "This isn't about me. It's about Benji."

"I picked out the headstone today," he mused in a soft growl. "Black marble. The engraver'll put the seal in the right-hand corner."

"I don't know if that's such a good idea."

"Of course it's a good idea. Benji lived and breathed the Agency."

"Mother Mary, give me strength." *What a good Catholic girl, sitting at a bar at five-thirty in the afternoon, an empty whiskey glass in front of her and a prayer on her lips.* She could almost hear her mother's soft, sarcastic humor, and in that instant she wished with everything she had for just a moment or two to bask in her quiet wisdom. If her mother were here, she would find a way to reach him. They had clung together in crisis; it had been the everyday business of dealing with life that had driven a wedge into the marriage. "I spoke with Wyeth this afternoon," London said quietly. "And it isn't good."

"Wyeth's a fine young man, Meg. You could do a lot worse."

"The investigation into Benji's death is almost over," she said, trying to break through his needling, to force him to hear her for once in her life. "They're going to try to pin an espionage rap on him."

Silence. His gaze remained glued to the television, and Maxwell Smart's nasally voice seemed overly loud.

London couldn't believe what she was witnessing. The disgust with her day, with Wyeth, and with the findings of the investigation hadn't left her, and this—this total lack of response—was the last thing she expected . . . the last thing she needed. He could have been as pissed off as she was, or, for her sake, for the sake of his son's memory, at least pretended to be. "That's it? Your son and my brother, who isn't here to defend himself, is about to be accused of espionage, and you sit there watching an old rerun of some stupid-assed show?"

"Show some respect! I'm still your old man."

"What about Benji? Doesn't he deserve some respect? He was a Llewellyn, Dad! Our flesh and blood."

"Don't you think I know that?" The gaze he turned on her was hard. "It pains me to say it, but Wyeth wouldn't blacken Ben's name unless there was just cause. He's a good man, and he was a good friend to Ben. Wyeth will sort it all out."

"*Benji* was a good man, Dad. Isn't it bad enough that he's dead, that the two of us are all that's left? Are you going to let them drag down his reputation, too? Without a fight? God . . . what is wrong with you?"

"I've got a daughter who shows no respect—that's what's wrong with me." He dug in his pocket and pulled out some crumpled bills, throwing them on the bar with a hand that shook. "I didn't put your brother in the ground, and I can't answer for any mistakes he may have made. It's between him and his God now. That's all I got to say."

"Put your money back in your pocket," London said softly.

"I pay for my own whiskey, and I answer to no one." Then he walked out.

Quincy, the bartender, brought the bottle of whiskey, refilling her glass. "On the house. You okay?"

She was far from okay, London thought. She was sick at heart and slowly losing faith in everything she'd ever believed in . . . family, the Agency. "Thanks for asking," she said aloud. "And thanks for the drink. I hope there's more where that came from. Looks like I'm gonna need it."

"Anything I can do?"

Quincy was a nice guy. He had a nice wife and two sweet kids, but she couldn't confide in him. "Not unless you know where I can find a man named Adam De Wulf."

"I know De Wulf." It was the guy who mentioned the Czech agent and the lock-pick trick. "What do you want with him?"

Always suspicion. If she told him De Wulf was the only witness to her brother's murder, she would get nothing from him. So she lied. "He's just come into some money, and I need to track him down. He's a hard man to find, but there's a half million in it for him."

"What's in it for you?"

"The commission," she said. "You a friend?"

"I don't know that he has any. We worked together—government work, a few years back. He seemed a decent sort. Kind of quiet and reserved, you know what I mean?"

"You don't say?" London's pulse kicked in, accelerating slightly. Her palm left a thin sheen of perspiration on the whiskey glass. "Have you seen Mr. De Wulf recently?"

"It's going on three years," he said, and London's breath ceased. "Then just last month a mutual acquaintance ran into him in New Orleans. Quite the coincidence."

She knew the hopes of getting the information that would make her search easier were slim, but she had to ask. "I don't suppose you have an address?"

"No address. Not even a name." At her blank look, he shrugged. "He's probably using an alias. Overly cautious."

Oh, God. He's paranoid. Great. Just great.

"You might try the French Quarter. It's exotic, and that might appeal to someone like De Wulf. He spent a lot of time overseas. Developed a taste for Turkish tobacco, as I recall."

"Thanks," London said, leaving her whiskey almost untouched, rising to go. She signaled Quincy, leaving a ten on the bar. "Keep his glass full as long as this lasts." Then she went home, packed a bag, left Colonel Sanders with a neighbor, and drove to the airport.

New Orleans, February

It was Adam's habit to walk from the apartment to the French Market for coffee each morning. The walk kept him mobile, making the slight hitch in his step a little less noticeable and a lot less painful. The limp was a grim reminder of a grimmer period in his life, the beginning of the end of everything. It had been four years since his fall off a rooftop in Tel Aviv, and he relived it each night in his nightmares. Somewhere just below the surface of his conscious mind, he saw the scalding white of the houses and shops shimmering in the midday desert heat, heard the sounds of congested streets, the distant babble of voices . . . Tel Aviv . . . the beginning, the end, of everything . . .

Resenting the intrusion almost as much as his inability to stop it from invading his thoughts, he forced himself to focus on who and what he was: khaki Dockers and a bright Hawaiian shirt in shades of green, blue, and scarlet, cheap sunglasses and a Minolta camera slung around his neck—the stereotypical tourist out to get a jump on his sightseeing agenda before the rest of the revelers in town for Mardi Gras awoke from their late-night debauchery and stumbled out of their hotels to fill the streets. The glaring white zinc oxide that covered his nose put the perfect cap on his persona. His own grandmother would have done a double-take. Not that Granny Perch had ever pried herself out of bed at such an ungodly hour.

Headed for the French Market, he paused in Jackson Square to watch an artist setting up his canvas. He snapped a few quick photos of St. Louis Cathedral and the glorious statue of Andy Jackson, then walked on, keeping an eye peeled for anything or anyone suspicious without seeming to do so.

At this early hour, there was a pinkish haze over the Mississippi. The levee was deserted except for a large, red-haired gent in a sharp gray suit. Built like a refrigerator, he stood by a park bench. "C'mon, Sal, damn it. Would ya hurry the hell up?"

"I'm comin', I'm comin', just as soon as I zip up." Sal, as dark as his friend was ruddy, shook it off and stuffed it into his fly. Adam snapped off a shot as Sal turned, struggling with his fly. "Criminently, my zipper's stuck!"

"Serves you right for pissin' in a public park. What if a cop caught your striptease? That's the kind of attention the boss sure as hell wouldn't like."

"It's the coffee down here. All that milk—it runs right through me. Beats hell out of me how an eight-ounce Styrofoam cup can make three pints of urine." Sal pushed in his huge gut and peered at the offending white shirttail protruding like a small flag through his fly. "Criminently, will you look at this? A five-hundred-dollar suit, and this is what I get?"

"I told you not to steal cheap," Freddie told him. "You come up with any leads?"

"Nada. Who'da thought findin' one live Aussie in the City of the Wet Grave would be such a friggin' pain in the tush?"

"Friggin'?" Freddie parroted. "Tush? What's with that?"

"I'm tryin' to clean up my language. My sister's kid's first communion's comin' up in a couple of weeks. I got to go to confession. What do you want me to do, go in there and say, 'Forgive me, Father, for I've fuckin' sinned'?"

Freddie shook his head. "For a man with a bladder-control problem, you're a real riot, d'ya know that? So, how do we find De Wulf? The man's like fuckin' vapor."

Adam didn't linger to hear the rest of the conversation. He bought his coffee, some fresh pastries, the morning paper, and some chicken wings and made a circuitous route back to his place, Joe Demano's muscle none the wiser.

"Joey the Finger" was a minor crime boss from Atlantic City with wide-ranging connections and three fingers missing on his right hand: forefinger, ring finger, and pinky. Word on the street had it that Joey had narrowly missed buying the big one in a Long Island car crusher, courtesy of a rival mob boss. The "accident" had damaged several tendons, giving him a permanent one-fingered salute.

Despite the image, Demano was not a man to cross. He was also not a man Adam normally would have dealings with, but the Lady of the Night made for strange alliances. It all made peculiar sense, if you thought about it. Joey the Finger had a passion for orchids; he also had an unlimited supply of ready cash.

Cash that Adam needed.

He'd hooked up with Joey through a neutral third party. Eddie Whitefish, Adam's landlord, was the consummate entrepreneur, dabbling in everything from running a thriving T-shirt business to a small-time numbers operation. If it hadn't been for Julia, Adam would have turned a deaf ear when Eddie mentioned that a friend of a friend was interested in the orchid and that there was a hefty commission involved for the man who could deliver the goods. Yet, if he were to be totally honest, the money had only been part of the allure. Poetic justice had rendered the caper damned near irresistible. Julia's orchid providing the money to drag her from the hell of her own dark world was bloody, fucking irony at its finest.

Get in; get the goods; get out.

It was supposed to be ruddy simple.

No masked gunman, no dead bodies, no beautiful but lethal ladies—just the orchid and a quick illicit flight to the Caymans, where the exchange would be made . . .

Then fate had intervened, and Adam never saw the Caymans. Joey the Finger had been very displeased—just displeased enough to send Laurel and Hardy to collect the orchid or break his bloody kneecaps.

But first they'd have to find him. They could have leaned on Eddie to get the information they wanted, if Eddie hadn't had a serious disagreement with his ex-wife's lesbian lover over past-due alimony payments. The ex's main squeeze was in city lockup, Eddie was in a coma, and Adam was in a world of shit.

Joey the Finger still wanted the orchid, but he'd dropped the going price by fifty thousand, forcing Adam to find another buyer. The type of care Julia needed didn't come cheap, and his resources were nearly exhausted.

Adam turned the corner at St. Philip and Chartres and narrowly missed colliding with the two apes he was trying to avoid. Freddie Caruso wolfed a jelly doughnut, sucking the stickiness from his thick fingers as Sal Antoine shook his head. "It's New Orleans, one of the most ethnically diverse cities in the whole U.S. of A., a hub of culture and decadence, and you're eating a jelly doughnut." He clucked his tongue, sounding like Granny Perch. "You really should step out of your comfort zone, my friend. Try a beignet. It's a doughnut type of thing."

"Hey, genius, what's this look like to you?" He held up the half-eaten pastry.

"Not the same thing. Variance is good for the soul."

"Variance is good for the soul?" Freddie said, not even trying to hide his sarcasm. "Where do you come up with this shit?"

"The universe is a mirror, Freddie. If you give off negativity, you'll get back negativity."

"Oh, Christ," Freddie muttered. "Somebody needs to whack that Tony Soprano. HBO gets into the waste-management business and suddenly therapy is chic? Next thing you know, the family's full of fuckin' couch potatoes."

Sal waggled a finger at his partner's skepticism. "Don't knock it till you've tried it. We all got issues— you need to learn to confront them head-on. It's unhealthy to keep everything bottled up inside."

"The only issue I got is gettin' my ass back to Jersey where I belong."

"Morning," Adam said with a nod and his best imitation of a Midwestern accent. The two blocked the sidewalk, with a few feet between them. He squeezed through sideways and kept on walking.

"Hey, pal," Freddie called after him. Then, when he failed to answer, "Hey, pal!"

Adam clenched his teeth, inhaling slowly, his muscles tensing as he turned back.

"Yeah, you," Freddie said, walking toward him. "You know some place that serves a decent breakfast around here?"

"There's a little place over on Decatur. Donovan's, I think. Yeah, that's it." He tried to seem pleased with himself but hesitant. "Anything else I can help you with?"

Freddie frowned, his eyes narrowed. Sal was staring up at the second-floor galleries overhanging the sidewalk, rife with greenery, lush and exotic. "Don't I know you from somewhere?"

"I think I passed you over by Jackson Square. Your friend there was busy on the slope of the levee."

"I don't think so," Freddie said. "But you do look familiar."

"Ever been to Battle Creek?"

"Wisconsin?"

"Michigan." Adam glanced at his watch. "Gotta run. The little lady's out of bed by now, and she won't be happy if I'm not there. Suspicious nature, if you know what I mean."

"Jealousy," Sal muttered. "That's poison to a relationship."

"Nice seein' you." Adam spun and walked away. Freddie's stare pricked the skin on the back of his neck, but he didn't look back. Turning the corner onto Dumaine, he stepped into the shade of a recessed doorway and let go of the breath he'd been holding. Hanging back in the shadows, he waited five beats, and when no one showed, he crossed the street and lost himself in the early morning pedestrian traffic.

Honz greeted him with raised hackles and bared fangs as he entered the second-floor apartment. "Take my head off, and there'll be no more wings for you." At the familiar sound of his voice, the weimaraner abruptly plopped down, cocking his boxy gray head while Adam fished in one of the bags, tossing the dog a *beignet*. As focused on food as he was lightning fast,

Honz caught the pastry and wolfed it down. "You've had dessert," Adam said, scratching the dog's head. "Now, for the main course." He unwrapped the wings, put them on a plate, then washed his hands and took his coffee and newspaper out onto the gallery to savor the mild February morning while Honz happily munched his morning repast.

Buried in the society pages amid debuts and an overwritten account of the mayor's fifty-first birthday party, it nearly escaped him completely. The photo was grainy, but it still caused his pulse to accelerate and his fingers to itch.

RARE ORCHID VISITS BIG EASY BOTANICAL GARDENS

A rare black orchid, the Lady of the Night, on loan from the London Botanical Society, will be the jewel in the crown of the Botanical Gardens exotic expedition. English socialite Alexandra Maltese, daughter of the Earl of Maltese and chair for the advancement of the society, acting as a goodwill ambassador, has been entrusted with the care of the exotic bloom during its five-city tour.

Adam read the article, then read it again, memorizing the Garden District address where the lady would be keeping the Lady. Then he folded the paper and started making plans.

The sting had been as meticulously planned as any Intelligence op in which London had played a part.

The mansion in the Garden District, an elegant relic of the postbellum period, belonged to a friend of a friend of a friend of Cid's. "You can have it for a few days, no sweat. They rented it to some movie types last year, and a rock band a few months ago. You being in Intelligence will be a relief, and the price is right: two Benjamins and that picture you have of J. Edgar in baby-doll pajamas and pink bunny slippers."

"It's a family heirloom," London had bargained. "How about a photocopy?" That photo, taken by her grandfather before he left the FBI for the clandestine service, meant everything to London. Harry Llewellyn had always claimed that J. Edgar's fondness for pink chiffon and stiletto heels had forced Harry's compass to point due north, and set him on the right track, to a fulfilling career where his talent for sneakiness and secrecy had become a valuable asset. He'd presented the photo to London, his youngest granddaughter—the only thing aside from the occasional quarter the tightfisted old man had ever given her. Whether the photo was genuine or doctored was any-one's guess. Harry had enjoyed practical jokes back in the day almost as much as his grandson.

Cid shrugged. "Scan-and-print will do."

"What's he want with it?" she'd started to ask. Then she thought better of it. Cid had wide-ranging connec-tions, a veritable network of ex-boyfriends, girlfriends, and relatives twice removed, all of whom she kept in contact with, and many of whom seemed to know someone slightly shady. As with the Humvee, Cid seemed to have the magic touch when it came to ob-taining the unobtainable. It was all legal and aboveboard, nothing unscrupulous, but the long and involved explanations gave London a migraine.

There was no doubt, however, that Cid was a good friend to have. She'd finagled the use of the mansion, and it hadn't broken the bank completely.

London eyed the orchid and wondered if it would fool anyone. After conning Fegan Broussard, a local reporter she'd first met in Chicago, into planting the phony story in the *Times-Picayune,* she'd bought the orchid from a nursery specializing in exotics: royal palms, bromeliads, orchids. Remembering the spidery, leglike roots of the plant in Vienna, she'd bought the ugliest damn thing she could find. Spotlighted on the south wall of a second-floor bedroom, it looked like a sick tarantula that had fallen in a vat of Nair: hairless and hideous, its roots a bark brown snarl. "You wouldn't fool a kindergartener," she said. "Not that I plan on allowing him a good look."

Everything was ready, every angle carefully considered, everything that could go wrong plotted, planned, anticipated, and strategically eliminated. She'd looked at every scenario twice. She'd packed light upon leaving the duplex: a few changes of clothing, a credit card, and some extra cash. She bought a five-round .38 revolver in a pawn shop near the airport, and the necessary tools of the trade. All she had to do was wait.

The house was dark.

Her clothes were dark.

Black jeans, a black T-shirt, and black sneakers. London pulled her hair back, twisting it at her nape, then pulling it up and tucking it securely under a dark stocking cap. If Benji could only see her now, he would have shone the flashlight up his nostrils and camped in a high falsetto, "I'm really scared."

But this was no witch hunt. It was the real deal, mega-serious stuff—so serious that the sheer notion that it might not succeed as she'd planned, the thought that he might not show, twisted her stomach into knots.

Crouched by the window in an advantageous position to watch the windows and door at once without being seen from the outside, London listened to the noise from the street. The crowd had started to gather early that morning, hoping for an advantageous view and a chance to catch the throws tossed from the floats. By evening, the curbs and sidewalks were lined with every conceivable size and shape humanity had to offer.

She peered through the louvers at the street below, searching for any sign of De Wulf.

Was he out there now?

Watching the house, waiting for an indication that the place was deserted, the perfect moment to slip in and steal the dreadfully ugly specimen London could only think of as the tarantula?

Her pulse quickened at the thought, her anticipation mounting steadily until she feared she'd go postal and run screaming into the street, firing at anything that remotely resembled an ex-CIA-current-second-story son of a bitch.

"Build the scam, and he will come," she said.

But would he?

De Wulf had a reputation as a crack spy, the officer of officers within the clandestine service, a man who carefully weighed every angle—observant, as patient as a monk, and twice as cautious. He didn't take chances, yet inexplicably, he had turned thief, crossing the thready line between right and wrong, good and evil . . . Darth Vader in cat burglar clothes.

Out beyond the reach of the city street lamps, the darkness beneath an overcast winter sky was utter and complete, but the length of tree-lined St. Charles Avenue was Christmas-tree bright. The parade went on for hours, Bacchus, the Greek god of the fermented grape, posturing as he waved to the raucous crowd and tossed strings of beads and handfuls of brightly colored doubloons minted in his own image. Inside the Maltese mansion, London's tension rippled over her in waves.

Was he out there yet?

Would he take the bait she offered?

Seconds, minutes, hours passed. The parade rattled away toward the Convention Center and the huge black-tie bash awaiting the upscale revelers; the crowds melted into the night, tourists staggering back to their hotel rooms, locals wending their way home, while London's patience bled out and her spirits sank.

At five minutes to midnight, she'd all but given up. For three days and three nights she'd worked tirelessly, barely sleeping, food a distant memory, dreams replaying the horror of an Austrian Eve of St. Sylvester. Her eyes misted, and she wiped them on her shirtsleeve. "I'm sorry, Benj. I tried; it just wasn't enough."

An arc of faint light swept across her peripheral vision. Sniffing, London raised her head, but it didn't come again. A passing car, an errant headlight beam reflected off the windows. She turned her head aside and heard the sound . . . a barely discernible scrape, like a foot on gravel or brick.

Brick courtyard, brick sidewalks.

London swallowed, tensing. The arc of light appeared again . . . just outside the long French windows, behind it something larger, darker, denser . . . the shadow of a man.

She held her breath, afraid to breathe, afraid to make even a whisper of sound. There was a soft screech as he plied a glass cutter and tapped out the circle in the pane, knocking it onto the floor. Slipping a gloved hand through, he unlocked the window and slid the window open.

Then, like the shadow he was, he stepped over the low sill and into the room.

Chapter Four

Adam went straight for the carefully fabricated display featuring what looked like a hairyless twig gone mad. "Shit," he said with quiet disgust. "I've been bloody well had."

The audible click of the revolver hammer being cocked preceded her raspy whisper. "Put your hands out where I can see them, and turn around. But do it slowly. Do anything to tweak my nerves, and I'll drop you where you stand."

Something in her voice told Adam that she meant what she said—the ragged edge of nerves exposed and raw, more than a taint of quiet desperation. He raised his hands to shoulder height, turning slowly. "Easy does it. No need to overreact. I'm not here to harm you."

She was flattened against the wall, the redhead with the spiky topknot and raccoon eyes who'd interrupted his fight with the assassin in Austria. She was thinner now—a little too thin, maybe—and he could feel the tension rolling off her in waves. Their gazes locked as he faced her. The mascara smears that had underscored her big green eyes in Vienna were gone now, replaced by dusty lavender shadows, her face so finely boned it triggered a strange ache deep inside him, and he couldn't help wondering when she'd last slept or eaten.

Julia had taken on a similar ghostly appearance, the

shadows and the gauntness caused by distraction as the voices that pummeled her mind made her too preoccupied to eat. But that was where the similarity ended.

Red's lovely cat-green eyes were sharp and angry, burning with a fierce light. "Take the glass cutter from your coat pocket and let it fall to the floor. Do anything stupid, and I *will* shoot you."

"So you keep tellin' me," Adam said evenly. "That piece looks a mite heavy for a twig like you. Wouldn't you like to give it a rest?"

"And have you muscle your way out of here?" She laughed, a brittle sound. "Not on your goddamned life. I had a hell of a time finding you, Mr. De Wulf." A flash of clenched white teeth. "I'm not about to let you disappear again."

"I see you've done your homework. What are you? A cop?"

Her cat's eyes narrowed, her full lips pursing into a rigid line. She was struggling hard to maintain control, fighting fatigue and Christ alone knew what. "You're not even close."

"You're with the Bureau?"

"You know, you could have saved us both a hell of a lot of trouble if you'd listened to me in Vienna. All I wanted was answers. I needed to know what you knew about the murder. I still do."

The veil lifted. Adam groaned. Jesus. She'd set the whole thing up specifically to lure him here. The newspaper article had been a plant. There was no orchid, not here in the States, anyway. No Lady Maltese. Just one small redhead with a killer ego and a very large ax to grind. And he'd leaped at the chance to take her bait. He shook his head, amazed at the sheer audacity of it all, at his own gullibility. "You've got balls any man would envy, I'll give you that—pursuing me halfway around the world, setting this whole thing up. If not for the fact that you've wasted what might have been a perfectly good evening, I'd be fucking flattered."

"Keep your fly zipped, Zorro. You're not my type. I like a man with scruples."

Adam chuckled despite his disgust with himself. "I'll just let myself out." It took the kind of balls he'd accused her of having to take that first step closer to the .38 she clutched with both hands. The pistol's bore was a huge dark hole, a gaping black eye that swayed with his every movement. A slug that size had stopping power and would leave an impressive hole. At a range this close it was damned hard to miss, and he was acutely aware that he might not walk away from the encounter. The hair on his forearms stood erect, and sweat snaked a maddeningly slow path from his nape to his shoulder blades, but he kept walking.

"Stay where you are, damn it." Her voice was rough, her nerves apparent, and for one brief second he wondered who the hell she was—and what she was on. She sidestepped to block his exit through the window, leaving little separating the muzzle of the weapon and his breastbone. "Don't make me shoot you."

They were inches apart, close enough for him to see the gold flecks around her black pupils, to reach out and brush the hair from her eyes. It slid through his grasp like a skein of silk, cool against the warmth of his fingertips. "Could you do that, Red? Could you pull the trigger and watch as I bleed out on the toes of your little black shoes?"

She remained stubbornly silent, but her mouth quivered, a hint of vulnerability, a subtle clue that she was not as hard as she liked to appear—not nearly heartless enough to kill him in cold blood for the want of answers he didn't have and wouldn't have given in any case. His own voice softened to just above a whisper. "You look worn out. When was the last time you slept?"

Silence.

She bit her lip to keep it still, gathering every ounce of strength she had, but it wasn't enough to stop him from reaching out. Pushing the gun barrel carefully aside, he closed his much larger hand around it, taking it from her, placing it on a nearby table. "Goddamn you," she whispered.

"You're too late for that. He already has." Adam stared down at her, sensing her desperation, trying not to care. Her problems were just that: her problems. They had nothing at all to do with him, and he had too many of his own concerns to take on anyone else's.

Still, something about her got past the icy detachment he'd carefully built up over the years, to strike at the very heart of him. He leaned in to steal a kiss, checking the impulse to stare down into that heart-shaped face and those pretty dark-lashed eyes. Her lips, soft and inviting, opened as she gasped in surprise, unable to resist, or rather, not wanting to make the effort. He pressed his advantage, cradling the back of her head in the heart of his hand as he brought her body hard against his.

"No," she said in a half growl, half moan. "No." But she didn't push away, didn't resist, and her response was every bit as hungry as his. She was unstrung, but she wasn't passive. Tangling the fingers of one hand in his hair, she backed him against the wall by the window, sliding the palm of the other over his shoulder and chest, seeking out buttons and popping them through their holes like a ruddy magician. There was no denying that the lady had a magic touch, and his reaction was instantaneous. Reaching down, he hooked a hand beneath her knee, urging it up.

London lost what little composure she had left; it went the way of her common sense and self-control. Weeks of tension and frustration had built inside her like magma inside a volcano, and what Adam De Wulf offered was a welcome release. She knew it was crazy. She knew that she needed a good head-shrinking for even considering it, but she wanted it . . . God help her, wanted him. "This is the most insane thing I've ever done. . . ." But she didn't stop.

Framing her face with his broad hands, he kissed her once, and then again, before nibbling his way to her chin. "The insanity was in tracking me down and bringing me here. Blimey, I'm glad you did."

With a sigh, London reached for the waistband of his jeans, loosening the rivet from the buttonhole, finding the zipper pull. Long celibate months stretched behind her. She was playing with fire, and she knew it, and De Wulf was a dangerous man. Yet, if she was going to be truthful with herself, she couldn't deny that his not being choirboy material was definitely part of the attraction. God, he was so sexy, and she didn't want to resist.

Downstairs, the door opened and softly closed. The floorboards creaked beneath someone's weight. De Wulf froze. "Are you expecting someone?"

"Just you," London said. She was still reeling from the encounter, and her pulse felt heavy and abnormally sluggish. As if she'd been drugged, and she just wanted to slide back to the comfort she'd found in his arms, his kiss. "I'm alone," she admitted, then wanted to pinch herself for telling the truth.

"Not for long." He pulled away, taking her hand as he slipped silently to the far side of the room. Taking her cue from him, she flattened herself against the wall. Reflex action, advantageous position. It would give them a second or two if the third person to enter the house that evening also decided to enter the room.

The footsteps came closer. The stairs creaked, and one huge, humped and deformed shadow crept up the stairwell wall. "Are you sure this is a good idea? 'Cause I'm not so sure. What if the old broad, Mrs. Falcon, is home? If she's in bed and we startle her, she's liable to scream bloody murder. Besides, I got to take a leak."

"You always have to take a leak. When you gonna get that thing fixed?"

"It's my prostate," Sal sulked. "Besides, that surgery causes impotency."

"Yeah, well there are worse things than a limp dick," Freddie assured him. "I'm gonna get you a box of Depends."

"What about Mrs. Falcon?"

"It's *Maltese,* not *Falcon,* you idiot. And if we get caught, we'll claim that we're lost. It's as simple as that."

"Doesn't sound kosher to me."

"Kosher, my ass," Freddie groused. "You wouldn't know kosher from pastrami."

"You shouldn't be so disrespectful. I got feelin's, too, you know. Doc Frack says that when one man insults and ridicules another, it's an effort to tear that individual down so the criticizer can feel superior—"

The shadow spun, morphing from one to two, the first one larger, more threatening. "Take those feelings and stuff 'em, Sal. I've had your pop psychobabble right up to here! You want to get in touch with your feminine side, then do it on your own time and leave me the frig out of it! Frig—aw, shit!" A sound of utter disgust. "Fuckin' pansy—now he's got me doin' it. I don't know why Joey puts up with you."

"Joey?" London whispered furiously. "As in Joey the Finger Demano?"

"That's the one." De Wulf then signaled her to silence with a finger to his lips. The pair came off the steps and moved cautiously toward the light spotlighting London's impostor orchid. Two very large men dressed like garish harlequins, Freddie and Sal moved past London and Adam and into the room. Freddie found the orchid. "Jesus, that's the ugliest goddamned thing I've ever seen. It looks like a demented centipede. It's a good thing Joey's gettin' it for nothin'."

"Yeah, it sure is ugly," Sal said, bending almost double to scratch his green-satin-covered shin.

London recognized the instant the costumed mobster realized they weren't alone in the room, but De Wulf saw it first. As the big-bellied clown bent forward, he shot a glance to the rear, his gaze narrowing. "Hey!"

For a man with a limp, De Wulf's reaction time was amazingly fast. He planted a boot on Sal's left butt cheek and gave him a shove. Off balance, Sal dove forward, plowing into Freddie. Freddie, the orchid, and Sal toppled like dominoes. "That's him! That's the thief! The guy who tried to scam Joey! Get him!"

De Wulf grabbed London's wrist, heading for the window, dragging her with him as the two struggled up, searching for access to the weapons hidden beneath the brightly colored costumes. "What are you doing?"

"Saving your life." He stepped over the sill and out onto the roof, as graceful as a cat on the slate. At the edge of the roof, he crouched down. "Down you go," he said, lowering her over the edge. For an unnerving instant, London dangled in midair, twelve feet above the ground, De Wulf's steely grip the only thing between her and a nasty fall. If he let go, the drop wouldn't kill her, but she could snap an ankle like a twig. Was that his plan? To disable his adversary and sneak off into the night?

But his grip never faltered, and then she found the porch rail and from there lowered herself to the ground. Overhead, De Wulf gripped the roof edge as Freddie loomed in the window. "Fucking sneaky, double-dealing bastard!"

He fired off several rounds, the slugs from the silenced pistol making *ping, ping* sounds as they rained all around De Wulf, shattering slate. De Wulf ground out a curse, swung down from the roof, and dropped to the ground beside London. "Now what do we do?" she demanded.

"We?" He laughed. "There is no 'we.' You found your own way in. Find your own way out."

London stared at him, the various ways of stopping him at her disposal careening madly through her mind, but the .38, her only real leverage, was lying upstairs in the Maltese mansion. She set her jaw, determined to tough it out. Joey Demano's "associates" ducked back in the window. In a minute they'd emerge and find them. "Go on, then. Get out of here."

He turned and took a few steps, glancing back, a look of frustration tightening his expression. "That's it? You're just going to stand there? Do you have any idea who those two are, or what they'll do to get their hands on the orchid you pretended to have? If you're lucky, they'll take you back to Joey, and you'll have another day or two, until he finds out you don't know anything and has those two seal you into a fifty-five-gallon drum. If they're feeling particularly impatient, you won't live to see New Jersey."

"I'm not your problem, remember?" London reminded him.

"This is true."

"So get on with your disappearing act."

"Bloody goddamned right I will." London watched

him walk to the fence and glance up at the house, and his face might have been carved from granite, his expression was so closed. But he didn't leave her there to face Demano's men alone. "Stupid, sentimental sap," he muttered, barely loud enough for her to hear. "Like you don't have your share of trouble. Like you couldn't pick a less hair-raising time to get chivalrous?" In the next instant, he grabbed London, pushing her down into the shadow of a large oleander.

The front door opened.

"You check the perimeter of the house," Freddie told his partner. "I'll check the back alley. They can't have gotten very far."

"There are bushes around the perimeter of the house. Aren't there snakes in Louisiana? I thought I saw something about it on *Animal Planet*—"

"You know, Sal, you're really starting to piss me off. I don't give a fuck what you saw on cable, but I can tell you one thing: If you don't straighten the hell up, I'm gonna have a little talk with Joey. You know how he feels about guys wimpin' out on him."

"All I said was—"

"The bushes, Sal. Or I tell Joey you cared more about your psyche than you did about catching that double-crossing lowlife who just deprived him of the orchid."

"All right, already," Sal grumbled. "I'm goin', I'm goin'." He planted his feet down hard, the leather soles slapping the brick walkway.

"Size twelves, no arch," De Wulf whispered. He was crouched beside London, so close that she could smell the leather of his jacket and the clean scent of soap. Their position—their predicament—was ridiculous, yet something about it felt natural, perhaps because she faced danger every day in her position as a CIA officer . . . or maybe it was him. The thought seemed odd, totally out of sync with her reality, but it refused to leave her.

To the left of the oleander, Sal struck a lighter and held it out. The yellow glow haloed his head, making it seem disembodied without penetrating the shadow. Then he lost his grip, and everything went black again. "I should have listened to Nanna and went to medical school. I could have fixed my own prostate by now." *Flick.* The flame appeared, dancing in the sudden damp breeze, kissing Sal's sausagelike fingers. "Criminently!" He dropped the lighter. "I should've brought a flashlight."

"Any luck out there?" Freddie's question preceded the first spatter of moisture on the bricks and shrubbery.

Sal's respiration picked up, as though he'd been walking hard. "Nothing in the bushes, or the courtyard, either. My guess is, they're halfway across town by now."

"We'll track him down," Freddie promised.

"Yeah, we'll get him. I got a real good look at him. He should be easy to spot. Hey, are you hungry? I saw a little restaurant a few blocks from here with a sign that said, *clean restroom.* It had real promise."

As their voices grew faint, the clouds gave up their burden and a chilly rain spattered the leaves of the white oleander. De Wulf slipped from cover onto the sidewalk, fully prepared to walk out on her and to take whatever information he had with him. Pleading with him wouldn't faze him. He was a self-serving hard-ass who looked out for himself, and to hell with everyone else—a man who had very effectively dropped out of sight for three years. He could do so again easily, and it occurred to London that the next time she might not be so lucky. "Could you give me a hand? I seem to be wedged in back here."

"Sure thing, but then I've got to run." He reached into the bushes, gripping the hand she held out—her left—as oblivious of the trap as a mouse with a raging addiction for cheese. She allowed him to pull her to her feet, his wrist exposed; then, before he could pull away, she clapped on the steel bracelet. "What the hell are you doin'?"

"Taking precautions," London replied, displaying her half of the handcuffs. "You aren't the only one who considers every angle, and I'm not through with you yet."

"I can hardly wait to see what comes next," he said, the comment on the dry side, heavy on the sarcasm. "I hope the hell it involves black leather and a good spanking."

"Don't get your hopes up."

"Do you have a name to go along with this shiny little fetish?" he asked, rattling the link between them, testing its strength.

"My name is Llewellyn, London Llewellyn, and I work for the government."

His eyes narrowed, and all the taut humor left his expression. "Government? As in CIA? You've got to be kidding!" He groaned. "Shit. I should have known."

"Don't be too hard on yourself. I didn't initially recognize you as Agency, either. In fact, I took you for a thief. Imagine that."

De Wulf glared at her. "Well, it appears you've got me. Now what?"

"I want answers, that's all. I want to know who killed my brother and why. If I get what I want, I'll be on the next flight out of here, and you can get on with whatever it is you do."

"Do I have a choice?"

"What do you think?"

Hunching his shoulders against the damp leather of

his jacket, he gave her what she wanted, but it was clear he wasn't happy about it. "All right. We'll talk, but not here. Demano's muscle may decide to have another look around, and I don't intend to be here if they do." Shoving his free hand into his jacket pocket, he pulled out a cellular phone and punched in a series of numbers.

"What are you doing?"

"I'm calling us a cab. It's a long walk in the cold rain, and you look as if you've had about as much as you can stand."

Joey the Finger was in the middle of a rousing game of canasta with his in-laws when Rosa, the maid, came discreetly into the room. A flighty brunette with deep acne scars, she paused beside his chair, craning to see his hand while waiting for him to notice her. "What's the fixation with this?" he snapped, waving his stiff finger under her long nose. "Ain't you ever seen a thumb and finger before?"

She jumped back, her eyes all ball and no lid, scared out of her wits. "Telephone, Mr. Joey. I think it's that fat man who always leaves the lid up in the first-floor powder room."

"Sal? Why didn't you say so?" Joey whipped the portable phone from Rosa's bony hands. He smirked at his father-in-law. "You'll excuse me, John? I gotta take this. It's very important." He got out of his chair, turning away from the table and his guests, nearly trampling Rosa. "Don't you have something to disinfect? You brought me the damn phone; now, vamoose outta here!" When Joey reached the far end of the great room, he put the phone to his ear. "Yeah?"

Background noise threatened to drown the caller out. "Sal? Is that you? Where the fuck are you guys?"

"It's a little jazz club on Bourbon Street. You wouldn't believe this place, Joey! You gotta come down here some time. It's a different world."

"You're partyin'? Where's the orchid? Tell me you didn't leave it alone in a hotel room. That prick De Wulf can't be trusted. He's liable to lift it again, just to prove he can do it."

"It's not at the hotel," Sal assured him. "The funniest thing happened. We tracked it down to a mansion where this socialite was staying, only when we got a good look at the orchid, it was the ugliest damn thing—"

"Damn it, Sal! Quit fartin' around and answer me! Did you get the fucking orchid?"

"Well, not exactly—"

"Not exactly. Not exactly? What the hell is that supposed to mean? Put Freddie on the phone."

"Look, Joey, you're not pissed, are you, 'cause we'll find it—"

"Put fucking Freddie on the fucking phone!" Joey shouted, then turned in time to field the jaundiced glances of his wife and mother-in-law. He lowered his voice and made nice. "Lemme talk to Freddie, Sal, or I'm gonna reach through this phone and rip your lungs out through your nose holes. Your nose holes, Sal. Do you get that? We're talking major agony here."

He heard Sal mutter something about hostility being unhealthy; then there was more noise, and the phone receiver changed hands. "Freddie, you find that orchid . . . no substitutes, do you get that? I want it here by Friday. It's Bitsy's birthday, and I don't want to disappoint her. You know how she gets."

"We'll do what we can, boss," Freddie said. "This guy's a slippery character. And I'm not even sure he's got the orchid. I think he fell for the same bait we did, which means he's lookin' for it, too. The way I figure it, if we tail him, he'll lead us right to it. Then we can relieve him of it. Without any more shenanigans."

"No more excuses, Freddie. You find him, and you get me that flower. I'm not gonna let some Aussie asshole get away with stiffin' Joey Demano. This is how rumors get started, and I can't afford to have the big boys in New York thinkin' I'm a pushover."

"Sure thing, boss. We'll keep lookin', no matter how long it takes."

Joey leaned over the receiver as though his threatening posture and don't-mess-with-me scowl could somehow translate through the wire. "Friday, Freddie. You get that rat De Wulf here by Friday, or your ass is grass and I'm the goddamned Weed Eater."

He hung up the phone and immediately shook off the foul mood that was rapidly descending. When he rejoined the group in the great room, he was all smiles. "Now, where were we?"

Chapter Five

The yellow cab pulled up to the corner of Dauphine and Conti Streets, and De Wulf paid the fare and handed the cabbie a fifty. "I was never here, you got that? And neither was she. The lady's got bondage fantasies and a jealous ex-husband. We don't want any unpleasant surprises, you know what I mean?"

The driver, a middle-aged, dark-skinned man with graying shoulder-length dreadlocks and a laid-back expression, gave a careless shrug while pocketing the bill. "Hey, man, it's Mardi Gras, you know what I'm sayin'? There's a million strange faces in N'awlins. Besides, you know all you white dudes look alike."

London watched the taillights fade to a red blur in the distance. "Bondage fantasies? You're a real gem, De Wulf."

He started off at a fast walk, cutting through a dark private passageway and into a bricked courtyard. The doorway was shrouded with ivy, a darker rectangle in a dark wall. De Wulf kept to the shadows out of habit. He was Agency to the core, a dyed-in-the-wool clandestine junkie still living the life without drawing the paycheck. London had seen her father do the same thing and knew that old habits died exceptionally hard. It took a certain personality type to make an ordinary man into an exceptional spy. Men like Patrick and De Wulf seemed born to it: the secretiveness, the sharp eye for detail, instincts honed to a razor's edge. They were hard men to live with, and nearly impossible to know.

But where had his instincts been this evening?

Had she really perpetrated the perfect sting?

Or was he losing his edge?

The thought made her nervous, and her heightened nerves slicked her palms with sweat. He opened the door and turned to glance back; London hesitated. "Having second thoughts?"

"Of course not," London said. But her mouth was suddenly dry, and she almost choked on the lie. Only a fool would intentionally follow this man into an unknown environment without considering the consequences. And London Margaret Llewellyn was nobody's fool.

De Wulf was a thief, sleek and muscular in body, handsome of face . . . but what else was he? A con man? A liar? Was he capable of murder?

The image of Benji lying facedown on the bed, eyes staring, flashed behind her green eyes, honing her fear, hardening her resolve.

It really didn't matter what else De Wulf was; he was her witness. The only witness. She couldn't walk away now. "Let's get on with it. The sooner I get what I came for, the quicker I'll be gone."

He preceded her up the darkened stairwell. London had to feel her way along and hope she didn't fall. "When was the last time you paid your electric bill?"

He snorted. "Come on, Llewellyn. Suck it up and quit complaining." They'd reached the landing and another door, this one locked. De Wulf took a key from above the door frame.

London laughed. "You've got to be kidding. You keep a key to your door above the sill? Could you be more obvious?" She conveniently ignored her own habit of keeping a key under the mat.

"Trust me. Break-ins aren't a problem," he said, putting the key in the lock and cautiously edging the door open. London could see the pale gray silhouette of a very large dog through the crack. The canine's lips drew back in a snarl, vicious-looking fangs white in the darkness; his low, throaty warning growl erupting in ferocious barking, he lunged for the opening.

London gasped, stumbling back as far as the handcuffs would allow.

"Hello, sweetheart. Adam's home." The ghostly hound backed away from the door but continued to watch their every move, ears pricked. "We've got company," De Wulf said. "Be a good bloke and come say hello."

The dog approached London, dropping onto his haunches in front of her, offering his paw. She took it hesitantly, amazed that it filled the heart of her hand. "You're allowed to keep horses in your apartment?"

"He's barely more than a pup. Honz used to belong to a musician down the street, but he had to relocate, and he couldn't take the big fella with him. I wasn't wild about the arrangement at first, but we got on well enough, and it's kind of nice havin' someone to come home to. Here you go." He reached in his jacket pocket and gave the dog a treat. "Good dog."

London's stomach rumbled. De Wulf looked sharply up. "You have a chihuahua in there?"

"Very funny," London said a little defensively. "Could we get on with this, please?"

"It's your dime," he said. "You're in, and I'm all yours. What do you say we break out the key to these things and talk like civilized human beings? Don't know about you, but I could use some coffee to chase the dampness."

"I'm fine, thanks, and we'll keep the bracelets a while longer."

He raised a brow, a definite challenge in his dark blue eyes. "I could take it from you, and the search to locate it wouldn't trouble me a damn bit."

London met his gaze without flinching or looking away first, but it took every ounce of strength that she could muster. The mere suggestion of his hands on her flesh made her shiver. He was bigger and stronger than she. He could easily overpower her, do anything he pleased with her, and he wouldn't be as easy to subdue as that jerk on the plane. He was capable and intelligent—an unscrupulous, mysterious, slightly shady character who hadn't left her when he'd had the chance, carried dog treats in his pocket, and may have been involved in her brother's murder. "Tell me what you know about Austria."

"I'm not sure there's much point in my doing that. You're not going to believe a word I say anyway."

"What were you doing in my brother's room that night?"

He was her brother, Adam thought. *That explains a hell of a lot.* Her desperation to find the answers, when there were no logical answers. Murder never made sense. She was CIA; she should know that by now. She was also on the edge, propelled by nervous energy, primed for total collapse. He recognized the signs, had felt everything she was feeling. It seemed like a lifetime ago, but the memories were still fresh, stirring a restlessness inside him that cried out for movement, action. "Damned if I'm not going to get that coffee. Come along if you like."

He moved to the kitchen, all but dragging her with

him, and he wouldn't allow himself to feel guilty. She'd asked for this. She'd barged into his life, his world, unknowingly probing into places where she had no bloody right to be.

She didn't back down, and she didn't give up, but neither did he.

She stood with her hip braced against the sink, glaring at him while he fumbled with one hand—his left hand—for the filters. "What were you doing in my brother's hotel room the night of his murder?"

"I needed an exit, and the door happened to be open."

"Because you had stolen the orchid."

Adam said nothing. The coffee was brewing, filling the kitchen with the heady aroma of arabica beans blended with chicory.

Llewellyn's stomach rumbled noisily.

"I've got some bagels and lox in the fridge," he offered, but she clung to her drill like Honz with a bone. The weimaraner didn't get a meat bone often, but when he did, Adam, who valued his fingers, left him strictly alone. He didn't have that luxury where Llewellyn was concerned, since it was his hide she was hell-bent on gnawing.

"What kind of connection do you have with the shooter? And don't lie to me. I'll know if you do."

Adam let his breath out in an impatient rush. "Do you ever listen? There is no goddamned connection! My presence in that particular room at that particular moment was sheer coincidence. It wasn't staged, and it wasn't planned, and I was as surprised as you were to find a corpse on the bed."

"But you were struggling with the assassin."

"Bloody well right, I was," he shot back, then, glancing at Llewellyn, softened his tone. "Look, I interrupted the bastard. If I hadn't grabbed the gun when I did, I would be as cold and dead as your brother right now. Believe what you want, but the truth is that I didn't have anything to do with his death. Somebody killed him, all right, but it sure as hell wasn't me."

"Why should I believe you?" she said, but he could tell that she did believe him. It showed in the sudden look of despair that entered her eyes as the truth of her situation registered. Her only lead, the basis on which she had built her hopes, had just evaporated, leaving her with nowhere to turn, no options.

Adam hesitated. His reluctance to trust made relationships difficult, and he hadn't been with any woman for two nights running in three years. Not since Julia. Women craved intimacy, and intimacy meant openness, and he'd lost that ability somewhere along the way—or maybe he was lying to himself. Maybe he'd never had it.

Julia had said as much, and no doubt she'd been right. He'd been a lousy husband.

Tel Aviv, and the cycle of tragedy and destruction that had followed, had left him wary. Loneliness was preferable to pain and regret, bitterness and guilt. So what was it about her that made him soften? Why did he feel compelled to reach out and brush her cheek with the tips of his fingers? Christ, her skin was so cold. Clammy, almost.

"Believe what you want," he said. "You will anyway, and I don't care enough to try to convince you. Who knows? Maybe having a scapegoat'll ease whatever's eating you up inside."

She bit her lip, but not before he saw its vulnerable quiver. She caught his hand in a grip that hurt and hung on so tightly that Adam winced. She was falling fast, her shaky emotional foundation being eaten away like a mountain of dust in a gale-force wind. She tried desperately to hang on to the threads of her composure. He saw the struggle reflected in her eyes and knew that this was the moment to turn away. He couldn't save her; that much was obvious. But he couldn't quite turn his back on her rapid slide, either. "Look, Llewellyn. I'm sorry about your brother. It's rough to lose someone you lo— someone you care about . . ."

Her lips parted in a silent snarl, her teeth clenched against a sympathy that was clearly unwelcome. She fought it; her whole body tensed, every muscle straining against the single tear hovering on the brink of her dark lashes. For an instant it hung there, mocking Adam's inability to detach himself from the struggle. "You play dirty, Llewellyn," he ground out, molding his palm to the curve of her jaw, brushing the liquid grief from her cheek with his thumb.

She would have pulled away, but the handcuffs kept her close, and then his voice softened slightly, his tone still rough yet silken, like crushed velvet; the fight left London in a rush. "All that hardness, the tough exterior—it's just an illusion."

"You don't know anything," London insisted. She might be in a bad way, but her survival instincts remained strong. It would be so easy to fall into his arms, his bed, to forget for an hour or two. He was good-looking in that overtly Australian-male sort of way: tall and broad-shouldered, as blunt and outspoken as he was sexy, more than mildly intelligent. There wasn't a damn thing he missed.

"I know that you'd be a real looker if it weren't for those shadows under your eyes. You know, Llewellyn, you're gonna be hard to forget. Coffee's done," he said as the pot gurgled behind him. "Damned if I don't like mine sweet."

London knew what came next. It was no surprise when his fingers found their way under her heavy, damp hair and lay warm against the chilled skin of her nape. The sensation was heady. London drank it in, hungry for more. It was a result of the tension she'd been living with for months, she adamantly told herself—the stark craving for physical contact, for a man's touch and whatever comfort there was to be found therein. It wasn't personal, and it had nothing to do with the man; only the moment.

She told herself all that and more, but she didn't believe a word of it. If she had been in a sultry New Orleans' state of mind, in the French Quarter with Wyeth, feeling strung out and wild with tension, she wouldn't have wanted to tear off his clothing and jump his bones right there in the kitchen. She couldn't imagine kissing Wyeth, let alone playing tongue tag with him while she strained to get even closer.

It was all about De Wulf—sexy, mysterious, impossible to find, and damned hard to fathom. De Wulf, whose free hand did a slow, sensuous slide down her spine and easily slipped into the waistband of her jeans. Warm, hard hand on soft, cool skin . . . The sensation was as intense as he was, a pleasure to savor, a whetting of sexual appetites. Groaning under the long kiss, London peeled the leather jacket off him, inch by inch, but with his one hand warming her buns and the other wearing the latest in law enforcement chic, bare skin was an impossible ideal.

De Wulf reluctantly dragged his lips from hers. "I don't suppose you've got a key for these things?"

"Of course I have a key," London said, rifling her pockets with one hand and coming up empty. "Just give me a few seconds. It has to be . . ." She pulled a face.

"Let me guess. Back at the Maltese mansion." He reached in his back pocket and produced a slim jack-knife, which he opened, revealing a variety of lock picks, as well as a small penknife.

"A lock pick?" London said. "You had it on you the entire time?"

He grinned, a flash of white teeth in a tawny face. London's breathing faltered. "Never leave home without it." He chose his blade, his touch as delicate and sure as a surgeon's. His cuff sprang open, and the grin grew wicked. "Now . . . where were we?"

She hesitated half a beat, and De Wulf let go an agonized groan. "Oh, Christ. You're having second thoughts. Just my luck that the Mata Hari who falls into my lap would turn out to be a freaking goody two-shoes."

London shifted, uncomfortable beneath the assessing weight of his stare. She wasn't sure she liked his comparison. Mata Hari maybe, but she hadn't been called a goody two-shoes since the third grade. The boy slinging the insults back then had ended up with a nosebleed. She'd gotten three days' detention and a good scolding from Patrick, but it hadn't taught her anything. The look she gave him was dangerous. "Be damned careful what you say, De Wulf. No one blackens my reputation and lives to tell about it."

"Oh, yeah? What are you gonna do about it?"

"This." Moving closer once again, she slid her hand over the damp fabric of his jeans, along the length of his left thigh to the telltale bulge in his crotch. "Or this," she suggested, undoing the riveted metal button that secured his waistband, easing his zipper down. It was a dangerous game they were playing: two relative strangers wildly attracted to each other, making love while they should have been getting acquainted. Somehow, London thought, it just felt right. As if they had been careening madly toward this instant in time since that first night in Vienna.

It was easy to rationalize her reasons for being in his arms; the truth was much harder for London to admit. Adam De Wulf was the only thing standing between her and a darkness she couldn't face. A few months ago, everything in her life had been clearly defined. She'd known who she was and exactly where she was headed. Now she couldn't be sure of anything.

The life, the career, the place in the world she'd constructed, were all built on shifting sand. There were no certainties and no guarantees. And truth . . . truth was just another illusion, with cold, black emptiness waiting beyond.

Cold, like a corpse. Black as a tomb. Empty . . . my God, she was so empty.

De Wulf was a lifeline, warm and solid and strong. London couldn't help thinking that in that moment she needed him more intensely than she had ever needed another human being in her entire life. Maybe if he held her close enough, she could absorb a little of that strength and regain her equilibrium. Maybe he could help her hang on to her sanity. For weeks he had been her only focus, her one best hope. Oddly enough, he still was.

It didn't matter that she didn't have a clue how he liked his coffee, or whether he wore boxers or briefs. All that mattered was the solid thud of his heart near her own, the urgency with which he claimed her mouth, the way he made her feel.

He was running his hands down her back, pausing at the curve of her waist, and sliding to the front to pop each button on her button-fly jeans. Then, hooking his forefinger through a belt loop and teasing her with kisses, he backed her toward the French windows, open to the second-floor gallery. Beyond the open windows, the city was alive with the light and sound of celebration. With her back braced against the window frame and the rain falling softly a few feet away, Adam De Wulf eased her jeans down, baring hips and a long length of thigh. As his hand found the heat of her, London sighed, letting the damp jeans slide past her calves to her ankles, carried by their own weight and the irresistible pull of gravity, then stepping free of them.

"No undies?" he said with a soft laugh. "A woman with a sense of adventure. I like that."

"Not that much adventure," London said, producing a slim foil packet, held between two fingers. De Wulf made short work of the condom, diving in for a deep, deep kiss, fondling her bottom, molding his strong and capable hands to her cool, damp cheeks. Rising on tiptoes, London strained to get closer, right knee crooked, foot hooked behind his calf as he eased into her.

Dear God, he was strong, and warm, and in sync with her every wish, the smallest, darkest most secret sexual desire. He made her feel the femme fatale, though nothing could have been further from the truth—sexy, vibrantly alive, even though she hadn't slept in days. He made her feel wanted, wrapped as she was around him—appreciated, cherished almost. Holding tight to his broad shoulders, she strained as he strained, one rhythm, one soft symphony of whispered encouragements and the sound of hungry kisses . . . and still, she couldn't get close enough.

Sensing her urgency, Adam lifted her higher, burying his face in the low scooped neck of her T-shirt as she settled slowly down on him, and he wondered what he'd done to deserve a night on the wild side. That was all it was, just a night. Now that she'd hit a dead end in her search for the truth, she'd be headed back to wherever the hell she'd been before New Orleans, before Vienna, and he would go back to his ghostly existence of back-alley deals and hating himself for failing Julia, meeting with his fence and doubling back to cover his tracks . . . doing his damnedest during the daylight hours to get on with his life, such as it was, and in his nightmares reliving the past.

Yet, fully taken by Llewellyn, her hot enthusiasm burning away all conscious thought, the rest seemed light-years away. The things she did to him were enough to make a whore blush, and he loved it. Thoroughly uninhibited, she proved a greedy lover, taking everything he had to give; reluctant to let him leave her for even a moment, she gripped him, wrung him of every last, ecstatic wave . . . tightening, tightening, then crying out as she went limp in his arms.

He paused for a moment, his miracle still clinging tightly to him, her legs locked at his waist, and her cheek on his shoulder, feeling the soft fall of her breath against his skin and letting a strange tenderness seep through him for the woman in his arms. Then, once his heartbeat had slowed to normal, he carried her to his bed.

Artificial light filtered through the cracks in the louvers, striping the smooth, naked shoulder of the woman on the bed with bands of soft gray and charcoal shadow. From his position by the French windows, Adam watched her. It was ten minutes past eight in the evening, and she'd yet to waken. If not for the lessening of the blue shadows beneath her eyes, and the faint, steady sound of her breathing, he might have been concerned. Instead, he walked Honz, checked with the hospital concerning Eddie's condition, drank coffee, and waited.

His notebook computer sat open, the screen saver

giving off an unearthly blue glow. With a last glance at Llewellyn, he walked back to the table, setting down his coffee cup, leaning down to stroke the touch pad. The screen saver evaporated, replaced by his instant-messaging program. He chose a contact and typed.

Bruno, are you on board?

Bruno came back in a flash with his usual greeting. *Where the hell have you been? I've been trying to reach you for days. Don't you ever pick up your messages?*

I've been preoccupied. Listen, mate. Are you still tapped into the Agency pipeline?

That depends.

On what?

On why you're asking.

I need some info on a chick named Llewellyn. See if she's on the payroll and get me any background info you can. And, Bruno? I need it yesterday.

An emoticon rolled around the message box, laughing hysterically. *Not that easy, pal. Some of this shit is highly classified.*

Which is why you love doing it. You're easily bored. You need a constant challenge. No doubt why you're on wife number four.

You suck.

No need for insults, mate. Just get me the skinny and there's a case of Foster's in it for you.

Adam signed out of the messaging program and began a search of his own. It took a bit of persistence, but he finally found what he was looking for. The stunning photo of the Lady that popped up on-screen had been taken yesterday in London. Fluted black petals nestled cunningly amid the spidery roots, soft as velvet, dark as midnight. Beneath the photo was a paragraph detailing the Lady's mysterious connection to the murder of an American citizen in an Austrian hotel room. Due to circumstances that sources close to the society were not willing to disclose, its location was being kept secret.

It was a little amazing how everything had worked in the current owner's favor. A shame about Llewellyn's brother, but a little mystery, a little murder, a hint of scandal connected to the orchid would only work to up the ante, making it even more valuable to Adam. They were afraid he'd try again, and they were right. The Lady was the one temptation he couldn't resist.

Another long look, and he got on with other matters. She was in full bloom, and she was still somewhere in the U.K. It would take a concentrated effort to find her, and even if he got to her quickly, the rigors of a transatlantic flight would likely be too traumatic for her to arrive stateside in top form—an undesirable turn of events that might irritate his potential buyer.

He flipped through his bank records with a few more clicks and checked his account balance. It was down since January, way down. The mishap in Europe had cost him time and money. There wasn't enough to do what he needed to do. Not nearly enough to assure that Julia got the kind of care she needed.

Picking up the portable phone, he thumbed in a number. A woman picked up on the third ring. Her voice was soft and had a lyrical quality, much like her daughter's had been before the illness. "Cerese, it's Adam."

A chilly pause, and she came back, all the softness gone from her tone. "How dare you call here?"

"Cerese, I'm concerned. How is she?"

"How do you think she is? Distraught, depressed, on edge . . . teetering on the verge of I know not what, thanks to you."

He'd hoped for better news. He always hoped for better news. Adam reached for the pack of cigarettes on the table and shook one out, but he didn't light it. "Cerese . . . if I could change things—if I could go back—"

"At least have the decency to tell the truth. Julia is in this situation because you were too consumed by your obsession to properly care for your wife and child."

Adam bent his head to light the cigarette, then shook out the match. He couldn't argue with her. Every word was true. "Can I speak with her? I want to help—"

"If you wish to help, then for God's sake, leave us alone! Julia stopped needing you three years ago, and I will be damned if I will allow you to do her more damage than you already have!"

The phone clicked, and the line went dead. Cerese had hung up on him, cut him off as Julia had cut him out of her life after Michael's death. With a hollow ache in the pit of his stomach, he dragged smoke into his lungs and tried to ignore the eerie feeling of being watched, but the crawling sensation at the base of his neck wouldn't allow it. He knew she was there, though just how much she'd overheard remained a mystery. "Sleep well, Cinderella?"

She was wearing one of his T-shirts and nothing else. It was only two sizes too big and hung down to the middle of her sleek thighs. Her hair, an intriguing and unusual shade of dark red and slightly mussed, hung loose around her shoulders. Even the shadows beneath her eyes had faded to a paler shade of blue. She looked delicious, and he ached to repeat last night, even though he knew it was unlikely to happen. Circumstance had brought them together, and since then everything had changed. Might as well attempt to put it in the past. Nothing, it seemed, was permanent, except his feelings of guilt, and he was beginning to think he would never be free from them.

She ignored the table and instead slipped onto a stool

at the island, her bare feet hooked over the bottom rung. Christ, she looked young. Too young. "What's wrong, De Wulf? You look like your dog just died." Honz, lying in front of the balcony windows, chose that moment to raise his head and let out a warbling canine groan. "Oops. Sorry," she said, "I didn't mean to imply anything."

"You must be hungry," Adam said. "There's some two-day-old takeout in the fridge, and a bagel or two in the bread box—or maybe you'd like to grab something on your way to wherever it is you'll be going."

She avoided his gaze, but he thought her eyes looked suspiciously bright. "Mind if I borrow that lock pick?" She rattled the handcuff still clamped around her slim wrist.

"No need. I'll do it for you." He reached for the steel bracelet, and his fingertips brushed the back of her hand. She glanced up, seemingly a little startled. Adam's mouth curved in a smile. "No worries, sweetheart. I've no intention of taking advantage of the fact that you're nearly naked, wearing nothing but one of my shirts, in my apartment. You don't know it yet, but I'm not that kind of fella."

"You could have fooled me," she said, and he couldn't quite tell if she was teasing.

"Last night?" he said. He could have made short work of the lock, but he purposely took his time, enjoying her nearness, the intoxicating smell of hot skin and shared kisses. "It was Mardi Gras. People do a lot of crazy things during Mardi Gras, things they wouldn't normally do."

"So you're telling me you gave up sex for Lent?"

"Not exactly." He met her gaze, and it was damned hard to tear himself away. He sprang the mechanism, the restraint opened, and still they remained inches apart.

"About that bagel," she said softly. "I am kind of hungry."

"Right. The bagels." For a moment Adam's gaze was locked with Llewellyn's, their breathing and the beat of their hearts perfectly synchronized. Then, without putting away the tools of his trade, he abruptly moved away, shattering the moment.

A little while later, he sat across the table from her, sipping his coffee while she finished the last bite of a third bagel and then settled back to wrap her slim white hands around a steaming mug of black coffee. "I don't know when I've tasted coffee this bad."

"After the first few pots, it loses its charm."

"You may have a point," London admitted, his gentle jab coaxing a smile from her. Caffeine had always been her drug of choice. For days, she'd been living on it and little else. *Living on the edge.* She'd been doing it so long, she wasn't sure she knew what a normal existence consisted of, yet De Wulf was in no position to judge her. She'd gotten a glimpse of his closet on her scavenger hunt for something to wear. It held an assortment of wigs, glasses, sunglasses, hats, and various devices. The man had more personae in his repertoire than Dana Carvey. "Coffee's my crutch, my security blanket," she observed. "But the life is yours. You've been out of it for a while—why the need for so much secrecy?"

He didn't have to tell her that it had become a habit. Old spooks never died, they just sank deeper into paranoia. De Wulf wasn't old, but there was no doubt that he was cautious. And maybe he had good reason to be.

"You ask a lot of questions," he said. He shook a cigarette out of a pack and offered her one.

London shook her head. "One bad habit at a time. Thanks anyway."

"So what's next, Llewellyn?"

"Another pot or two. Only this time, I'll make it."

It wasn't what he meant, and she knew it. He was talking about the investigation into Benji's murder. She'd hit a dead end, and they both knew it. Only London wasn't quite ready to face what came next, and she dreaded seeing Patrick. She'd failed, and failure didn't sit well with her. Llewellyns outperformed normal mortals. Duty came first—duty to family, to country, to the legend that was the clan Llewellyn.

"You've come up blank," he said carefully, "yet you don't strike me as the type to just roll over. It's something to think about, however. Maybe the time's come to just let it go, get on with your life."

The mere suggestion touched a raw nerve. London's temper flared, and her glance hardened. "Bury my brother and get back to business as usual? Put his murder in the past and try to forget it ever happened. Like you've done with the orchid?"

The jab hit its mark. She saw the shades come down. His expression changed subtly; his features grew taut, his blue eyes wary . . . and London wondered what lay behind his obsession with that damned orchid. "Apples and oranges, sweetheart. You're in dangerous waters— in all probability you are out of your depth—and whatever it was that got your brother killed could easily do you, too."

"I'm not your sweetheart," London assured him, ignoring that they had a great deal more in common than either of them was willing to admit. "And I seem to recall a pair of goons in satin small clothes who were hot on your ass not long ago. You want to talk dangerous? Let's talk Joey the Finger Demano, and your involvement with one of the most ruthless mob bosses on the Eastern Seaboard. Dangerous waters, De Wulf? That's the freaking pot calling the kettle black!"

He sucked hard on the cigarette and then blew out a stream of soft gray, stubbing it out in a potted plant with at least half a hundred discarded butts, all of them half smoked. "You're going to kill that palm if you keep that up."

He snorted, and some of the tension between them lessened. "Better it than me. I'm tryin' to quit."

London breathed a little easier. Thoughts of last night's passionate interlude, of the poignancy in his touch, were never far away. Something was happening between them—something she didn't fully understand and wasn't yet ready to let go of. "Level with me, Adam. What's with the suits? What do they want with you? They didn't exactly look like part of Demano's collection agency, and you don't strike me as the type to get mixed up in anything stupid without a really good reason."

"Honz needs to go out," he said quietly, and there was something about the way he said it that touched a chord deep inside London. Whether from habit or some inherent tendency, he wasn't a man who easily allowed others access to any part of his life, yet he'd brought her here to his apartment; he'd cared for her, made love to her, and guarded her sleep.

"Honz is fine," London argued. "And what's more, I don't think he appreciates you using him as a way out of answering my question. Are you in some kind of trouble?"

Without acknowledging a very legitimate question, he reached out and teased the curve of her cheek with a lazy finger. "Blimey, Llewellyn. The only trouble I have at the moment is trying to keep my mind on business, and my hands off you. Hey," he said softly, "no need to look like that. You haven't lost your best friend. We barely know one another."

"Actually, I have," she said. "Benj was more than my brother; we were friends." She fought the catch in her voice and lost. "For as long as I can remember, he was there to rag on me, to make my life harder than it needed to be, to do all the things big brothers are supposed to do. Now he's gone, and I can't even clear his name."

Adam's head came up. "Clear his name? From what?"

Llewellyn's pretty green eyes, glassy with tears, narrowed. "They've accused Benji of being a double agent."

He whistled softly. "That's a bit rough. Any chance they're right about him?"

"No way. Not Benji," she insisted, emphatic. "There's no way he would have been involved in something that dirty. Benji wasn't just a straight arrow; he qualified for sainthood. And the Agency wasn't just his job; it was his life. A calling."

"Sounds like a real stand-up fella, if you ask me. But you may not be the best judge of Benji's character, you bein' his sister and all."

"I knew him better than anyone, with the possible exception of Wyeth."

"Wyeth Pinchot?" Adam couldn't quite believe his ears. He hadn't heard that name in three years, and certainly hadn't expected to hear it come from Llewellyn. "What's he got to do with this?

"You know Wyeth?"

"You could say that," Adam admitted. "We worked together a few times." He didn't bother to tell her that there was no love lost between them. Pinchot had been brought in from administration when Adam's case officer suffered a massive coronary. John Bridow had been something of a legend in the Directorate of Operations, and his shoes had been impossible to fill. Pinchot had done a poor job of it, and Adam hadn't made his job any easier. He'd been too consumed with his search for a rogue operative to concern himself with coddling Pinchot's shaky ego. Besides, Adam had been DO through and through, and highly independent. Unlike Bridow, Pinchot was a born and bred paper pusher, with limited experience in inspiring a spirit of cooperation among the ranks. In other words, he'd been a first-class arse about pushing his bloody weight around.

"Wyeth and Benji were close friends," she said softly. "He's almost family."

Something in the way she said it triggered a twinge of envy within Adam. Pinchot was lucky to have someone who felt that way about him. How long had it been since he'd had that kind of connection to anyone? Not even with Julia, he thought. In reality, not since his parents died.

Llewellyn's cheeky bravado had collapsed. She sat there looking small and uncertain, and all he wanted to do was hold her, kiss that fragility away. He was aware of her emotional state. She was vulnerable, and he was a genuine heel to be thinking of wild, uninhibited sex at a time like this. He couldn't seem to help it, though. She had that effect on him. There was a soft, faraway look in her eyes, a breathy quality to her voice, and at intervals—when the strain on her became too much—she caught that full lower lip between her teeth, pausing until she could safely go on. It was driving him crazy.

She was driving him crazy.

"We've known him forever. In fact, we practically grew up together."

"What's Pinchot think about all of this? The charges against your brother, I mean."

A shuddering sigh. "He believes it. All of it. He was the one who broke it to me and presented the evidence."

Adam watched her closely, aware that he shouldn't put her through this. But she seemed to need to talk, and at the moment he was her only option. He tried not to think about what that said—about both of them. "Evidence?"

"Bank deposits. More money than he could have possibly made legitimately. Witnesses who claim that Benj was working with the Ghost."

It was the last thing he expected her to say, and the one thing that turned his blood cold.

Chapter Six

"Come again?" Adam said. "I can't have heard you right."

"Wyeth hinted that Benji may have had some connection to the Ghost. The Ghost was a double agent active a few years ago, whose identity is still unknown."

"No kidding. What the hell led them to that conclusion?"

London shrugged, but there was an air of dejection about the gesture. "An informant—an Austrian agent, who claims to have firsthand knowledge."

Adam shrugged. "So your brother went over to the other side."

"It wasn't like that."

"Look, it wouldn't be the first time something like that happened. Grudges and interdepartmental rivalries, a sense of not being appreciated, money . . . Like I said: it happens."

"Maybe—to other officers. But not to Benji." In an effort to make him hear her, she leaned forward, grasping one of his hands with both of hers, holding his gaze just as unrelentingly. "You didn't know him, Adam, but I did, and I swear to you, he's innocent."

The pain in those pretty green eyes was as obvious as it was impossible to ignore. Why it was so crucial to her that he believe her—and believe in a dead bloke's innocence—remained a mystery. He was a stranger, a thief, more at home in the shadows and back alleyways than in the sunlight until he had stepped over a window casement and into her life. It had happened in a split second, and he would be just as quickly gone. It didn't make a damn bit of sense that she should hang on his reply with that look on her face, as if she would shatter if it turned out to be the one thing she couldn't stand to hear. . . . But none of it made a damn bit of sense—not the murder, not her dogged persistence in tracking him down, not the crazy urge to hold her for as long as she would let him.

"I believe you," he said, watching as the breath she'd been holding went out of her. For a moment, they sat quietly, Llewellyn as relieved at his admission as Adam was perplexed by her need to hear it. "What I don't get is why it matters to you. Why do you care what I think? I'm nobody. In fact, nobody would probably be a step up."

"You're not nobody. You're all I have."

Adam took another cigarette out of the box lying between them on the table and shoved it between his lips, trying to avoid focusing on what she'd just said. But he couldn't quite smother the soft sarcasm of his conscience. *Check that ego, De Wulf. You can't afford to let a simple, offhand comment turn your head around. She's a woman, that's all—a warm, shapely body in the darkness, a delicious, temporary distraction—and you can't allow her to become anything more than that.*

He lit the cigarette, a Turkish tobacco he'd become fond of overseas, and let the match burn down to his fingertips, dropping it a fraction of a second before the flame could kiss his skin. A long drag and a short pause later, he raised his gaze to hers. "If that's the case, sweetheart, then you're in a hell of a lot of trouble.

Look, Llewellyn, it's been fun. In fact, you're the best time I've had in a long time, but there's a brick wall at the end of this dark alley, and no other way out but the way you came in."

His brusqueness didn't shake her at all, and he thought that she was quite possibly the most stubborn woman he'd ever had the misfortune to be handcuffed to. "You could come back with me," she said.

Adam could tell by the way she said it—softly, intently—that it wasn't a harebrained idea she'd come up with this instant. Oh, it was harebrained, all right, but it was also something she'd been thinking for quite some time. *Oh, Christ,* he thought. *Was that the real reason she'd come to New Orleans? To drag him back to Langley?* The thought made him queasy. "Back?" he said suspiciously.

"You're exactly the type of man I need to help me break this thing," she argued fiercely. "The only man. You have the experience. You're respected, and you know more about the Ghost than anyone."

He knew about the Ghost, all right. More than he wanted to know. He'd spent the better part of two years pursuing every lead he could dig up, and he'd come within a hairbreadth of catching him. He'd come too close . . . and it had cost him. In fact, the price he'd paid for his obsession had been too high, and he wasn't the only one who'd suffered because of it. His failures had a way of spilling over onto other people . . . people he cared about—and he wasn't about to let that happen to Llewellyn. "You're forgetting that I've got plans—obligations. I can't put my life on hold for some crazy redhead who's got a hard-on for getting her pound of flesh. And anyway, why would the Ghost break a three-year hiatus just to come back and kill your brother? He dropped out of sight a long time ago. Why come back now? It doesn't make sense."

"Since when did any of it make sense? Somebody's got to pay, Adam. My brother's dead; his reputation is shredded."

Benji was dead, all right, but so was Michael.

"But you're alive. Look, I can't bring him back, and neither can you. The smartest thing you can do is to deal with your grief and get on with it. I'd lay odds that's what good old Benji would say if he were here right now."

It was easy to hand out advice when your heart wasn't the one being torn in two, and hard to deal with it when it was happening to you. He knew how she felt. He'd been there . . . or very nearly so. A brother. A child. It was the same, and it was different. Both were lives unlived—one cut short in his prime, the other a promise unrealized. Adam rubbed the spot where a scowl had formed, dead center in the middle of his forehead. For a half second, he saw the small white coffin. So small, it couldn't be real . . . too small to contain a life. "I can't help you, Llewellyn. Not with this. I won't."

"I could have turned you in, and I didn't do it. I could have had you arrested."

"And I'm supposed to be grateful for that?" He shook his head, the image of that shiny white box and brass handles still with him. "You've no fucking idea what it is you're dealing with."

Or what she was asking.

"I know that you can do this," she said.

Adam put the cigarette in the ashtray, where it streamed smoke to the ceiling. She was still holding on to his hand, her grip painfully tight, as if he were important to her survival, her hold on reality. Maybe he was. Maybe he was all that was standing between her and disaster. The only one who could stop her from throwing her future away. "You're beautiful," he said, coming half out of his chair, leaning across the table to graze her mouth with his, unsurprised when she met him halfway and braced a hip on the table. Her empty coffee mug rolled off the table and onto the floor, joined by the ashtray, and neither of them noticed. "You're unbelievably sexy . . . a real firecracker. You've got your whole life ahead of you. What the hell kind of man would help you throw all that away?"

She broke from him, just enough to look into his eyes. Her pupils were large, her lashes damp . . . the green of her irises soft and inviting, like deep water, and Adam sensed that the danger of drowning was incredibly real. "I'll change your mind, De Wulf. I'll make it so you can't resist me."

"I'm halfway there already," he admitted. "Go on, give it all you've got. It won't make a damn bit of difference."

London heard the warning, but she didn't listen. His knowledge was vast, his experience unequaled, and he'd been well connected during his days with the Agency. He could help her find Benji's killer, if only she could convince him. The kiss had started as a ploy to lure him in, but it quickly went far beyond that. Adam was ruggedly handsome, lean and hard-muscled, sexier than he was cooperative.

London had had a lifetime of experience in dealing with hard-nosed, hard-assed, pigheaded males, but she'd never met anyone quite like Adam De Wulf, and as his weight pressed her back onto the table, she sensed that the stakes in the dangerous game they were playing were far greater for her than for him. He was secretive, emotionally distant, so closely shielded as to appear completely invulnerable. Her own defenses, on the other hand, were tattered and worn, her vulnerability at an all-time high, and the physical escape he provided so thrilling, as intoxicating as a narcotic—and just as potentially lethal. He was exactly the sort of man she'd been careful in the past to avoid, and the type to which she'd always been fatally attracted.

The dangerous type.

An ego buster.

A heartbreaker.

The type of man she might never be able to get enough of.

It terrified London, yet instead of putting the brakes on her passion, the fear just added another dimension to the insatiable craving for the warm, hard feel of his hands on her flesh, the heady rush of her blood surging madly through her veins.

He kissed her hard, relentlessly, his hands working the T-shirt up to bare her breasts. London held her breath. The apartment had been dark last night when they'd made love with the rain falling softly outside, and the shadows had been deep; and with their sexual currents running high, there had been little time for him to take notice of the padding in her black lace Wonderbra, or breasts that were, on her most optimistic day, a cup size smaller than she would have liked them to be. The kitchen light was on, a glaring seventy-five-watt bulb throwing a blue-white illumination on every corner of the kitchen, keeping the cockroaches at bay and revealing all her imperfections.

De Wulf didn't seem to mind. He left her breathless, her senses spinning, and kissed the blue-marbled white softness with an infinite tenderness. London caught a ragged breath, running her fingertips along the flat planes of his cheeks, gently caressing the corners of his mouth, where skin burned bronze by the subtropical sun met pale flesh that rarely saw the light of day. His lowered lids raised, and the hunger in his eyes astounded her. Then he left off the foreplay, swept her off the table, and carried her to his bed.

There, in the sweetly scented semidarkness, amid sheets rumpled from her long sleep, Adam made love to her. Llewellyn was an impatient lover, but Adam didn't rush to completion. He liked the feel of her softness cushioning him, the cool touch of her small hands on his skin, and he wanted to prolong it. As much as she aggravated and nagged him and tried to manipulate him into helping her, he had a soft spot for her. Llewellyn, all wild red hair and big green eyes. She was a treasure, all right, a rare bit of balm for a lonely heart, a peach of a distraction to take his mind off his troubles—but he was acutely aware that it wouldn't last.

She would be leaving soon, heading back to Langley and the life she'd left behind in order to find him. In a few weeks or a few months, she would have forgotten him, and this night would be a vague memory.

It wouldn't be as easy where he was concerned. He'd never met anyone quite like Llewellyn, and he knew that he would savor the memory of her scent, the sound of her breathing in the darkness, the catch in her throat as she gave herself over to ecstasy and her body went limp beneath him—for a long, long time.

When London woke, she immediately knew that something was wrong. Sunlight was slanting through the louvers, but there was no rich aroma of roasted beans brewing, and the apartment was deathly quiet. Lying naked in a tangle of sheets, she rolled onto her back and glanced at his pillow, where the imprint of his head was still visible. The bathroom door was open, but the room was dark. "Adam?" Throwing off the sheets, she fumbled for the oversized T-shirt he'd stripped from her last night, and slipped it over her head. "Adam?"

Barefoot, she padded to the kitchen. Honz's nylon lead was missing from its place by the door, and so was the leather case that held Adam's notebook computer. Ignoring the chill foreboding that snaked up her spine, she tried to convince herself that he was just walking the dog. "He wouldn't dare leave now," she assured herself, "not after last night." But a small, cynical part of her knew differently. Her pulse kicking up an angry notch and a sickening ball of cold dread in the pit of her stomach, she stalked to the closet in the bedroom and threw the door open. The clothing had been rifled, and there were a suspicious number of empty hangers. Pinned to an empty wig stand was a note. London lifted it off and read:

> *The rent's paid till the end of the month. Stay as long as you like. Thanks for the ride, Llewellyn. It was a blast.*
>
> *A.*

"It was a blast?" London crumpled the paper, heat rising along with her anger. "Fucking arrogant bastard. I'll show you a blast."

Eddie Whitefish came out of his coma in time to bitch about his hospital lunch. His physician had stopped by a half hour earlier to remark on Eddie's miraculous recovery. Eddie didn't know shit about miraculous, unless one took into account the fact that that butch bitch Helga had beat him senseless with a dildo. "Like it ain't bad enough that I'm in this cockroach palace because of a freaking fake cock, they expect me to eat this crap?" He poked at the squares of green Jell-O with the tip of his spoon, shooting a glance at his roommate. The guy had to be eighty if he was a day, and he slept even more than Eddie had during his stint in la-la land. "You hungry, Bobby? 'Cause I ain't eatin' this shit." Eddie checked the hallway outside the room for activity, then scooped up a green cube and, using the spoon as a catapult, shot the Jell-O into the old coot's grizzled maw.

"Now, is that nice?"

Eddie glanced at the large men suddenly filling the small doorway and grinned a little too widely—a lame attempt to hide his nervousness. "Freddie, Sal! It's great to see you!"

"Eddie, you're a hard man to find," Freddie said, his gray eyes slitted in his round, freckled face. "We been lookin' for you, Eddie. Where you been?"

"Who, me? I been right here, sleepin' off a hell of a hangover." Eddie shifted in the hospital bed. In the next bed, Bobby let out a loud snort, then settled to snoring again. "I'm flattered that you came to see me, but what brings you here? I ain't done nothin' to piss Joey off, have I?"

Sal motioned to the closed door on his right. "You mind if I have a look at the facilities?"

Freddie rolled his eyes, and Sal spread his hands wide. "What?"

"Get on with it, will you?" Freddie ground out.

Sal shook his head on the way to the bathroom. "All that hostility's gonna get you an ulcer, my friend."

"I'm not sure Joey agrees with you, Eddie. You know how he feels about broken promises. That guy you hooked him up with who was supposed to deliver the orchid? Well, he didn't come through for him, and Joey—he's not a happy man. And when Joey's not happy, I'm not happy." The statement was punctuated by a loud flush and the rush of retreating water.

"Adam stiffed Joey?" Eddie swallowed hard, his Adam's apple bobbing convulsively.

Sal emerged from the bathroom, zipping his fly. "Yeah, and he almost got away with it. He's a slippery character, that Australian. A little too careful, if you know what I mean. We've been askin' questions, and we've come up empty—nada, zero, out of pocket—"

"He gets the picture," Freddie snapped. "And that's where you come in. You know this guy, and you know where to find him. Unless you're anxious to take another long sleep, you'll share that information with us."

Eddie looked from Freddie's flushed face to Sal, who shrugged. "Freddie's got issues he hasn't dealt with yet. They make him cranky."

"I can see that," Eddie agreed. He'd begun to sweat. He could feel perspiration collecting under the thin hospital gown. Joey the Finger was ruthless when it came to getting what he wanted, and Freddie and Sal lived to carry out Joey's orders. One of Eddie's friends from the old days in Jersey had decided to hold out on Joey, and he'd ended up in a vat of red wine vinegar. The coroner's report had cited drowning as the cause of death. Eddie hadn't been able to look at vinaigrette the same way since. "Hey, listen, guys. I don't owe this guy my loyalty. What's he ever done for me? I'll be glad to tell you everything I know about Adam."

Eddie waited until Joey Demano's muscle departed the hospital room, counted to ten, and picked up the bedside phone. Finger poised over the buttons, he suddenly realized he couldn't remember Adam's number.

Kicks Merlot was a regular at Jackson Square. Like most of the artists and musicians who hung around on the city streets, Kicks could usually be found seated on the hard concrete walkway outside the black wrought-iron fence, not far from the statue of Andy Jackson, his dark glasses hiding a sightless stare, clarinet case open to donations as he made slow, hypnotic love to his horn.

Dressed in a bright Hawaiian shirt and plaid polyester pants, his graying hair stringing from under a flat-crowned black felt hat, Kicks wrapped up a medley of tunes with his usual flair, ignoring the eerie protesting howl of the large dog that lay by his side. Several tourists had gathered around, and Kicks heard nervous titters as well as the flutter of currency into the open clarinet case. "Always a critic in the crowd somewhere," Kicks said in a voice gone smoky and soft.

The tourists moved on, and the Weimaraner grumbled low in his throat. "Blow this gig, and you'll be back on the kibble." Llewellyn was going to be plenty pissed; he just hoped the hell she wasn't pissed enough to trash the apartment, or he'd have little hope of getting his security deposit back.

"Would you look at that? Blind as a bat, and he plays like an angel."

"How the hell do you know he's blind? Maybe he's just hungover."

"Are you kidding? Look at that incongruous combination of patterns and plaids. Only a blind man would dress like that. You got a C-note on you, Freddie?"

"What the hell do you want with that kind of money?" Freddie demanded. Kicks could see the man's shoes. Expensive. Italian. Bruno Magli or some such pretentious shit. The dark guy wore loafers, highly polished.

"I'm gonna give it to him. Such determination and God-given talent should be rewarded."

"Reward him out of your own take, you big, dumb fuck."

"Hey. No need to get nasty."

"Stay and swoon all you like. I'm goin' over there to Conti to kick that Aussie's ass all the way to Baton Rouge."

The Bruno Maglis retreated from his field of vision. Sal sighed. "Listen, don't take it personally. Freddie doesn't deal well under pressure, and he doesn't know how to enjoy the finer things in life. It's nothing personal. You're really very good." He dug in his pocket and pulled out a five. "Have a nice day, now." Then he hurried to catch up to Freddie.

Adam lowered his smoky shades to look at Honz. "So Llewellyn's at the apartment? She's no babe in the woods, you know. Not like she needs anyone to help out." He shifted his glasses back into place, picking up the horn and snapping off a jazzy-sounding stanza before lowering it again. "She's trained to survive and trained to kill. Unless they get the drop on her, she'll be right as bloody rain—if she's even there. She might be halfway to the airport by now. There's no good reason for her to stay, and nothing for her in New Orleans."

The weimaraner laid his chin on the concrete and put his paws over his eyes, as though it pained him to look such a fucking liar straight in the eyes.

Adam couldn't blame Honz. He hadn't believed a word of it, either. Llewellyn didn't need a legitimate reason to stay. It hadn't mattered to her that he didn't have the information she'd tracked him down in order to obtain; his not knowing the killer's identity hadn't sent her packing, and he wasn't at all convinced that his abandoning her would, either. He'd figured she'd get the message if he just disappeared, but he'd discounted her innate capacity for stubbornness, and he could imagine her waiting for him to return, dressed only in one of his T-shirts, all long bare legs and sexy, come-get-me smile.

There was an excellent chance that she and Joey Demano's aging Italian stallions were about to have a head-on collision. Honz slid one paw down and rolled that pale eye at Adam. "We're a pair, you and I," Adam said with a sigh. "A pair of saps, that's what."

He put the horn in the case, closed it with a snap, and dropped it by a goateed gent with an acoustic guitar. "Keep an eye on this for me, will you?"

"Sure thing, man."

Then, taking Honz's lead, he started out in the direction of Conti Street at a dead run.

London was halfway out the apartment door when she realized she had no clue how to find Adam De Wulf if he did not wish to be found. He had been living in New Orleans, while she was a stranger to the city. He would have familiarized himself with every side street and back alley, every easy escape and area of possible concealment.

Every wily fox had two exits to his den, and De Wulf had covered every angle a dozen times. She couldn't hope to outwit him. Getting to know a city this large would take time—time she didn't have. He had taken the things that were important to him: that amazingly ugly hound and his notebook computer. Chances were excellent that he wasn't coming back.

She showered and changed, made coffee, and sat at the same kitchen table where they'd nearly made love the night before, musing over her cup. Of all the information she dug up on De Wulf, personal stats were nonexistent aside from his educational info and that uncle in Ohio . . . though John LaMonte, the retired spook from the bar who'd pointed her compass toward New Orleans, had mentioned an ex-wife in connection with Adam. No indication, not the slightest inkling if this wife was living or dead—someone he'd contact or avoid—and the details of Adam's life remained a well-guarded secret.

While her half-finished cup of coffee cooled on the table and formed a thin and undrinkable scum, London pummeled herself mentally for screwing up. She'd spent forty-eight lust-filled hours in the most intimate contact with De Wulf, and she hadn't asked a single question or gained a single microscopic scrap of the sort of pertinent information that would clue her in to how she might locate him. "So, I was a little distracted," she said irritably. "It isn't often a woman comes across buns that tight."

She closed her eyes and breathed a silent prayer of thanks that Patrick was in another time zone. She'd just committed a cardinal sin as far as he was concerned: allowing herself to succumb to great sex. For one sacrilegious second, she wondered if Patrick had ever—then, horrified, she forced her thoughts to take an abrupt U-turn. *Trust me, London, you do not want to go there.*

Instead, she made up for being lax and distracted by rifling the apartment. She didn't find much. There was a short stack of *Popular Mechanics,* and another, more high-tech magazine she didn't recognize in the small bedroom closet. Neither stack had mailing labels.

No subscription. That was unsurprising. He would ignore the thrift of mail delivery in favor of increased security. She'd wager that his computer had a fortresslike firewall, too. She was in the middle of ransacking his underwear drawer just for the sake of petty revenge when a footstep sounded in the hallway. London looked up sharply, a pair of black silk boxers in hand. *Maybe he changed his mind,* she thought, giving herself a hard mental shake for being so hopeful.

"Don't be such an ass, Llewellyn," she muttered, turning back to what she'd been doing. "He's not coming back, and you'd be an even bigger ass than you are if you let yourself care about him. He's fucking, big-time trouble, and you need that about as much as you need a killer case of hemorrhoids."

But she did need him. She needed the expertise that only he had, the knowledge she suspected he possessed but had shared with no one. She'd done all the research she could possibly do—paper files, computer files, and Cid's vast connections—and she'd come up surprisingly empty. There had been a few documents concerning the Ghost, but nothing that wasn't already common knowledge or part of Agency scuttlebutt. It was almost as if the files concerning the Ghost had been dumped or destroyed.

But that made about as much sense as her getting involved with a former spy turned cat burglar.

Why would Administration destroy the files on an open case? How long had the files been gone, and had De Wulf known anything about it? She'd sensed he knew a great deal he wasn't telling, and with him gone there was little chance of her learning any of it. "You couldn't pick a boring, stay-at-home kind of guy to get involved with? De Wulf is about as communicative as a mime with laryngitis. And you're getting nowhere with this."

She glanced around the apartment. It was shaded, the shadows deep and comfortable, the rooms and furnishings slightly shabby in a time-worn New Orleans sort of way. Sounds of midmorning traffic mingled with an occasional snatch of conversation from pedestrians strolling through the quaint streets of the French Quarter. Honz's huge rawhide chew bone occupied one corner of the kitchen, and the potted palm was drooping from an overdose of nicotine.

God, she was going to miss this place.

A board creaked under someone's weight, and as London turned, the door crashed in and Joey the Finger's associates came barreling into the kitchen.

London spun for the bedroom and the French windows open to the balcony and the street, two stories below. The drop was a lot more serious than the leap from the porch roof at the Maltese mansion, but Demano's muscle were packing, and she didn't have time to stand around and wonder about her options. She ran to the railing and flung a leg over; then Freddie's sausagelike fingers closed over her arm.

"Where the hell do you think you're goin'?" His piece, a shiny chrome-plated 9mm automatic, caught the lazy morning sunlight as it broke through a rent in the clouds. "For a minute there I was afraid nobody'd be here. I'm so glad to see that you're home."

"Nice place you got here," Sal said, indicating the rumpled bed with a nod of his dark head. "Though it could use a bit of straightening. Clutter invites chaos— bad chi, you know? Negative energy." He sneezed hard. "You got a dog?" Sneeze. He blew his nose on a white monogrammed handkerchief—a sound like honking geese. "I'm allergic to dogs."

"Would you shut the fuck up?" Freddie snarled. "You're pissin' me off with this sensitive shit." His hard little pig eyes slid to London. "Where's that prick, the Aussie?"

"De Wulf," Sal corrected.

"What?"

"Eddie said his name was De Wulf."

"What the fuck ever. I don't care what the fuck his fucking name is!"

London tried to twist from his grasp, but he was relentless. "I don't know where he is, but you're right about one thing. He's a prick—an arrogant, blockheaded Australian asshole, and if he were here right now, you wouldn't have to kill him. I'd do it for you."

"Sounds to me like there's trouble in paradise."

London spun on Sal. "You know, he's right. You really should shut up. I don't know where he is. He left early, without telling me anything."

"I don't know if I believe her, Freddie. I saw her bite her lip just now—a sign of indecision in body language."

"You know what?" London said. "I'm sick of this bullshit! You lost the orchid. So buy another one! You either let me go and we call it even, or you're gonna be dealing with a major case of PMS."

"And lose our best bargaining chip?" Freddie said. "You're shacked up with this guy. He'll come back for you. I think we'll wait for him—together."

"Bad decision," London said, grabbing a handful of Freddie through his trousers and twisting hard.

"Fucking bitch! What the hell is wrong with you?" Freddie cuffed her hard with his free hand, the one that held the pistol. The blow caught her on her forehead, just above her left temple, and stung like hell, but London didn't break her hold on his genitals—not even when a mouse-colored streak flew over the carpet, grabbing up the chew bone.

Freddie went to his knees. "Oh, Christ! Oh, Jesus! Kill me!" Freddie screamed. "Just kill me now!"

Sal had his hanky in one fist, his weapon in the other. He sneezed continuously and could barely keep his eyes open. "Shit!" Sal said. "*Ah . . . sniii!* Freddie. I think our guy's here. *Ah . . . sniii!* Listen, friend. If you know what's—*ah, sniii!*—good for you, you'll stay—*ah, sniii!*—put."

Outside on the balcony, Llewellyn was in big trouble. Adam launched himself across the room and onto the gallery, grabbing her with one hand, flinging her out of the way as he hit Freddie with a punishing right. His face purple, Freddie gagged for air, his eyes rolling up into his head as he fell back, twitched twice, and lay still.

Inside the bedroom, Honz had the sneezing Sal trapped on the bed, which he circled, baring his fangs in a warning growl. "Call him—off—*ah, sniii!*—will ya? Crimen—*ah, sniii!*—ently! I'm dyin' here!"

Freddie moaned and held his crotch as Adam grabbed Llewellyn's wrist and dragged her out of there. At the apartment door he whistled sharply, and Honz left off harassing Sal and bolted down the hallway.

"Jesus, Llewellyn, now you've done it!"

"Now, *I've* done it? Excuse the hell out of me for defending myself. What did you expect me to do?"

"Anything but bust the balls of one of the most ruthless mobsters on the East Coast would have been acceptable."

They pounded down the stairs and across the courtyard, where Llewellyn lost a shoe. She balked, hopping on one foot. "What the hell are you doing?" She'd broken away, turned back to the shoe lying faceup a dozen feet away.

"I'm not leaving it!" she said. "They're Italian."

"I don't give a shit if they're Donna freaking Karan! There's no bloody time—"

A bellow of pure rage funneled out of the stairwell. Adam swore, grabbing Llewellyn and throwing her upside down over his shoulder, then sprinting for the gate. He shot a glance to the rear. Freddie staggered out of the dark passageway into the light, his pistol clutched in one hand, the other still holding his crotch as he shouted a stream of foulmouthed obscenities, punctuated by Sal's back-to-back sneezing. "Sum-bitch!" Freddie howled. "I'm gonna kill both of you!"

"Ditto. *Ah, sniii!*"

Adam was six feet from the gate when Freddie started shooting. Bullets struck the courtyard wall, splintering brick and raining dust and razor-sharp shards all around him. He heard Llewellyn suck in a breath; then they were through the gate and on the street. "All right," she said. "I get it. The shoe is history. Just put me down."

Adam set her on her feet. She brushed her hair out of her eyes. "Where's your car?"

"Don't have one," Adam said.

"You don't have a car? How can you not have a car? It's positively un-American."

"So sue me." A yellow Checker cab appeared down the block. Adam grabbed her hand, whistling sharply as they dodged traffic. The cabbie pulled to a stop, and Honz leaped onto the seat; Llewellyn followed, and then Adam. "The airport, and step on it!"

Chapter Seven

"So, how about another double mocha latte with extra whipped cream? You look like you could use it." Cid looked London up and down and shook her head. "Maybe you should lay off that stuff and try a protein shake."

"Health shakes?" London shuddered. "You've got to be kidding. Besides, two's my limit. I'm trying to quit." She stared glumly at the pair of empties in front of her and thought of the potted palm at the New Orleans flat, its soil white with cigarette butts, its foliage drooping from the nicotine. Adam's voice echoed distantly in her head: *"Better it than me. I'm tryin' to quit."*

London immediately regretted her lapse. She'd sworn she'd stop thinking about him . . . but he'd been such an adventure . . . and such a disappointment. Nothing and no one could have convinced him to return to Virginia. The look in his eyes had told her that, and despite putting forth a heroic effort, she hadn't been able to change his mind. She'd failed—in more ways than one—and all she could do was regroup, decide her next move, and try to forget him.

She glanced at Cid, who was wearing an interesting mix of desert camouflage and flourescent pink tie-dye, which made London's gray pinstripe blazer and trousers seem ultraconservative by comparison. The Agency's new casual dress codes wouldn't have permitted something so wild, but it was after hours and Cid was on her way to the gym. "So, what's new in your life?" London asked. "Any buff new bods on the horizon?"

Cid's expression changed subtly. A lift of her dark brows, a noncommittal shrug. "Well . . . there *is* this guy."

"Oh, yeah? Now, that's intriguing. Is it someone from the health club?"

"No. This one actually has a neck." Cid sipped her carrot juice. "He's got a brain, too."

"There's a change," London said. "What happened to Snake?" Snake was an ex-cop with a cobra tattoo and bulging biceps. He'd been good-looking, in a bad-boy-be-careful-what-you-wish-for kind of way. Perfect for Cid, who, from all indications, seemed to enjoy a regular walk on the wild side.

"Snake? He's history."

"You two broke up?"

"Weeks ago. It was for the best." Cid shrugged. "He decided on a career change, and the clash in our life choices was just too big to overcome. You know, a vocational gap."

"From a cop to a biker—what's he doing now, opening a chop shop?"

"I wish. He's enrolled in Santa school. He got religion and he's training to be a bell ringer for the Salvation Army. Snake in a Santa suit. Can you imagine? I tried to tell him the red suit was gonna clash with his hair, but would he listen?" She stirred her cup with a green-striped swizzle stick. "I don't want to talk about it; it's too depressing. Let's talk about you. You've been weird since you got back. Quiet. In fact, too quiet. What happened in Louisiana?"

London frowned at the thin brown thread around the seam of her cup. If she combined the contents of both empties, it would almost make a dribble, and she wanted that new paint job for her old Porsche more than she wanted another coffee. Her savings account still hadn't recovered from the trip to New Orleans. "Weird? Gee, thanks." Patrick had said the same thing, only at ten times Cid's decibel level.

"Well, not *bad* weird, just weird. You know." Another shrug. "You haven't been to the clubs; you work late; you come in early. Pinchot says he spoke to one of the security guards, and your car never left the parking garage night before last. What's with that?"

"I had some research to run on the system." She wasn't about to tell Cid that she spent the biggest part of her nights going over the same questions, reviewing the same facts she'd reviewed the night before, in the impossible hope of uncovering anything new—and the rest of the time trying not to think about a certain retired spook. There was a chance that Cid might understand about her preoccupation with Benji's death, about Adam, but she couldn't risk it. And she didn't need a lecture about the virtues of acceptance and getting on with one's life, or the futility of dead-end love affairs, on which Cid was an expert.

The expectations friends and family dumped on her were way too high. Impossibly so. How could she get on with her life when so much was still unresolved?

Benji was dead.

Adam was gone.

And she was alone in her search for the truth.

For one fleeting second, she couldn't help thinking that maybe if he'd agreed to help her, maybe if she had his expertise, his skills, maybe things would have been different. . . . But he hadn't, and she had about as much chance of finding him a second time as she did of finding the Holy Grail.

"Wyeth means well, but he really needs to get a life so he can stop dissecting mine."

Cid blinked, all fake-lashed blue eyes and spaciness. "Pinchot's concerned about you, Lon. A little too concerned, maybe. I don't know, but I think he's got the hots for you."

"Wyeth?" London snorted. "You're kidding, right? We've known each other for half of ever. He spent as much time making my life miserable as Benji did when I was growing up, and that kind of intimacy doesn't make for good relationships. There's no room for mystery when you know someone as well as I know Wyeth."

Cid shrugged. "You might be surprised."

London squirmed in her chair. Starbucks was crowded, and Cid's observation made her vaguely uncomfortable, though she wasn't sure just why.

Thankfully, Cid let it drop. "Speaking of Mr. Mysterious, you haven't said a word about him, which is a pretty good indication that you found him. So, what's he like? Tall, dark, and secretive? Is he good in bed? Is he creative, or a snore?"

It was the one subject London had hoped to avoid, and the one thing she couldn't seem to stop thinking about. The way he touched her, the sound of his hoarse whisper in the dead of a New Orleans night, the way he'd made her feel. "He was . . . a dead end, and my trip was a bust."

"You're kidding? No new leads about what happened to Ben?"

"I already know what happened to Benji. He was murdered."

"But you said he was there in the room when Ben was killed. Doesn't he remember anything about the shooter? Height, weight, stats? His impressions, maybe?"

"Nothing that made any difference," London said. "Listen, I can't talk about this. In fact, I have to run. I'm supposed to meet Dad for dinner in thirty minutes."

A few minutes later, she hurried across the parking garage and climbed behind the wheel of the Porsche. She turned the key in the ignition, and nothing happened; then she turned it off and tried again. The engine growled but didn't start. London kept coaxing. It was a game they played, a battle of wills, and the old car never tired of it. She was just about to try again when someone rapped on the driver's window. London fumbled for the door latch; then Wyeth leaned close and peered in at her. London released the breath she'd been holding, and wound down the window. "Damn it, Wyeth. It's not a good idea to be sneaking up on me like that."

"You headed to Patrick's?"

"Yes, and I need to get going. I'm running late, and you know how he hates that."

"Mind if I beg a ride? I had to call a tow truck for my Audi. I think it blew a fuel pump."

"*You're* going to Dad's?"

"He invited me to dinner. I couldn't say no." He bounced on the balls of his feet, hands shoved into the pockets of a Levi's jacket. The heat was down in the parking garage. "Did you know it was supposed to get this cold? The weather report said it was supposed to be warm today. Who knew it would get this cold?"

London sighed. "Get in. If we don't make it to Patrick's by six, he's gonna rip us both a new one, and I still have to stop by the market."

Dinner at Patrick's was a nightmare. London and Wyeth arrived late, and Patrick was already well steeped in a recently opened bottle of scotch. In the kitchen

London found an alarming number of empties, in the trash, under the sink. Patrick was drinking; it wasn't social drinking, and it wasn't moderate drinking. They were going to have to discuss it, and she wasn't looking forward to it.

She spent an hour cooking pasta, making salad—a vain attempt at bringing one evening of normality into what remained of their shattered family. Her efforts weren't appreciated. "This pasta's too limp," Patrick grumbled.

"I think it's fine," Wyeth put in. "In fact, it's really great pasta."

Unfazed, Patrick fixed London with a bleary gaze. "Your mother always made the pasta al dente. That means you cook it just till it's fork-tender. This is overcooked." He stabbed a fork-full and held it up. "You could bait a hook with that."

"But why on earth would you want to?" London took a deep breath. It had been a lousy day, and the last thing she needed was Patrick's needling. "Mom spent a lot of time in the kitchen. I've been a little too busy with my career to learn to cook perfect pasta."

"Don't be a wise-ass, Meg. Something worth doing is worth doing right."

"Dad, for Christ's sake," London shot back. "It's spaghetti. The fate of the free world doesn't hang on whether it's al dente or not, and maybe if you'd set aside that chip on your shoulder long enough, you'd realize that."

He bolted the last two inches of scotch remaining in his highball glass and pointed an accusatory forefinger at her. "You watch that mouth, Meg. That kind of talk makes a woman look like trash, and I won't have it coming from my daughter! Always gotta have the last word. Never figured out that sometimes it's best for a woman to keep her mouth shut. Not like Ben. Ben was never cheeky to his old man. Ben learned respect."

"Benji knew how to work you."

"What the hell's that supposed to mean?"

"Nothing. It didn't mean anything. Forget I said it."

Patrick, feeling his whiskey and spoiling for a fight, wasn't about to let it go. "It meant something, or you wouldn't have said it."

London put down her fork. "All right. If that's the way you want it. Benji showed you what you needed to see, Dad. He knew how to avoid confrontation. It was one of his most valuable talents, keeping the peace in this family." She looked him straight in the eye. She wasn't angry, not really, just tired of their constant sparring. They couldn't have a simple dinner together without it resulting in a brouhaha. Just once, why couldn't they manage a simple dinner? "It's obvious that I don't share that particular talent for keeping all the balls in the air. Hell, I can't even cook pasta."

"So, now I have to be managed?" Patrick demanded, voice rising. "Is that it? Like some worn-out and worthless old man?"

"I didn't say that," London insisted.

"It isn't what you said that's important, Meg. It's what you meant."

Wyeth looked as if he wanted to crawl under the table. "That was the best pasta I've had in ages," he said a little too enthusiastically. "Meg, do you mind if I have seconds? Patrick, have some garlic bread."

London's look was frosty. "It's London, not Meg."

Wyeth smiled apologetically as he put down his napkin, clearly embarrassed. "Sorry. I didn't mean to overstep."

Patrick stiffened, and the hand that refilled his glass trembled. "You see what I'm saying?" Patrick asked

Wyeth. "Nothing but disrespect. I'm glad her mother isn't here to see what's become of her."

It was the worst thing he could have said. Something inside London broke open and bled. It was the one weapon he had that hurt her, and the one he always resorted to when she didn't live up to his great expectations. "I don't know about you," she said to Wyeth, "but I've certainly had my fill." Sickened by his desire to wound her, and by the violent urge she had to fight back, she threw down her napkin and came out of her chair, her father's argumentative voice sounding off behind her.

"Where do you think you're going? You haven't been excused!"

London laughed, but there was no humor in it. "You don't get it, do you, Dad? You're not talking to a twelve-year-old, and I don't have to take your crap anymore. No wonder Mom left you."

Wyeth stood. "I'll come with you."

London would have relished a few minutes alone, but she didn't argue the point. She'd already snapped at Wyeth once that evening when he seemed to be working hard to maintain the peace between her and Patrick . . . *stepping into Benji's place, Benji's shoes.* She wasn't sure why the errant thought rankled.

She walked as far as the oak tree in the front yard, the same one she used to climb when she was a kid. It was solid under her hand, steady and permanent. It would always be there, while human relationships were fragile and uncertain. *Here today, gone tomorrow. My God, Benj. How did this happen?*

After a moment, Wyeth broke the silence. "I know it may not seem like it, but he's worried about you—and quite frankly, so am I."

"Yeah, well you both have an odd way of showing it."

The fact that he'd been discussing her with Patrick hadn't been lost on her, and she wasn't happy about it.

"Okay, so maybe talking to your dad was a mistake, but I didn't know what else to do." He let out a hurried breath. "They want to send you back out on assignment. Kirkland thinks it will do you good to be operational again."

It was the last thing London expected. "Where?"

"His exact words were, 'anywhere but Austria.'" He took a cigar from the inner pocket of his sport jacket and held it up. "You mind?"

London shook her head.

He struck a match and puffed the cigar to life. Then he shook the match out and flung it to the curb. "Listen, London. I argued against it—not because I approve of this thing with Benj, but because I don't think you're ready for an overseas op. You know what it takes— you've got to be in top-notch physical shape—"

"But it isn't my physical condition that concerns you," she said.

"No, quite frankly, it isn't." A pause followed the admission, and she wondered if he was wishing he hadn't said what he was thinking. "Look, at the risk of being repetitive, I know how hard you're taking this, but maybe it's time to let it go. Get on with your life, your career."

Unable to find a suitable reply, London walked to the Porsche. "Tell Dad I said good night." She drove away without looking back, leaving Wyeth to find his own way home.

The evening had turned cold and crisp, with the sort of clear golden light that could only be found in autumn and spring. In New Orleans, the azaleas would be in full, glorious bloom, the days would be warming, balmy by turns, the sun would be warm on exposed skin, and the breeze as gentle as a kiss on the cheek.

Where was Adam? Was he still in New Orleans? Or had he moved on, to another city, another identity, another persona?

She'd thought about him endlessly in the three weeks since she'd returned to Virginia—daydreamed about him, and at night he haunted her dreams. He was a weakness, an obsession, and she wondered how long it would be before she stopped thinking about him, before the sweet warmth of his touch faded, before she could no longer see his face in her mind's eye.

She drove for nearly an hour, not really caring where she went as long as it was far away from Patrick. Then, when she'd exhausted her options, she went home.

Colonel Sanders was draped over the back of the couch, indulging in a snooze when she walked in. He opened one eye, staring at her without moving a muscle; then slowly the eye drifted shut again. "Glad to see you, too," London muttered.

Later, in the quiet of the kitchen, London went over the files she'd found in Benji's apartment after the murder. The files contained reports and notes on Benji's old cases, but nothing particularly helpful. London read until her head hurt and her vision began to blur. Then she paused, rubbing her eyes with the heel of her hand.

Her concentration had been so acute that she'd blocked out everything—all sight, all sound . . . but there was no sound. The house was totally, utterly silent. Not a noise, not a breath, not a creak to be heard. Unusually, unnervingly silent. The quick pad of running paws preceded Colonel Sanders' stubby body into the kitchen. With a disturbed *mer* he flew under the table and leaped onto a chair, completely concealed by the hunter-green-and-tan checked tablecloth. London sighed, reaching under the table to smooth his ruffled feathers, and the cat growled menacingly. "Hey! What's with you? PMS? DID? I suppose that next you'll be telling me your name is Chico, and you have a brother named Harry, and that you've never heard of a cat called the Colonel."

The Colonel was in no mood to be messed with. In fact, he swatted at her hand, and when she bent under the tablecloth to look at him, every hair seemed to be bristling. "You look like an overgrown hedgehog," London said.

As she was bent over, staring at the suddenly neurotic feline, something flitted past her peripheral vision. It went quickly, there and then gone, a pale blur in the dark field of the windowpane. Her instincts screamed for her to look; years of training kept her from giving in to the urge. Instead, she forced herself to breathe normally, remaining calm as she pretended to go back to her reading. When she'd entered the house, she'd gone straight to the kitchen and dumped everything at the table, including her Gucci knockoff handbag, which, during the course of her research, had been placed by the leg of her chair. She needed that bag and the pistol inside it, but she couldn't be obvious about it.

Someone was outside, just beyond the halo of light shining from her window, watching her. She didn't have to search the shadows. The shivery touch of their curiosity crawling along the skin of her forearms was sufficient proof they were there.

But who could it be?

It wasn't a bad neighborhood, and having a cop living on the other side of the wall was a definite plus. "If that's a peeper out there, he's about to get more than he bargained for." She hooked the strap of the bag with a finger and slowly hauled it up and onto her lap without seeming to do anything.

No sudden moves. If the watcher had a weapon other than the pistol in his pocket, she didn't want to startle him. She slipped her hand into the bag, her fingers closing over the cold steel of the weapon, and the crawly sensation fled. "Don't know about you," she said to the cat, "but I could use a glass of water." The sink was a foot and a half from the back door. London moved toward it as casually as she could. The door lock was a simple dead-bolt mechanism—too simple, Patrick had groused time and time again. He would have had her cloistered like a nun if he'd had his way, knitting afghans behind locked doors instead of being an active participant in life, her biggest thrill another new season of *Jeopardy*.

Almost there.

Her attention on the dark windowpanes, London threw the dead bolt, flinging herself down the back steps. As she struck a shooter's stance, the heel of her left foot found a fresh dog turd, and she slid, cursing as she went down like a bag of rocks . . . and the shadowed figure slipped out the other side of the back alley and melted into the darkness.

London picked herself up off the damp pavement, wincing at the pain in her ankle and the unsightly state of her new shoes. They were butter-soft suede, and now they were covered in dog do—ruined. She'd never been a crier, not even during the hormone-laden days of puberty, when girls became women and emotions always seemed to be running at high tide. But the disastrous dinner with Patrick and the heartbreaking loss of an expensive pair of pumps were almost more than she could stand. She stomped, shoeless, back into the kitchen, throwing the dead bolt, killing the light and leaving the kitchen.

Her bedroom faced Rialto, a well-lit middle-class street in a quiet middle-class neighborhood. Still feeling rattled from the episode in the kitchen, London drew a hot bath and indulged in a long soak, then threw on her favorite pajamas and wandered to the window. The streetlight bulb broken a few weeks ago had been replaced, and the sidewalk below was cast in its weak blue-green artificial glow. She scanned the street; the trees and bushes stood stark black and motionless. It all seemed normal . . . and it left her feeling restless.

Turning her back to the bed, she stared through the windowpane at nothing in particular, but saw the terminal at New Orleans International Airport instead. She'd been convinced that he was coming back to Langley. They'd gotten away from Freddie and Sal, and putting several states between them and Demano's enforcers seemed like the wisest move, but Adam had had other ideas. London's first clue came when he got out of the cab, leaving Honz in the backseat and instructing the cabbie to keep the motor running.

"You aren't coming with me, are you?" A simple question, straightforward—perhaps foolishly so. The answer was obvious.

"You don't need me, Llewellyn. Bloody hell, you don't need anyone." He smiled, and she had the vague impression that the expression was bittersweet. "And I don't need Langley. There's more than one ghost back there." He caressed her cheek with his thumb and sighed. "Better run. You'll need to get through security. Long lines these days."

London's throat ached. This was really it—they were going in opposite directions and she wouldn't see him again. She should have anticipated it; in fact, she should have been prepared to face it. But she wasn't, and it hurt. "There must be something I can say that will change your mind."

"Chin up, ay? and don't look so lost. You'll find your answers." He'd kissed her by the curb at the terminal gate—just a brief brush of his mouth against her cheek. Then he stepped into the cab and was gone.

London closed her eyes, leaning her forehead against the cool glass. He'd been so wrong. She wasn't doing all right. Her investigation into Benji's death was fizzling, and Wyeth was applying pressure for her to drop the matter altogether. He'd claimed it was out of concern for her, but London suspected there was more behind it than just Wyeth's worrying about the state of her sanity. The brass at the Agency were like all branches of government. What they didn't like, they did their best to bury. Failures, foul-ups, scandals—it hardly mattered. The rule was: keep it quiet, and keep it within the Company.

Her continued interest in a matter the DDO and DA considered closed was making people nervous, and some of those people wielded considerable power. They could make things damned uncomfortable for her if they wanted to. If that weren't enough, her relationship with Patrick was disintegrating. They couldn't talk without fighting, and they'd never learned to fight with the gloves on. As a result, someone always emerged from their arguments bruised and bleeding.

She hated it, hated the animosity. But she didn't know how to stop it. She couldn't make him proud of who she was any more than she could bring Benji back.

In light of everything that was wrong in her life, she'd completely forgotten the face in the kitchen window until the scrape of something heavy dragging across the shingles shocked her out of her inertia. Leaning closer to the glass, London strained to detect the source of the unusual noise, but the roof was empty. She'd almost given it up as something she'd imagined, until the pair of gloved hands grasped the ledge, and the lean, dark-clothed figure swung itself up and over the roof ledge. London slipped behind the cover of the heavy winter draperies and tried not to dwell on the pistol lying on the kitchen table.

She was an experienced operative with one of the most highly specialized, highly sophisticated intelligence agencies in the world, and she never seemed to have her weapon when she needed it—a dangerous habit that certainly spoke well for her level of distraction.

She could hear footsteps on the roof outside—quiet, careful treads that brought the prowler nearer to the only available entrance. Whoever he was, he certainly had balls—big brass balls, breaking into the residence of a government employee when said employee's car was parked out front and a police officer lived next door. She thought about calling Topper, but the phone was on the far side of the bed. Besides, his rattletrap Cougar hadn't been at the curb in its usual spot, and it was a safe bet he was pulling afternoon shift, which meant he wouldn't return until after midnight. Topper's wife, Betsy, was away, visiting her folks in Manassas for the weekend, and the last thing London needed was to talk to their machine; so she opted for the porcelain figurine of Lawrence's *Pinkie* sitting on her nightstand next to her packet of oral contraceptives and a half glass of tepid water.

Clutching Pinkie's thin waist, London held her breath. The casement bumped and then slowly slid up, and a thin beam like that of a penlight slid around the room, lingering on her pillow for the space of a breath and a heartbeat. When he ducked through the window and into the room, she struck, the statue arcing up and then sharply down as he began to turn.

Adam heard the swish of the draperies and caught a blur of movement out of the corner of his eye as she came at him—Llewellyn, nearly lost in the ugliest men's flannel boxers and oversized pajama top he'd ever seen, a porcelain doll held over her head like a weapon. She would have crowned him with it, too, but he raised his forearm and deflected the blow, knocking the statue out of her hands. It flew several feet and landed with a crash on the hardwood—nothing left but sharp splinters. "Hey, Red. Nice to see you, too. I'd been thinking of a 'Hello, Adam' kiss, but I suppose your trying to bash my head in will have to do."

She punched him in the stomach, then followed it with several open-handed blows aimed at his head. "Damn you!" she said. "What the hell do you think you were doing just now? Sneaking in my window! I could have killed you!"

"With that?" he asked, skating a glance at the pile of dust and rubble. "I like to think I'm a bit tougher than that. Unless, of course, I die laughing at that getup you're sporting." He looked her up and down, and he was in no hurry to meet her gaze again. "You're lookin' good, Llewellyn. Did you miss me?"

She wasn't ready to let him off the hook. He could see it in her face: her expression slightly petulant, a twelve-year-old's pout on a leggy beauty. Adam watched her for the space of a few breaths, drinking in that impish face and sleek, almost boyishly thin form. She turned to close the window. "Next time try a more unique approach: ring the bell."

"Yeah, well, I might have, but there's an SUV across the way, and he appears to be watching the house."

She went cautiously to the window and peered out, then swung and hit him again. "You are such a liar!"

Laughing, he hooked an arm around her waist and kissed her deeply, his hands quite naturally finding the smooth skin of her thighs, the soft curve of her ass. Her response was instantaneous: the parting of her lips, the hurried breathing, a soft, almost inaudible groan . . . and then she pushed away from him. "You're a shit, do you know that? Even worse than being a shit, you're an unrepentant shit! You left me at the airport, and now you show up out of the blue and think you can break-and-enter your way back into my life . . ."

He waited out her anger. She had every right to be ticked off, and there was no way he could explain his reasons for being here. He hadn't planned on returning to Virginia. In fact, he'd sworn when he turned his back on Langley three years before that he would never set foot on Virginia soil again. He'd fooled himself into believing that he'd left it all behind: the tragedy and frustration, the sorrow and the loss . . . and then Llewellyn walked into his life, and everything changed . . .

The fury burned out, but her wariness remained. She was afraid to hope. Afraid he would walk out on her again, and he couldn't deny that she had a valid reason to think it. "Why are you here, Adam? Level with me."

Adam shrugged, his tone even. "Unfinished business." He sounded casual, but he wasn't fooling anyone. Neither of them believed a word of it, and there was no way he could tell her the truth.

That he'd missed her. Her face, the way her green eyes tilted upward at the outer corners the smallest bit, giving her a slightly exotic look, the way she could look both serious and skeptical at once, the fact that she got totally lost in his T-shirt . . .

It had come as something of a surprise, missing Llewellyn. He'd known that she'd linger in his memory for a long time, but he hadn't expected to feel anything but an overwhelming relief that she was out of his life for good.

Kicks Merlot had reappeared on the streets of New Orleans a few hours after Llewellyn caught her flight back east. Kicks, in the company of the mouse-colored Weimaraner, played clarinet for tips in Jackson Square until twilight, then hung out at a homeless shelter till dawn.

He didn't bump into Freddie and Sal again, though Eddie Whitefish had left a message on his cell voice mail that two of Demano's men were in town asking questions. Eddie suggested that Adam might want to think about a nice long vacation—someplace tropical, like Tahiti.

Palm trees and soft trade winds had a certain appeal, and a nice long stretch of lazy days and long nights with ample time to come up with a plan to get his hands on the orchid would have been the smart thing to do. But Adam couldn't seem to tear his thoughts away from Langley and a certain redhead with a knack for finding trouble. She'd set a course for treacherous waters, and the thought of her going it alone refused to leave him.

"You still haven't answered my question."

"Christ, Llewellyn. I go to the trouble of finding you and all you want to do is ask a lot of bloody questions." She bent a look on him, and Adam gave her what she wanted . . . at least in part. "All right, damn it. I thought you might want to know that Freddie Caruso's attachment to ice packs and boxer shorts is history. He's back on his feet, and word on the street is that he wants revenge on you more than he wants the orchid."

"That's it?"

Recognizing that glint in those green eyes of hers, Adam smiled. "Well, now that you mention it, there is something else."

"Something that can't wait?"

Hooking a finger in the waistband of her boxers, he tugged gently, bringing her closer, then slid his hand over her belly and into her warmth. He gazed down at her for a moment, savoring the shiver that ran through her, and then she was wrapping her delicious self tightly around him, and they tumbled as one onto the bed.

The doorbell startled London awake. The room was dark, and for a moment she didn't have any idea where she was, or what time it happened to be. She did know that she wasn't alone in the bed, and she was oddly reluctant to leave the cozy nest.

Snuggling deeper into the pillows, she drank in the solid warmth of the body lying beside her and listened to his deep, even breathing, and the idiot on the front porch laid on the bell a second time.

London came out of bed with a soft mumbled curse, searching frantically for her scattered pajamas, fumbling into them and throwing on a short kimono-style robe as she stumbled from the room. The bell sang again. "Damn it. I'm coming!" She reached the door, flicked on the porch light, and checking the peephole, groaned. "Damn it, Wyeth, do you have any idea what time it is?" she said, jerking the door open.

"Actually, it's after two, and I've been calling you for over an hour. I keep getting a busy signal, and the operator said it was off the hook."

London glanced at the desk phone on the bureau. The receiver was lying beside it. "It must have been the cat. I didn't check it when I got in."

Wyeth's gaze went over her, and London couldn't suppress the urge to close and belt the robe. He caught the move and frowned. "Is everything all right? You seem a little undone."

London released an impatient breath. "I was sound asleep, that's all. I'm fine; the Colonel's fine; the house is fine. It's late, and if you don't mind, I'd like to go back to bed."

"All the same, maybe I should just come in and have a look around. I need to have a word with you anyway, and I'd rather not spill it out here, in front of the whole neighborhood."

London kept a firm grip on the doorknob and didn't offer to let him pass. "Spill what?"

Wyeth craned his neck to look around her, his mouth gone suddenly slack. London turned to look, then groaned.

Adam, barefoot and tousled, his bare shoulders gleaming in the low light, realized they were no longer alone and paused at the foot of the stairs, a hand on the newel post. "You got any coffee in this place?"

"In the cabinet to the left of the sink."

When she turned to face Wyeth, he was still gaping after Adam. "Dear God. You know him?"

"You could say that. We're—friends."

"Friends. Friends? London, do you have any idea? No. Of course you don't, or you wouldn't be—Jesus. I can't believe this."

London, thoroughly out of patience, started to close the door. "Say good night, Wyeth."

She would have pushed the panel shut, but Wyeth caught it. "Wait! It's Patrick. He must have gone out after I left. They found him on the street a couple of hours ago. He has a slight laceration to his scalp, and his wallet's missing."

"Oh, God. Somebody rolled him." Patrick, hit on the head and robbed in a dark alley. What in hell was happening to them? London turned away, all her anger dissolving. "Thanks for letting me know. I'll get dressed and be right there."

Chapter Eight

"What do you mean, you lost him?"

Freddie winced at the razor's edge in Joey the Finger's voice. He held the telephone receiver away from his ear until his boss had exhausted a long string of obscenities. "Damn it, Freddie! Where the hell are you?"

"I'm here, Joey. I must have lost the connection there for a minute. It's Louisiana. They don't have all the comforts of home down here like we got up in Jersey. They eat crawfish, for Christ's sake, and you ought to see the size of the cockroaches."

"Do you really think I give a damn about the cockroaches? What the hell's the matter with you? Have you lost your mind? You know how important the orchid is. You know that I promised Bitsy that she'd have it for her birthday. But the day came and went, and no orchid. She was disappointed, Freddie, and you know how I hate to disappoint her. Maybe you'd like to explain yourself. What the hell happened?"

"It was the woman's fault," Sal said into the extension. "She almost killed Freddie—you should a seen it, Joey. Man, it got ugly."

Freddie hissed and made threatening gestures at Sal. "What woman?" Joey demanded. "I send you down there to do a job, and you two are gettin' laid? What the fuck is wrong with this picture?"

"It wasn't like that," Sal insisted. "She had his nuts in a vise. Almost twisted 'em off. In fact, the doctor said a few more minutes and the flesh might have mortified. Turned gangrenous—lack of blood supply, you know? It could have led to amputation."

Freddie winced.

"Sal, put Freddie back on the phone."

"Cocksucker," Freddie mouthed at Sal. "Oh, God, Joey, no, not you." He grimaced at Sal, who sat on the green and orange paisley bedspread, and wrung his fists together as if he were wringing a dishrag, then pointed at Sal. "No, I'd never call you a—yeah, I know."

"You better fix this, Freddie," Joey said. "Or I'll find someone else who will. And you know what that means."

Freddie swallowed convulsively as he hung up the phone. They were holed up in a shit-bag little roach palace motel just north of New Orleans. The decor was puke ugly, and the construction so shoddy that when the planes passed overhead, the walls shook. Freddie hated the dull green walls and the dirty orange carpet, but not half as much as he hated Sal. "You had to tell him that? Do you want to get me killed?"

"Your hospitalization was in the local papers. I figured the honest, straightforward approach might be best under the circumstances."

"What circumstances?"

"You know . . . during this period of rehabilitation. Till you get back on your game and figure out if everything's in working order."

"You know what's in working order, Sal?" Freddie said, a dull red creeping up his thick neck and into his face. "My trigger finger, that's what! And if you want to avoid bein' alligator bait till we get out of this mosquito-infested cesspool, you'll keep your big mouth shut!"

"All I was saying—"

Freddie walked to the bed, where Sal sat in a lotus position, looking like a dark-skinned Buddha. Leaning down menacingly, Freddie put a fat forefinger under Sal's nose. "You talk too damned much! Now, get over to the airport and find out where the hell De Wulf disappeared to. I don't care how you do it—just do it!"

"Just drop me at the door. I don't know why you had to play chauffeur. I could've called a cab. It's no big deal."

"I'm not dropping you at the door, and it is a big deal. You got off easy, Dad."

"The asshole that hit me got off easy. Hit me when I wasn't lookin', or this never would've happened."

He was uneasy with the conversation and wanted just to slough it off so that he could go back to doing what he always did: playing the tough guy, ignoring his problems, burying his pain. London had always accepted Patrick for who and what he was . . . only this time, it wasn't that easy. "I know you don't want to talk about what happened tonight, but I'm worried about you. At least let me walk you in."

"Will you cut me some slack?" he shouted, then groaned and put a hand to his head, shooting her a sidelong look. "What? I have a headache, but I'm not an invalid. I can see my own friggin' self into my own friggin' house."

"No one said you were an invalid, but you have a concussion, and the doctor says—"

"Doctors! What the hell do they know? I've had worse than this, and no medical attention was even available. Not like a man can worry over a hangnail when he's working a covert op in the Sudan."

Patrick had suffered a minor concussion and a massive blow to his ego. "I'm coming in," London insisted. The argument had gone on for the past twenty minutes, since she had walked into the emergency room. Seeing Patrick—who always seemed bigger than life to London—bitching about the acute rear ventilation of his paper gown as the doctor stitched the cut above his right eyebrow had given London a jolt. She could see the toll Benji's death had taken on him. He wouldn't admit it, but he was hurting, just as she was . . . and she couldn't turn her back on him as long as there was a slim chance that he needed her.

"You're making too damn much of this. I slipped on a dog turd, that's all."

"You, too, huh?" Then, when he looked at her, "never mind." She couldn't tell him about the face she'd seen in the kitchen window, or her suspicion that someone had been watching her from the deep cover of the dark alley. He'd freak and insist on camping out in her living room. It was bad enough that Wyeth knew about her connection to Adam. She wasn't ready to share that piece of news with Patrick. She could always remind Wyeth that her personal life was none of his business; Patrick wasn't as easily managed.

"Turn the corner at the Quick Mart, and duck into the alley."

"Why? Are you out of aspirin?"

"Am I out of aspirin? Are you telling me you didn't notice that tail? Dark-colored sports car. Looks like a new model, foreign make. He's been tailing us since we left the hospital parking lot."

London glanced in the rearview mirror. A shiny black Mitsubishi Eclipse Spyder trailed them at a discreet distance, but it was impossible to see the driver from that distance, impossible to tell if it was a tail or merely coincidence. A frisson of uneasiness zigzagged its way along her nerves. The pale blur in the window could have been Adam, but if that were the case, why would he have disappeared only to find his way through her bedroom window? It didn't make sense.

"Maybe it's a coincidence," London suggested, but she knew the comment stemmed more from wishful thinking than from any real belief or rock-solid possibility.

"A coincidence? At four in the morning? Wyeth's right. You're losing your edge."

London ground her teeth so hard her jaw creaked. What exactly had Wyeth been telling Patrick? That he feared for her sanity? That she was unfit for the clandestine service, that her career was in jeopardy? The same things he had said to her earlier that same evening? "Screw Wyeth Pinchot," she ground out. "I am *not* losing my edge." She geared down and revved the engine, running the yellow light at the corner of Fifth and Severe Street just as it changed to red. The Spyder stopped, and London hung a hard right, cutting down the first alley she came to, doubling back, and reappearing several car lengths behind the dark sedan. She trailed behind for eight blocks, then breathed a sigh of relief as the driver pulled into a Shoney's parking lot.

"Wyeth's becoming a real pain in my ass," London said. "I'd think someone in his position would have something better to do than gossip about his coworkers."

Patrick snorted. "Forget Wyeth. You mind tellin' me what you're working on that has someone tailing you in the dead of night?"

His tone had changed, and he hadn't even scolded her about her less than genteel language. She found it oddly encouraging, and for a moment London forgot their never-ending animosity toward each other. "You put a lot of years in at the Agency," she said.

"Thirty-two, to be exact."

"Did you ever once question the wisdom of Administration?"

"I trusted them to sort out the right and wrong of it. I was there to carry out orders, to do a job . . . that's all. That's why you're there, too. Not to question, and not to be disrespectful . . . and not to bring more pain to this family."

"Pain." London sighed. "Is that what you were trying to do tonight? Drown the pain you feel about Benji?"

"I had a drink or two," he said, immediately defensive. "Since when is it a crime for a man to have a drink or two?"

"When that man carelessly puts himself in a dangerous situation and ends up facedown in an alley, that's when." London got hold of her frayed temper and deliberately took a deep breath. It wasn't her intention to make matters worse between them. If anything, she'd hoped to find some common ground. "Look, Dad. I don't want to argue."

"Then don't." Patrick dug his keys out of his trousers pocket, got out of the car, and stalked up the sidewalk to the two-story frame house where London and Benji grew up, Ella died, and Patrick still lived.

London watched him go. His normally purpose-filled stride was slower, with a hitch in his step that reminded her briefly of Adam. When she'd closed the door on Wyeth and turned around, he'd been gone, vanished, leaving only a ghostly whiff of cigarette smoke in the air and the bruise of his passionate kiss on her lips. She'd been torn between disappointment and self-recrimination since. *Well, what did you expect, London? Did you really think he'd hang around and be the proverbial pillar of strength? Ward Cleaver, he isn't.*

Sarcasm didn't help, and the sense of disappointment didn't fade.

The lights went out in Patrick's house, replaced by the flickering blue incandescence of the TV screen. He'd parked his butt in the recliner, just as he'd done every night of his life since her mother's death. Immersed in a weird and unexpected sadness, London didn't notice the Mitsubishi until it stopped beside her. Its lights were suspiciously out, the inside of the vehicle impossible to see through the smoked glass of the passenger window. London fumbled for her bag, but as her fingers found the cold steel of the handgun, a cigarette flared briefly, and the window whirred down.

Adam. London's pulse faltered, and relief flooded her solar plexus.

He leaned across the passenger seat, and the door opened. "Get in."

London hesitated. Encounters with Adam always seemed to culminate in one thing, and she was beginning to get concerned about where all this was leading. She wasn't the clingy type, with the phone number of a wedding planner on her Rolodex . . . but she wasn't an advocate of casual sex, either, and she didn't even know if her mystery man was married. She could almost hear Benji, who had never missed an opportunity to bust her chops about her taste in guys: *For God's sake, London. What were you thinking?*

She stared at Adam. What *was* she thinking?

That he was hard, and masculine, and sexy. That his secretiveness and the fact that he was so impossible to know intrigued her, even while the caution lights flashed and the warning bells rang in her head. He was dangerous, and she was a fool for depending on him, for trusting him. "Some of us still punch a time clock, you know," she said, knowing how lame it sounded. "I have work in a few hours, and it isn't good to leave my cat alone too long. He gets a little spastic when I'm gone."

"Sure thing. You go on home and baby-sit your neurotic fur ball. I'll just check out the lead on my own. Maybe I'll drop by tomorrow, clue you in about what went down."

That got London's attention. "Lead? What lead?"

"A dead drop . . . James Madison Park, half an hour."

"Are you sure your information's credible?" James Madison Park was a favorite for agents from the now defunct Soviet Union, but she hadn't heard of it being used in years. It was a prime location for a drop, however. Its footpaths were rambling and poorly lit, and because it was located a few blocks from a major roadway, it was easily accessible and provided a solid, reliable escape route. London pulled her keys from the ignition and locked the Porsche, sliding into the buttersoft leather bucket seat of the Mitsubishi, closing the door. "Are you saying what I think you're saying?"

"You bring your handcuffs? If you're bent on interrogating me, we could at least make it interesting." He shot her a look. "Just because I'm out of government doesn't mean I've given up my connections, and my sources seem to think that things are heating up again."

London buckled her seat belt. With Adam behind the wheel, she suspected she was in for a wild ride. She'd done all the research. After several years of sporadic espionage, the Ghost's activities had fallen off, the last incidence having occurred thirty-six months ago . . . just about the same time De Wulf left the Agency and went underground.

Something about the connection sent a chill through London. She glanced at Adam.

Adam disappears, and the espionage ceases.

He reemerges on the scene, and suddenly the biggest

threat to national security since the Cold War ended is back in business?

How much did she know about him really?

The implications of the thought registered, sinking deep into her subconscious before she could shake them off.

Get a grip, London. This is De Wulf you're thinking about, Super Spy . . . a legend in his own right, and the notion that he and the Ghost were intimately linked is beyond ridiculous. . . .

Wasn't it?

Of course it was, she told herself emphatically.

"The Ghost has been out of action for three years. Why would he resume his activities now?"

He looked at her, his stare dark and impassive. "Who said it's a he?"

It was London's turn to stare. "You think the Ghost is a woman?" She snorted, but he wasn't laughing.

He shrugged, and his leather jacket creaked softly. "I don't know what to think, but where the Ghost is concerned, I've learned not to rule anything out."

Doubt yanked at London's psyche again. Like breaking and entering, botanical larceny? Like trouble with the East Coast Mafia? Like a whole host of clandestine activities that law-abiding citizens would never dream of participating in?

Okay, that was all questionable, but it also wasn't espionage against his own government. Besides, he hadn't exactly succeeded at getting his hands on the orchid, and most of his breaking and entering had been a prelude to foreplay . . . at least the instances she was aware of . . . and she sure wasn't complaining. She just wouldn't let herself think about the larcenous areas in which he succeeded. "Don't ask; don't tell" really wasn't such a bad concept in certain areas. The DDO hadn't been privy to the existence of the football pool last Super Bowl season, and London had come out three hundred dollars in the black.

Adam eased the car into a lightless area and killed the headlights.

London tried not to think about being in a dark, deserted area with him . . . a man she barely knew . . . a dangerous man for whom she had an irresistible attraction—and a truckload of doubts.

"Adam?"

"Yeah?"

"You've never explained why you left the Agency. You had a distinguished career; you were making a name for yourself. . . . Why not stick it out until retirement?"

The muscles at the corner of his mouth flexed—a sign of irritation. "It's simple, really. I didn't turn my back on the Agency. It turned its back on me." Adam homed in on something in the shadows, and then there was no time to question the cryptic remark. "Did you see that?"

"It's a statue . . . a bronze of some dead president, I think. It's difficult to tell with no light. What happened to the streetlights, anyway?"

"The courier's handler would have arranged to put them out . . . stolen bulbs, pellet guns . . . what have you."

"Everything looks deserted. How do you even know this is the right spot?"

"Blimey, Llewellyn," he said with a laugh. "You're a regular babe in the woods. Look at the lamp post."

"A smiley face?" London said, seeing a circle, two dots, and a squiggle. "You've got to be kidding. How do you know it's not just graffiti?"

She had no more than asked the question when something stirred in the shadows to the west of the life-size bronze of James Madison. The sky was gray now. In half an hour, the sun would be putting in an appearance, and London had a feeling she was going to be late for work. She concentrated on the transient in the trench coat. If he aimed it in her direction and whipped it open, she was gonna be pissed at De Wulf for dragging her out here. Trench Coat followed the path for a few yards, weaving slightly. When he reached a low shrub, he turned slightly and shot an arc of urine onto the ground, then settled onto a park bench to snooze.

"So much for your sources," London said, watching him lean forward.

His gaze was fixed on the deeply shaded area just to the left of the park bench. She thought he was being stubborn until Trench Coat abruptly straightened, then stood. A figure moved out of the shadows, dressed completely in black . . . a bulky hooded sweatshirt, sweatpants, and tennis shoes—it was impossible to tell if it was male or female. Watchful, moving with a mixture of stealth and purpose, the phantom approached the trench-coated courier. The two exchanged envelopes.

"Stay here." Before London could argue the point, Adam was out of the car and sprinting toward the pair. Fumbling for her pistol in the bottom of her bag, London followed.

Adam moved fast, too fast for London to keep up. He shouted for both agents to stand where they were. The trench-coated man turned and, mouth torn open in surprise, stumbled back, toppling the bench, landing in a clump of shrubbery. The figure wearing the sweats sank into a defensive crouch, pivoting on the balls of its feet to face Adam. Its face a hideous Halloween mask with sunken black holes for eyes and howling mouth, it brought a gloved hand from the pocket of the sweatshirt and squeezed off a shot at Adam, then turned and ran into the shadow-filled heart of the park. Adam followed.

"Damn it, De Wulf!" London shouted, groping in the shrubbery for the trench-coated agent. She caught a fistful of his coat, and he slipped out of it; she grabbed his pants leg, and he kicked her hand away. Her weapon went flying, and the man shoved her hard.

London stumbled back and fell. Fifty feet along a gray, dimly lit path, Adam was about to launch a full-body tackle when a jogger came out of the mist. A middle-aged man, wearing a Notre Dame sweatshirt and bright red bicycle pants and breathing hard, he seemed stunned at the surreal scene he'd stumbled upon. "What the—"

Before Adam could shove the jogger out of the way, the agent grabbed him, locking an arm around his throat, holding the weapon to his temple.

Adam was tempted to rush them. It was the closest he'd come in three years, and he would have to let him go. Reluctantly he took a step back. "All right. Easy does it. I'm backing off."

"The weapon." It was a rasp, inhuman-sounding, mechanical, androgynous.

Adam sucked the mist-filled air into his lungs. Back along the path, he heard Llewellyn grunt and curse as she fought the courier. She hadn't listened. She'd followed, and he could only hope she had the sense to let the bastard go. The spook who held the jogger hostage jerked its grotesque head at Adam's gun hand. "Just let him go." Adam moved his arm out away from his body, opened his hand, and let his weapon drop to the grass.

A hiss of triumph, and the dark figure backed into the bushes, taking the jogger hostage.

The light was changing. The deep charcoal of predawn was lightening. Objects and shadows couldn't be discerned from one another. The mist closed in, thready and lending heavily to the surreal atmosphere. Adam picked up his handgun and carefully made his way along a shadowed path into the heart of the park. Pursuit was dangerous, but he couldn't leave it like this, couldn't just let it go, no matter the consequences.

His every sense felt magnified. He could smell the faint taint of wet wool and knew it was the smell of fog in early spring, damp cold earth, and a world that hadn't quite recovered from its winter's sleep. The scrape of a shoe on cement sounded a few yards away, startling a sparrow from the low branch of a maple. The bird took flight with a noisy flutter, Adam spinning to face the perceived threat, pistol palmed and ready to fire.

But it was only Llewellyn. "I lost him," she said, limping toward him. Her shoe was minus a heel—the second pair she'd ruined that evening. "I can't believe I lost him."

"There seems to be a lot of that going around." Adam stuck the pistol in the waistband of his jeans, center back. "Stay here. I'll be right back."

London glared at his retreating back. "In your dreams," she said, and with a quick hop and a skip, she caught up. "Do you have any idea how much I paid for these shoes?" They were making noise when she walked, so she paused to take them off. When she glanced up, Adam was gone. "De Wulf?" she whispered, scanning the area. "Now, where the hell did he go?"

A few feet ahead, the path forked, slanting slightly as it moved through a heavily wooded area. She surveyed both directions and tried to figure out which path he'd taken, then decided on the heavily wooded section. "De Wulf?"

Something caught her attention—yards ahead, barely

visible through the mist, a figure crouched by some low shrubbery. She thought she saw black leather and released the breath she'd been holding. "What were you thinking, deserting me like that?" The form twisted, its grotesque mask seeming to scream as weapon and silencer rose.

"Shit!" London brought her .38 up, but not before the spy squeezed off several rounds. She felt the rush of air as a bullet sped past and buried itself in the trunk of a tree at her back. Then she hit the ground. When she looked again, the figure was gone, vanished. The only signs that it had been anything more than a figment of her imagination were her ghostly pallor and a pair of running shoes protruding from the shrubs where her assailant had been.

"Oh, God. Adam?"

He trotted in from the opposite direction, his limp barely even noticeable. "I heard shots. Are you all right?"

"Yeah. I'm not sure how, but that thing managed to miss me. Looks like its hostage wasn't quite so lucky."

Adam took her by the arm, but London shrugged from his grasp. Something drew her to the man lying facedown on the mulch, a sick feeling in the pit of her stomach. The shot to the back of the head had been unnecessary and beyond cruel. There was just enough of his face remaining on the right side to identify him. London sat back on her heels and closed her eyes, fighting down a violent wave of nausea.

"You recognize him?"

She nodded, pulling herself together. "Yeah. Fred Johnson. We've shared a cubicle since my return. Fred's—was—a good guy, family man. He's got kids."

Adam took her hand and got her to her feet, away

from what was left of her coworker. "Where are we going?" she said. "We can't just leave him there—"

"We're not leaving him. But we've got to get back to the car and the cell phone. Somebody's got to alert our good friend Pinchot, and call the police."

Chapter Nine

When Wyeth arrived, the Alvira Police Department was just wrapping up. A short, dark-haired man in a tan leather jacket, white polo shirt, and khaki trousers chatted with the crime scene photographer, asking about angles and lighting. Then he saw Wyeth and came quickly across the grass toward him. "Mr. Pinchot? Detective Viagra—no jokes, please. The guys in the department bust my chops enough as it is. You'd think they'd have a little respect for a man's birthright. So the stiff is one of yours?"

Johnson, slightly ridiculous in red bicycle shorts and Notre Dame sweatshirt, lay facedown on the grass. Wyeth had joked with him just last week that he wouldn't be caught dead in that getup, and now Johnson had been. Acid roiled up in his stomach. He purposely skipped breakfast, knowing he was headed down here and what he would find; now he was beginning to regret it. Death didn't sit well on an empty stomach, either.

The coroner's assistant stopped long enough to unwrap a stick of gum and shove it in his mouth and chewed with manic energy. He nudged Wyeth with an elbow to gain his attention. "Ever see the damage a .357 does to a pumpkin at close range? Kinda looks like that."

The detective tapped Juicy Fruit on the shoulder, a

two-fingered jab that bordered on belligerence. "Look, Michaels, just take care of business and get him out of here. If you're not careful, I'll see to it personally that you're enrolled in sensitivity training."

Jesus Viagra had worked Metro Homicide for twelve years, and the grim nature of his job had continually worn away at his sense of humor until it was the size and scope of a mustard seed. He'd stopped beside Wyeth, but his black, pupilless stare was reserved for Juicy Fruit. "What the freak are *you* looking at? Do your job, or I'll find someone who will. I hear they got a new chimpanzee down at the zoo who's lookin' for part-time employment. I'll have your people give his people a call."

"You're a real stand-up guy, Viagra." The attendant grabbed his crotch before helping with the body bag. "If I had a name like yours, I couldn't change it fast enough!"

"Yeah, well, I had it first! Damn drug companies. Now, take your handyman routine and moon-walk on out of here." He turned back to Wyeth. "Everybody's a freakin' comedian these days. Jack-off."

Wyeth glanced at the attendant, at the gurney, the ambulance—everywhere but at Johnson. "Could we get on with it, Detective? I have a press conference in less than an hour. I can't afford to be late."

"Media circus, huh? Yeah, well, better you than me," Viagra said. "Listen, I've been talking to our witnesses. They're your people, too, I take it, as was the vic? Kind of surprising. But I guess you guys are everywhere."

He indicated a young woman and her tall companion— a dark-haired man with a leather jacket, jeans, and sleek half boots. Aviator shades hid eyes that Wyeth knew from experience were intensely blue. London's hair was pulled into a hasty, spiky tail on the top of her head. Gold hoop earrings caught the sunlight shifting through the budding tree branches overhead. As she turned and shot him a glance, he noted that she looked ragged . . . as if she hadn't slept. *Damn De Wulf.* Without any effort, he was dragging her in, and his world was not a safe place for someone like London. Wyeth clenched his teeth, his gaze sliding back to Adam De Wulf. "The female officer is London Llewellyn, but her companion has no current connection with the intelligence community that I am aware of."

Viagra's heavy brows shot up. "No current connection? Does that mean he's a G-man too?"

"Treasury?" Wyeth snorted. "Hardly. He'd never get clearance for any position where credibility is a requirement. Rogue operative—former, not current. Do whatever you like with him, but go easy on Ms. Llewellyn."

"I meant *government man,*" Viagra informed him. "So, you really don't like this guy De Wulf?"

That was putting it mildly, Wyeth thought. He hated the air that he breathed, and if he could have snatched it away from him, he would have. Aloud he said, "As a professional courtesy, could you give me a rundown on what you have so far pertaining to Johnson's murder?"

"Off the record? You mentioned the press."

"Certainly."

"Well, one thing's for sure. We can rule out suicide." Viagra patted down his jacket pockets, then frowned his disappointment—the look of a man who just remembered he'd quit. "One shot to the back of the head at close range, execution-style. The missile blew away part of the skull in front, so it's a good guesstimate that Mr. Johnson was dead before he ever hit the ground." He nodded at London. "So, Ms. Llewellyn is CIA, huh? Is she married, by any chance?"

"No, she's not."

"Too bad," Viagra said. "I am. Speaking of which, I'm meeting my wife for brunch at a little Italian place near here. I'll be in touch." He walked past London, his perpetual scowl never wavering as he did a double-take.

Wyeth shook off the residue from the interview, but his lousy mood didn't lessen as De Wulf laid a hand on London's shoulder and spoke quietly to her. The contact was brief, a comforting squeeze; she glanced up at him and nodded, and Wyeth stifled the impulse to reach for his Tums and instead made short work of the space between them and himself.

London saw him coming and straightened. She was feeling the effects of twenty-six hours with no sleep, and the last thing she needed was yet another lecture from Wyeth. Her eyes felt gritty and her reactions were slowing. She needed a caffeine kick, and even her usual double mocha latte wouldn't suffice. She needed espresso, and she needed it yesterday.

De Wulf stood a little behind her, seemingly unfazed by all that had occurred—as solid and silent as Gibraltar, and almost as supportive. She supposed she should be grateful that he had stayed, given his normal disappearing act, but with the death of a colleague still fresh in her mind, gratitude came exceptionally hard.

Wyeth didn't wait until the crowd of cops and the coroner's people dissipated. He just lowered his voice and jumped right in. "I hope to Christ you have a good explanation for engaging in the surveillance of a foreign agent with no authorization and no backup!"

"I can explain," London said quietly . . . but could she? They both knew that the reason she was in this mess was standing right behind her, looking lethal and sexy and spoiling for a fight. Adam didn't like Wyeth any better than Wyeth liked him, and he wasn't the type to respect the position if he didn't respect the man. She caught the hardening of his jaw and sensed that he'd had enough.

"For pity's sake, Pinchot, can't you see she's wrung out? If you want to chew on something, then have at this. Llewellyn was with me. *I* dragged her into it. *I* got her involved. But that's what has you so steamed, isn't it?"

Wyeth's temper flared at Adam's interference. Or, perhaps, at his defending her. He took a step toward Adam, a threatening advance that didn't faze De Wulf. He stood his ground, and his animosity toward the younger man was readily apparent. The only thing left to the imagination was the underlying reason for it.

"Exactly who the hell are you?" Wyeth demanded. "You aren't government, and you don't have the clearance or the authority to meddle in things that obviously are none of your concern."

"The Ghost *is* my concern," Adam said quietly.

"The Ghost?" Wyeth snorted. "That's what this is about? A case that was shelved three years ago? A man lost his life because you're hanging on to the past?"

"Another murder, execution-style," Adam said. "Does that sound familiar, Pinchot? Just like Ben Llewellyn. Both CIA, both killed the same way."

"This is insane!" Wyeth grated out. "You can't link Benji's death to what happened here last night, De Wulf! He was killed by a single gunshot, felled by an intruder, possibly someone he was working with."

"It was the same actor."

"How do you know that?" Wyeth lost it, grabbing a fistful of black calf leather, getting in Adam's face. "How the hell do you know that?"

"Simple. Because I was there," Adam said softly,

planting a hand on Wyeth's chest, shoving him away. "C'mon, Llewellyn. I'll take you home."

He'd put himself between her and Wyeth—a gallant but unnecessary attempt to shield her from the consequences of her own actions. Despite his interference, there was no way of avoiding what came next. Johnson was dead; she'd been involved, however inadvertently. She would have to answer for it. "Go on. I'll take care of this and catch a ride home with Cid."

"Right," he said, and with his glasses hiding his eyes, she couldn't tell if he was disappointed or relieved.

Wyeth waited until Adam was out of earshot before he turned his attention to London. "Do you care to explain to me how the *hell* you ended up in the middle of this?"

"Adam had a tip about the courier, but it turned out to be more than just a dead drop. It was a meeting. The other agent showed almost immediately, and that's when things got out of hand. Adam went after the agent with the mask; then Johnson appeared, and the agent grabbed him."

"And De Wulf pushed a volatile situation into murderous territory, jeopardizing not only your life but one of our officers'."

"Johnson showing up when he did was a fluke," London insisted. "There was no way either of us could have predicted it." She wasn't sure why she felt the need to defend him, or why she hadn't mentioned the shots fired when she'd stumbled onto the masked phantom crouched over a lifeless Johnson. Instinct urged that she give Wyeth the minimum, the bare basic facts and nothing more.

"He set this whole tragedy in motion. A man is dead,

London—a capable senior officer with a family—and
now I have to go and speak to his wife. . . ." He took two
steps, turned, and came back, his strides impatient, his
temper hanging by a thread. "Do you have any idea?
No, it's obvious that you don't."

"If this is about Adam—" London began, but he cut
her off with a laugh, a humorless bark of a sound.

He was clearly upset, the veins popping in his temples and just above the collar of his white shirt and the
impeccable knot of his navy blue tie. "Oh, it's about
De Wulf, all right. He's a loose cannon, Meg. A risk
taker. And a damned dangerous man not known for his
rational thinking."

"He's a good man. He was at the top of his field three
years ago. I saw the photo with the DDO. It was taken
at the White House. He had top clearance; he was one
of the most trustworthy officers the CIA had." And now
he lived on the edge, something inside her warned—a
second-story man with a shady past and a lust for exotic
orchids.

"*Had* being the operative word where De Wulf is concerned." Wyeth planted his feet wide, as if bracing for
his argument. "I'm not denying that he was good at his
game, but all of that ended when this obsession of his
took over."

"The Ghost," London said, brow furrowing.

"It ended, Meg, but De Wulf wouldn't let it go. There
was talk that he had personal problems. Maybe that's
what sent him over the edge; I don't know. I do know
that if you get involved with this guy, you'll be begging for disaster."

They had moved only a few yards into the park. Johnson's body had been removed, but the yellow crime
scene ribbon fluttered in the morning breeze. "We're not
involved." It wasn't a lie. The truth was, she couldn't ex-

plain her connection to Adam. It was mind-numbing sex, uncontrollable attraction, mystery, and intrigue— things Wyeth had probably never experienced and certainly would never understand.

"Not involved." Wyeth scratched his head, his expression skeptical. "Is that why he came down your stairs half naked?"

London flushed. "Does the phrase 'none of your business' mean anything to you?"

"I care about you, and that makes it my business. He's responsible for this mess—"

"He would never hurt me, and you know it," London insisted.

"I don't know it!" Wyeth shouted, then lowered his voice when one of the cops still at the scene turned to stare. "And neither do you." He softened his tone, changing tactics, becoming the surrogate big brother now that Benji was gone. "What the hell did he mean back there? He said he was 'there.' Where is there? In Vienna?"

London took a deep breath. "I told you there was a witness when Benji was murdered."

"A witness." Wyeth's gaze narrowed. "De Wulf? De Wulf was in the room when Benj was killed? Jesus H." He shook his head. "And you tracked him down. That's why you were out of town." He shook his head, changing his tactic. "Look, Meg, De Wulf is the kind of guy that makes a great distraction. He's older, he's been around, and he's dangerous. I'm sure his rantings about the Ghost must seem legitimate, but you have to believe me when I say that they are just that: rantings."

He made it all sound very cliché and a little pathetic, and his patronizing tone raised her blood pressure. She wasn't an impressionable virgin, awestruck by the experienced older man, and she'd heard enough. "At least have the decency to say it straight out."

"Adam De Wulf is a lunatic. At best, he's a paranoid who functions without treatment. At worst, he's irrational. Do you need to hear more? If so, then you're a good deal denser that I thought, and far too thickheaded for your own good."

London stared at him for a wordless moment. His scathing criticisms cut deep, possibly because she sensed they might contain a kernel of truth. It wasn't as if she hadn't had doubts about Adam, but the attraction was stronger and always seemed to override caution. "I've changed my mind about coming in today."

"That might be best for everyone. Maybe you can manage to get some shut-eye." As she stalked off, he hurried to catch up. "I'll give you a ride home."

"Thanks, anyway. I think I'll pass."

Upset with Wyeth, she stepped off the curb, directly into the path of a green metal monstrosity. Brakes screeched on warming pavement. The driver put her spiky blond head out the window. "Do you have a death wish, or what?" She adjusted her lavender-colored glasses. "Lon, hon? Is that you?"

London opened the passenger door. "I need a lift home. Can you help me out?"

"Sure thing. Hop in. Was that Pinchot back there? Hey, what's with the shoes?"

He wasn't sure where the sense of urgency had originated, but it had seized him halfway through his meeting with a former Soviet scientist, when he'd heard the child crying. Thin and pathetic, a continuous, plaintive wail, it turned his hackles straight on end and made his blood run icy cold. Imagination . . . it had to be his imagination . . . some trick of the wind, or a weary, overly stressed mind. He'd been putting in a lot of overtime, so much that he was barely ever home—a circumstance that kept Julia's nerves on edge and the two of them at each other's throats.

The marriage had been strained from the beginning. Julia's complaints that he was married to the Agency had turned from soft and tearful to angry and strident, and Adam's promises that it would all be over soon had quickly worn thin. There had been several hot leads in the past few months. He was certain that the Ghost was someone who worked at the George Bush Center, someone he knew. He was getting close; he could feel it, and he couldn't slack off now . . . not even when Julia begged him to.

Her pregnancy had given him hope that things might change between them. The baby seemed to give her life new focus, a purpose beyond her passion for orchids, and Adam had hoped that the child would bring them closer. But now all that was ended. . . .

Their son was gone, as were Adam's delusions that their marriage could be salvaged.

The thought was punctuated by the eerie wail that even the radio couldn't drown out. Heart pumping so violently it felt ready to burst through the wall of his chest, Adam slammed the SUV into park and ran up the walk. He took the steps two at a time.

The house was dark. Not a glimmer of light in any of the windows. Maybe she was sleeping.

Dear God, let her be sleeping.

The front door was open. He let himself in, quickly checking the downstairs rooms for signs of intrusion. But there was nothing. Not a single whisper of sound. His senses, on overload for weeks, kicked up a notch. Raw nerves pushed him closer to the emotional edge.

Something wasn't right. The house had an air of expectancy, as if it were waiting. But waiting for what? "Julia?"

Through the dining room and into the kitchen. A step at a time. An eternity passed as he reached out a hand and pushed open the hinged half door that led to the kitchen. It creaked on its inward swing. He released it as he stepped into the room; then he turned and saw her crouched in the corner by the cabinets. "Julia? What is it? What's happened?"

Dark strands lay all around her bare feet. As Adam took a step toward her, she lifted another lock and hacked it off with a carving knife, an inch from her scalp. She looked wild and unkempt, her dark eyes irrational. Adam softened his voice. "Julia, it's Adam. Darling, give me the knife."

She hacked off another dark strand with a sawing motion and allowed it to fall at her feet. "Michael. I want Michael."

"Michael's gone. Don't you remember?"

"I remember," she said. "You took him. Where is he? I want Michael! I want my son! What have you done with my son?" She tore frantically at her long hair, severing the thick hanks an inch from her scalp, as if the shearing could somehow undo the damage that had been done—as if somehow, by punishing herself, she could bring Michael back.

"Julia, for God's sake. Give me the knife. I know you miss him. I miss him, too—"

"God?" she cried. "There is no God! If there was a God, if there was any justice in this world, my baby wouldn't be dead—you would!"

Her words might have stung if he hadn't been so numb, if he hadn't said the same thing to himself a million times over the past month. It was his fault that this had happened. It was all his fault. Michael's death. Julia's insanity. Their shattered marriage . . . She was a victim, just like Michael. She hadn't asked for any of this. In fact, she had begged him to stop.

How many times had she begged him to stop, to leave the Agency?

How many times had he put her off?

"I'll call the doctor," he said softly. "He'll give you something to help you sleep. You need to sleep."

"I don't want the doctor! I want my baby, Adam! What have you done with him? What have you done with my baby?"

With an ear-splitting screech, she sprang from the corner. Her white nightgown a ghostly blur in the darkness, she threw herself at him. Adam grabbed for the knife, and she pulled it back a fraction of a second too soon. He felt the bite of the blade lay his palm open, the warm, steady flow of blood that smeared her pale forearm and made his grip unsteady. He caught her wrist with his uninjured hand, and the knife went flying, landing on the kitchen tiles, bouncing once, then skittering a few inches before it stopped.

Adam got his arms around her and held her in a bone-crushing embrace until she stopped struggling, but her voice, a hoarse and ragged whisper continued to rage. "You fucking bastard! I hate you! Do you hear me, Adam? I hate you."

Adam straightened and glanced at his watch. The illuminated dial glowed an unearthly green in the dark room. Three A.M. He felt as if he'd been caught in the nightmare for hours, but he'd last looked at his watch at five minutes after two. He couldn't resist the urge to glance around the farmhouse kitchen, but the shadowed corners were empty.

He was alone in the house, and there was no one in his life to give a damn whether he lived or died.

As if on cue, a large gray shadow lifted itself off the floor by the hearth and came to his chair, insinuating its nose under his hand. The Weimaraner. "Thanks," Adam said. "But I'm not sure you count." Honz dropped onto his haunches, gazing up inquiringly at Adam. "Like it here, do you?" The dog whined. "Well, I don't. Too many memories. Too many ghosts."

He should have unloaded the place long ago, but it had been purchased shortly after he'd married Julia, and he'd never felt quite right about it. "I s'pose it'll keep the rain off, and it gives you a place to hang out while I'm otherwise occupied."

He got up and made coffee, and while the pot gurgled and belched, he flicked on the computer. The message program started flashing. Bruno.

Where the hell have you been? I've been trying to reach you for days!

I've been preoccupied, Adam told him. *What do you have for me?*

The Lady's bloom is almost exhausted. Experts say she won't flower again for months, maybe years. What kind of shape is your portfolio in?

Adam snorted. *What else?*

Well, there is something else, about another lady. Seems like Cerese wasn't exactly telling the truth when you spoke with her last. She couldn't possibly know how Julia is, because she hasn't seen her in two years.

Adam frowned. *Why would she lie?*

Gee, I don't know. Maybe because she hates you and blames you for what happened? Or because she's a deceitful bitch? Shall I go on?

Adam shook his head. *Anything else?*

One small detail. Julia was last seen in the D.C. area. You think she could still be there? Adam? Adam?

Adam shut down the computer, and even a scalding cup of black coffee couldn't chase the chill that claimed him.

Julia in the D.C. area. How was she? Where was she? And did he really want to know?

Cid unlocked the door to her apartment at five minutes after three. Spudzy, the bouncer from Inkspot, her favorite nighttime haunt, had followed her home. After she fielded a few kisses by turning her head and giving him a shove, he'd taken the hint and stalked off in a sulk. Spudzy was good for an occasional laugh, but Cid wasn't into comedians, and she only had time for one man.

The apartment was dark. She didn't bother turning on the light. She liked the shadows. There was something oddly comforting about varying shades of gray. Everything seemed less harsh in the dark, as if the world had finally worn off the hard edges.

"Where have you been?"

She didn't even flinch at the sound of his voice. She'd known she'd come home to find him waiting. "I could ask you the same thing. How did you get in? I don't remember giving you a key."

He held up a credit card. "Tricks of the trade. We all have them." He patted the chair he slouched on. "C'mon over here. I need to know that you're all right."

Cid hesitated, then moved slowly toward him. It was all part of the game they played. He pretended to worry about her, and she pretended not to care. It was all an act. She did care. He was her one constant, the only living, breathing being in this life who understood, and she didn't want to lose that. She didn't want things to change, didn't want to go spinning out of control.

"I thought you'd be tied up tonight," she said, her voice a lazy purr. "You said you'd be at the office, but details drive you crazy, don't they?"

"I missed you." A hand slid over her small breast, then over her abs and belly to where he really wanted to be. "Who was that guy outside? Should I be jealous?"

"Jealous? Of Spudzy? That's funny."

"Not from where I sit. Tell me you love me."

Cid laughed—a brittle sound. "You don't give a damn if I love you or not, as long as you get what you came here for. It's not about love, Wyeth. It's about power, and we both know it. You need that rush as much as I do."

"It's about power," he agreed. "And it's about pain. You love to inflict it; I can't escape it. You have me where you want me, just like always." Wyeth brought his free hand up to grip her jaw, his fingers and thumb digging painfully into her face. "Tell me you love me."

"I love you," she whispered, sighing as he let go, and the game began in earnest.

Chapter Ten

It was Friday morning, and London was running late. She wasn't sure what it was about Fridays that threw everything off balance. Maybe the anticipation of the weekend was screwing with her subconscious, she thought, then snorted. "Get real," she said, juggling a shoulder-strap handbag as big as a small suitcase and stuffed far too full, and a portfolio full of Benji's papers. The fob attached to her car keys was tucked under her chin. "Your weekends are so dull you make the Bushes look like party animals by comparison."

Cid had been badgering her to get out more, and London knew that the platinum blonde was probably right. As flaky as Cid could be at times, she often had an offbeat sort of logic that London couldn't dispute.

Head down, chin tucked tightly over the keys, London caught sight of the mess on her porch in time to save her mannishly stylish oxfords from a fragrant disaster of the canine variety, and London from a serious case of déjà vu. She did a quick hopscotch, balancing her load while glaring down at the messy dog pile on her porch. "Damn it, Cosmo!" she said, shooting visual daggers at Topper's basset hound, who eyed her impassively from the other side of the banister. A closer inspection, and London apologized, bending to retrieve the soft plastic and very realistic-looking dog pile. She turned it over. On the bottom was a hidden compartment, and inside the compartment, a message comprised of words cut from a magazine and pasted onto a plain white sheet of paper:

Meet me for lunch at Quincy's. We have something important to discuss

"Patrick," London said. "I wonder what it would be like to have a father who just picked up the phone and dialed?"

The morning crawled by. London spent several hours being debriefed by Wyeth and the DDO before she returned to her desk. She was supposed to be writing a report on the events of last night and the circumstances leading up to Johnson's death, but she couldn't seem to concentrate. His pens and pencils were still in the *All-time Greatest Dad* coffee mug he used as an organizer. His umbrella hung from its strap on the Peg-Board, held there by a huge thumbtack, and London kept imagining she heard the slap of his number twelves in the hallway outside.

A genuinely nice guy who was well liked, he'd had an effect on his coworkers, and the air at the center was tense yet subdued. London shook off thoughts of Johnson's wife and kids, wondering if anyone else could sense the dark undercurrent simmering just beneath the surface at the center.

"You're spending too much time with Adam," she said to herself.

Cid, passing in the hall, paused in the doorway. "There's a name I haven't heard before. Who's this Adam? What gives? C'mon, Lon, give over and spice up my morning. It's like a tomb around this place."

London sighed. "Cid, we lost a man last night." It was a little amazing that she had to remind her.

Cid's expression remained blank. "Oh, yeah. Johnson. I heard about that. Don't you think that was all a little weird? I mean, what was he doing in the park before dawn, anyway?"

"Jogging, like he did every morning. His wife worked the early shift at County Hospital. He liked to cook her breakfast before coming in. . . ." London shook her head, pressing her fingertips to her eyes. "I can't talk about this."

"Your call. So, listen, are you busy later? I'm meeting some friends at Inkspot downtown, and I thought you might like to tag along. Willie Freid is stopping by. He's a real hottie. I think you two might just hit it off."

Willie was a musician Cid talked about sometimes, a friend-of-a-friend-of-a-friend, way-out kind of relationship. But then, everything in Cid's world was way out there. She was waiting for an answer, and London couldn't think of a legitimate reason to refuse.

It wasn't as though she had anything pressing, or even anything to look forward to. God alone knew when or if she would see Adam again. He was as predictable as PMS mood swings and unlikely to give her a heads-up on anything.

Besides, it wasn't as if there were anything between them . . . well, nothing normal, anyway, and she wasn't about to sit home waiting for the phone call that never came.

Come to think of it, he never called. He didn't have her number, and if he did, he probably wouldn't use it. He'd think the wires were tapped. She thought of the fake dog pile on the porch and the cryptic message from Patrick, and wondered if she really wanted to become involved with someone as Agency-ingrained as her father. "Why not?" she said suddenly. "It's not like I have any plans, and I don't have to bathe the Colonel until next week."

It was settled. London sat back with a feeling of satisfaction as they finalized their plans. If he broke and entered again with the idea of a hot night, he'd find she wasn't home.

Quincy's was deserted at noon. The regulars, primarily government retirees like Patrick, didn't normally begin filling the stools and dark corners until after *The Young and the Restless* was over. Patrick had foregone his usual stool at center bar and instead was seated at a table near but not in front of the one-way mirror/window overlooking the street. The window had been Patrick's brainchild. It made him and his cronies more comfortable, knowing they could look out but no one could look in. The change of locale, combined with his aspect, sent London's antennae into red alert. He wasn't just clean-shaven; he was glowing, his ruddy face alive with expectancy, his crew cut bristling at attention. Something was definitely up. London held her breath.

"Well, are you going to just stand there?" he said in a voice less edgy than his usual growl. "Or will you sit down and take a load off?" His head swiveled toward the bartender. "Hey, Quincy! Will you bring my little girl a whiskey? We're celebrating."

"Little girl?" London said suspiciously. He hadn't called her his little girl since she was five years old and she'd executed her first dead drop, arranging with some of the neighborhood kids a game of hide-and-seek through clandestine means. "What are we celebrating, Dad? Did the Democrats finally buy into the theory that

Iran-Contra was all just a dream? And I can't have a whiskey. I'm on my lunch hour."

"Order something from the grill. Quincy makes a mean pepper steak."

"I think if it's all the same to you, I'll just have the salad. I'm really not very hungry." She asked him twice, but he kept his surprise under wraps until she had a mouthful of lettuce and sweet onion.

"Oh, by the way, I'm selling the house."

London almost choked. When her sputtering subsided, she dabbed her watery eyes with a tissue and then blew her nose. "What did you just say? Because it sounded like you said you're selling the house."

"That's right," he said. "I put it on the market this morning, first thing. The realtor called an hour later to say he's got a potential buyer."

"But I don't understand," London said, trying to fathom what was happening. At some point in time, she'd left the bar and entered the twilight zone. "You loved that house!"

"Your mother loved that house," Patrick corrected. "It was okay when you kids were at home, but with—" He broke off and cleared his throat. "It's too damned big for one old man. I feel like a pea in a coffee can."

"But where will you go?" London demanded.

"That's easy," he said with a self-satisfied look. "I've thought it all through, and I'm doing the logical thing. No fussy retirement home or gated community for me, no, sir. I'm moving in with you."

London signaled Quincy to refill her seltzer. It was early, far too early for a whiskey, but she had a sick feeling she was going to need one. "Moving in with—I'm not so sure that's a good idea."

"Of course it's a good idea," Patrick countered. "Unless, of course, you don't want me around?"

Not want him around? Why would she not want him to live with her? Other than the few hundred reasons that immediately leaped to mind, she could think of only one thing. "Dad, think about this. It's me, London. You and I can't get through a simple dinner without tearing each other's heads off. How on earth will we share a bathroom?"

"You've got a guest room, and I don't go to bed early, so I get up late. You shower in the morning; I shower at night. We're family, for Christ's sake. Family sticks together. But if you really think it's a bad idea, I might be able to convince Quincy to rent me the attic. It's a little chilly in the winter, but my arthritis hasn't been too bad lately. I can get by."

London closed her eyes. Did she think it was a really bad idea? Oh, yeah. It was a really bad idea. In fact, it was the worst idea she had heard in at least ten years, and she couldn't refuse without drowning in guilt. She was his daughter, and she was Catholic. Though she battled it valiantly and sometimes won out from sheer stubbornness, guilt was engraved on the Llewellyn crest. Or would have been, had they had a family crest. "Not want you to live with me?" London choked out. "Where would you get that idea? Of course I want you to live with me. Like you said, we're family, and families stick together." But privately she wondered how she was going to survive the adjustment.

"Then, it's settled!" Patrick said with a rare smile. "I'll head on over as soon as we leave here. My suitcase is in the car, and there's no need to give me a key. I can get in."

London sipped her seltzer and tried to dismiss the eerie notion that somewhere nearby, Benji was laughing his ass off.

* * *

London spent the rest of the afternoon finishing and polishing the report on the incident in the park, and then after work she stopped by the small brick residence on Haley Avenue where Johnson's widow quietly grieved.

The house was full to bursting with "government" personnel—the code word for Agency to the outside world. Five of her coworkers were gathered in a loose knot in the dining room, drinks in hand, chatting quietly about their golf games while their wives attempted to comfort Helen Johnson, Fred's widow. Yannick sent a glare her way and left the group for those gathered out back on the patio. Ed Malek and Jim Fritz nodded, Murphy looked right through her, and Peterman hung his head. Johnson had been well liked, and the chill in the room was arctic in its intensity.

On the far side of the dining room table, Wyeth stood with one hand in his trousers pocket, listening to something Cid was saying. He glanced up and caught sight of her, his jaw tightening as he excused himself and started to thread his way through the gathering toward her. London abruptly turned away, but he caught her before she could get very far. "Damn it, Meg," he whispered furiously, "what are you doing here? I thought we agreed you were going to keep a low profile?"

"I'm paying my respects," London said. "Surely that's allowed? And under the circumstances, I think it's appropriate. I worked with Johnson, and I feel terrible about what happened."

"It's allowed. I'm just not so sure it's a good idea, that's all. Helen's awfully distraught." He combed a hand through his blond hair, the same hand he'd kept in his pocket while talking with Cid—a hand that bore a livid bite mark ringed by a deep-blue bruise.

"My God," London said, grabbing his hand. "How on earth did that happen?"

He pulled his hand from her grasp—nervously, she thought. "This? It's nothing. My neighbor's kid was about to run into the street, and when I caught him, he nailed me."

"He's got a mean set of jaws. You might want to suggest that Eloise buy him a muzzle."

"Eloise?"

London's smile faded. "Eloise? Your neighbor? You did say it was her three-year-old who bit you?"

"Yeah. Yeah! Listen, don't make a big deal out of this. I'm fine, really. Could we step outside, please? I was going to stop by on my way home. I really need to talk to you—"

"That makes two of us. Miss Llewellyn." Helen Johnson was a tiny woman with a thinning head of dark blond hair and a spine as straight as a ramrod. London had seen her several times, and she'd always exuded an air of poise and grace. This afternoon, she looked haggard and deflated, as though someone had pricked her with a pin and let all the air escape, and London suspected that if not for the pair of CIA wives who flanked her, she might have fallen. Tension rolled off the trio in waves.

"Mrs. Johnson," London began. "Helen, I can't begin to express how sorry I am about all of this—"

Helen Johnson slapped her—a ringing blow that clearly conveyed the hatred, frustration, and hurt that wracked her—so forcefully it made London's ears ring. London pressed a hand to her stinging cheek. "I'm truly sorry for your loss," she finished softly.

"You have no right being here," the older woman spat out. "No right at all. Has it occurred to you that if you and your boyfriend hadn't been in the park that Fred would still be here? If not for you, my Fred would still be here. He'd still be alive, and I wouldn't be alone!"

"He's not my boyfriend," London said. Her tone was soft, almost pleading. "I never meant for any of this to happen. Please, you have to believe me."

Helen's eyes were dull and pitiless. Empty of everything but grief and inconsolable loss. "Get out. Someone get her out of my house!"

London stood rooted to the floor, her face white with embarrassment, unable to do anything but stare at the stricken woman until Wyeth took her arm and guided her from the house. "Oh, God. You were right. I shouldn't have come here."

Wyeth squeezed her shoulder. "Don't be too hard on yourself," he said, abandoning the confrontational tone he'd used before. "You did the right thing, paying your respects. Johnson liked you; everybody knows that, including Helen. She's not herself." He sighed heavily, and London knew there was something on his mind— something he was reluctant to say.

She wiped the moisture from her cheek with the back of her hand. "There's more, isn't there? You said you wanted to talk to me."

"You've been suspended."

"What?"

"With pay, pending the investigation into Johnson's death." He seemed unable to say it fast enough. It was an unpleasant task, and he wanted it finished. "I just got word this afternoon. I asked them to let me break the news. I thought that somehow, coming from me—"

"It would soften the blow," London finished for him.

"I guess that's not possible," he said. "If you want, I can speak to Patrick."

"No. I'll tell him, but not now. It's my responsibility to let him know how badly I fucked up—I'm just not ready to face that yet." She had broken the news about Benji. She would tell him that she'd lost her job, that her actions, her decisions, her life, were being subjected to a microscopic inspection. She would tell him as soon as she got the nerve, but right now she couldn't get out of there fast enough.

It was falling apart. Her life was disintegrating, and she was beginning to feel panicked. "I have someplace to be. I guess I'll be in touch."

"It's not over yet, Meg," Wyeth called after her as she hurried down the sidewalk to her car. "Hang on to that. Maybe it'll help."

It was meant to comfort her; instead, it added to her sense of unease. He was right about that much. It was a long way from being over.

By the time she left the Johnsons' residence, her spirit was frayed and ragged, her mind full of recriminations.

Rationally, she knew that Johnson's death was not her fault, yet a part of her couldn't help speculating on whether he would have been seized by the Ghost and killed if she and Adam hadn't been at the park, just as Helen had suggested. The idea made her uneasy, and the uneasiness blossomed in her chest, crowding her heart and lungs, making her restless and wild. She had to resist the urge just to break and run—a mindless sprint with no thought beyond the exhaustion of mind and body and the easing of the anxious tightness in her chest. It took every ounce of willpower she possessed to get behind the wheel of the Porsche. A turn of the key in the ignition, and the engine growled. "Not now, damn it." She tried again. It leaped to life.

Benji's apartment was on the second floor of a neat white house in Overbrook, fifteen minutes away and a half hour away from London's duplex. London had spoken to Mrs. Morrow, Benji's landlady, shortly after the funeral, and since she had no plans to rent the apartment until the renovations on the house were complete, she'd graciously agreed to store Benji's things. London had been grateful. She'd been to the apartment several times, yet until now she hadn't been ready to face finishing going through his things. A message on her machine from Mrs. Morrow yesterday had changed that. The renovations were complete, and she'd found a renter for the space.

London dialed Goodwill from her cell phone and donated Benji's things, arranging for them to pick them up the next day. Then she used Benji's key to let herself into the three-room walk-up.

Soft spring sunlight flooded the living room, pooling on the sand-colored carpet. The space was orderly and well cared for. *A place for everything and everything in its place* . . . oh, so typically Benji. He'd gotten all the neatness genes in the family. God, she missed him. She stood inside the door, hand on the knob, trying to imagine she heard his low whistle coming from the kitchen, the splash of water in the sink . . .

Then she forced herself to break away, heading for the bedroom closet and the box of personal effects she'd taken from the drawers the last time she'd been there. Benj had been into gadgets, a bit of a cyber-geek, but more of a minimalist than a collector of anything that didn't whir or bleep. He'd left a state-of-the-art desktop system that she'd carted home a month ago, a notebook computer, a closet full of clothing and shoes. In vivid ironic contrast was the modest stereo system that was so dated it had a turntable and some Sinatra records. London wrinkled her nose at them, but left them in the closet. She took some framed photos from the end tables and several undeveloped rolls of film . . . a pathetically small offering to a life cut short.

Cradling the shoe box containing those few mementos, London sank onto the chair beside the telephone.
"God, Benji," she said, a tear spilling over her lashes and
sliding down her cheek. "Everything is such a mess. I
wish you could talk to me." Another trickle of tears, another attempt to stop them. "What's going on here? First
you, now Johnson . . . Who did this? And why? It
doesn't make sense. It doesn't make any freaking
sense!"

She hadn't cried since that night in Adam's New Orleans apartment, and she didn't want to cry now. Tears
didn't solve anything, and they made her feel weak,
drained. She struggled hard to hold it together and
barely succeeded. Dark emotions swirled immediately
below the surface of her enforced calm. She wanted to
scream, but if she started screaming, she feared she'd
never stop, so she perched on the edge of the chair while
the shadows lengthened outside, clutching the box with
those few precious items far more tightly than she
needed to.

A long, silent pause preceded the tap on the door.
Pulling herself together, London put down the box
and walked to the door. "Mrs. Morrow, I'm nearly
finished—"

But it wasn't Mrs. Morrow. He struck a match, lit his
cigarette, then shook out the flame. "We thought you
might like some company," he said simply.

He was wearing his signature black leather jacket
with a close-fitting white T-shirt and faded jeans. The
leashed Weimaraner sat beside him. "How did you find
me?" London demanded, a little shaken by his sudden
appearance, yet strangely glad to see him. Could she
ever make a move that he didn't know about? Would
he ever fail to make her mouth dry with nerves, her
knees weak with wanting him?

He shrugged. "A good tail is worth its bloody weight, and that antique you drive is as easy to spot as a flashing neon sign. Didn't they teach you better than that at the Farm? You need something that blends in if you want to avoid detection."

"You sound like my father," London said. "And I'm not so sure I like the idea of being followed. Have you been watching the house, too?" She hadn't forgotten her doubts about him, or the white blur of the face at her kitchen window, and Johnson's death and Wyeth's warning this morning hadn't helped. If he was following her, what else was he doing that she didn't know about?

"Well, in this case your old man's right. Get yourself a new set of wheels if you want to get by unnoticed. Something a little more unremarkable."

"You haven't answered my question," London reminded him, on edge from the encounter at the Johnsons', from her suspension. "Have you been watching my house?"

"What the hell's got your tail in a twist?" He crushed the cigarette out in an ashtray. "Don't tell me . . . our man Pinchot. Exactly what did he say anyway? That if it wasn't for me the Cold War would have ended years sooner? That I'll break your heart and ruin your life?"

"He said that you're trouble," London said candidly, "and that I should avoid getting involved with you. And then he told me I've been suspended pending the investigation."

"Suspended? Now, there's a tough break." He reached out, running his fingers along the underside of her jaw to her ear, then down her throat to the place where her white shirt was buttoned. "Are you all right?"

"No. I'm not. But I will be." London shivered. She couldn't stop her body from reacting to him. His touch was warm, his fingers supple and strong. The heat he summoned in her was alluring, hard to resist, and she had to remind herself that this was Adam, a man she'd chased halfway around the world, whom she'd made love to, whom she couldn't stop thinking about. *A man she barely knew.* "I don't know what to think anymore, or believe. I don't even know if you have a family, if you're married. And I'm warning you, I have a strict rule: I don't get involved with married men, ever."

"Divorced. Three years. I guess that means you're safe with me."

But was she?

His fingers played up and down her throat, his touch teasing, a reminder of the night before . . . before the nightmare in the park began. He shifted positions, bending just enough to nuzzle the erogenous zone below her ear. "I'm sorry about the suspension," he said, "but Pinchot's wrong about me. I'm not the enemy."

But in a way, he was the enemy, the biggest threat to her well-being, her sanity. Until he stole into her life, everything had been clear and unmuddled, with lines that were meticulously drawn, and principles that couldn't be breached or broken. Her life had been neatly compartmentalized: career, social life, family, the cat's monthly bath day, the occasional blind date. Then she met Adam, and everything had changed. Her family had been shattered by heartbreaking loss, her social life consisted of late-night rendezvous with a second-story man—a man she might or might not be able to trust— and her cat smelled strongly of tuna. As for her career, it was currently doing a rapid spiral down the tubes, along with everything she'd worked so hard to achieve. "I really—should go. I need to go home . . . and I need to find Cid."

"Boyfriend?"

She shook her head, and he frowned. "Hey . . . have you been crying?"

"Who, me?" she managed, but even that brief attempt at humor fell short and sounded suspiciously watery. "Yeah, I guess you could say that."

He sank onto the arm of the sofa and would have pulled her down onto his lap if she hadn't resisted. "C'mon, out with it. What's wrong?"

London drew a shaky breath. "I can't—Adam. I just can't do this anymore. The Ghost, the craziness. Maybe it would be best if we stop this now, before someone gets hurt—mainly me."

Adam reached for her, and she jerked back. Their hands touched, a brush of his fingers against hers. "You're giving up?"

"I didn't say that." The tears were coming in earnest now, a hot cascade over the cheek that still burned from the slap she'd received from Johnson's widow.

"What about your brother's murderer? Does the bloke just walk? Do you really think that Pinchot and the rest of those clowns at Langley give a rat's behind if the case gets solved? Sweep it under the rug is what they'll do, and get back to business as usual." He stood up and, this time, managed to catch hold of her hand. "Don't do this, London. You need me, and goddamn it, I need you. I'll stop by the house later; we can work this through."

"I won't be home."

"Tomorrow, then."

"Please don't. I need time to get my life in order, and I can't do that rationally with you popping in and out."

Then she turned and walked from the house. Adam looked from the door to the shoe box that sat forgotten on the sofa. He picked it up, lifting out one of the photos. Llewellyn as a freckle-faced adolescent grinned at the camera, camping it up with an older male version of herself, her beloved Benji. "She'll miss these," he said to Honz, who rested his chin on Adam's boot. "No harm in returning them to her, is there?"

Nestling the framed photo carefully back in beside the undeveloped rolls of film, he tucked the box under his arm and, with Honz, left the apartment.

Warehouse Row was a trendy spot, thanks to the revival of the club scene. Just a few years before, the empty factories and warehouses had seemed destined for a gradual disintegration. Then a pair of entrepreneurs with a pocketful of ideas and a Rolodex full of connections to bankroll them had stepped in to snap up the run-down property. The result was a string of trendy establishments housed in the modified buildings.

A short drive from D.C. and the surrounding Beltway, the row, with its air of city sophistication and lack of crime and traffic congestion, was an instant hit, and Inkspot was the reigning diva. Everyone who was anyone in the tristate area eventually found their way to Inkspot. All the hot bands booked there. Even Ozzy had been scheduled, then had had to cancel to do Barbara Walters—a turn of events that mystified the airheaded Cid.

"I still can't figure out why anyone would want to do Barbara Walters," she said. "Anyway, I thought Ozzy and Sharon were happily married."

London rolled her eyes. "I don't think that's quite what they meant." She thought about explaining, but any attempt would likely sail right over Cid's head.

Cid signaled the barmaid and ordered another round. "Spudzy seems kind of sulky this evening. Did you two hook up or something? He keeps stealing glances in this direction."

Spudzy, the bouncer, stood sentinel by the entrance, his huge arms folded over a massive fifty-two-inch chest. He was good-looking in a blond all-American-boy kind of way—perfect for Cid: quick with a joke, not terribly cerebral. "He's not looking at me," London pointed out, "and if you don't stop trying to fix me up, I'll have to stop hanging out with you."

The gaze Cid turned on London was intensely amber, like a cat's. Glamour contacts. Why did that surprise her? Everything about Cid was just a fraction on the wild side, an eclectic mix of Butch Wax, tanning butter, and bodybuilder chic. From the inch-long buzz-cut per-oxided hair to her outdated thrift store find of black parachute jacket and pants, she was impossible to ignore. "I like you, Lon. You deserve to have someone special in your life. Besides, you've had some rough breaks lately, with Ben getting himself killed like that, and then that thing in James Monroe Park."

"Madison. It's James Madison."

Cid shrugged. "Right church, wrong presidential pew. I still can't believe they're blaming you for killing Johnson."

Cid's translation of the facts made London want to cringe, and Helen Johnson's screech echoed in her head: *"If not for you, Fred would still be alive!"* "They aren't blaming me for killing him. They're blaming me for being in the right place at the worst possible time."

"What's with Pinchot's part in this?" Cid wanted to know. "He couldn't wait to break the news? I thought he was your best bud."

"He's a friend of the family, but you're right. He hasn't exactly leaped to my defense in any of this."

Cid took the celery straw from her tomato juice cock-tail and took a bite. "Gee, Lon, looks like you really are all alone in this. Have you told your dad yet that your career's kaput?"

Cid was the soul of tactlessness and witless repartee, but it was hard for London to hold that against her. Her heart was in the right place. It was her common sense and social skills that were severely lacking. "Not yet, and I really should be getting back. If I avoid him much longer, he'll come looking for me. I think he put a tracking device under the dash in my car, and I didn't have time to sweep it for electronic equipment. The radio had so much static coming here that I had to turn it off. I don't know how I'll survive this with my sanity."

Onstage, the lead singer of Dirty Socks stepped up to the microphone. The crowd went wild as the slicked-back James Dean lookalike sent up a frenetic, string-busting, head-banging tune at an ear-splitting level, then melted into a funky retro rendition of "Saturday Night Fever." London slung her macramé bag onto her shoulder and stood, but as she turned toward the door, it opened, and *he* walked in.

"Oh, God." She didn't realize she had spoken aloud until she glanced up to find Cid watching her with a puzzled frown.

"Hey. Are you okay? You look like you've seen a ghost, or something equally freaky. Do you want another round?"

He was heading for their table, and there was no way for London to make a discreet exit without piquing Cid's interest and triggering a game of twenty questions. It was easier just to try to ride it out. "Ladies," he said, but his gaze never left London.

Cid's antennae went up; London groaned. "Hey, there, tall, dark, and sexy. You two know each other?"

"You could say that," Adam replied. "Mind if I join you?"

"Would it matter?" London asked.

"Probably not. Can we have a word?" He grabbed a chair, pulling it close to London's, sinking into it. "You'll pardon us," he said to Cid, and then to London, quieter, more intensely, "C'mon, Llewellyn. It's business. We need to talk."

"I can't believe you followed me here," she said, thoroughly exasperated with him. "Wyeth was right. You are obsessed."

"Fuck Wyeth," he said easily. "Do you really think I give a shit what that pea-brained, white-livered, paper-pushing ninny thinks? Figures he'd be mixed up with HUMINT and appointed to watch the rest of you. He doesn't know anything about human nature, not having a bloody life of his own."

"That's not fair. He's just trying to do his job."

"If you trust him so much, then why didn't you tell him about this?" He dug in his pocket and held up a small plastic evidence bag. Inside was a chunk of metal, slightly flattened from impact but still recognizable. "That's right," he said. "It's the slug from the park—the one that almost took you out. Level with me. Why didn't you tell him?"

London frowned. "I don't know. Maybe it was the shock of finding Johnson—"

"What a load of manure. You're trained to pay attention to details, just like me. This is a murder investigation, and there's not a chance in hell you would let something like a spent slug from an assassin's weapon slip by you. You can defend him till you're blue in the face, but the truth is, you don't trust him any more than I do." He got up, jerking his chin at Cid, having one last shot at London. "It's from a nine-millimeter, just like the one that killed your brother. But since you're so ready to let it go, you don't care about that, do you?"

Then he was gone, melting back into the crowd. London searched the faces with no luck. She knew that she should let it go. She *wanted* to let it go, and as she stood, she cursed herself for the deep need always to have the last word. "Cid, I need a favor. I need to borrow the Humvee. You can take the Porsche home. I'll bring it by tomorrow, first thing." She shoved her keys across the table toward Cid.

"Sure, but what for?"

"I need to catch a thief, and I can't do it in my car. It's too easily recognizable. I'll bring the Humvee back tomorrow, I promise."

Then, before Cid could reply, London grabbed Cid's keys, pushing through the entrance and into the parking lot in time to see the black foreign make back out of a parking space and snake from the parking lot.

"Oh, no," London said. "You don't get away quite so clean this time." The Humvee started without any of the temperamental crap she'd learned to expect from her Porsche, so she was able to stay a few car lengths behind without losing him.

As she passed the lot attendant, a dark-colored sedan turned into the club's lot, and two large, well-dressed men got out. "Listen," the shorter of the two said. "You suppose this place has a men's room? That green tea I had with dinner went right through me."

It was late, but she was wired and ready to freak. She sensed it coming, dark and malevolent, ultimately destructive . . . fury, an anger so deep that it filled her, spilling out of her eyes as she looked in the mirror, vibrating through muscle, nerve, and bone. She splashed cold water on her face, trying to get a grip, but control was far beyond her reach, and attempts to contain the dark force within her were futile.

For what seemed like an eternity, she stood there, gripping the edge of the sink so forcefully that her knuckles creaked, the silence of the apartment pulsing with the rhythm of her rapid breathing. Her trapezoids stood out on her shoulders, every muscle defined and straining against the threatening explosion, until she freed the beast and let go with a primal scream so shrill and inhuman that it shook the neighbors from their beds and brought at least one of them running. Consumed by the emotional riptide surging through her, she swung a can of hair spray at the mirror, the furious pounding on her apartment door a deep bass accompaniment to the sound of shattering glass.

"Miss Blankenship! For Christ's sake, it's three o'clock in the morning! Miss Blankenship! If you don't settle down, I'm calling the cops!"

Cid quieted, glancing into the spider web of shattered glass still clinging to the frame. A thousand tiny fragmented and distorted Cids stared back at her with wild eyes. For a moment, she was horrified. The woman in the mirror was a stranger, no one she recognized. And then she remembered it all: the bruises, the swelling, the forfeiture of her identity.

He'd triggered this. "Damn you," she said, staring into the glass and seeing his face. "I hope you burn in hell."

Chapter Eleven

London was three car lengths behind and all but hidden by a hulking white SUV. By looking through the Dodge's windows, she could just make out the taillights of the black Mitsubishi Spyder. She followed him through town until, at the outskirts, the Durango made a right turn; then she dropped back a little, putting another two car lengths between them, and hoped he wasn't paying attention.

For twenty minutes she tailed him, far beyond the Alvira city limits, where there were no street lights and few houses. She was beginning to suspect that he was aware of the tail and leading her on a wild-goose chase, when he made a left turn onto a gravel road. London drove past, counted to five, then turned the Humvee and followed. Accustomed to the snug, comfortable feel of her sports car, driving the Hummer was like driving a life-size box of Saltine crackers mounted on a heavy-duty suspension, and the shock of the rough road rattled her teeth.

For three miles she followed at a discreet distance, guided by the cones of light that were his headlights; then, abruptly he left the road, passing through a narrow break in the trees. London killed the headlights and slowed to a crawl. The night sky was clouded, but she could just make out a hard-packed driveway. The driver of the Mitsubishi was a mere shadow figure moving toward the house. She waited on the road until he disappeared inside; then she closed in.

The farmhouse wasn't exactly well provisioned. He'd been in town for a few days, but he'd lacked the time or inclination to stock the fridge. He did have a six-pack of beer, a loaf of bread, five pounds of raw chicken wings, and a bottle of Jim Beam. "Want a beer?" Adam asked the Weimaraner. "He popped a can and poured a saucer half full; then, as his housemate began to enjoy, he took down a slightly dusty highball glass from the wormwood cupboard and partially filled it, still talking to the large hound, a ghostly gray shadow in the dark room. "I need something a bit stronger. How was your evening, ay? Mine sucked. Llewellyn's an okay sort, but she hangs out with some genuine flakes, and I'm not sure I like that Cid. A female on steroids . . . can you imagine?"

"I hang out with flakes? Is that it? What does that say about you?"

He threw an accusing glance in Honz's direction. The Weimaraner let out a low "woof" of an apology and thumped his short tail on the hardwood floor. "How the hell did you get in without Cujo here tearing a limb off? Do you have a T-bone in your pocket?"

"He likes me," she said, reaching down to ruffle Honz's ears. "And the feeling's mutual. Should you be giving him alcohol?"

"He likes me." Now, there was a freaking understatement, Adam thought. It was more than unusual for the Weimaraner to allow any intruder to leave with both legs. The exterminator in the French Quarter had taken to wearing Depends when he had to spray Adam's build-

ing. Yet, Honz was glad to see her, and Adam had the weird impression that the canine thought she belonged here, that they were a team, a pair . . . a trio. They were going to have to have a long talk. But then, Honz was a dog, so what the hell did he know?

"I didn't expect to see you here," he said to Llewellyn. "Especially after you brushed me off—twice in one day, I might add."

She wouldn't give him anything willingly, but if he was being totally honest, that was a major part of the attraction: a fraction of mutual mistrust, grudging admiration, and a ton of sex appeal. It was the perfect relationship. Almost. "You're not the only one who knows the value of a good tail." She straightened and glanced around, taking in the generally dejected air of the place. "Nice place you've got here. You do something to piss off your housekeeper?"

"Who said it was mine?" He wouldn't give an inch, either. It wasn't just a protection mechanism. It was survival instinct, a habit so ingrained in his personality that he couldn't have stopped if he wanted to. Somewhere along the way, he'd forgotten how to lower those barriers, to drop his defenses, to let anyone in. Everyone was a potential threat, a probable enemy.

Even Llewellyn.

"Give it up, De Wulf. You came through the front door. If this place belonged to someone else, you would have come through a window." She ran a finger over the countertop and grimaced at the grit on her fingertip. "I have to give you credit: You sure know how to pick them. This place has all the charm of a mausoleum. Is that intentional, a ploy to discourage guests? Or haven't you gotten around to settling in?"

"It keeps the rain off," he said with a shrug. "As for settling in, I don't intend to be here that long." He was feeling defensive. Who the hell did she think she was? She didn't have a right to answers. He valued his privacy. It was damn near sacrosanct.

More than that. His secrets were the only things that he had left.

She turned from her inspection of the dust and cobwebs to meet his gaze. "Was this your wife's kitchen?"

The image of Julia with the carving knife flashed behind his eyes. "You sure know how to make conversation. Julia was a lifetime ago. What's it to you?"

She shrugged, and the boatneck cashmere sweater she was wearing slipped off one shoulder. It was a deep shade of coral, and very becoming. She looked soft and sweet in the half-light of the kitchen, easy to hurt, and even while the urge to lose himself in her built to an unbearably painful crescendo, his first instinct was to push her away. Distance meant a marginal safety, even though he suspected that supposed safety was nothing but a sham. Sex was one thing; emotional vulnerability was quite another. He couldn't allow himself to care for her, for his sake, for hers.

"I'm curious. You're extremely guarded. A little too guarded, even for a man in your position. That kind of caution is usually a red flag, an indicator that you're hiding something. I'd like to know what it is."

"There's no mystery you can't solve with a simple conversation. If you want to know about me, all you have to do is ask Pinchot. I'm sure he's pissing his pants to give you the lowdown on me."

She walked to where he sat, and stood there looking down at him, so close that he could smell her perfume— lotus blossoms with woodsy undertones. "I'm not asking Wyeth, Adam. I'm asking you. I checked your records. They were sealed three years ago. It isn't exactly standard procedure for an officer's personnel files to be considered classified documents."

"Jesus Christ, Llewellyn. What do you want from me?"

"Simple. I want to know the man I'm sleeping with. What's so wrong with that?"

There was nothing simple about it. Everything about his past was complicated, including—*especially*—his relationship with Julia. She had to be protected—at all costs. By giving Llewellyn what she wanted, he would be betraying a woman he'd once loved, the woman who had given birth to his son. *A victim of circumstance and his own blind obsession. An innocent who got in the way, a pawn in a life-and-death game.*

A part of him screamed that he was deifying Julia out of some warped need to play the heavy, that he was making excuses for behavior he didn't comprehend and couldn't explain, that he hadn't had a choice in what happened . . . but the larger part of him wasn't quite ready to listen.

"It was part of the deal. Quid pro quo—one hand washes the other."

She reached down, her fingertips gliding over the back of his hand, the sensuous kiss of heated silk on hungry skin. The contact was almost more than he could bear without responding. He wanted her, dreamed about her. She filled his thoughts, his world, and it scared him beyond all reason. Llewellyn didn't play fair, and women like her could be dangerous. They had a way of working their way into a man's life and then destroying him. "What deal, Adam?"

Deliberately he caught the hand that teased him, and pressed it to his cheek in a wordless plea for mercy. "They wanted to distance themselves from me; I needed to disappear. It was personal, and if you give a damn about me, you won't ask for more information than that. It's over and done with. Let's leave it at that." He kissed her hand, nipping the finger that traced the hard line of his lips. "Is that the only thing you came here to satisfy? Your curiosity?"

His tone was suggestive, provocative. The heaviness that came with passion's arousal settled into London's vitals; her pulse accelerated, and her hands tingled with the need to touch him, to tangle her fingers in his hair, to touch the hard planes of his face. She resisted as long as she could, then slowly allowed him to ease her down onto his lap. She leaned in, straddling him, her skirt riding high on her thighs as she teased him with a kiss.

His hands slid with an infinitesimal slowness down her spine to her bottom, and he dragged her closer, until the only barrier between them was the thin veil of her scarlet silk panties and the soft worn denim of his jeans. Then he was pushing the chair back, lifting her onto the edge of the table, running his hands up and down her inner thighs.

Hooking his forefingers in the elastic at the curve of her hips, her pulled the flimsy covering down and off, parted her knees wide, and kissed her until she thought she would lose her mind. Braced on her elbows, half reclining, London held her breath. The rough heat of his tongue, the scrape of his beard, just hours old, the selfless way he brought her to a shuddering explosion made him seem something of a miracle. How had she found him? How had he come into her life?

When would he leave, disappearing again without explanation?

Still breathless, London sat up, freeing him from the restraint of his jeans, guiding him into her, clutching his shoulders for support.

Adam kissed her mouth, her eyes, her cheek. Supporting her weight with an arm at her back, the other braced on the table beside her hip, he lost himself in Llewellyn and the moment—a perfect moment when extreme caution and nightmares, waking and otherwise, ceased to exist.

"Stay a while," he said, and in that moment Adam realized that he'd never wanted anything as much as he wanted to wake in her arms.

"I can't. Dad moved into my guest room this afternoon. If I don't come home, he'll ask a lot of uncomfortable questions. Questions I can't answer."

"An hour or two," Adam coaxed, nuzzling that spot at the outer edge of her collarbone that drove her crazy. "C'mon, Llewellyn. You're a big girl . . . your pop doesn't need you . . . but I do." He kissed her, framing her face with his hands, drinking her in. "Stay. We have a lot of ground to cover, a lot to discuss."

London thought about her doubts and misgivings, but they seemed petty compared with the persuasion in his kiss, the genuine need in his voice. Even Wyeth's cryptic warnings seemed to melt like the last patch of snow under a warm spring sun. Responding to the grave light in his blue eyes, she gave him what he wanted. "All right. An hour or two, and then I have to get back."

The room where they'd made love a second time was more orderly than the rest of the house. Someone had taken the time to put clean sheets on the bed, and the drop cloth had been removed from a chair near the window. The curtains had been cleaned and were drawn tight, leaving the room in total darkness. Unable to sleep, troubled by the events of the day and too many unanswered questions, London gently disentangled herself from Adam's embrace and slipped from the bed, picking up her clothing piece by piece as she stumbled over it, making her way to the window.

Beyond the closed door, the Weimaraner whined, then let go with a low, suspicious "woof." Honz had been restless for almost an hour, and she wondered what he heard that she hadn't. Her sweater clutched to her chest, she parted the curtains and stared through the dark window glass, but all she could see was a sliver of orange moon hanging low over the treetops. The yard and driveway were utterly dark. Nothing moved; nothing stirred, but the dog didn't relent. A warning growl, and he pranced to the top of the stairs.

London turned toward the bedroom door.

Had she heard something downstairs?

The soft click of a door being closed?

Or was it just her imagination? With a frown, she threw on her sweater, crossed to the door, and went into the hallway.

Honz stood at attention, tail pointing, ears pricked. The fine hair from the base of his neck to his tail bristled in alarm, but he was noticeably reluctant to leave the hallway outside the bedroom where Adam slept. "What is it, boy? What's down there?" She paused to listen, but she didn't hear anything.

His odd, light eyes sought hers. "Woof."

"All right. Come on, then. If it's bothering you that badly, maybe we should check it out." London started down the stairs, the Weimaraner a ghostly gray shadow moving in sync with her.

The dog reached the bottom of the stairs first and trotted to the hall closet; then, nose to the floor, he went straight to the kitchen and a hidden alcove London hadn't noticed before. In the alcove was a door, and the door was slightly ajar. "I'm just not that stupid," she told the dog. "Hang on a minute." She padded back to the kitchen, sliding out drawers until she found what she was looking for: a carving knife with a nine-inch blade. Then she pushed the door open and entered another dimension.

It was some sort of greenhouse/workroom with glass walls and ceiling. Concrete benches lined the walls, and a central work space with sink and tap occupied the center space. Empty pots, unplugged lights, and potting soil were everywhere. Honz made a quick circuit of the aisles, stopping to sniff the shards of broken glass littering the tiles, lapping at the puddle of water spreading slowly from the sink base to the wall.

"Oh, God, the sink!" A thread of water ran from the tap into the stoppered basin, creating a dark, glassy pool. Something bobbed just below the surface of the water, pale and pathetic. London turned off the tap, then reached in with a troubled frown and fished it out . . . a baby doll, similar to one Patrick had bought her for Christmas the year that she turned eight, only this one's eye sockets were empty; its eyes had been gouged out.

London dropped the doll, backing away from the sink and into something warm, alive, solid. With a startled cry, she dropped into a crouch and spun, still clutching the carving knife.

"London? What the hell are you doing?" For one sickening instant, Adam saw Llewellyn, saw the terror in her eyes and the raised knife, and flashed back three years. Another lifetime, another woman, a similar threat . . . and then she recognized him, and she dropped the knife, grabbing his arms as though she needed the very real feel of warm, living flesh, the reaffirmation of life. "What is all of this?" He glanced from her to the water, to the eyeless doll, and stepped on a shard of glass and swore, leaving a scarlet stain where he stepped. Ignoring the blood, he reached past London, taking the doll by the foot for a closer inspection, his face losing its color.

"I turned off the tap, but there's water everywhere," London said. "You're bleeding. Come on. Let's get out of here." Adam flinched when her fingers encircled his arm, but it snapped him out of the trance he'd fallen into, as did the look of concern on her face. "Your foot. Adam, you're bleeding."

He glanced down at the stain fading from red to watery pink over the wet tile. "Yeah, right."

Honz led the way from the greenhouse, then sat by the door. London got Adam into a chair and then opened the door for the dog, and simultaneously, somewhere in the distance, an engine leaped to life. "Do you have any antiseptic?"

"In the cabinet by the sink."

She found a bottle of alcohol, some cotton, and bandages. "This is going to sting." She extracted a small glass fragment, then cleansed the wound with alcohol.

"What were you doing back there?"

She didn't look away from what she was doing. "Honz seemed upset by something down here, so I came down to have a look around. He led me to the greenhouse. You must have left the faucet on."

"I checked it earlier today," Adam told her. "It was dry as a bone."

"Well, someone turned it on." She didn't mention the eyeless doll, and neither did he. "A greenhouse is kind of an odd addition to a farmhouse."

Adam ran a hand through his sleep-tousled hair. "It was Julia's workroom."

She glanced up. "Julia? Your ex-wife? She liked to garden?"

"Orchids. She had a passion for orchids. She used to propagate them."

Llewellyn smoothed a bandage over the cut securing it with adhesive tape. A small, sick smile played over her lips. "Orchids. Rare, black orchids?"

Adam was silent.

"Bingo." She laughed. "It's a rule I never break. Don't get involved with married men. So what do I do? I get involved with a divorced man who's still obsessed with his ex."

She got to her feet, one arm full of first aid supplies. Adam took hold of the other. "It isn't like that."

"Oh, no? You risk your life, twice, attempting to steal an orchid worth a fortune that just happens to be like the orchids your wife grew? How richly symbolic."

"Not like. The Lady of the Night is Julia's orchid. It's a fluke. She invented it."

"If she invented it, then how did it end up in England?"

"She fucking gave it away—that's how. She donated it to the Royal Society."

She glared down at him, and Adam knew how insanely illogical it sounded. The exploits of a paranoid rogue operative and his mad ex-wife. "And you were stealing it back for what reason?"

"It was my only option," he ground out. "What in bloody hell does this matter? I don't have the goddamned orchid . . . and I don't want to lose you. Not for something like this. It isn't about Julia. She has nothing to do with the two of us, and what we have is too good to walk away from."

"What do we have, Adam? Sex on the table? Sex in the bedroom? Sex anytime you feel like it? I don't know who you are. God, I don't even have your phone number! This isn't normal. Flooded greenhouses and drowned dolls with their eyes missing—it's just too damned bizarre, even for me."

"Llewellyn."

"I have to go now. I have to get back to what's left of my life." She pulled her hand from his grasp and straightened. "Who knows? Maybe there's something I can still salvage."

She walked out, not turning to look back. Adam stood too quickly. Pain knifed through his foot, but he still managed to limp to the door and open it in time to see her taillights disappear down the drive. Honz slipped past him and stood waiting for him to close the door. What the hell had just happened here? he wondered. How the hell had it all gone so insane?

The answer was clear.

Julia.

He didn't know how or when, but she had to be behind it. He shut the door and leaned heavily against it, staring at the darkness at the top of the stairs.

Those few hours in Llewellyn's arms had meant more to him than she would ever know . . . a speck of normality in a life gone completely haywire, and the first time in as long as Adam could recall that he'd slept without dreams.

Shaken and irritated from the eerie scene in the greenhouse and her confrontation with Adam, the last thing London needed was to pull in at the curb behind Wyeth's baby blue Audi. She sat for a moment, weighing her chances of sneaking in through the kitchen and making her way upstairs without being noticed; then she remembered that it was *her* house, not Patrick's, and decided to brazen it out. Uninvited guests seemed an unavoidable part of her life these days, and she would just have to learn how to deal with the intrusions until she could find a workable solution to the problem of Patrick.

What she couldn't deal with was nearly tripping over her nineteen-inch television as she entered the shadowed dining room. Squeezing between it and a mammoth entertainment center, London glared at the pair in the living room who were busy manhandling a big-screen set that looked suspiciously new. "I'm gone for a few hours and you've turned my living space into Circuit City? For heaven's sake, Dad, what do you think you're doing?"

Patrick threw her a hard glance. "Just making a few improvements, that's all. No need to get your colon in a twist. They were having a sale at Sears. I've been wanting a new set for years. Now that I've sold the house, I can finally afford one."

"But I liked my small set," London insisted. A wave of defensiveness swept over her, and she felt like a chatelaine defending her castle against the threatening hordes. He'd been here one day, and he was already taking over, infringing on her territory, her private space. "This *is* my house. Did it ever occur to you to ask if I wanted an electronic monstrosity in my living room? That thing is so . . . *huge!*"

Patrick's expression hardened. "You think we should have talked about it? Since when do we talk? Huh? Since when have we had an open dialogue about anything? We should have discussed this, just like we discussed the fact that you're up to your neck in hot water? I've got to learn from somebody else that my daughter's mixed up with some suspicious character and may or may not have caused a fellow officer's murder? Don't talk to me about a lack of communication, Meg. You're the queen of 'don't ask; don't tell.' "

Until now, Wyeth had busied himself removing the

cardboard crate from the television set and stacking it to one side. Yet, as Patrick's scathing monologue ended, he glanced up, catching London's hostile glare.

"There's no need for me to share the details of my life with you, Dad. Looks like you've got your own pipeline." She threw one last glare in Wyeth's direction before stalking to the stairs.

"Damn it, Meg, wait!"

London heard Wyeth scrambling to get over the debris in what once was her living room, but she didn't stop, and she refused to look back. She'd had enough of men and their attempts to manipulate and ruin her life. In fact, she was so fed up that in her next life she was considering coming back as a lesbian.

He must have somehow managed to get through Patrick's obstacle course, because she heard his attempt to take the stairs two at a time, until the Colonel shot from the hallway and tripped him. He slid down several treads before he managed to catch himself and got to his feet again. Then London slammed her bedroom door and turned the latch.

"C'mon, Meg, will you open the door?"

"Did you break anything?"

"I don't think so."

"Too bad."

"I wasn't the one who told Patrick," he insisted. "I'm here because he called me to help him with the stuff he bought. I agree with you that he should have asked, but he wanted to surprise you, and it wasn't my place to tell him what to do. It also wasn't my place to give out details about your suspension, and I didn't. I swear. You know I don't operate that way. Well, not after the last time anyway." He pounded a few times on the panel. "Come on, Meg. Please. Just open the door. Look, if you don't believe me, then ask your dad. He may be a grouchy old pain in the ass, but you know he won't lie to you."

London relented, opening the door a crack. "Watch what you say about him. He's still my father, even if he has taken over my living space."

Wyeth laughed. "Sorry. I was just agreeing with you. Can I come in?"

"I'm still pissed off at you," London told him.

"I know."

She pushed the door open and stepped back, but she only went as far as the foot of the bed, where she stood with arms folded and one shoulder leaning against the post. He glanced around, every bit as uncomfortable as she was. "So this is the inner sanctum?"

"What do you want, Wyeth?"

"To talk. Just to talk. We used to talk all the time, not so long ago. I miss that. I miss you not being my friend, Meg."

What he meant was that things had changed since Benji's death, since Adam De Wulf had entered her life. What he didn't realize was that her life was no longer simple. In fact, it had all suddenly become unbearably complicated—worse, she didn't know how to sort it all out, and she wasn't in the mood to reminisce. "You said you didn't give Dad the information, and I'll accept that. What else is there for us to say to one another?"

He settled back against the dresser, his fists shoved into his jeans pockets. The USC sweatshirt he wore had the sleeves cut out, and he looked tanned and fit. "I'd like to know that you're okay."

"I'm fine," London said. "Just fucking fine. How else should I be? My brother's dead and I don't have a clue as to who's responsible; I've got a career that's on the skids; and my old man moved in with me, which means my freedom, not to mention my personal space, has been severely curtailed. All in all, I'd say I've pretty much hit bottom, and things will start to turn around any minute now."

"What about De Wulf? How does he fit into all of this?"

She threw him a look that clearly conveyed that Adam was a boundary they would not cross. Wyeth took the hint. "All right," he said, holding up a hand to still any comment she might make. "I'm going to assume that you know what you're doing, and leave it at that."

But did she know what she was doing where De Wulf was concerned? She thought of the defaced doll, the shattered glass on the greenhouse floor, and her discovery about the orchid, and sighed. "Why did the Agency want rid of him?"

"Meg, De Wulf's records are sealed. It's something I'm not at liberty to discuss."

London pinned him with a look. "Damn it, Wyeth, you owe me that much."

He capitulated with grace and gave her what she wanted. "Off the record, De Wulf started out as a crack officer. From what I've heard, there was no one who could touch him. He was like a chameleon. He could set up an op anywhere, and his cover was unshakable. He didn't just play a role; he became it. It's part of what makes him so dangerous. He distinguished himself in several hot spots, aiding the guerilla fighters against a Guatemala dictatorship and shutting down a drug cartel, getting valuable information in Israel. But somewhere along the way, something happened. I don't know. Maybe he just spent too much time abroad. Maybe it was a result of the accident in Tel Aviv. When he came back to the States he was already heavily immersed in a case involving a double agent."

"The Ghost," London said. "I did some digging of my own."

"For some reason, catching this guy became a crusade for him. It wasn't until his personal life fell completely apart that he became a liability. He was burned out, and the element of trust so crucial between an officer and his superiors was gone. We tried to arrange a leave for him, time to get his life in order, but by that time it was already too late. His wife divorced him and disappeared, and he seemed resigned to do the same."

"Julia?"

"Julia Wilkes. He told you about her?"

London frowned. "Sort of. You said she disappeared?"

"Without a trace. There was speculation at the time that she must have had help. No one disappears that completely on their own. As for what caused it all, you'd have to ask De Wulf. All details of a personal nature were wiped from the records before they were sealed. He was tight with the director, so they respected his wishes."

He scratched his head. "So, how about it? You in for the company softball game?"

"What?" Lost in thought, London glanced up. "Oh, the game. I haven't decided yet."

"Think about it. I'm playing for the skins team, and we could use a good shortstop. Besides, Yannick's been taking bets on whether you'd wear that bikini top you wore last year."

"Yannick's an ass."

Wyeth grinned. "I'll tell him you said that. Listen, I need to help your dad and then get out of here. I'm meeting someone later." He did the unexpected then, crossing to where she stood and gently kissing her cheek. "I'm glad we're okay again. I missed that."

"Yeah," London said, chafing her arms. "Me, too."

At the door, he paused and turned back around. "Oh, yeah. I almost forgot. The Ghost? There was some speculation at the time that it was all an elaborate hoax De Wulf concocted to gain a little glory. There was never any proof, or he'd be in a federal pen now instead of here in Virginia."

With a troubled frown, she watched him go out. He'd answered a few of her questions, but it hadn't solved or simplified anything. Instead, it raised more questions. Questions only Adam could answer, and he wasn't exactly talking.

Chapter Twelve

"So, what'd you do to Mr. Mysterious last night when you finally caught up with him?"

It was twenty minutes after one, and London had spent most of her morning looking for Cid. She had gone to the blonde's apartment, but it had been tightly locked and no one answered, even though the Porsche was parked in the building's parking lot. London had called a few mutual acquaintances from her cellular, then checked the usual hangouts. After an hour of looking everywhere, she'd finally found her at Beef Cookie's Gym.

Beef Cookie's catered to the fitness crowd's softer set. With the heavy metallic rattle of the free weights, the whir of the treadmills, and the smell of sweat, it wasn't the sort of place London would have chosen as her kind of haunt, but it was very fitting for Cid. The buff blonde, flat on her back, bench-pressing 210 pounds, was in her element.

The young African-American woman spotting Cid threw London a skeptical glance. "She don't look like she's got enough muscle to do a whole lot of damage to anything bigger than a gnat."

"I can handle myself," London said, feeling a little defensive and a lot uncomfortable under the weight of the other woman's skeptical stare. "Anyway, it's not always about size or muscle. It's about strategy."

The young woman of color just hooted; then, as Cid finished her set and racked the weights, she tossed her a towel. "Yeah, honey, I hear you. Girlfriend," she said to Cid, "I'll catch you in twenty minutes."

"Never mind Cookie," Cid said, rising to straddle the bench. "She's got a membership drive going." She mopped her streaming face with the towel, then ran her hands madly through her stand-up do. "So, what about this Adam? Did the tail pan out?"

"Yeah. I found him."

"Gee, Lon, try not to sound so enthusiastic. What happened? Did he sprout horns, or something? Not that it would be a bad thing. I knew this guy once who used to get all wild-eyed and crazy on me. It was a real turn-on."

"My God, you are so sick," London said. "Have you ever dated anyone who didn't have psychotic tendencies?"

Cid passed the comment off. "Loosen up, Lon. Have a little fun for once in your life. You never know—you might even discover that there's a wild side under all that anal you carry around."

"I'm not anal," London insisted. "I can relax, and I like to have a good time as well as the next woman—just not necessarily this morning."

"Bad night? So what happened anyway? You gonna clue me in or keep me guessing?"

A shrug. "It just didn't turn out like I expected, that's all."

"Now that's telling," Cid said with a vague frown. "I thought you liked this guy."

"I do—at least I think I do. But maybe 'like' is too strong a word. God," London said, pressing her fingertips to her temples. "I don't know what to think. He's . . . different. I'm attracted to him, but . . ."

"But?"

"What do I know about him? Aside from the fact that his coffee is dreadful? He might be an ax murderer for all I know."

Cid gave her a blank look. "You think Adam's a Lizzie Border type?"

"Borden. Lizzie Borden, and she was acquitted." London sighed. "I was trying to make a point, but it's obvious I didn't do a great job of it."

"Look, you said the last guy you dated was a real snore, and the one before that had knuckles that dragged the pavement. As for different, Snake and his Santa suit were different." Cid hung her towel around her neck. "Aside from the accent, this guy seems normal enough. So cut the crap, Lon. What's the real problem?"

"I'm scared," London admitted. "I think I could fall for him, and it might not take much. I'm just not so sure that I want to get in line behind an ex-wife he isn't completely over and that damned orchid."

"An ex and an orchid, huh? Do they have any kids?"

"I didn't even think to ask, but I don't think so. I kind of got stuck on his fixation with his ex-wife and her orchid. That's why he stole it, or tried to—because it's connected to her. She created it, like Doc Frankenstein and his experiment. It's complicated. Look, I'm sorry," London said. "I didn't come here to unload on you."

"What are friends for?" Cid asked, her voice going from its usual nasal quality to something a little softer. "You ever think about having kids, Lon?"

"Yeah, I guess," London said, sensing the strange shift the conversation had taken. "I mean, not for a few years maybe, but kids would be nice. Patrick would be a pretty good granddad."

But Cid had zoned out. "Yeah, real nice."

She'd been more honest with Cid than she'd been with anyone, even with herself. It felt a little odd opening up like that, out of character. Cid was a bubble-brain, but she was also nonjudgmental. Maybe it was due to her own dating escapades, but unlike Wyeth, the platinum blonde hadn't been shocked by London's involvement with Adam.

What she hadn't told Cid was that despite all the strangeness surrounding Adam, despite everything she didn't quite grasp, he needed her. She could sense it when they were together, feel it in the way he kissed her. She couldn't predict the outcome, didn't know what the next week or even the next day would bring. The only thing she knew for sure was that it wasn't over between her and De Wulf. "Listen, I've got somewhere to be," London said, her voice soft and sad and her mind on other things. "I put the Hummer in your building lot and picked up the Porsche. Can I give you a lift home?"

"Thanks, but Cookie'll drop me. We're going down to the East Street salad bar to do a little grazing. I'll catch up with you at Inkspot later?"

"Maybe, but don't hold a seat for me. I may be tied up."

"Sounds intriguing," Cid called after London. London must not have heard, because she didn't turn around. Probably a good thing, Cid thought, for both of them. For a few seconds she found it impossible to maintain the moronic blank expression. Then she pulled herself together, and the mask slipped slowly back into place. She had some place to be, too, and she had better get moving.

* * *

Adam spent an hour mopping up the mess in the greenhouse, and another forty-five minutes exercising the Weimaraner. Honz's quality of life had improved since they'd come north from New Orleans. He'd been constantly leashed in the city, and every groundhog hole and scampering gray squirrel that crossed his path proved a grand fascination for the canine. Adam watched Honz stretch out his legs and bound full speed in pursuit of the grouse that burst from the brush, and wondered what Julia would think about the mouse-colored mooch living under her roof.

Julia wasn't anything like London, he thought. She didn't have a speck of fondness for animals—then he stopped himself. *Hadn't had,* past tense; he didn't have any idea what she was like now. Maybe she had reinvented herself. Maybe she was whole emotionally.

Maybe by now she'd forgiven him.

"Nice try, De Wulf. Forgiveness is just too damned easy." And he couldn't quite erase the specter of the doll, white and lifeless, its eye sockets black voids. Was it someone's idea of a sick joke? Or was it something more sinister?

The only certainty was that someone had gotten into the house while he and London slept. After they'd made love in the kitchen. Had the intruder been there even then, watching? Or had she come in after?

She. The thought bit deep. *Julia.* It had to be. Nothing else made sense. The Ghost was one thing, but he hadn't wanted any of the craziness that had gone on in his life to touch Llewellyn. She was special. A one-in-a-million kind of woman, and though it might be the best thing for her, the last thing he wanted to do was drive her away. It was strange, but he kept hoping that things would change: that Julia would show up, cured of her psychological problems; that she wouldn't need him anymore, and he'd be free to pursue some sort of semi-normal life.

The idea of normality was so alien at the moment that he wasn't sure what that was. Waking up to the same woman every morning, maybe? For a split second he allowed himself to visualize a drowsy redhead lying next to him, her pretty green eyes shuttered in sleep, and then he put the fantasy away and got back to reality, ending the Weimaraner's romp in the open field and heading back to the house.

Once inside, he broke out the notebook computer. "Heads up. Incoming."

Adam? Where the hell have you been?

Walking the dog, actually. He needs a good run now and then.

Speaking of running, I haven't found a trace of your ex since she hit the Beltway. I've checked under both names, married and maiden, and nothing. No credit cards, no hospitalizations, no arrests, not so much as a whisper. It's like she dropped off the planet. Listen, I hate to do this, but I gotta ask. Are you sure she's still alive?

Gotta be. Her parents couldn't cover up a death, nor would they want to. Cerese never misses an opportunity to turn those thumbscrews. She's out there somewhere. Keep on it, will you?

It'll cost you.

Doesn't it always?

Adam signed out of the messaging program and walked to the door of the greenhouse. He'd swept up the broken glass, but the doll still lay on the potting bench, and his ex-wife was still out there, just as fragile, just as damaged. Maybe he was fooling himself. Maybe there was nothing he could do to help her. Maybe the best thing he could do, the kindest thing, was to leave her alone. There was someone he *could* help, though at the moment he doubted she was speaking to him. He closed the door on the workroom and turned to find Honz sitting a few feet away, looking totally perplexed by him. "She's not wild about us at the moment, you know. She's got people tellin' her we're a couple of hot dogs."

The canine let go with a warbling groan.

"What'dya say, mate? I'm thinkin' our image could use a bit of an overhaul."

Patrick was immersed in an episode of *Star Trek* when London got back to the house. "Would you look at that? That sneaky bastard Spock's ears have got to be ten inches long!"

A low voice answered him, and London gave an inward groan. He had a guest. Oh, God, some fried old government guy from Quincy's was parked in her living room, staring with mindless male fascination at that towering monstrosity Patrick called entertainment. The best that she could hope was to sneak quietly past and hide out in her bedroom until Patrick threw him out and the house became her home again. Eyes straight ahead, a doughnut in her mouth and her arms overflowing with purse, cat treats, and a Styrofoam cup full of steaming coffee, she walked slowly toward the stairs. Her foot just touched the bottom step when Patrick boomed from the living room: "There you are! I was wondering when you'd get in. Come on in here and be hospitable. We've got company."

Taking the pastry from her mouth, London turned toward Patrick's voice. "This is my daughter, Meg. Meg, Officer Adam De Wulf. De Wulf here was with the Company but took an early retirement a few years back . . . kinda like me."

There was an easiness about the way Patrick referred to him that triggered a shock wave that rippled through London, followed by a strange sense of dawning dread. "You two know each other?"

"Know each other? Why, this man single-handedly saved my ass in the Sudan. He was a brash young officer then, fresh from training, but what he lacked in experience he made up for in ba—" Patrick broke off, his ruddy face taking on a deeper color. "Intestinal fortitude."

"Oh, he's got balls, all right," London muttered.

"Patrick's far too modest," Adam said with a smile. "He taught me everything I know."

"God help me," London said under her breath.

"What's that?" Patrick demanded with a hawk-eyed glance in her direction.

"Nothing," London insisted. "Not a damn thing." As De Wulf raised his brows in silent question, she smiled nastily. He hadn't let on that he knew her, let alone intimately. She should be grateful for that, yet his cheek in coming here and ingratiating himself with Patrick rubbed. Especially after their disagreement this morning. "Mr. De Wulf. I'd shake your hand, but at the moment mine are both full. Some other time, perhaps."

He came to his feet, and London couldn't help doing a double-take. God, he looked good. Dressed in a dark suit with narrow lapels and a narrow dark tie, his hair slicked back and his shoes highly shined, he in no way resembled the freewheeling thief whose bed she'd left this morning, and the change was as startling as it was disconcerting.

This was Adam De Wulf, the Agency legend, the career professional who'd taken a wrong turn somewhere along the way, then cut a deal to disappear without a trace. "Why are you here?"

"Where the hell are your manners?" Patrick complained. "It's a courtesy call, between old friends. Adam heard about what they're trying to do to Ben, and he wanted to know if there was anything he could do to help out."

London stared at Patrick. "Oh, really? What happened to not questioning the Agency? What happened to us being there to serve, not to question?"

"A man can change his mind," Patrick told her. "Anyway, who's saying the brass are wrong? I'm just saying we turn over a few rocks and see what we find. What's wrong with that?"

"Other than the timing, not a damn thing. Look, Mr. De Wulf, it's been nice, but I'm worn out, and I really need to get some sleep. Why don't you stop by in, say, a week or two and we can discuss this?"

"Don't be ridiculous," Patrick said, pushing out of the recliner, taking Adam by the arm. "Listen, do you still have a taste for whiskey? I've got a bottle of Irish whiskey in the cabinet just waiting for a special occasion. So, tell me all about yourself. You been keepin' busy since leaving the Agency?"

Eyes narrowed suspiciously, London watched the two disappear into the kitchen. He might fool Patrick, but he didn't fool her. He wasn't here about Benji. He was here to further complicate her life.

As Adam De Wulf was making himself comfortable in the Llewellyn kitchen, Wyeth was waiting impatiently for his lover's return in an apartment across town. She'd been gone for several hours, and he was starting to get antsy. He'd tried to stress the importance that they lie low. Too much activity would increase the risks, but she was getting harder and harder to reach, harder to control. An adrenaline junkie, she thrived on risk. Wyeth like to keep things low-profile, having gotten his fill of living large years ago.

Ironically, she'd been the one who'd brought him back down to earth. One rash decision years before had brought them to this. The experts called it a codependency, and maybe it was. In a weird way, he needed her, and there was no doubt she needed him. He kept her from a total meltdown, from falling off the tightrope she was always walking. And he was constantly aware that he was responsible for her, for who and what she was. It wasn't an easy awareness, and there was no escaping it.

Checking his watch for the thousandth time, he watched the sunlight fade and the shadows lengthen; his nerves stretched a little tighter. Where was she? What had she done now? How the hell would he ever get them out of this?

As the questions mounted, the key turned in the lock, and she slipped into the apartment. The atmosphere immediately changed. The dark energy she exuded seemed to make the shadows pulse and throb. Wyeth felt angry but intoxicated, fascinated by the monster he'd created. "Damn it, Julia, where the hell have you been?"

Her eyes got a little misty at his use of that name. "You must be upset with me," she said, her voice whiskey-soft. "You haven't called me that since Switzerland."

He walked to where she stood, quietly taking her hand, but it was smooth and without cuts or abrasions. "I saw the bathroom mirror."

She shrugged it off. "I had an accident."

Wyeth didn't believe a word of it. "Did this accident have anything to do with Adam?"

Her mouth tightened. "What does Adam have to do

with anything?" When he didn't reply, she shrugged. "I didn't expect to see him . . ."

"You didn't expect to see him with London," Wyeth corrected. "That's it, isn't it? Seeing Adam with London set you off." He was pushing her to make a point, and that was dangerous, but he had no choice. He had to be certain to get his point across. "No more indulgences, Julia. You've already gone too far. You know how this works. Get too confident, and it all falls apart."

A twitch of her mouth, a bright glimmer of pain that entered her eyes. "And who would know better than you? Your ego got a little pumped, didn't it? That's how we got here, isn't it, Wyeth?"

Wyeth put his arms around her, and she let him. One rash decision. One desperate mistake that would haunt him the rest of his days. "I can't ever make up for that. I can't ever do enough. . . . It was a mistake."

She clung to him for a moment, then pushed back, pulling herself together, hiding her fragility. "Past history, right? Let's forget it ever happened." Calm words, sensible words, but there was no escaping their slight tinge of bitterness. "Why don't you tell me about your day? Where were you this morning? I tried to call."

"I had to help out a friend."

Cid sighed, resting her head on Wyeth's shoulder. *Not a friend. London. There was a very big difference.*

"Have another whiskey, Adam. You look like you could use it." Patrick topped off Adam's glass, then refilled his own. When he turned to London, she put her hand over her glass.

"I've had enough, thanks," she said. "And quite frankly, so have you."

The gaze Patrick turned on her was a little unfocused.

"It's a celebration. It's not every day someone of this man's stature comes to visit. To better days!" He drank it down and splashed it partly full again, sobering slightly as he raised his glass. "To Ben. The best damn son a man could ever have."

London felt a catch in her throat as she touched her glass to her father's and Adam's. She drank, but as Patrick reached for the bottle, she grasped its neck. "Dad, please, don't."

"Please don't. Please don't what? Have a whiskey? Since when can't a man have a whiskey in his own house?"

London lowered her voice, hating De Wulf for witnessing it all when it should have been a family matter—private, between her and the father whose life was falling apart. "It isn't your house, Dad. You sold your house, remember? There's a recliner in my living room, a TV the size of an elephant, and the cat's taken up permanent residence under my bed. You live here now, remember?"

She was taking a risk, trying to control his drinking in the middle of an obvious binge. It was usually at this point that he went off like a Scud missile. Instead, he stared at her for a minute, then sighed. "You sound just like your mother. She always hated it when I went on a bender." But it wasn't said unkindly, and he let go of the bottle. "I think I've had enough anyway. Got to keep a clear head if we're going to crack this case. What d'ya say we order a pizza and some of those poppers from that place on Water Street?"

Over pizza they got down to business. London thought it had all the quirky charm of a Coen brothers classic: she and her lover, who happened to be an old friend of the father she couldn't seem to get along with, who knew nothing of their heated liaison, calmly discussing her brother's murder. At any moment she'd turn on her pillow and squint at the clock as she tried to shed the weirdness she'd fallen into while she slept.

But it wasn't a dream.

"Any clue as to what Ben was working on prior to his death?"

London sighed. "He'd been working a high-ranking official in a Middle Eastern government who'd been feeding Benj information. He couldn't say, but I think he was an Iraqi. The man wanted to defect, and Benji was making the arrangements. I talked to him a day or two before, and it was pretty much in the bag. Another week or two, and he would have been back home."

"What do the brass say about it?" Adam asked.

He was asking the question for Patrick's sake, keeping up the deception. He'd barely taken his eyes off her, and it was having a far greater effect on London than the double shot of Glenlivet whiskey she'd drunk. "The official line is that Benji had something going on the side, that his motive was money, and that they have proof, but it's all circumstantial. It could easily be something to provide cover for the truth after the fact."

Adam stroked his chin. "You think he was set up."

"I don't know what else *to* think," London said. "It's the only thing that makes sense. I didn't get a good look at the assassin, but I saw enough to get the sense that this was no amateur. He wasn't there in that hotel room by chance. He was there specifically to take Benji out."

Until now Patrick had been silent. Frowning, he shook his head. "That doesn't make sense, Meg. Everybody who knew Ben liked Ben. Who would want to kill him? The Iraqis?"

"I don't know," London said. "Maybe. Maybe not. I just don't know."

Adam didn't buy it. She could see it in his face.

"What else was going on in his life? Friends? Relationships?"

London shook her head. "Friends all over, but no one he hung out with on a steady basis, unless you count his Wednesday night bowling league. And Wyeth, of course."

"There must be something somewhere. What about his personal stuff? Files? Papers? Phone records?"

Patrick nodded, his eyes gleaming. "I told you he knew his stuff." He pried himself out of his chair with a groan. "Think I'll shut my eyes for a few seconds. I hope you'll excuse an old man, Adam. Meg, you take good care of him. We've got a lot of catching up to do."

Patrick disappeared, the recliner clanked, and he began to snore.

London glared at De Wulf. "Old friends? Taught you everything you know? You lying bastard. You ingratiate your way into my father's good graces so that you can get to me. You lie to him by pretending we don't know one another. That's low, De Wulf, even for you."

"What was I supposed to say? Oh, by the way, Patrick, I'm enjoying a bit of slap-and-tickle with your daughter? C'mon, Llewellyn, level with me. Do you really want your old man to know about us?"

She got up and went out onto the back steps, where she sat down. It was a fine afternoon, pressing hard on the close of day, warm and damp with a promise of new green everywhere. Her half of the duplex had a long, narrow strip of backyard, bordered by the alley. A few daffodils planted by the previous tenant nodded their yellow heads by Topper's fence. London breathed in the warm spring air and consciously released some of her tension, willing herself to calm down as the door opened and closed quietly behind her. Of course he would follow. Did she really expect any less? Hitching up his trousers, he sat on the steps beside her. "Would it help if I said I didn't make the connection between the two of you until I knocked on your door and Patrick answered?"

"Why are you here, De Wulf?"

"You know why," he said, taking a pack of smokes from his shirt pocket, shaking one out, lighting up. "I haven't been able to get you out of my mind since you stormed out this morning. I couldn't just leave it like that."

She hadn't been able to forget him, either, but she wasn't about to admit it. Her life was falling apart, damn it, and Adam, with his spooky house, shrouded furniture, and eerie goings-on, wasn't helping. "Well, maybe you should have. Coming here wasn't just a bad impulse, Adam. It's the worst thing you could have done. What am I supposed to tell Patrick?"

"You could try telling him the truth. Of course, he'll insist on knowing my intentions, but I think I can survive it."

"Well, maybe I can't," she said, then wished she hadn't.

"You can't run from this, London. It's too late for that."

"Running," she said with a laugh. "Who's running? I'm trying to catch a breath." Oh, yeah. She was definitely running, or trying to, but he kept drawing her back in, and she couldn't seem to resist him.

"You scared? 'Cause you act scared."

Frightened? Oh, God, yes. In fact, *terrified* might have been a better word. It was all about him. She was afraid of him. Of caring too much. Of getting hurt. "I'm not scared. I'm cautious."

"To hell with that," he said flatly. "You know what your problem is? You think too much," he said. "You need to learn to go with your gut. Listen to your instincts. It's what Patrick would do."

"Patrick's instincts told him to sell his house and move into my guest room—me, the daughter he can't stand. How sane is that?"

She pressed her fingertips to her temples in a lame attempt to stop the whirring activity of her brain, but it didn't work, and those instincts he mentioned screamed at her not to throw it all away because she was scared. She didn't listen, and she couldn't follow his lead, no matter how good he looked in his dark suit. "You came here from Louisiana because of your ex-wife, didn't you?" It was a shot in the dark, but worth the attempt.

"I'm not looking to rekindle anything with Julia, if that's what you're driving at. We're ancient history, and there's no going back."

"A straight answer, Adam. You owe me that much."

He muttered a few choice four-letter words, then reluctantly gave her what she was demanding. "Word has it Julia's somewhere in the D.C. area. She's the reason I came, London, but not the reason I stayed. You are."

London gave a sick little laugh. "I couldn't lure you with sex; no argument I made was convincing enough, yet you find out your ex is here and you hop the next flight? And I'm supposed to believe it's over between you? Give me a little credit, will you? My taste in men may be suspect, but I'm not quite that naive." She ran her fingers through her hair, pushing it back from her face. "What I am is tired. I need to regroup, Adam, and I can't do that with you here."

He searched her face for a moment, perhaps hoping she'd change her mind, or trying to think of a way to change it for her; then he took a matchbook from his coat and wrote something on the inside flap. "It's my cellular number. If you change your mind, give me a call."

He left by way of the alley, not bothering to enter

the house. London stared at the matchbook until the numbers wavered and swam. Slow footsteps sounded in the kitchen. "Adam?" Patrick said. "Now, where did he get to?"

London blinked back irrational tears as Patrick joined her on the porch. "Where's Adam?"

"He had somewhere to be," she said, clearing her throat.

"But I thought we were going to work on Benji's case." Patrick countered with a heavy frown. "He said—"

"He must have changed his mind." London got up, brushing past him into the dimly lit kitchen. *Please, oh please, just let it go*, she thought. *Please don't press me on this*. But she could hear Patrick's grumbling behind her.

"Changed his mind? De Wulf would never do that! He would never renege on a promise—especially not to me. He's a man of his word!"

"Maybe that's the problem," London shot back before thinking. Groaning, she turned to the cabinet above the sink, took down a packet of Alka-Seltzer, and plunked the tablets into a glass.

"You got a problem with a man who keeps his promises?" Patrick thundered. "Didn't I raise you better than that?" Then his eyes narrowed, and the lightbulb came on. "It's De Wulf you have the problem with, isn't it? You don't like him!"

"I like him, Dad. I don't trust him. There's a difference."

"You don't trust him? You don't know him! How the hell can you not trust a man you never laid eyes on before today? And don't hand me that women's intuition shit."

"I can't talk about this now," London said. She was tired, worn out, emotionally, physically. She didn't want to think, and she didn't want to explain her way out of the mess a few unthinking remarks had gotten her into. She downed the fizzing liquid, put the glass in the sink, and made for the stairs, ignoring Patrick's shout that rang out behind her.

"Damn it, Meg! What the hell's going on here?" He watched her go, wanting to follow yet painfully aware that she was female, with all of the strange and incomprehensible thought and behavior patterns that accompanied it. Bewildered, Patrick grabbed a beer from the fridge. "Not trust Adam? She's lost her fucking mind. I trust him. I'd trust him with my life . . . I'd even trust him with hers." He popped the top and took a long swallow, shaking his head as he sat down at the table. "Women."

Chapter Thirteen

Freddie shot a cold-eyed glance around the van. "There's no way this is gonna work, Sal. Even if we run into the Aussie, we won't be able to do shit in a compound like that. It's paramilitary, and this time they've got the guns."

Sal offered his seat to a blue-haired grandma in a flowered muumuu and flip-up sunglasses. The old lady huffed, "Thanks, junior, but I don't take candy from strange men, either." She motioned for the elderly women in the middle seat to squeeze in, settling her broad backside on the end nearest the window to the accompanying groans of her companions.

Sal shrugged. "How else are we gonna get in? Who would've thought De Wulf was CIA? He's gotta show up there, doesn't he? I mean, these guys are all workaholics. They don't know how to relax—kinda like you. You gotta learn to kick back, my friend. Enjoy a little leisure time. If it helps, try to think of it as a learning experience."

Freddie eyed Sal with disgust. "I don't want to expand my horizons, Sal. My goals are simple. I just want to kill one Aussie. Is that so much to ask?"

Sal shrugged, hitching up his khaki trousers, settling his bulk on the seat beside Freddie. Unlike his friend, he'd gone tourist, opting for a bright Hawaiian shirt and

mirrored shades that threw Freddie's frown back in du-
plicate miniature. "If it's meant to happen, it'll happen.
If not, we'll have to accept that it isn't in the cards. You
win some; you lose some. It's a universal truth, my
friend. We do our utmost, and sometimes things fall
through. Then we roll with the punches and pull ourselves up by our sock garters again."

"You really are full of shit," Freddie said, earning several wrinkled frowns from the two forward seats. "And
it's not just regular shit, Sal. It's emu shit. Do you have
any idea how bad that stuff smells?" He lowered his
voice. "I've had it right up to here with your life lessons,
Sal. Who do you think you are? Gary Zoloft?"

"As a matter of fact, I read that book. It was very en-
lightening. If you like, I could lend it to you."

Freddie groaned.

"Think positive thoughts, my friend," Sal said.

"Yeah, yeah, I know. The universe is a mirror, and
you're an asshole. It doesn't solve our problem." Freddie's coat pocket began to bleat out the theme song for
The Godfather. He took out his cellular phone and
scanned the caller ID, shoving the phone at Sal. "Jesus.
It's Joey. You answer it."

Sal pushed the button and threw a jovial hello the
caller's way. "Sal, where the hell have you been? I've
been tryin' to get Freddie for two fuckin' hours. I'm not
sure I like it when my soldiers are unaccounted for.
You're not ratting to the feds, are you, Sal?"

"Who, us? Not a chance. As a matter of fact, we're on
a tour bus headed for the Central Intelligence Agency
compound—"

"W-w-what?"

"You know . . . CIA?" Sal shot a surreptitious look
around and lowered his voice to a bass whisper. "Fred-

die got a lead on that guy De Wulf. Turns out he's CIA—imagine that!"

Joey was pacing the hardwood floor of his office back in Jersey. Freddie could actually hear his slippered feet scuffing the polished surface from two feet away; sweat broke out on Freddie's scalp and trickled over his temples and brow. He dabbed at it with a monogrammed silk handkerchief. "Sal, put Freddie on."

Freddie shook his head.

"I think he's in the bathroom," Sal said. "You know, he hasn't been the same man since New Orleans, Joey. Who knew one little broad could do so much damage to a tough guy like Freddie?"

"Sal," Joey's voice rose through the receiver. "Put fucking Freddie on the fucking phone or I'm gonna come down there and tear your fucking prostate out with my bare hands. Your prostate, Sal, do you get that?"

"Got it. Catch up with you later."

Sal handed the phone to Freddie, who winced as Joey chewed him out. "Damn it, Freddie, I had to buy Bitsy a chrysanthemum for her birthday. A crysanthemum, Freddie! She's threatening to change the lock on our bedroom door. Do you know how humiliating it is to have to sleep on the sofa in my own house?"

"I'm sorry, Joey. I don't know what happened."

"You wreck my marriage and all you can say is 'I'm sorry, Joey'? You make me sick, you know that? Sick!" Joey banged the receiver on his desk for emphasis. "That's your head, Freddie, if you don't get me that goddamned orchid!"

"Yeah, boss. I'm losin' the signal. I'll call back later." He shut off the cellular and returned it to his pocket. "That goddamned Australian is gonna die for this, and that red-haired little bitch can go right along with him.

And before I kill him, I'm gonna cut off his balls and make him suffer. If it's the last thing I do, I swear to you, Sal—"

The old broad in the fuchsia flowered muumuu scowled over the seat at him. "Young man, if you don't knock off the profane language, I'm going to ask the driver to have you ejected from this bus!"

Freddie turned three shades of purple, but he didn't reply. Sal smiled at the scowling matron. "Sorry, ma'am. It's our first field trip, and my friend here gets very excited. Mint?"

She hadn't planned on becoming an insomniac, yet there was no denying that her sleep patterns since becoming entangled with Adam De Wulf had been turned completely inside out. She would have laughed it off as part of his doubtful charm, yet she didn't find it especially funny. Not all that long ago, her bedroom had been a haven, a cozy nest in which to forget about the job and all its hassles, to curl up and read or watch TV. These days, she'd have a better chance of sleeping in the middle of I-95 than in the queen-sized four-poster bed.

Stretched full length on the firm mattress, London couldn't cajole or even threaten the tension to leave her long enough to grab a nap. Her brain whirred, her muscles clenched, and every errant breeze brought her upright, where she sat fully expecting to see a black-gloved hand slide the window up and Adam to step over the sill.

"Great. Just great." She flung a forearm over her eyes to block out the light. "If I don't soon get some sleep, I'm going to feel like a zombie."

She lay in a stupor for a while, dreadful thoughts running through her mind. She hadn't slept truly well since New Orleans. What if she never slept well again without the long, tall Australian in her bed?

It was a sobering thought, and not one any independent single woman would welcome. "You're giving him too much importance," she groaned. "Sure, he's gorgeous, but you don't need him—for anything. You can do this on your own." It sounded good, yet as she dragged herself off the bed and pulled Benji's notebook computer out of the bedside table, she had to admit that had he come to her right now with lust on his mind, she wasn't sure she would have turned him away.

Maybe sleep was for other people. Employed people, with real lives and real jobs, and boyfriends who didn't have their own private fence—unless, of course, it was the chain-link variety instead of one who sold stolen goods. The kind of existence she used to have, B.A. Before Adam. "Try and concentrate, London."

She hacked her way into phone company records and got a printout of every call made from Benji's apartment in the past year, long before he'd left on the overseas assignment. She went over the numbers twice, but there was nothing unusual in the list of contacts—no flashing neon sign that would signal a connection that didn't quite belong. The same went for his cellular accounts. There were calls to Patrick and Wyeth and London's former residence in Prague, Benji's dentist, and his ex-girlfriend, but nothing to arouse suspicion or provide any clues that there was anything going on in his life that London didn't already know about.

By the time she closed the notebook computer and put aside the phone records, she was working on a case of eyestrain that demanded she take a breather. Not quite prepared to let go, she dug through the drawer in her bedside table for her reading glasses and instead found Benji's PDA, the same PDA that Austrian officials had confiscated from Benji's hotel room in Vienna and later released to her. In the days following the memorial service, it had lain on the nightstand, a none-too-subtle reminder that Benj was gone. Finally, as she became more preoccupied, more on edge, she had placed it out of sight, in the drawer, where it was eventually forgotten in lieu of more urgent things.

Now London took it out, the pebbly black shell cool in her hand. She'd resisted owning one herself, and she'd ribbed Benji about being the personification of the young, upwardly mobile professional who couldn't find his way to the can without his personal digital assistant. The image was rapidly becoming a modern cliche, and an entire segment of the world's population was becoming dependent on AA batteries. None of her arguments swayed Benji, the original gadget guy. If it was on the cutting edge of electronics and had buttons, beeps, and a stylus, he'd be compelled to possess at least one. She'd rarely seen him without it, which was the reason she'd put it away. It had been too painful a reminder of his absence.

London took out the stylus, flipped back the front cover, powered it up, and stared at the screen:

System lockout. Enter password to access this handheld computer.

"Password. What password?" She took a chance and tried his e-mail password: *Spiderman.*

Password assigned. Show records. She tapped the home icon, and the icon grid came up.

"Elementary, Benj. Anyone could have figured that one out. Address." She paged down through a long list of addresses, phone and fax numbers, and e-mail addresses, then checked the date book. The months from September through November indicated two meetings per week with "Aries," the name of his contact, and then nothing until the second week of December, which had a flurry of appointments. Crammed in the midst of agency abbreviations and locations was the short message *Call Wyeth. Geneva Clinic, Dr. Hans Fritz. JDW?*

A quick Internet search revealed that Geneva Clinic specialized in cosmetic and reconstructive surgery.

London sat back on the bed. Geneva Clinic? Switzerland? Why would Benji be asking Wyeth about a clinic in Switzerland that specialized in plastic surgery? There was only one way to find out. She picked up the phone and dialed. It was ten P.M. in Geneva, definitely after hours, but worth a try. A crisp feminine voice answered. *"Doktor Fritz, bitte?"*

"What nature is your business?"

"Ah, you speak English." London gave the receptionist an encapsulated and slightly altered version of the truth: that she was calling on behalf of Benjamin Llewellyn concerning a matter he and the doctor had discussed on 13 December.

The receptionist put London on hold, then in a moment came back. "I am sorry, *junge Dame,* Doktor Fritz is unavailable."

She couldn't say why, but something about the episode set her teeth on edge. She'd had the distinct impression that it was the mention of Benji's name that had caused the door to be slammed in her face. The question was, why?

What business did Benji have with a Swiss plastic surgeon? Had he discussed it with Wyeth?

Or did a killer keep him from ever making that call?

Still holding on to the receiver, she cleared the line and dialed Wyeth's number.

Across town, *she* sat in the shadows of Wyeth's apartment, waiting. It was a game they played, this cat-and-mouse. He came to her, and she kept him wait-ing, wondering. She needed him, and he was . . . where? By the time he arrived, she'd be wild with an-ticipation, wild for him. She had no doubt that it was an unhealthy relationship, and she didn't give a damn. What was healthy? London's pining for a man she didn't know, wouldn't love, couldn't hold? *Healthy* was mundane, boring . . . as boring as a marriage to a man who was never there, a husband in name only.

The phone rang, and Julia jumped. Her heart rate ac-celerated; her breath stilled. On the fourth ring, the machine kicked on: *"Pinchot . . . leave a message and I'll get back to you."*

"Wyeth, it's London. I need you to call me as soon as you get in. I don't care how late it is. I think I may have found something in Benji's PDA . . . a Swiss doctor by the name of Fritz. He's a plastic surgeon who works out of a clinic in Geneva. Wyeth, I don't get it. Why would Benj be contacting a plastic surgeon? Especially one that expensive?"

London's voice trailed off, and the machine clicked, rewound, then beeped to signal that it was ready to record again. Reaching out, she pressed Play, the sound of London's voice reverberating inside her head.

"Wyeth, it's London. . . . Wyeth, it's London. . . . Wyeth, it's London. . . . a Swiss doctor by the name of Fritz . . . Wyeth, Wyeth, Wyeth . . . it's London. . . ."

A key rattled in the lock. He flicked on the light, and she threw herself into him, knocking him flat, but he wasn't that easily deterred. They grappled for a few minutes in fierce physical combat, Wyeth finally gain-ing the upper hand. He pinned her to the carpet, and she let him. She could have thrown him off; she was strong enough. The weight training had given her that, pro-viding a sham security, a sense that she would never be weak or vulnerable again. "What is it?" he asked in a rough whisper. "What's got you so unwound?"

She stared at the green light on the answering machine, the telephone she'd unknowingly knocked off the cradle. "She knows," she said. "London knows."

Heat up, a flurry of activity, and the trail would get cold again. That had been the pattern in the past, until it stopped completely during the dark days after Julia's illness. The pattern had been carefully calculated, never altered, unchanging—each lull a cooling-off period of several months in which Adam's tension had gathered, reaching unbearable levels because he knew that first strike was coming. He just never knew when. The operative known as the Ghost had sold secrets to the Russians, to Israel and Iraq. He'd obtained specifications for a new U.S. missile defense system that was so highly classified that few in government were aware of it—a circumstance that caused bickering and unease on the floor of the House when it finally leaked. The plan was scrapped, and Adam seemed to be the only one unsurprised by it.

"Hot and cold, hot and cold," Adam murmured. "A few meetings, a transfer of documents or information, and then lie low again. Go about your daily business while you await another opportunity. Then, when everyone is lulled into a false sense of security, you get back to business as usual."

But the spying wasn't business as usual. It was extracurricular, an interesting and profitable sideline. The one true and unshakable fact pertaining to the Ghost that still applied was that it had to be someone on the inside.

Someone at the CIA.

Someone highly placed and highly knowledgeable, with an eye toward minimal risk—or at least until recently.

Adam jotted down past activities—places, dates, and security breaches—indicated the three-year lull in the Ghost's activities with a flat dividing line, then traced recent movement. Dead drops, arms sales, security breaches, killings . . . Starting with Ben Llewellyn in Austria and culminating in the murder of Officer Johnson two nights ago, when he'd interrupted the drop. If the old pattern held true, all activity would cease, and it would be months before it resumed again.

He ought to be relieved, Adam thought, but he wasn't. Instead, he felt edgy and restless, waiting for the drop of the second shoe, and he couldn't quite shake the impression that he was missing something, some crucial difference between the events unfolding now and incidents occurring three years ago.

The question was, what?

Where did the difference lie?

There was no denying that the level of violence was escalating. It was something that had been rare in the past. The Ghost had killed, but only when cornered. He thought about London's account of the park shooting. The shooter had grabbed the jogger when confronted by London, but the killing was unnecessary. Off duty and taken by surprise, Johnson had been unprepared for a violent assault. He hadn't been armed, and it was doubtful he would have put up a struggle. London was no hot dog and would not have forced the shooter's hand. The double agent had had the option of shoving Johnson away and disappearing, yet he'd chosen to kill the unarmed officer. London had said later that it seemed like a taunt, as if the assailant was flaunting his control over the situation—even when nearly caught.

Power.

Johnson's killing was about power. He'd chosen to kill Johnson to show that he didn't fear London or Adam. But what about Ben Llewellyn? The single shot to the back of the head had been delivered before Adam entered the room. There had been no one to impress with his lack of fear, his control over the situation. If the motive for Llewellyn's killing hadn't been power, then why the hell kill him at all? There had to be a reason. What was it?

Execution-style murders sent a message, made a statement, frightened others involved in something larger, and kept the victim quiet.

But the murder hadn't sent a message or frightened anyone. Had Ben been silenced? What had he known that would be dangerous enough, valuable enough, to cause his death. And who would have benefited the most from his being eliminated?

The Iraqis? A single assassin wasn't their style. If they'd been responsible, a group of goons with black masks and semiautomatic weapons would have stormed in and kidnapped him, then either tortured him in order to get information or made some outrageous demands to the government in order to get him back. They also would have claimed responsibility by now, and it would have been splashed all over the U.S. newspapers.

There had to be something else. Something that only Ben knew about. Something the murderer didn't want leaked.

Adam had done some digging into Ben Llewellyn's background, and London had been telling the truth. Her brother was squeaky-clean. No gambling, no prostitutes, no whispers of a double lifestyle. He'd been honest to a fault, without a single blemish on his career record. "It's about the Agency," Adam said aloud. "It has

to be. Ben Llewellyn knew something he wasn't supposed to know, and that something got him killed."

JDW meant just one thing to London: Julia De Wulf.
But why would Benji be interested in a woman who had
disappeared three years ago? And what connection, if
any, did Adam's ex-wife have to Dr. Fritz and the
Geneva Clinic?

She scrawled the name on the back of an envelope
and shoved it into her pocket. Julia De Wulf. The name
just kept popping up, first because of Adam's obsession
with the orchid, and now with Benji. Adam was closely
guarded, and reluctant to divulge what he knew, at least
with her, but there were other ways of gaining information. And it might be a good time to do a little
research on her own while she waited for Wyeth to return her call.

She threw on a pair of faded jeans, her Georgetown
U. sweatshirt, and sneakers. With her hair caught in a
low-slung tail, and shades to hide the fact that she
hadn't slept, she flung out of the house and headed
straight for Langley.

She might be suspended, but she hadn't lost her security clearance. She drove to the main gate and flashed
her ID and building pass. Johnson's memorial service
had been scheduled for one o'clock. It would be over by
now, but most of the officers would gather at Quincy's
afterward for a few drinks; and few if any of the regulars who knew Johnson—like Yannick, Wyeth, or
Cid—would be coming in today. She'd just have to go it
alone and hope she could dig something up.

Al Falcon was working personnel. With three ex-
wives and two sets of dependents under the age of
eighteen, Al usually worked weekends for the over-

time. He'd told London not-so-jokingly several times that it was the only way he could afford to eat. Yet even three marriages down the tubes didn't put Al's roving eye to rest.

He whistled when she approached, pushing back in his chair and locking his hands behind his head. He was nice-looking in a broken-nose-lantern-jaw kind of way, but he was no Adam, and London was only interested in one thing. "Well, if it isn't the Lone Ranger. Heard about your adventures in the park, babe. Nice goin'."

If it had been anyone else, London would have shot him down with a few choice words, but Falcon was as sincere as a desk jockey with a bad back could get. "Too bad about Johnson. It bites the big one bein' at the wrong place at the wrong time. A little like my second marriage. If I'd been in St. Louis instead of Las Vegas, it never would have happened." He sat up, glancing around, lowering his voice. "Level with me, one spook to another: You get any leads on this guy? I asked Pinchot about the case's status, and he almost took my head off. What's with him these days, anyway? He seems preoccupied."

"No leads that I'm at liberty to leak—um, I mean, share," London told him. "As for Wyeth, it's probably hormonal."

Falcon's brows shot up. "He's got *those* kinds of problems?"

"I don't know," London said. "Why don't you ask him?"

Falcon was slow, but eventually he caught on. He shook a finger at her. "You're pulling my leg. I bet you'd be a lot of fun between the sheets," he said with a grin.

"Maybe, but you're not going to find out. Listen, can we stop clowning around? I need some information on a dependent of a guy who worked here a few years ago. His name is De Wulf."

"Adam De Wulf's wife?"

"You know them?"

"Hey, babe, I been here fifteen years. I've guzzled beer at every office party, softball game, and backyard barbeque. Of course I know Adam. I knew Julie, too, back in the day. Wanna talk about a match made in hell? Whew! You gotta wonder why a chick who hates the biz would marry a spook's spook like Adam. Not exactly good thinking on her part, but then, we're talking about Julie here."

London pushed her glasses down and considered him over the rims. "Details, please."

Falcon shrugged. "Well, she was pretty weird, and it got worse with him gone so much. She wouldn't go with him. Said she didn't trust foreigners. Can you imagine? Married to an Outback Jack and she didn't trust foreigners?" He laughed, then sobered again when he noticed that London hadn't joined in. "Anywho, after the fiasco in Tel Aviv, he came home for good, and that's when it really started to fall apart. Him with a bum leg from that spill he took, and her knocked up? Had to be a hell of a shock to come home from a ten-month stint overseas and find your wife with somebody else's bun in her oven—oh, wait, that happened to me, too. No wonder I had such empathy." He shook his head and sighed.

"A baby," London said. "He never mentioned it."

"I'm not surprised," Falcon said. "It's a guy thing. Masculine pride and all that."

"What happened to her, Al?" London asked with a troubled frown. She couldn't get the image of that sightless doll out of her mind.

"From what little I heard, it was a premature birth.

The little guy only lived for a few days. Julie took it pretty hard."

"And then she divorced him and disappeared."

"Yeah," Falcon agreed. "But first she tried to kill him." He nodded at London's surprised look. "Oh, yeah, babe. Stabbed him with a kitchen knife. Yeah . . . I'd say she lost it, all right."

"Any idea where she went?"

"Now, that I *don't* know." He sat back again, looking rather rakish and weather-beaten. "So . . . you goin' out with me, or what?"

"Not in this lifetime," London said, pushing her glasses back up. "The last thing I need is my heart broken. But thanks for clueing me in."

"Hey, babe, leavin' so soon?" Falcon called after her as she turned away. "I got a really interesting story about Yannick, guaranteed to be unfit for mixed company!"

London turned the corridor corner and nearly collided with a tour group. Tours were limited, tightly scheduled, closely watched, but welcomed by the DA as an essential part of their public relations program. An elderly lady with hair the vibrant pink of a new Brillo pad and with painted black brows nudged her companion in the flowered muumuu, slyly slanting a nod in London's direction. "Geeze, Georgia, wouldn't you think a place this lovely would have some sort of dress code?"

"If you'll be so kind as to look to your left, you'll see the great seal of the Central Intelligence Agency almost underfoot. . . ."

Sal followed the tour guide's directions and caught sight of a slim redhead. "Hey, Freddie, would you look at that!"

"It's a floor," Freddie groused. "Show me De Wulf, and I'll get excited."

"Not the floor, the redheaded broad over there . . . the

one who's casually dressed. Isn't that the girl from the Big Easy? You know, the one who nearly succeeded in making you a gelding?"

Freddie turned three shades of pink and, before Sal could stop him, barreled for the exit. "Here, here!" the guide shouted after him. "You must stay with the tour! No wandering around the compound is permitted!"

"I don't think my friend is feeling well," Sal told the guide. "It's a sudden attack of scrotum-itis. I'll just go make sure he's all right."

As he hurried after Freddie, the pink-haired lady raised her artificial brows in a disbelieving arch. "Scrotum-itis?"

"Oh, don't be so dense, Iris," her muumuu-wearing friend said. "That young man has had his nuts in a twist since he got on the bus."

Freddie was seeing pure, unadulterated red. He'd had a bad feeling about the tour since Sal first mentioned it. Ever skeptical, he'd known there had been a slim chance of finding what they were looking for, and he'd been right. De Wulf was nowhere around, but the gods had done him one better and dropped that ball-busting little bitch from his nightmares right into his lap. He'd zeroed in on her and was in hot pursuit when Sal's fat hand pulled him up short.

Freddie glanced down at the hand wrinkling the sleeve of his expensive suit, then into Sal's dark face. "Let go of me, Sal, or you're gonna regret it."

"I'm just delivering a reality check, that's all," Sal said. "Look around, Freddie. There are men with guns here, remember?"

"If you start spouting some line of shit about live-and-let-live, I'm gonna drag you all the way back to

Jersey and stick *your* balls in a vise! Then we'll see how *you* like it!"

Sal let go of Freddie's arm. "Take it easy; take it easy. I'm only sayin' we have to walk softly here, that's all."

"*You* walk softly, Sal. I'll handle this my own way!" He sprinted off after the redhead, but Sal had delayed him too long. He'd never catch her on foot. "Freddie! Freddie, wait! Oh, my God. Oh, my God." Sal caught up with Freddie as he flung himself into the driver's seat of the van and began tearing wires out from under the dash.

The tour guide was jogging across the parking lot. "Have you lost your mind? You can't do that! Get out of that bus! Security? Security!"

The van screeched to life. Sal threw himself inside as Freddie stepped on the accelerator and laid down rubber, but the redhead was approaching the gate. Unaware she was being pursued, she made a right onto Dolley Madison Boulevard. Freddie slammed the accelerator against the floorboard. The van streaked toward the gate. Sal's heart pumped so violently, he thought it would explode. Uniformed guards with automatic weapons screamed for Freddie to stop, while behind them a steel barrier rose from the ground. "You'd better stop, my friend!" He shot a glance at Freddie, whose teeth were tightly clenched, his eyes gleaming with a fierce and insane light. The guards leveled their weapons, screamed one more time for them to halt, then sprayed the van with machine-gun fire as Freddie rammed the gate and the van's front end disintegrated.

Freddie hung on to the wheel, but it was no longer attached to the steering column. "Out of the vehicle! Now! Get down on the ground! Down on the ground! *Get down on the ground!*"

Stunned, Sal stumbled from the van. His nose was bleeding, and he had a cut under his left eye. Freddie looked no better. His fury had worn off, and as Sal flattened on the pavement, he looked a little pathetic. "She got away, didn't she? The bitch got away?"

"Yes, my friend. She got away . . . but I'm afraid we didn't."

Chapter Fourteen

Adam waited while the shadows grew long and the house became eerily quiet. The cellular was on. He checked twice, then checked it again. "I would have thought she'd have rung us by now, wouldn't you? She asked for the number, and I gave it to her. What the hell good is that if she doesn't intend to use it?"

The Weimaraner cocked his head and groaned. He glanced at the fridge, where the raw chicken wings resided, then back at Adam, and licked his lips.

"It's a test; that's what it is," Adam declared. "She's playing with us. Stringing us along. She shows up here and draws me back in. I go to her with a legitimate offer of assistance, and she shows me the fucking door. She said it's because of Julia and the orchid, but that's just a clever bit of subterfuge for what she's really up to. Mental torture. That's what this is. Demented female mind games. It's like a Chinese water torture, only slightly farther south."

Honz sank to the floor and covered his eyes with his paws.

"Don't look so defeated. We've got our own agenda, and we'll let Llewellyn stew." He took the leash off the peg by the door before he turned back. "Well? Are you staying here or comin' with me?"

With the Weimaraner riding shotgun, Adam drove to

the one place he could think of where he might pick up a new lead on what Ben Llewellyn was really up to in the days before he died.

Quincy's was an Agency haunt. Quincy's old man, who'd been with the Company since shortly after its conception, had bought the place upon retiring. Within a few months, it had become the place to go to unwind and toss back a few with one's own kind. Quincy's old man was gone now, only a silent, lonely presence in the photo, above the bar, of John walking alone on a snowy, deserted Moscow street. The tradition he started, however, continued, and it was understood by all that nothing spoken or implied within the paneled walls of Quincy's ever left the bar.

It was the weekend, and the place was packed. Adam saw a few familiar faces in the crowd, but not the man he was looking for. If anyone knew what Llewellyn's brother had been into in the days before his murder, it would be Wyeth Pinchot. Llewellyn had indicated more than once that the two had had a long-standing friendship, and since Wyeth was Ben's handler, the two would have had few secrets between them . . . unless Administration had it right and Ben Llewellyn had turned. London was adamant that he'd been clean, and from all indications, she might be right—yet the double agent's loved ones were usually the last to know, and he couldn't vouch for Ben Llewellyn's innocence on her word alone.

"Adam! I haven't seen you in half a decade. How the hell have you been?"

"All right, Sam, and you?" Sam Easy had been an instructor at the Farm when Adam was in training. A big man with a direct stare and a soft voice, Easy was a real straight shooter, unquestionably trustworthy.

"I gave up complaining a few years back." He

grasped and shook Adam's hand. "Not like anyone listens anyway. Who's your friend there?"

"This big fella?" he said, with a smile for Honz. "Just someone I picked up along the way. Doesn't talk a lot, so it's not like I can't trust him to keep secrets." The waitress came by and took Adam's order. "Double whiskey, straight up, and my friend here'll have a Heineken."

She raised her eyebrows, but she didn't argue.

"You always were a unique bastard," Sam said with a laugh. "So what brings you back here? You weren't exactly thrilled with the business when you left us. In fact, I believe you said you'd be back when hell froze over. It was a tough winter, Adam, but not that tough."

"I came back because I was looking for someone," Adam admitted.

"Did you find that someone?"

"No, I didn't, and it seems to have been a wasted effort." The waitress brought Adam's whiskey, beer, and a shallow bowl. He poured the beer into the bowl and set it in front of Honz, then knocked back his whiskey. "Sam, you know a man by the name of Ben Llewellyn?"

Sam shook his head as he watched the canine lap up the brew. "Now, that's the damnest thing I ever did see. Won't he get drunk?"

"Honz?" Adam snorted. "Holds his liquor better than I do."

"Did I know Ben Llewellyn? Hell, I trained him, just like I trained you. Ben was a good man, real good. Damn shame about what happened."

"You buy the Agency line on it?"

"On the record, I have to go along with what my superiors say—you know that."

"And off the record?"

Sam leaned forward, bracing a forearm on the table. "No way did Ben Llewellyn turn. No way."

"What about Wyeth Pinchot?" Adam wondered. "They were friends, I take it? What did Pinchot know about this?"

"Good friends. And nothing as far as I know, but it's hard to tell about Wyeth. Still waters, if you know what I mean. He's not the type to come in here and hang out. Not like some I could mention." Easy's gaze slid to a figure hunched over the bar. "Now, there's one I worry about."

"Hey, Quince. Set me up, will you?"

Quincy poured half a jigger into a shot glass, slid it in front of Patrick, and handed him the portable phone. "How 'bout we call London? Just to let her know where you are."

"She'll figure it out on her own," Patrick said. "No need to tell that one anything. She's already got all the answers. Or at least she thinks she does."

"How about a trade, then? Even Steven. You can have all the scotch you want if you give me your keys." The bartender kept his voice low to avoid embarrassing Patrick, but Patrick seemed beyond recognizing it.

"If I give you my keys, I can't get home. This is a lousy neighborhood. If I leave my car here, the punks in the hood'll strip it for drug money."

"Hang around till closing, then," Quincy suggested, "and I'll drive you home in your car. My wife'll follow us over and drive me back. That way, your car'll be there for you tomorrow, and everybody's happy."

"It's all right, mate. I'll give him a lift home. I'm goin' by there anyway."

Patrick's expression cleared, and the argument he would have made was instantly forgotten. "Adam!

Where'd you get to earlier? I thought maybe Meg had tried to run you off."

"Me? Intimidated by a woman?"

"Meg's a hard case, but she means well. She just doesn't have Ben's finesse with people."

"Chip off the old block, ay?" Adam couldn't say much without risking arousing Patrick's suspicions, and with everything so uncertain, he felt it was best to operate on a need-to-know basis. If the older man got wind that Adam and London were more than just passing acquaintances, he was bound to ask a lot of questions. Uncomfortable questions. Questions Adam couldn't answer. "You ready to go?"

"No reason to stay." He shot a smug glance at the bartender as he slipped off the stool. "No worries about my car, Quince. Adam here'll take care of everything. He always does. C'mon, De Wulf, let's blow this joint."

That might have been true in the past, Adam thought as he slipped the bartender a bill and he and his two companions left the bar. But things had changed. *He'd* changed. At thirty-nine, he wasn't as young as he used to be, and he no longer looked at the world as his playground. Maybe he was more responsible, or maybe he was wearing down, wearing out, more frayed around the edges than he even cared to admit. The intrigue just didn't thrill him as it once had, and he thought more about his options than he ever had.

"Options? What options?" It was Julia's voice, bitter and shrill, that rang in his head. *"You have no options, Adam! You're a puppet! At the mercy of the Agency, and you'll never have a life of your own!"*

"You're wrong about that. A man always has options." He didn't even realize he'd spoken aloud until he slid behind the wheel of the Mitsubishi and caught Patrick's troubled frown.

"You okay, Adam?"

Adam patted the Weimaraner's muzzle when Honz stuck it over the backseat. "Right as rain," he answered. "Why do you ask?"

Patrick waved it off. "Ah, no reason. You just seem a little different, that's all. Like something's botherin' you."

"Ever have a case you couldn't solve, Pat? Something that kept you awake at night so long you just wanted to let it go?"

"Yeah, as a matter of fact, I did. But it wasn't a case—it was my wife's death. Losing her was a lot like that. I felt kinda lost. Like my internal compass quit working."

Adam understood that feeling. He'd been like that since leaving the Agency. The thing that had been his life, his everything, was suddenly gone. He'd tried to tell himself that he'd adjusted, but he hadn't. He'd just sort of gone on doing what he'd always done, not really worrying about the legalities of his actions . . . only without the sanction of the government. "What'd you do about that? Fixin' it, I mean?"

"You can't fix somethin' that big. I just keep getting up every morning," Patrick said. "Just like that . . . and every now and then, I allow myself a glimmer of hope that Meg will find some decent guy and settle down. I'd like a grandson or two before I kick off, though with Meg's attitude, my odds of winning the lottery would be a whole lot better." Patrick's glance slid Adam's way, judging, weighing. "I don't suppose you and—ah, never mind. Must be the whiskey."

"Yeah," Adam said, "alcohol does funny things to a man." But he'd only had two shots of whiskey, and he was thinking the same thing. It was the most preposterous notion—more than that. It was crazy, and he'd best get it out of his head immediately.

Beside him, Patrick sighed. "You hungry, Adam? I know this little coffee shop that stays open all night. They serve the best grilled cheese in the whole world."

Adam glanced at his old friend. He got the message. Patrick wasn't ready to go home, wasn't ready to face Red.

At half past three Adam nosed the Spyder to the curb behind Llewellyn's ancient Porsche. She could have afforded something a little less antiquated, yet her frugal streak had won out. Real estate agents advised savvy buyers to "buy the worst house in the best neighborhood," which Llewellyn had translated into autospeak, and she bought a wreck with a lopsided rear bumper that was a fashion statement in name only. Its paint had lost all its gloss due to too much exposure to the elements, and when she turned the key, the ignition groaned and complained like a ninety-year-old trying to get out of a low-slung hammock.

Her stubbornness in hanging on to the junkyard chic made no sense to Adam, but his inability to get Llewellyn's lopsided logic was an indisputable part of the attraction. Adam opened his door and got out, the Weimaraner trailing him. "Watch your step," he told Patrick. "These foreign makes are low in the carriage."

"Yeah, and these knees aren't what they used to be." He groaned a little as he peeled himself out of the car and stood, still not as steady as he should have been, despite a couple of pints of black coffee. "You're comin' in, aren't you, Adam?"

Adam hedged. He could see London's silhouette in the front window. Her arms were crossed over her chest—defensive body language—and she looked angry. "I'm not so sure that's a good idea."

"But we got to get our game plan together for this investigation. You're not backin' out on us, are you?"

"Back out? Not a chance." He took a deep breath and followed Patrick up the walk, Honz beside him. Adam glanced at the hound. "If we're gonna get on her good side, you've gotta be nice to the cat."

Honz warbled an answer low in his throat, but he looked almost as wary as Adam felt.

She met Patrick at the door, dressed in striped blue drawstring pajama bottoms and a white camisole top—a slight improvement over the hideously ugly boxers. The glare she sent his way said none of this was going to be easy, but it was nothing compared to what she gave Patrick. "Where the hell have you been? I've been looking all over for you!"

Patrick was immediately defensive. "Now, is that any way to talk to your father?"

"It is when my father's been out drinking and I've been worried sick about him! I drove by Quincy's. Your car was in the lot, and the place is closed. What am I supposed to think?"

Patrick's ears were tipped with red, a sure sign he was getting pissed. "You might try remembering that your old man can take care of himself and doesn't need his daughter to tell him what to do! I was with Adam. We had coffee. End of discussion."

He stomped to the living room and flicked the remote to turn off the TV, which had been tuned in to the soap channel. "You? Watching the monstrosity?"

It was her turn to pinken. "It was background noise."

Patrick just looked at her. "I got to go to the can. Adam, you make yourself at home, and don't mind my daughter. It must be that time of the month."

He disappeared up the stairs, and London turned on Adam. "Did you encourage this?" she demanded.

"Encourage what?" Adam replied. "The fact that he had a few too many? Is that really what's got your knickers in a twist, or is it the fact that he invited me in?"

"Both," she shot back. "At least I had some control over the situation before you two became such good buddies. Now you're popping in and out of here like you own the place, and you're using the front door. I'm not sure I like that. What if he catches on?"

"Oh, I get it. This isn't about my being here; it's about my being here with Patrick. You're jealous. You want me all to yourself, is that it?"

"I am not—I am *not* jealous! And you are so egotistical!"

"Maybe, but I'm right, aren't I?" Adam did the unthinkable and reached out to cup her cheek, his smile fading as he leaned in to steal a kiss. "No need to fret, sweetheart. I'm all yours whenever you want me."

The fight was leaving London, the anger being replaced by a desire she didn't welcome and couldn't control . . . a desire so intense that it frightened her. That's why she held back. "Don't."

"Think about it, Llewellyn," Adam said, his tone soft, suggestive. "Think about us, and the way it can be . . . the way it's been since the beginning. Then tell me to stop." He kissed the corner of her mouth, and she softened.

"I hate you for this," she whispered even as she met the next kiss halfway. "You know that, don't you?"

"Careful where you tread with those emotions, Red. You know what they say about that thin line." She was nearly his; he felt her giving up the fight, giving in, and her surrender was incredibly sweet.

"Is that what happened to Julia? Did she cross over that line?" She pushed back far enough to meet his gaze. "I know, Adam. The marriage, her mental state, her infidelity. Why didn't you tell me she tried to kill you?"

She got what she wanted. She'd stopped him cold. Adam ran a hand over his face, but it couldn't erase his frustration. "Nothing like a rousing discussion of the crazy, homicidal ex-wife to nip the thought of sex with the girlfriend right in the old bud."

"That's not exactly an answer."

Like Honz with his chicken wings, she wasn't about to give it up. "I didn't tell you, because Julia's my problem, my responsibility. It has nothing to do with you. *She* has nothing to do with you, and I intend to keep it that way!"

"Responsibility?" she said, her eyes widening. "How the hell are her mental problems your responsibility?"

"Because it's my fault! I'm the one who caused it! I'm the one who made her that way!" It was almost a shout, and Patrick chose that moment to reappear in the doorway.

He looked from Adam to London, standing inches apart, both caught in the teeth of some mysterious, heated confrontation. "What's this about? Why are you shouting? What the hell's going on?"

"Look, Pat, it's late," Adam said abruptly. "I think it's best if Honz and I just go. I'll call you tomorrow, and we'll set something up—away from here."

"Oh, no," London ground out. "You're not getting off that easy this time, and we're not through here."

He stalked out, the dog bolting too, while Patrick gaped. "What the—Jesus Christ. Will someone tell me what the hell is going on around here?"

"Damn it, Adam!" Uncaring that she was dressed in pajamas and fuzzy pink slippers, London went after him. She caught him by the curb as he was about to open the passenger door of the Mitsubishi. She grabbed his arm and wouldn't let go, forcing him to face her. "You can't just drop a bombshell like that and then leave without explaining!"

"Not here, and not now," Adam said. He was wishing that for once she'd let well enough alone, when the small red dot flitted over her face like a scarlet firefly, finally lighting on a spot in the center of her forehead. Adam swore, diving at her, knocking her down a fraction of a second before the driver's and passenger windows simultaneously blew out.

Adam got up and pulled her up with him. "Pat, get her inside. I'm going to have a look around."

"If you're going, then so am I."

Adam nodded at Patrick, who bullied her into the house. "Damn it, Meg. For once in your life will you listen to reason? Adam's right. Whoever that was might still be out there."

"Someone just took a shot at me," she snapped. "Me, damn it! I can't let them get away with that!"

"You're going in the house, like Adam said, and you're gonna wait there until he says it's safe for you to be somewhere else."

"Damn it, it's my life we're talking about here!"

Patrick gave her a shake, his glare fierce. "It's your life, but you're my daughter. Hasn't this family lost enough already, for Christ's sake?"

London met his gaze. There was fear in his eyes, and something else: a silent plea that spoke clearly to her. He wasn't just trying to control her; he was trying to protect her. He'd lost her mother, and he'd lost Benji. He didn't want to lose her, too.

She blinked, trying to answer past the tightness in her chest. "All right. I'm going. But I don't have to like it."

She turned back to the house as Wyeth's Audi pulled in at the curb. He got out, glancing at Adam's windowless Mitsubishi and the glass scattered over the pavement. "My God. What happened here? Is everything okay?"

"Hell, no, everything isn't okay. Someone took a shot at Meg. If it hadn't been for Adam, she wouldn't be here." He scrubbed at his bristling crew cut. "Damn it, Meg! Will you go into the house like I asked? It isn't safe for you to be out here in the open. Not until Adam catches the bastard that did this."

"Patrick's right. You need to get inside while we sort this all out." Wyeth took her arm and guided her up the walk, but it was obvious she wasn't happy about it.

"So, I'm supposed to take cover while the big, strong, invincible males circle the wagons? Do either of you realize how ridiculous this is?"

"You were the one in those sights!" Patrick bawled. "You were the target! Wyeth, you're her superior. Order her to get inside."

"I'm going," London snapped, "but I hate this."

"He's just trying to protect you," Wyeth told her once they were inside. "That must have scared the hell out of him just now." He raked a hand through his blond hair. "Didn't do much good for me, either, and I wasn't here to witness it. He doesn't want to lose you, Meg, and quite frankly, neither do I. There's been enough tragedy in this family. I don't think Patrick could survive it if anything happened to you."

"Nothing's going to happen to me." Brave words, but she was still running on adrenaline. When the rush finally passed, she would be as shaken as he was. "I'm glad you came by. I need to talk to you about Benji."

"What about him?"

London dug in her handbag and handed him an electronic device. "This is Ben's PDA."

"Where'd you get this?"

"The Austrian officials confiscated it during their search of his room, and they were holding it for evidence. After the investigation concluded, they sent it to me, along with a few other personal effects. I'd almost forgotten I had it; then the other night I came across it again and decided to check his date book."

"And?"

"And I found this notation."

She turned the apparatus on, and the screen displayed the message: *Call Wyeth. Dr. Hans Fritz, Geneva Clinic. JDW.*

"That's odd," Wyeth said. "I wonder why he never called."

"I think the *JDW* stands for Julia De Wulf, but I can't seem to make the connection. Why would Benji be interested in a woman who dropped off the planet three years ago? And what's with the Geneva Clinic? They specialize in plastic surgery."

"Have you asked De Wulf about it?"

"I haven't had a chance," London admitted. "I was hoping you could clue me in."

Before Wyeth could answer, Patrick came in with Adam. The latter barely acknowledged Wyeth, not giving him more than a glance, speaking directly to London. "You all right?"

"I wish everyone would stop asking me that!" she snapped, then sighed. "Okay, so I admit it. I'm a little on edge. What did you find?"

"It's too dark to tell if there are footprints," Adam said. "We'll have to wait till daylight to go over the area, but I did find this at the base of the oak tree in the vacant lot across the street." He handed her the empty brass casing. There's every reason to think it belonged to the sniper. Must have been positioned to watch the house."

London shook her head. "But why? That doesn't make any sense. Why would anyone want to kill me?"

"Because you've been looking into your brother's murder. You've been making the blokes over at Langley more than a little nervous."

"That's reaching, don't you think?" Wyeth asked. "Why would anyone want to kill London?"

"Stranger things have happened," Adam said, his gaze so intense it cut right through Wyeth. "Like you arriving right on the heels of the sniper's shot. Want to tell us where you were five minutes ago?"

"I don't owe you an explanation," Wyeth said coldly, "and I don't like being accused of things I had no part in. I'd never do anything to hurt London, and she knows that, even if you don't want to believe it." He clapped Patrick on the shoulder and stopped in front of London. "I need to get out of here before I say something I shouldn't. Take care of yourself, will you? I'd never forgive myself if something happened to you."

"I'll call you tomorrow," London said, closing the door after him. For a solid minute, Wyeth stood on the darkened porch, letting his fury wash over him; then he got in his car and went in search of *her*.

Johnson's memorial service earlier that afternoon had sapped Wyeth emotionally. Because he'd worked closely with Johnson over the course of several years, he'd stood beside the grieving widow, stoic and respectful, offering silent moral support while he cursed himself for the worst sort of hypocrite. She'd collapsed in Wyeth's arms when the captain of the honor guard presented the flag from the coffin, and it had been all Wyeth could do to watch Johnson's nineteen-year-old son accept the triangular red, white, and blue.

For the thousandth time in three years, he looked at his life and felt helplessly caught in a hell of his own making, a hell he had no chance of escaping. Not even a pint of vodka could soothe the sick feeling that had taken root deep inside him. It was an odd feeling, knowing that you were rotting from the inside out. No one sensed the decay as Wyeth went through the motions of his life, but it was there, eating away at the last ounce of decency left in him.

He wasn't just a failure; he was a fraud.

The incident at the Llewellyns' underscored that fact. When he got home, he was no less furious. The Hummer was parked down the street.

She was crouched by the sofa when he walked in, her arms locked around her knees as she rocked back and forth. Wyeth went to her, getting down on her level. "You crazy bitch!" he said, and slapped her so hard her head bounced off the arm of the sofa.

Her lip puffed immediately, a smear of scarlet on her teeth where the blow had cut her, but it didn't seem to register that he was angry. "Wyeth. Where have you been? I needed you."

"Out." He couldn't tell her that he'd been watching the house where she'd lived with Adam, downing Absolut and debating a confrontation with her ex-husband . . . a coward's way out, but a way out. Adam was the only one who could stop her, the only one she couldn't destroy. She'd already done her worst to De Wulf, and he'd survived. One word to Adam De Wulf, one hint that his ex-wife was ass deep in espionage and murder, that everything he'd believed for three years was a lie, and it would all come crashing down around them. "They put Johnson in the ground today, and I had to be there to clean things up. That's what I do, isn't it? Sweep up after you. Before I came here,

I stopped by the Llewellyns', and everything was in an uproar. It seems someone tried to kill London, and if not for your ex-husband, she'd be dead by now."

His heart pulsed with sickening thuds as he dug his fingers into the sinewy flesh of her upper arms. "Why? Why would you do something so insane? Tell me!"

"Because she knows," she said. "London knows. She's dangerous—to me, to you. I can't let her ruin it for us. Someone had to stop her."

Wyeth hit her again, not bothering to close his fist. "She can't prove anything; don't you get that? She doesn't know anything . . . just like Ben didn't know anything." He sat back, breathing hard. His anger was starting to fade, but he felt no regret for hitting her. She deserved that and so much more. Reaching out, he took her by the underside of her jaw, tilting her head up with the same hand that had bloodied her mouth. "Understand me, Julia. If you hurt London, I swear, I'll—"

"You'll what, Wyeth?" she demanded softly. "Hurt me? Do you think that frightens me? You've done your worst to me. Nothing else can compare."

He pushed her away roughly, the accusation as painful for him to hear as it had been for her to endure. "You're half right. We've done our worst to each other. The deception, the lies, half-truths, and evasions, the secrets, Julia! This is insanity—it's like a disease, eating away at us . . . and for what? Where's the payoff? A few thousand dollars for my best friend's life, my integrity . . . It hasn't been worth it."

"It was never about the money."

"No. It was never about the money. It was about Michael, the child we lost—together, Julia. Not just you. I lost him, too—I mourned him."

"It was the Agency's fault, and Adam's. They did this—"

This time he wouldn't let her shove it off onto some-one else. "Cut the crap! We did it to ourselves, and it has to stop. Do you hear me, Julia? *It has to stop.*"

"After London . . ." she insisted. "We can go some-where . . . disappear . . . just the two of us."

Wyeth shook his head. "It's too late for that. It's be-come a sickness with you. You'd only surface again, and I'd spend the rest of my life covering for you. I don't want to live like that—I can't." He sat down by the phone. "You know, it's almost funny, but you're every bit as obsessed as Adam ever was. Maybe more so . . . At least he was on the legal side of things. You're just a murderess. With you it's all about power."

"How can you do this to me? After all we've been to each other?" He was choosing London over her. She al-most didn't believe it, though the truth was there, on his face, in his voice. He would sacrifice her life to save London's. "How can you choose her, Wyeth?"

He laughed, and that was harder to take than his sar-casm, his hatred. "You really don't get it, do you? It isn't just about London. It's about Benji and Patrick, and all that they are. You know, when I was a kid, I used to hang out there, and I'd watch them interact, and I was so en-vious. I wanted to be part of the family, not some kid with nobody who gave a damn about him, who they took pity on. I wanted to be one of them. Hell," he said softly, bitterly, "I still do." He sighed as he picked up the phone. It was over, he thought with a rush of relief. So this was how freedom felt. It was finally over.

"What are you going to do?" she asked softly.

"What I should have done three years ago. I'm going to end it. I'm going to tell them everything."

He turned away from her as he started to dial. The phone was pressed to his ear when the bullet struck him—one clean shot, and his heart exploded. Wyeth slumped forward onto the table. One arm hung limp at his side. A trickle of red soaked his sleeve, ran over the back of his hand, dripping from the tip of his index finger onto the white linoleum She took the receiver and placed it back on the hook, then put her cheek against his. He was warm, and as long as she didn't look down, she could pretend that he was sleeping. "We were so good together," she whispered, with no one there to witness the single glistening track that dampened her cheek.

Chapter Fifteen

"There's nothing over there to find—a few scattered bits of broken bottles and some cigarette butts, but nothing even remotely fresh, and nothing left by our shooter. Definitely a professional hit." Adam had just returned from his inspection of the vacant lot across the street. Patrick was on the phone, working the grapevine of former colleagues, retired and active, to see if word of the shooting had been leaked. His contact list was almost as extensive as the D.C. phone listings, so it was going to take a while.

London could hear his voice, lower than his normal grizzly growl, droning in the background, a reminder of how serious the situation was. "A professional hit. Then, it's CIA related."

"Not necessarily," Adam said. "There's a chance it could be your pal, Freddie Caruso. From all indications he wasn't too happy about having his balls twisted nearly off. Makes it hard for a man to forget a woman, coming that close to castration."

London snorted. She was dreaming of an espresso, something dark and rich and exploding with caffeine, since she still hadn't slept. "Those two clowns are at the bottom of the list. They couldn't manage to get out of their own way; how could they pull something like this off without bungling it, or leaving a blazing neon trail behind?"

"List," Adam frowned, homing in on that one word. "You said 'list.' Who else do you know that wants you dead?"

London shrugged, not really wanting to admit to him that she might have more enemies than friends. It wasn't that she was a social scene dropout. She just hadn't met that many individuals outside the Agency circle intriguing enough for her to want to hang out with them. Besides, when talk turned to her occupation and she gave the vague reply that she worked for the government, it ended any chance of normal interaction, and most civilians either became annoyingly intrigued or overly suspicious. "I may have pissed a few people off, but I can't imagine anyone would want to take me out for that. Besides, we haven't established that they weren't shooting at you. They sure made a mess of your car windows."

"This is serious," he told her.

"You're telling me," London groused. "I mentioned going out for coffee this morning, and Patrick threatened to lock me in my room. He hasn't done that since I was fourteen."

"That's not exactly a bad idea."

"Excuse me? Who pays the rent here?" She blew out a frustrated breath. "I just wanted some coffee."

He watched her for a moment, his expression as serious as she had ever seen it; then he crossed to where she was standing. When he laid his hand on her shoulder, she flinched. "Patrick did you a favor. You need some sleep, not more coffee."

Oh, yeah. She needed sleep, and she'd entered this weird place where she couldn't seem to rest without him in the room. It wasn't what she wanted, to be de-

pendent on a man for anything—especially this man—
but she hadn't wanted Benji to die, either, or Johnson.
And she didn't like the feeling that someone, somewhere out there, wanted her dead. Nameless, faceless
. . . it could be anyone, and none of it made sense. So
many things had just occurred that she hadn't anticipated or even considered . . . like Adam's growing
importance to her. Her life was spinning out of control, and there wasn't a damn thing she could do to
stop it. Depressing thoughts. London sighed. "I need
to keep going. I need to find out who killed Benj, and
then I'll think about sleep."

She hadn't moved away, and he hadn't taken his
hand from her. It stayed on her shoulder, a warm, solid
weight, oddly comforting, and she had the irresistible
urge to step closer. The gesture seemed to say that
they would get through this together . . . but that was
a false impression.

They weren't together, not by the wildest stretch of
the word, and she doubted they ever could be. They
were too much alike, capable of driving each other
crazy. Besides, relationships built on lust didn't last.

That's what it was—lust. That's why she ached for
him to wrap his arms around her and just hold her. It
was lust all right . . . or at least, it was the only name
she was willing to attach to what she felt for Adam.
Anything else would thrust her into the category of
hopeless romantic, and no way would she buy into
that. "Sleep's overrated, anyway," she mumbled. "I'll
be fine, as soon as I figure out what Benji wanted with
Dr. Fritz. I found a notation in his PDA. It was a reminder to call Wyeth about a Dr. Hans Fritz at Geneva
Clinic."

"Pinchot's considering reconstructive surgery? Good

choice. Maybe they can make him look a little less like a choirboy."

"Not funny," London said. "Besides, I asked Wyeth when he stopped by last night, and he didn't know anything about it. Apparently, Benji never got the chance to make that call."

Adam was skeptical. "That, or Pinchot isn't telling the whole truth."

"Wyeth and Benji were friends. He knows how much this means to me. Why would he lie?"

"Judas and Jesus were friends, too," he said softly. "It didn't keep things from getting ugly. I'll drop by later today and have a little talk with Pinchot. Maybe I can pry the truth out of him."

London couldn't quite get Adam's suggestion that Wyeth might not be telling her the whole truth out of her mind. It might have been the fact that she had been awake for what felt like an eternity, or the residue from last night's traumatic events, but Adam's suspicious nature was infectious, and she wasn't completely immune.

It *was* possible that Wyeth was keeping something from her out of some misguided urge to protect her. He seemed to have made it his mission in life to look after her, even though she was more than a few years removed from her naïveté. And that overprotective impulse of his had only gotten worse since Benji's death.

"There's one way to find out." She picked up the phone, then decided instead that a one-on-one confrontation might be best. She needed to be able to look him in the eye when she asked him if he'd been less than truthful with her. God help him if she found out he knew about Dr. Fritz and hadn't shared that information with her.

It was impossible to escape Patrick's suddenly vigilant eye. He'd kept tabs on her throughout the day, and if he discovered that she was planning on going out alone, he would insist on going with her. Getting Wyeth to admit he was keeping secrets would be an impossibility with Patrick present. If that didn't make things difficult enough, Adam had promised to pay Wyeth a visit, and she needed to get to him before Adam arrived and turned the bid for truth into a testosterone-laden pissing contest.

Patrick had always thought highly of Wyeth. He wouldn't make it easy for her to ask the pointed questions she needed to ask, or for Wyeth to give honest answers with the stern Llewellyn patriarch glaring down his nose from across the room. If she was going to accomplish anything, it would require careful planning and execution.

Since his retirement, Patrick had become a creature of habit. Two P.M. was nap time. Every day at the same time, the recliner clanked and Patrick began to snore. He slept for forty-five minutes, no more, no less, showered, and drove to Quincy's for an early beer and a late lunch.

At five minutes to two, London paused at the top of the stairs. The recliner launched, her father sighed, and a few minutes later, she slid behind the wheel of the Porsche.

Three-thirty-six Palmetto was a one-story brick with white trim and no shutters. London rang the bell, then waited impatiently for the sound of Wyeth's footsteps. A minute ticked by, but there was no answer. She rang the bell a second time. The Audi was parked in its usual spot. A long, annoying buzz, too persistent to ignore.

She rapped on the door. "Wyeth! Come on, Wyeth. It's London! Will you open the door?"

Wyeth's neighbor, Bill Uttley, killed the motor on his lawn mower. "Hasn't been anyone in or out all day. Kinda weird, too. I always pick up the paper as Mr. Pinchot's starting on his morning run. Not this morning, though. Maybe he isn't feeling well. You want me to call his landlord, or somethin'?"

"That won't be necessary," London told him. She tried the knob. The door was unlocked. She eased it open, pausing to take in the silence. "Wyeth? You there?"

Not a stir of air or a creak of a floorboard. The house was utterly still, waiting. Mr. Uttley followed London onto the porch, where he stood, weaving back and forth on the balls of his feet, craning his neck to catch a glimpse of the apartment's interior.

London closed the door in his face. The living room opened via a wide arch into the kitchen. Wyeth was seated at the end of the table, his back to her. Light streamed into the living room, but the kitchen shades were drawn and dust motes did a lazy dance in the buttery beams playing over the space of hardwood floor between them. "Wyeth?" she said foolishly. She knew it was unnecessary. She could see the dark stain an inch above the back of the chair, dead center between his shoulder blades, and she felt a little sick as she stopped beside him. "Oh, God, Wyeth."

Somehow, he'd managed to remain upright, despite his breastbone being blown half away. His eyes were closed, his face pale, and there was a trickle of blood congealing at the corner of his mouth. London pressed two fingers to his jugular, aware before she felt his unnatural chill that he was dead.

She took out her cell phone and dialed. "Dad?" she

said softly. "Dad . . . it's Meg. I'm at Wyeth's and I need you to come here. He's dead, Daddy. Wyeth's dead."

"We'll have to wait for the coroner's report, but it looks like he's been deceased for several hours." A plainclothes officer stood by an unmarked car, talking into the radio microphone, lending the scene an air of the unreal. No lights. No sirens. Just Jesus Viagra, looking uncharacteristically rumpled in his pilling navy Dockers and striped short-sleeved shirt. His belt was in its last notch, and the half-eaten tuna-and-cheese-melt sub he was munching probably wasn't helping.

He pinned London with a look. "I didn't expect to see you two again so soon. Two days, two stiffs. That's gotta be some kind of record."

"Believe me, Detective," London replied, "it wasn't planned that way."

"Mind tellin' me where you were last night . . . just for the record?"

London felt a firm touch on her shoulder, a warning not to say too much. She glanced up as Patrick answered for her. "As a matter of fact, she was at home, with Adam and me. I just got a new big-screen TV. We were watching the Travel Channel and reminiscing."

"And you are?"

"I'm her father. And Wyeth Pinchot was a friend of the family. A good friend."

"Mr. Pinchot was CIA, Ms. Llewellyn is CIA, and you—"

Patrick thrust out his chin, and his eyes took on a hard glint. "Past tense," he said pointedly. "I'm a man of leisure these days."

"What about him?" Viagra jabbed a thumb in Adam's

direction. He was leaning against the wall, his fists shoved in his pockets as he closely watched the exchange.

"What *about* him?" Patrick demanded. "He's a friend of the family, just like Wyeth."

"Detective, I don't see what any of this has to do with Wyeth's death. I've told you everything I know, and if you don't mind, I'd really like to go home." London was a little shocked at how calm she sounded, how rational. It was the numbness. It had to be the numbness. She felt as if she'd been shot full of novocaine—body and soul. When it wore off and she started to feel again, she would fall apart. She didn't want to be here with this man when that happened . . . or with Adam, for that matter.

They were on an uneven footing these days. There was still so much unsaid between them, so much that was unresolved.

"I didn't know the CIA was so family oriented." Viagra pointed his pencil eraser at London. "You guys got day care?"

Patrick stepped between them, strangely protective. "What's it to you?"

"No need to get testy, Mr. Llewellyn. Just curious, that's all." Viagra glanced at his notebook. "I guess I got what I need—for now. Ms. Llewellyn, stop by the station when you get a few moments. Just routine follow-up stuff."

It was 10:33, and the hours since London had discovered Wyeth had passed in an unrecognizable blur. She was functioning, but she found that a little disturbing. Wyeth was dead, and she spent the afternoon making phone calls, alerting her peers at the Agency on a need-to-know basis. Everyone else would find out soon enough. Cid was the last on her list, mostly because London was dreading breaking the news, and she felt she owed it to her friend—and, in an odd way, to Wyeth—to break the unwelcome news face to face.

Not that Cid and Wyeth were particularly close, but they were on friendly terms. Besides, London thought, getting it all off her chest might help clear her mind so that she could sleep, though these days sleep was more a concept than a reality.

Spudzy nodded and grinned as she entered. Road Kill Raccoons, a local band, was the featured act that evening. What they lacked in four-part harmony, they more than made up for in volume. Blue strobe lights flickered above the stage, while a revolving spotlight spun and flashed over the dance floor, highlighting dancers at random in shimmering, unearthly lime green. London spotted Cid on the far side of the room. Deep in conversation with Beef Cookie, she seemed oblivious to the tragedy that had been visited upon Wyeth's friends earlier that morning.

Cid looked up as London approached. "Hey, Lon. How goes it? I was beginning to think you were bored with the club scene. You haven't been by in ages."

"I was here night before last," London said with a frown. "Anyway, I've been—busy."

Beef Cookie got up. "I'm headed to the ladies' room. I'll catch you later. Girlfriend," she said with a skeptical glance at London, "order yourself a steak. You need some meat on them bones."

London ignored her, sliding into a chair. A waiter came by, and she ordered a whiskey, straight up.

"That's some strong stuff," Cid observed. "Listen, are you okay? You look kinda ragged. That man of yours isn't giving you a hard time, is he?"

"He's not my—" London stopped and sucked in a breath. Her temper was frayed, but that wasn't Cid's fault. She'd had no part in any of it. "Look," London said softly, "that's not why I'm here. I've got some bad news. Really bad. It's about Wyeth."

"Pinchot?" Cid's voice was irritatingly level, and London had to remind herself that the blonde didn't know.

"Yeah." She rubbed the frown line forming between her brows, as if it would somehow ease the ache behind her eyes. "I went by his place this morning to talk, and I found him—he'd been shot, Cid. Wyeth is dead."

Cid blinked. "Pinchot . . . a suicide? You're kidding, right? I mean, he seemed to have it all together—just a regular guy."

London shook her head. "Not suicide. Murder. Just like Benji. Someone shot him from behind while he sat at his kitchen table."

"But who would want to kill Pinchot?" Cid asked. "That doesn't make sense, Lon. Are you sure about this?"

"Damn it, will you listen to what I'm saying for once? Wyeth is dead! I saw him! I saw the blood, and the bone fragments, and—" She realized how she sounded, saw the blood drain from Cid's face, and reached out. "I'm sorry. I don't mean to take it out on you. It isn't your fault. None of it is your fault." The flashing strobes lent the scene a nightmarish quality. There was an anger building inside her, a feeling of impotent rage so overwhelming that she knew, if she didn't escape the noise and the lights, she'd go on an insane rant that no one needed to witness, least of all Cid. She grabbed her purse, and at the same time the door opened and Adam walked in. "Listen," she said, "I have to get out of here. I'll call you—about the arrangements."

"Yeah. Sorry about Pinchot, Lon. I know how close you two were."

"Yeah. I'm sorry, too," London murmured. "You ever notice how it's the ones who least deserve it who seem to end this way?"

"I guess. Or maybe it's just that when bad people die, nobody cares." Cid's blue gaze followed London to the door, where she glanced at Adam, who turned and followed her out. "And sometimes it just can't be helped. It's fate, you know."

Outside, the quiet descended over London. She'd thought that by leaving the noise and the lights she could still the rage, but it wouldn't be contained, and all she could think of was running, as far and as fast as she could, away from Cid's blankness, away from this place and from Adam. He only added to her confusion, making her feel things she didn't comprehend and couldn't control. She walked away from him, her Bass loafers silent against the asphalt parking lot. But Adam wasn't about to let her go.

"Llewellyn?" When she didn't reply, he grabbed her arm, stopping her desperate retreat, forcing her to face him. "What the hell's wrong with you?"

"Gee, I don't know, Adam. What could possibly be wrong with me? I lost my job, I haven't slept in days, my father has moved in and taken over, and I just found my brother's oldest friend splattered all over his kitchen. . . ." She closed her eyes against the blinding pain that knifed through her. "I'm sorry. I seem to be lashing out at everyone."

"Don't apologize," he said quietly, patiently. "It isn't necessary—not between us."

"Us," London laughed, and there was a desperate,

edge-of-hysteria quality to it that they both recognized at the same time. "That's part of the problem. I don't know where to put 'us,' Adam. Are you my friend? My lover? My father's best friend?"

"Why categorize it?" he said simply. "I'm here. It's what matters, isn't it?"

She pulled from his grasp, his coolness and patience suddenly an irritant too strong for her to tolerate. "It matters, okay? I need to make sense of it! I need to make sense of something! Benji and Wyeth . . . nothing makes any damn sense these days!"

He caught her arms and held her still when she had the mad urge to run into the night. He didn't say anything. He just held her until she had exhausted the rage and spent her resistance; then he opened the door to the Mitsubishi and helped her in.

Picking up the car phone, he dialed. "Pat? It's Adam. She's with me. Yeah, she's all right. No worries, ay? I'll take care of everything."

"He's going to ask questions," she said when he hung up. "You know that, don't you?"

"I know. But he's worried about you. He has a right to know you're all right, and I don't want him out looking for you when you're with me."

But she wasn't all right, and they both knew it.

Adam accepted it. He not only understood; he'd been where she was now: desperate, confused, so burned out physically and emotionally that he'd feared he would never find his way back to a semblance of normality.

Llewellyn was strong; all she needed was time. He was convinced that she could survive damn near anything, given a little time to adjust. *She's strong,* he reminded himself again, not totally convinced. She just needed to rest, to catch her breath.

He took her to the one place he knew where they

could be alone. She didn't argue. The starkness, the haunted air of the farm house seemed to suit her mood. The dark living room, the deep shadows that whispered of his own tragedy, the waiting, expectant silence, spoke to her in a voice filled with commiseration and understanding. Nothing she could say would surprise him, and she knew it. "How did you know where to find me?" she said, her voice brittle.

Adam shrugged. "Simple deduction. I figured you'd need to tell your airheaded friend about Pinchot, so I drove by every body shop I could find, then checked the club."

"Sounds like a great deal of effort for so little payoff."

Adam reached out to her, brushing her hair behind one ear. "You're here, and you're all right. Somehow, that's enough. Would you like some coffee?"

A slow shake of her head. "I want everything to be like it was. I want to answer the bell and see Benji's face; I want to laugh at his stupid jokes. I want to walk into the Center and run into Wyeth. . . ." Her voice grew soft and strained. "I want things to be like they were before all of this started. I want to be able to sleep, and I don't want to hurt anymore." Her eyes glistened. She sniffed and groaned, trying to fight the emotional swell that was rising in her, but it was too huge, too overwhelming—months of suppressed grief, rage, disappointment, frustration. "What's wrong with me, Adam? Why can't I just close my eyes, block it all out? Why can't I just sleep?"

Adam had no answers, no solutions. He could only gather her against him and hold her while the tears ran and silent sobs shook her, kissing her damp cheek, her silky hair. "Let it go," he said. "Let it all out."

After a few minutes, the sobs ceased. London wiped her eyes on the clean handkerchief he handed her, and blew her nose. She felt drained and a little desperate, and if it hadn't been for Adam, she might have succumbed to a full-blown emotional meltdown. He was her lifeline, her slim link to sanity, living proof that they could withstand anything. His strength and resiliency were magnetic. More than that, she needed it, needed him, and there was only one way she could communicate that need to him. If she spoke, she would break apart—she was that fragile—so she framed his rugged face with her hands and kissed his cheek, the corner of his hard mouth.

He hadn't shaved, and his beard abraded her skin. London reveled in it. She wanted—*needed*—to feel something, anything but this horrible emptiness.

With a sigh of surrender, he buried his face in the soft fall of hair at the curve of her throat. Then, without a word spoken between them, he lifted her and carried her up the dark stairs.

In the stark shadows of the bedroom, London slipped out of her jeans, slid her sweater over her head, and turned, offering herself to Adam.

Sinking down on the mattress, she sighed as he covered her body with his and covered her face with kisses. There was not an inch of skin left neglected, not an erogenous zone he missed worshiping within a hairsbreadth of ecstasy, and when he came back to her lips, he kissed her until she felt dizzy and weak. "Make love to me, Adam," she whispered against his ear. *Make me feel alive.*

Much later, London lay amid the damp, rumpled sheets, her cheek pillowed on Adam's chest. His arms were around her, and the covers drawn around her shoulders. She felt warm and drowsy, relaxed for the first time in days. As she drifted off, Adam's whisper filled her ear, underscored by the solid, steady drum of his heart. "It'll be all right, sweetheart. Everything'll be all right."

Patrick rang the bell, but the damn thing must have been disconnected, so he let himself in and stooped to let the Weimaraner off the lead. Honz bolted for the stairs while he walked to the kitchen. The house was quiet despite the fact that it was almost eight-thirty in the morning. "Now, where did that goofy-looking mutt get to?" He trudged toward the stairs and started up. As he reached the top landing, Honz pushed against the closed door, which slowly swung open. For a brief interval, Patrick stood, stunned by the sight of his only daughter in bed with the one man he admired above all others. Then he turned and noiselessly went out.

"Meg and Adam. Jesus. No wonder things seemed so strained between them. They only just met—it must have been one hell of an attraction."

He knew that he should have been pissed, but Meg had always been decisive and tough-minded. She knew what she wanted, and she went after it. "And she wanted Adam. Poor bastard," Patrick said with a small and satisfied glint in his eye. "With that Llewellyn charm, he never stood a chance."

They'd have to have a talk, man to man. It was a fatherly thing to do, and who was he to mess with tradition? In the meantime, he'd do what he could to help things along. Meg's car hadn't been parked at Adam's, which meant it was wherever she had left it. The tracking device he'd planted under the dash so he could keep an eye on her whereabouts was still activated, and pinpointed the location. "The least I can do is bring the old heap home," he reasoned aloud. She was strangely protective of that damned car, and knowing that it was home safe and sound would take a load off her mind—give her more time to spend with Adam.

Patrick parked his car in front of the duplex. Topper, Meg's next-door neighbor, was mowing the grass. Patrick moved in for the kill. "Hey, Topper, how's it going?"

"It's not," Topper replied, settling his do-rag more firmly on his balding head. "Wife's got me mowing the grass. Jeez, I hate yard work. Was there somethin' I can do for you?"

He looked hopeful. Easy prey. "Yeah, actually. I could use a lift over to a place called Inkspot. Do you know it?"

Topper grinned. "Know it? I had it staked out the other night. Let me grab my keys. This yard'll just have to wait."

When Patrick arrived, London's car was parked in the parking lot. Cid's Humvee was across the lot. The blonde was about to slide under the wheel, but when she saw him, she hesitated. It seemed that she might come over to ask what he was doing there instead of Meg . . . then she seemed to reconsider. She got in the Humvee, started the engine, and drove from the lot.

"Thanks, Topper. I can handle it from here."

"You sure?" He pulled on his diamond stud earring. "'Cause I'd be glad to hang around."

"I'm sure. I got it covered." Patrick waved him off, opened the door to the Porsche, and triggered the mechanism. There was a flash of red fire, a deafening roar, and everything went black.

At 10:23, Adam's cell phone rang. He picked it up, hoping Llewellyn would sleep through it. She'd had a rough couple of days, and she needed as much rest as she could get. "De Wulf."

"Adam?"

Adam put down his coffee cup, the hair on his nape standing straight. "Julia?"

"You recognize my voice. I thought, perhaps—it's been so long."

"Where are you? How are you?"

"Does it really matter?" she wondered. "I mean, it's not like you give a damn. I know you have someone else . . ." Her voice dropped, sad-sounding, perhaps a little unsteady. "She's very pretty. Congratulations. Does she want children?"

Adam's pulse hammered in his ears. He saw the wildness in her dark eyes, the glint of the carving knife before it sank deep into his flesh. "You were here in the house; you left the doll."

"You don't like to be reminded, do you, Adam? You'd love to forget all about me, about Michael. A dead baby is more convenient than a live one. That way you don't have to explain that he belonged to someone else."

"I never wanted that," Adam ground out. "I wouldn't have hurt an innocent child, and you know it."

"You should have died on that rooftop," she said. "If you hadn't come home, they'd still be here."

"They? What does that mean, Julia? Michael *and* his father? What the hell have you done?"

The receiver clicked, and the line went dead. Adam put the phone down, bracing his fists on the table, hanging his head as he tried to contain the wave of fury rippling through him. "She's not in D.C.; she's here," he said, sensing that he was no longer alone. "She was here in this house the night the tap was left on in the workroom."

"She left the doll," London said softly. "She blames you, doesn't she? For the baby? That's what it means."

"She blames me for the wreck our marriage became, for Michael . . . for everything. If not for me, she and her lover could have started fresh. It would have been so much more convenient if I had died in the fall in Tel Aviv, but I survived, and I came home—a broken man with a career that was beginning the long slide, a bum leg, and a wife who was careless enough to get pregnant by another man."

London frowned. "Tel Aviv. Wyeth mentioned it."

"I'm sure he did. Pinchot was the reason I was there. The Ghost had started his activities a year or two before. At first it was small stuff. So small that no one took notice, but it didn't take long for it to escalate."

London knew what he was saying. Most double agents started out small, each success another ego stroke, another reason for them to believe that they couldn't be caught, another reason for the activity to escalate.

"I asked to be assigned to the case, and Pinchot granted my request. He'd just taken over as my handler, and our approach was vastly different. He was fresh from Administration; everything with him was by the book. I'd always figured that the end outweighed the means. Getting the job done was all that mattered. Not that I was making great inroads into solving the mystery of who was selling us out. I'd come close a few times, but the bastard always seemed to have one over on me. It was like he knew what I was going to do before I did it, like he had access to the information I fed to my case officer."

"Your case officer," London said. "You don't think— Wyeth? The Ghost? You're joking!" She laughed, but he didn't join in, and his expression said it all.

"It was the perfect setup," he insisted. "The very man I was hunting down overseeing my every move? I started to put it all together in Tel Aviv, about a week before the accident. Just by chance I stumbled upon a man named Aziz, a former official in the Israeli government who'd purchased documents directly from the Ghost. My last meeting with Aziz was supposed to take place on the roof of the hotel where I was staying. When I got there, he was on the ledge. I made a grab for him as he stepped off—lost my balance and went down with him. I spent a month in an Israeli hospital. As soon as I was able to walk again, they flew me back to the States, back to a marriage that was falling apart, to a wife who was in love with another man. Maybe if I had ended it there, the baby would have lived. . . ."

"What happened, Adam?"

"I'm what happened. I went back to pursuing the Ghost with everything I had, and I got close—too close. Julia was in the third trimester of her pregnancy when she disappeared. She was missing for three days, and when I found her, it was too late. She was out of her mind with the drugs he'd given her, not even aware that she'd delivered the child in a filthy abandoned warehouse. I named him Michael Alexander De Wulf. Such a big name for a tiny little fella. He lived for thirty-five hours, and died before Julia got to see him."

"I'm sorry, but she shouldn't blame you for it. You didn't give her the drugs that caused her to miscarry so late in the pregnancy."

"No," he agreed. "But I cornered him. He used her as a hostage, a way—the only way—to convince me to back off. Julia was always fragile. The drug was something new—a strong hallucinogen. It pushed her past fragility and over the edge into a full-blown psychosis.

She isn't just angry; she's a danger—to herself, to anyone who's fool enough to get close to me."

"Close to you . . . like I am?"

He looked at her, and the truth was there on his face. "Julia has lost everything, and she holds me responsible for it. She'll want retribution, and there's only one way for her to do it: through you."

"You're overreacting," London said with a shake of her head. "We're involved, but it's not like—"

"Not like I'm falling for you, or anything?"

"Adam."

He shrugged. "Don't look like that, Llewellyn. After all, it's my problem, and I won't let it complicate your life."

London tried to ignore his admission. She wasn't sure what that meant or where it might lead, and she didn't want to ask. Better to forget it for now and deal with it at some future time, should it ever arise again. It could have been an impulsive thing. Yeah, that was it. He was worried about her, and thought he'd just throw it out there for emphasis. Now, if she could just get her pulse to stop racing. "I still think you're giving her way too much credit. A doll with its eyes put out may be creepy, but it isn't exactly lethal."

"It was just the beginning." He reached for his phone. "We can't take any chances. We'll alert Patrick and get him out here. I'll set Honz out to patrol while I try to figure out how to find her."

At the mention of his name, Honz jumped off the couch and trotted to Adam, his leash in his mouth.

"I thought you said you left him with Patrick," London said.

"I did."

"Then how'd he get here?" She squeezed her eyes shut. "Oh, Christ, no." The pocket of her sweater gave a half-drowned bleat. She fished out the cellular phone and answered. "Llewellyn."

"London?"

"Topper?"

"Yeah. It's me. I'm at the hospital. Jeez, honey, I just don't know how else to put this: I have some really bad news. It's about your dad . . ."

Chapter Sixteen

The intensive care unit at St. Aloysius was blindingly bright. Too damn bright, London thought. Jesus. What were they thinking with all the lights? How was anyone supposed to rest and recover lying under three hundred glaring, unnatural watts?

The weirdest thoughts ran through her head as she followed the nurse through the double doors and down a short corridor. They hung a left at the nurses' station. Someone had brought in a box of doughnuts, and they were lying on the counter with the lid open while a gnat flew in a holding pattern a foot above the open box.

Someone really should close the lid. I know he won't eat much, but how sanitary is that? Or maybe it was a she. Did gnats have a sex, or were they androgynous? Of course they did. How else did they make more little gnats? And how did it get in here in the first place? Why didn't someone notice? And why wasn't there anyone keeping an eye on the monitors? Maybe it was some sort of game. Maybe the nurses tried to be as far away as they could manage; then, if a monitor signaled someone crashing, they all raced back like rats in a maze running toward the cheese in the center.

They were dumb thoughts, and not terribly complimentary to the attractive middle-aged blonde who led her calmly to Patrick's room. At the door, she turned, offering London a reassuring smile. "Ten minutes every hour. He needs his rest."

It was ten past three in the morning, and Patrick had just come back from Recovery. The anesthesia had worn off, but he was groggy and in and out of consciousness. London pulled the aluminum chair next to the bed and sat down. The right side of his face, neck, and upper torso had sustained the worst of the injuries. Four hours of surgery to remove the shrapnel and reattach the fingers of his right hand. It would be a few days, the surgeon had assured her, before they could be sure the operation had been successful. There was still a chance that he would lose a portion of his hand.

After a few minutes of just sitting quietly, listening to the beep, beep, beep of the cardiac monitor, she noticed his breathing change, and he turned his head, his uncovered eye slitting open. "Oh. Meg, it's you. What are you doin' here? Where's Adam?"

"That's all you can say is 'Where's Adam?' " she asked softly. She carefully avoided pointing out his precarious situation, or that Adam wasn't family and that visitors to ICU were restricted. It wasn't that Patrick didn't know that already or couldn't take it; it was self-preservation. He was her father, her one link left to the past, and she was terrified of losing him.

"Gotta keep tabs on him. That's potential son-in-law material. Gotta make sure you don't do somethin' stupid, like tryin' to dump him because you're too damn proud to let him know you care."

London snorted. She couldn't let herself think in that vein. It wasn't realistic, even after what Adam had said at the farmhouse. He said he was in love with her, and it frightened her. That kind of fear was counterproductive, especially when there were more important things to think about—like who'd killed Wyeth, and who wanted her dead. First the sniper, and then Patrick. There was no doubt in her mind that the device in the Porsche had been meant for her. Somehow, she managed to keep her concern from infecting her voice. Her tone was quietly dismissive. "De Wulf and me? You've got to be kidding! Those must be some heavy-duty drugs they're giving you."

"Stranger things have happened. He's a good man, Meg. You remember that."

"How can I forget it? You're constantly reminding me."

"Always a joke with you. Be serious for once in your life."

"C'mon, Dad, really. You don't have to worry about Adam. He's the original tough guy. He can take care of himself."

"You're pretty tough, too, as I recall. First in your class. First place on the firing range—always something to prove. Always a competition—with Ben, maybe even with your old man. It's that damn name. London. What the hell kind of name is that for a good Irish Catholic girl? Shameful, and your mother did it just to spite me." He rolled his head on his pillow and indicated the nightstand. "I miss her, Meg." He sighed. "Can't a man get a drink around here?"

London rang the nurse, who brought some ice chips. "Ice chips," Patrick bitched. "What the hell is that?"

"*That*, Mr. Llewellyn, is all you're allowed until the anesthesia wears off completely and we evaluate how you are doing. Doctor's orders. Now, you behave yourself."

He grumbled, but London could see he was grateful for the little moisture he was allowed. "Dad? Do you remember what happened?"

"Sure I remember. I might be retired, but I haven't lost my edge yet. I dropped Honz at the farm," he said with a wink, "and then I decided to pick up the Porsche.

My good deed for the day, sort of, to keep you from having to do it. I know how preoccupied you've been lately—because of this thing with Ben, I mean. Topper gave me a ride to the club. Swell guy, that Topper—damn good neighbor."

"But I had the only set of keys," London reminded him.

"Since when have keys been necessary? I'm a resourceful guy."

A resourceful guy who'd planned to hot-wire her car, and she didn't want to dwell on his motives, or the fact that he admitted being at the farm. The thought made her squirm. But the one thing he hadn't planned on, and couldn't possibly know, was that the Porsche had been rigged with plastique, so that when the door was opened, the explosive was detonated. There was no doubt that the explosion had been meant for her, and Topper had made it chillingly clear that had it been she who had opened the door of the Porsche instead of a much larger Patrick, she probably wouldn't have survived the brunt of the blast. As it was, Patrick had been knocked back by the force of the explosion—the contributing factor, along with a good deal of luck, in saving his life.

"Do you remember anything else?"

He was getting tired. She could see it. His lids were heavy, and his voice a little slurred. "Yeah. One thing. I saw that friend of yours, the butch blonde. It looked like she'd come over; then she must have changed her mind. Left in a kind of a hurry."

"Cid was at Inkspot? That's weird. The club doesn't open until six."

Listen . . . how about givin' your old man a kiss? I'm gonna sleep now."

The request was one she hadn't heard since she was a knock-kneed kid, and it brought tears to London's eyes.

She bent down and kissed his cheek. "I love you, Dad, even when we make each other crazy."

"Of course you do," he said. "We're blood. In this clan, that means something. Llewellyns stick together, through thick and through thin. You remember that . . . and you tell De Wulf I need to see him, will you? We need to have a talk, man to man. It's important."

"I'll do that." For a few minutes she sat there on that comfortless metal chair, watching him sleep and being thankful that he was alive. Then, quietly, she got up and went out.

Like a glass house in an earthquake, it was all falling apart. It didn't seem to matter how meticulously she planned it, something always went terribly wrong. The marriage to Adam, the affair with Wyeth, Michael . . . It had all gone so wrong! *How had it gone so wrong*?

She paced the breadth of the room, not pausing even for the space of a hurried breath before turning again, as panic threaded through her veins, wrapping itself around her vital organs. Wyeth . . . She'd call Wyeth. Wyeth would know what to do. Wyeth would help her, calm her.

She ran to the phone and dialed. It rang three times, and then she remembered. Wyeth was gone. He couldn't help her anymore. He couldn't love her.

Her panic was suffocating now, crowding her lungs, squeezing her heart until she feared it would explode just as his had. She slid to the floor and sat hugging her knees. There had to be a way to fix it, she thought wildly. There was always a way out. Wyeth had shown her that. She just had to stay calm and think.

A weak cry penetrated her chaotic jumble of thoughts. Barely heard, the thin, pathetic wail still had the power to get her full attention. In one jerky motion, she unlocked her arms from around her knees and came to her feet, opening the cabinet door, selecting a doll from the collection she kept there, each one missing an eye, a head, a limb. "Michael," she said, crooning down at the small, pale face. "I'm here. Mother's here."

For a moment, she could see him calm, his tiny rosebud mouth curving in a sweet baby smile. . . . Then, gradually, the vision cleared, replaced by the deep gaping hole in the center of his forehead as she threw it across the room and slowly backed away, but the ghostly echo of a long-dead child persisted, and nothing could block it out.

"You know, Ms. Llewellyn . . . I'm beginning to think being anywhere near you isn't healthy. First, the man in the park gets his head blown off, then your good friend Mr. Pinchot has the misfortune to get himself fatally wounded, and now this car bomb thing with your father. Oh, and let's not forget that someone took a couple of shots at you night before last—an incident that you conveniently neglected to tell me about. Tell me again why you decided to withhold information in an ongoing investigation. I'm assuming that you had a very good reason, because as you know, that's a serious breach of law enforcement etiquette, not to mention it making you appear like an uncooperative witness. Normally, when a witness won't cooperate, it indicates that they are somehow involved. I would hate to think that of you, so feel free to disabuse me of that notion."

Viagra had insisted on dragging her down to police headquarters, a two-story brownstone with stylish tinted windows and a modest sign out front. It was a nice enough place as far as police stations went, but not the sort of place where London wanted to spend the morning. "I'm not directly involved in any of this," she insisted. "I wasn't anywhere near when my car imploded, or when Wyeth was killed, and as for De Wulf's windows being shot out, we have no proof that it was anything more than some neighborhood punk out to have a little thrill at his expense."

"Uh-huh. Well, the explosive planted under the hood of that Porsche wasn't planted by some punk. We're not talkin' gasoline in a soda bottle here. It was sophisticated—like maybe something the CIA might use."

"What is that supposed to mean?" London shot back, then calmed at Topper's discreet cough.

The detective hitched up his Dockers and sat on the corner of his desk. It was a warm day, and the fan circulating overhead stirred the hair he'd combed over his bald spot. "Why don't you tell me?"

"I thought getting the answers was your job, Detective."

"You've got an answer for everything, don't you, Ms. Llewellyn?" He got up suddenly, shoving a hand in his pocket to jingle his change. "Two bodies in less than a week, and a victim of an explosion, and they all have one common thread: you. I'm not so sure I like that."

"Yeah? Well, I have a few questions of my own. Wyeth Pinchot was murdered two nights ago in his own home. What the hell are you doing about that, besides harassing me?"

He shot a frown at Topper, who had offered to stay. Since Adam had left the hospital after getting the news that Patrick was expected to survive his injuries, and she hadn't heard from him since, London had taken him up on it. Topper possessed what, at the moment, she lacked: a level head. She was feeling dangerous and reckless, and she wanted answers, which she wasn't getting sitting here in Viagra's office. "Is she always like this?"

Topper had abandoned his yard gear for an Orioles ball cap, jeans, and a T-shirt. Except for the shoulder holster and service revolver, he didn't look much like a cop. "Beg pardon, sir, I think she may be a little stressed out. Her dad's in ICU, and her friend Mr. Pinchot is deceased. It'd be quite a lot for anyone to digest."

"Thanks," London said, "but I've got everything under control—at least for the moment. Detective? Are we through here? I have some things to take care of."

"Go on, get out of here! But, I'm warnin' you: no more bodies, Ms. Llewellyn," Viagra said with a shake of one pudgy finger. "I don't want to see you back here in connection with another case."

Topper caught her as she was leaving the building. "Hey! London!" He trotted over as she turned. "Listen . . . I feel real bad about your dad. Are you sure there's nothing I can do?"

His concern was so genuine, she couldn't help a small, fleeting smile. "Thanks for the offer, but I think we have everything we need."

"You'll call if you change your mind?"

"I'll call. I promise."

London went home long enough to pick up her mail and check the answering machine. There was nothing suspicious or leading, no messages, no cryptic letters indicating who had planted the plastique or why. . . . There was also no message from Adam. She fed the cat, called the insurance company, and made a phone call to check on Patrick. The nurse said he was sleeping. London hung up the phone but didn't let go of the receiver.

Where was Adam?

Was he trying to track down the elusive Julia? What would happen if he found her? He'd said he loved London, but his ties to the disturbed woman were strong, and she could only wonder if they were strong enough to pull him back in. She closed her eyes. She could still lose him to a poison relationship and a woman he didn't love. Sometimes obligation was far stronger than emotion. Her parents were a fine example of that. Ella had come back to Patrick in the end. It hadn't mattered that the marriage had ended years before.

It could happen with Adam and Julia, and it wouldn't matter that she loved him. There it was: the thing she'd been fighting for weeks. How they felt about each other really didn't matter. In the end, he could get dragged back in, and he would take her heart with him. She had a moment of sadness so profound that it wrung her spirit, leaving her with the deep need just to hear his voice. Fate wasn't about to cut them a break, and there was no way out for either of them.

She picked up the phone and started to dial; then, before it could ring, she hung up again. "God, London. Are you really that desperate? You should be glad he's not hanging around, complicating everything . . ." A sick laugh, a shake of her head. "Like life isn't already complicated enough."

Benji's PDA was lying on the dining room table. "Oh, God, Benj. What happened? What went wrong?" If only he were here, he would know exactly what to say, what to do. Impulsively she turned on the device—a pathetically small attempt to be near some part of him, to share the closeness of rival siblings. The date book and its notations came up on screen.

Benji's final notations.

Call Wyeth. Geneva Clinic. JDW.

Julia De Wulf. What did Benji know about Julia, and what did it have to do with the Geneva Clinic?

She picked up the phone again, and this time dialed the clinic. "Herr Doktor Fritz," she said.

"May I say who is calling, please?"

She didn't hesitate. "Julia De Wulf."

"One moment." The receptionist rang her through.

A man answered, his voice deep and heavily accented. "Julia? How may I help you?"

"Dr. Fritz."

His voice changed. "Who is this?"

"Dr. Fritz, don't hang up. My name is Llewellyn, and I work for the Central Intelligence Agency."

"I have nothing to say to you."

"I think you do," London said quickly. She was thinking on her feet now. Just keep him talking. "Is Julia De Wulf a patient of yours?"

"I do not discuss my patients—with anyone."

"Then Ms. De Wulf *was* a patient at Geneva Clinic? You can either speak with me or with my superior, Mr. Pinchot."

"Do you take me for a fool? What reason would there be for me to answer Mr. Pinchot's questions? He already has all the information pertaining to Mrs. De Wulf, and this conversation is ended."

The phone clicked, and the dial tone buzzed in her ear. Dr. Fritz had cut her off, but his words wouldn't leave her. *"Do you take me for a fool? What reason would there be for me to answer Mr. Pinchot's questions? He already has all the information pertaining to Mrs. De Wulf . . ."*

He was mistaken. How could Wyeth possibly have known about Julia being a patient at the Geneva Clinic?

She tried to shrug it off but couldn't let it go. Somewhere deep in her psyche, the pieces were falling into place. It was starting to make a dreadful kind of sense. Benji had made the notation, a reminder to call Wyeth about Geneva Clinic, in connection with JDW, Julia De Wulf. Yet, when she had questioned Wyeth about the call, he'd denied it. In fact, he'd claimed that he never heard from Benj, and he had seemed a little uneasy about the question, as if anxious to dismiss it, to put it behind him. The question was, why?

Why would Wyeth lie about Benji calling him?

Their friendship had been exceptionally close, and he'd been fully aware that she'd been struggling to put all the pieces together. What motive could he possibly have had for keeping that scrap of information from her . . . unless he was somehow involved . . . ?

"Involved in what?" she said aloud. "Benji's murder? You're reaching with that one." She bit a thumbnail. No, not Benji. Julia. This didn't have anything to do with Benji. It was about Julia De Wulf.

This time when she picked up the phone, she didn't hesitate. She dialed Adam's cellular phone. There was no answer.

He claimed Julia was here, watching, waiting, and she had doubted him, half-convinced that his claims could be the result of his suspicious nature. Then there were Wyeth's admissions that Adam wasn't to be trusted, his warnings that she shouldn't get involved with him, that he was dangerous. He'd even gone so far as to let her know that Adam had been suspected of fabricating the Ghost's activities in order to pad his own reputation.

She'd chalked it up to some sort of weird male intra-Agency rivalry. But what if Wyeth's warnings had stemmed from a different motive altogether? What if there was something more behind it? Much more?

It had been clear from the first that the two men disliked and mistrusted each other, but could Wyeth have been wary of Adam's presence in Virginia—and particularly in her life—because of some information he had had about Adam's ex-wife? She could think of only one way to find out. Grabbing Patrick's keys off the table, she headed to Wyeth's. If there was any evidence of Wyeth's connection to Julia De Wulf, she would find it at Wyeth's apartment.

"Two days in the slammer and that suit'll never be the same. It's wilted, my friend, and it doesn't smell so fresh, either. You should look for a good dry cleaner."

"I can't afford a dry cleaner, Sal. It took every dime I had to bribe that skunk of an attorney into seeking bail. What the hell kind of an attorney refuses to arrange bail?"

"The kind that got wind of your somewhat lengthy rap sheet, perhaps?" Sal suggested. "Besides, I think those intelligence guys were bent on riding you right to the pen for destroying government property. Of course, your sworn and solemn oath to show at the hearing went a long way toward redeeming your character in the eyes of the law."

Freddie's eyes narrowed, shifting from the deep wrinkles in his tan silk suit to Sal, who spread his hands in a subdued Italian shrug. "What?"

"I'm not looking to reform, you ass-wipe! I'm looking to get that fuckin' flower and keep my ass out of a sling. Do you have any idea how pissed Joey is at us right now? Bitsy filed, Sal. She's divorcing him because of that damned Australian gigolo."

"De Wulf and Bitsy?" Sal said. "I can see it. Yeah, I sensed that about him. Joey must be devastated."

Freddie squeezed his eyes shut and imagined killing Sal. A slow manual strangulation definitely had its merits, but at the moment it was running a close second to ripping his tongue out and beating him senseless with it. "Shut up, Sal. Will you just shut up?"

Sal looked a little hurt. Huffing along beside Freddie, he seemed on the verge of breaking the silence, then seemed to think better of it. Finally, when they reached a bus stop, Sal raised his hand. "What the hell is this? Kindergarten?"

"There's no need to be so cutting. My question is very pertinent to our undertaking."

Freddie waited, but Sal went no further. *"Well?"*

"Well, I was just wondering if you had a plan to find De Wulf."

"I got a plan, all right. I made an even trade and got the information we need to find De Wulf."

"I thought you said you were broke."

Freddie tapped his left wrist where his watch had been. "One of the guards had a guy run the plates on the red-haired little bitch's Porsche. He says her name's Llewellyn. London Llewellyn, and I got her address. We'll just take the bus over there to 1371 Rialto Street and surprise her. If we find her, we'll find De Wulf."

Adam had stayed at the hospital until Patrick was moved from the recovery room into ICU. He'd been a little torn about Llewellyn. A part of him had longed to hang around, just in case she needed a strong shoulder—someone to lean on, or to catch her should she fall. She didn't fall, though, just bit the bullet as she always did, relying on a deep reserve of inner strength to get her safely through a difficult time. She didn't touch his hand, give him a kiss, or even glance back as she followed the nurse through the double doors and into the intensive care unit.

Adam, standing with his hands shoved into his pockets, got the message. His services were no longer required.

There was the slight stab of disappointment to be endured at that. She might have thrown him a bone of some sort, the assurance that he would see her later so they could pick up where they left off that morning. But that might have given him the misguided notion that she actually needed him on some level, and Llewellyn was very much the feminist, women's-rights, don't-need-a-man type, and all that. The only thing left to him was to take himself on home and do the manly thing—sulk, while he tried to put together the pieces of the damned puzzle he was living in.

He checked in with Bruno first thing to see if there was any word of Julia's whereabouts, and Bruno came back to say that his ex-wife still hadn't surfaced. *I did develop the film you gave me,* Bruno's message read. *Interesting stuff.*

A moment later, Adam's e-mail indicated that he had mail. He opened the attachment and scanned the photos. Scenic shots of Vienna and of Ben himself, leaning against a lamppost on a deserted Austrian street. Ben looked happy, an adventurous young man who was clearly in his element. He saved the file for Llewellyn. He'd get the originals from Bruno later. Then he cut to the second file, sinking back in his chair as a familiar pair of faces came up on-screen; Wyeth Pinchot and the scattered blonde Llewellyn sometimes hung out with, Cid.

The photos were taken in a rural setting that might

have been right here in Virginia or halfway around the world. They were deep in conversation, the blonde stoic and Pinchot's expression intense, and he could only wonder why the pair were meeting in secret. The likelihood of its being Agency business was slim. Pinchot had been well established and would have had little use for a secretary outside the Agency walls . . . unless . . . unless their meeting had nothing to do with the Agency.

Adam scrolled through the file, shot by shot. Thirty-six photos of two Agency employees who were completely unaware they were being caught on film—photos taken from a distance with a telephoto lens by Ben Llewellyn, Wyeth Pinchot's best friend. The last shot showed the pair embracing. In fact, the blonde was clinging to him, the hand on the back of Pinchot's neck clearly visible. Adam transferred the file to a photo program and zoomed in on the last frame. The blonde's nails were bitten to the quick, just as Julia's had always been. She'd even tried hypnotism to stop the compulsive biting, but she'd never managed to break the habit.

Adam felt sick.

Bruno? I need a favor, and I need it fast. The blonde in the photos. Her name is Blankenship, Cidney, with a "C." Run a check on her and see what you come up with.

Adam called Llewellyn at the house, but there was no answer. Then he dialed the hospital and asked for ICU. Patrick's condition was stable, and his daughter had gone home.

The messaging window popped up. *Adam?*

What do you have for me?

Just curious. Is this chick in preschool? If she isn't, she should be. As far as I can tell, she didn't exist be-

fore twenty-nine months ago. Do you want me to keep looking?

That won't be necessary, and you can drop the search for Julia. I've found her.

Chapter Seventeen

The police tape still circled the outer perimeter of the house. London ducked under it. Wyeth kept a spare key in the mailbox, in a small magnetized box that adhered to the side of the box. Not terribly secure, but easy to access. The street was quiet—not a great deal of activity or traffic. She wasn't supposed to trespass upon a crime scene, but she doubted Detective Viagra would have granted her permission to go in and look around had she asked. He wasn't exactly thrilled with her at the moment. One glance at the street, and she retrieved the key and went inside.

It was odd how a house changed the moment it became unoccupied. It was almost as if the sticks, bricks, and mortar had some knowledge of what had occurred here: that Wyeth had gone away and wasn't coming back. The quiet was more than a home awaiting its owner's arrival; it was hopeless and melancholy.

With no family to mourn his passing other than London and Patrick, Wyeth had left specific instructions there was to be no wake, no memorial service. Following the autopsy, his remains would be cremated and scattered on the grounds at Langley, once the sight of Langley plantation, Robert E. Lee's ancestral home.

It saddened London that Wyeth had stipulated that he did not want his life commemorated. With no living family, he deserved to be remembered and grieved by the people who knew him best and cared about him: his friends and colleagues at Langley. He'd been a fine man, a fine officer, and she still couldn't fathom what had gone so hideously wrong. Maybe the clues were here, in this house . . . or maybe she would never understand the role Wyeth had played in Julia De Wulf's disappearance. She knew only that she couldn't let it go until she was satisfied that she had exhausted every lead, until she discovered what it was that led Benji to make the notation on his PDA.

Call Wyeth. Geneva Clinic. JDW.

Julia De Wulf had been a patient at Geneva Clinic—that much London knew—and there had been a mutual dislike between Wyeth and Adam. But it didn't explain the clinic. Why had Julia De Wulf gone to a clinic in Switzerland that specialized in cosmetic surgery and facial reconstruction? Dr. Fritz had referred to her as a patient, but that revealed little. What procedure had she had performed, and why?

London began her search in the living room, a room so sparse in its furnishings that it barely seemed lived in. She conducted a thorough search, peering in drawers, taking books off the bookcase and rifling the pages, even using a small flashlight to look under the sofa. The TV was a big-screen type, and he had the latest entertainment equipment. London flicked the remote's power button, and Mr. Spock came on, complete with Cleopatra bangs and ears nine inches tall. "What is it with men?" she said aloud. "Why do they always seem to think bigger is better?"

The room was clean. She turned off the television and moved on. The bedroom always seemed to reveal the most about a person. It represented the comfort zone, a private sanctuary, a place to relax that outsiders rarely intruded upon . . . a place where secrets were shared, revealed, kept. Wyeth's bedroom was masculine, tastefully decorated, and understated. Bisque-colored walls and plush carpeting a few shades darker created a striking contrast with the ebony wardrobe, bed, and dresser. The closet was spacious and well organized: Wyeth's collection of suits, shirts, and casual wear hanging neatly above a shoe rack with a half-dozen pairs of highly polished shoes. Storage containers lined the top shelf, but they held sweaters and cold-weather gear along with a few miscellaneous mementos from childhood that he couldn't bring himself to discard.

London looked in every conceivable space, but there was no damning evidence, no explanation, nothing to indicate how he knew Julia De Wulf or what his connection to her might be. . . . Just a photograph, on a table near the bed, of a startling dark beauty in a vibrant red dress. London picked it up. The woman was clutching the arm of a tall, dark-haired man in a tuxedo and smiling coyly over one shoulder at the camera.

London ran a finger in a soft caress over the image of the woman's companion. Even with his back turned to the camera, Adam cut a handsome figure. But it was the woman who caught and held London's interest.

So this was Julia.

She was breathtaking, and it was easy to see why both men had fallen in love with her—first Adam, then Wyeth. It was the only reason London could think of for Wyeth to have the photo of another man's wife by his bed. He'd been in love with Julia De Wulf, yet that still didn't explain what had become of the vibrant brunette, and the photo wasn't about to provide the answers. She carefully replaced the photo on the table by the bed, and as she stepped back, a scrap of bright pink caught her eye, peeking out from beneath the edge of black cotton comforter.

Reaching down, London picked it up, a terry sweat-band with the word *Nilo* emblazoned on it. Nilo fitness equipment, the same brand of equipment Beef Cookie bought for her gym. Cid had been wearing a sweatband just like it that day at the gym.

"It's strange, how overlooking one small detail can ruin everything."

London turned toward the woman's voice—more cultured, less nasal than Cid's, but shot through with a hollowness London recognized. "I didn't realize until a little while ago that I had left it here."

"How did you get in?" London, firmly caught in the surreal moment, was unsure how to react. Cid was a friend, wasn't she? A confidante. London had confided in her, telling her things she hadn't been comfortable sharing with anyone. Cid had proved to be a wealth of information over the past few months. She'd even helped her find Adam.

Cid held up a key, a smile heavily tinged with sadness lingering on her lips. "I knew the password."

"You and Wyeth?"

"You sound surprised, but that's okay. There's a lot you don't know. Wyeth and I have a history. You might even say we were soul mates." Her eyes glistened with unshed tears—brown eyes, London noted, not blue. Eyes that were strikingly similar to the woman's in the photograph. She seemed to recognize the instant when the last piece fell into place for London, because she smiled. "That's right. I've been right here all along, and no one caught on. My own ex-husband didn't recognize me. Dr. Fritz isn't just a cosmetic surgeon; he's an artist. It's the reason I sought him out."

London shook her head. "I don't get it. If you and

Wyeth were in love, why not just start over? Your marriage to Adam was finished. Nothing stood in your way."

"That's where you're wrong," Julia said, looking so much like Cid, sounding like a stranger. "We couldn't just start over. Adam wasn't about to let it go. He was obsessed."

"Adam's obsession," London said. "You mean the Ghost. What did that have to do with anything?"

"He would have ruined Wyeth, but not because of the espionage—because I loved him. I never loved Adam the way I loved Wyeth. Do you know what that's like, Lon? To love someone so much that you would sacrifice anything to keep him safe?"

"Yeah, I guess I do." She loved Adam, despite the obstacles standing in the way of their relationship, and she couldn't help wondering if she would have the chance to tell him. Cid—she stopped herself, amending—*Julia* was as unpredictable as she was unstable.

"If I had known you'd fall for him, I wouldn't have been quite so willing to help you find him. But who knew? I was a little surprised that he'd stepped over the ethical line, even though it's in perfect keeping with his character. He never cared about the methods he used, as long as he got what he wanted. I learned a lot from him. No one stands in my way." She sighed. "Did he ever get his hands on the Lady of the Night? No, I guess not. Pity, she was my crowning achievement. But that was a lifetime ago."

London frowned. "You said you would have sacrificed anything to save Wyeth. What did you mean by that? Wyeth has always landed on his feet. His career was on the fast track from the beginning."

"That wasn't enough for him. He needed a challenge. That was how it began. The information was always at his fingertips—easy access; buyers were everywhere. The real challenge was in getting away with it."

"Getting away with it?" London laughed, but the sound was hard and flat and infected with disbelief. "Adam suspected Wyeth. He told me as much, and I didn't believe him. Oh, God . . ." she said as the final piece of the puzzle fell neatly into place. "Benji found out, didn't he? About you—about Wyeth? That's why he mentioned Geneva Clinic."

"Ben wouldn't have had to die in that hotel room if he'd just stayed out of it. But he found out Wyeth and Cid were involved, and he started looking into Cid's background. It was the one thing we overlooked . . . Cid's history. It began where Julia's ended. Wyeth always meant to complete it, but he got me into Langley so easily that I guess he figured it didn't matter."

"Wyeth killed Benji because Benj had figured it out—the Ghost . . . you . . ."

"Not Wyeth. He loved Benji. He loved your family. He would have gone to prison before he would have harmed a Llewellyn."

"Not Wyeth . . . you." Suddenly, it all made sense. The masked assailant in Benji's hotel room and the assassin who murdered Johnson were the same person, not a man but a muscular woman. "So you made the sacrifice. That's what you meant a moment ago. You said you'd do anything for Wyeth, and that included murder. You killed my brother, and you killed Johnson."

Julia's brown eyes were deep wells of misery. "Your brother sealed his own fate by insisting that Wyeth turn himself over to the authorities. He said it was the right thing to do, the only thing. So sanctimonious—just like Adam. The Agency meant more to him than his best friend's life. I couldn't let that happen, so I kept him from spilling our secret. Only afterward did I realize that it couldn't stop there. The Ghost provided the perfect cover. Johnson's death made Ben's seem logical, like it was part of something bigger."

"And Wyeth blackened Benji's reputation in order to protect you."

"He loved me. We made a child together." As she said it, she turned her head slightly, as if she were listening intently for something London couldn't hear. "Did you hear that?"

"Hear what?" The house was as quiet as a tomb.

"A baby crying. I thought I heard a . . ." For a moment, the facade of control slipped, and London got a glimpse of Adam's nightmare. This was why he'd been so desperate to find her. He'd known how dangerous she could be, how totally unpredictable, and so had Wyeth.

"What happened to Wyeth?" London asked, struggling to keep her voice level and calm.

"You did, Lon. Kind of ironic, don't you think? You got in the way, just like your brother. You started digging around, and then you got Adam involved in it, too. When you found out about the clinic, I knew it was just a matter of time. I had to do something. When he found out, Wyeth was angry. I was here when he came back from your place, and he said it was over, that he wouldn't allow me to hurt you or your fucking family any more than I already had. He said he was going to tell them everything."

"So you killed him . . . and then you made a second crack at me by planting plastique in my car—only you got Patrick instead."

"I had no choice," she insisted. "No choice. Just like now." She brought the weapon up, concealed until now at her side—a deeply blued pistol and silencer. "You first," she said with a short jerk of the barrel. "We'll take the Hummer. I don't like your father's car. It smells of cigars. Doesn't he know how bad they are for him?"

No one was home at Llewellyn's duplex. The house was quiet, the cat taking a snooze on the back of the sofa. Patrick's car was conspicuously absent from its usual spot. Adam made a quick circuit of the second-floor bedrooms, already certain what he would find, then just as quickly went back down the stairs.

Where the hell was she? Had she gone back to the hospital? Or had she gone in search of Julia?

The second possibility triggered an instantaneous sensation of dread in the pit of his stomach. With Pinchot gone, Julia would be especially close to the edge, maybe just desperate enough to want to hurt someone, to inflict the same pain that she was feeling, and who was left in her life but London?

He'd written down the address Bruno had sent, the address to an apartment on the north side of town that belonged to Cid Blankenship. It was in the warehouse district, and he couldn't get there fast enough.

As the Spyder sped away from the house on Rialto, a bus pulled up at the corner, and two men got off. "Hey," Sal said, pointing to the speeding black sports car. "Doesn't that guy look familiar? And he's got a dog just like De Wulf!"

"Idiot!" Freddie snapped. "That *is* De Wulf!" Freddie glanced around wildly, his eyes lighting up when he saw an older gentleman approaching on a moped. Sal groaned as Freddie ran after the cyclist. "Police!" Freddie screamed. "I'm confiscating your vehicle!"

The older man put up a noisy protest as he was dragged from the moped, and Freddie and Sal sped off in lukewarm pursuit of the black Mitsubishi.

* * *

"Don't worry. It's just a precaution. I know how hopped up on caffeine you get, and I don't want you to do anything rash, like throwing yourself from the moving vehicle." Julia circled one of London's wrists with duct tape, then bound it to the other in front of her. She'd already patted her down for weapons and relieved London of her .38. "Do you think Adam will be surprised to see me after all this time? Oh, that's right—he's already seen me, sort of, at the club. Why do you suppose he didn't recognize me? I mean, you would think he'd know the woman he married. Maybe he's losing it, burning out."

"I liked you better when you had the EQ of a kumquat," London told her. "At least you didn't flap your jaws so much. You're giving me a migraine."

"Get in, Lon."

"Do I have a choice?"

She still held the pistol, and London knew from experience that she knew how to use it. Johnson and Wyeth were proof of that, and if she could kill Wyeth, a man she professed to love, she could kill anyone, without a thought, without remorse. "Well, I can eliminate you right here if you'd like that, but then you won't get to see Adam again. You do want to see him again, don't you? You'll want to say good-bye."

"London stared at her. "You really are a piece of work, you know that? Espionage, high treason against the government, murder. Is there nothing you won't do?"

"Nothing I can think of at the moment," she said; then her expression hardened. "Get in, Lon. Who knows? Maybe if you're a good girl, I'll let you go. Maybe I'll let you both go, and I'll just disappear . . . again. It can be done, you know. There are other clinics abroad. For enough cash, they could make me look like you if I wanted."

London sat facing forward in the front passenger's seat of the Humvee, intentionally blocking out the drone of Julia's voice. She was talking, just talking. She had no intentions of letting her go—or Adam, for that matter.

Especially Adam. She blamed him for everything; that much was clear. There was no way she'd let him live now that Wyeth was gone. Adam would pay for Wyeth's death with his life, even though Julia had been the one to pull the trigger.

She wasn't rational.

Julia got in and drove. They were headed out of town. London knew what came next, and her stomach knotted into a fist-sized lump just thinking about it. She would take her somewhere secluded, lure Adam there, and kill them both. London knew far too much to be discounted as a viable threat . . . and Adam . . . If Julia killed her, Adam would never let it go.

Unless she could manage to talk her way out of it. "Why not just drop me off along a deserted road somewhere?" London suggested. She struggled to keep her voice steady, tone level. Hysteria was contagious. If she freaked, Julia might do something drastic. "There are a hundred roads like that around here. It would give you time enough to disappear. You could be on a flight out of the country before anyone even knew."

"It sounds good, Lon, but it won't work. They're *here.* I can't leave either of them."

"They? I don't get it. Your family?"

"Michael and Wyeth," she said. "What kind of mother would leave her son and go away?"

London watched her, checking for chinks in her facade, but she was utterly calm.

"Michael?" London repeated with wonder.

"Our son. Mine and Wyeth's. He's in the car seat."

London glanced over the front seat, her eyes widening as a chill snaked slowly up her spine. The pale form of the doll was strapped carefully in. A doll whose eyes had been glued shut to feign sleep. Creepier still was the huge, gaping hole in the side of its head. It looked as if it had been struck with a blunt object numerous times. London's eyes widened slightly as she turned back around. It was Jesus on the plane all over again, only this time it wouldn't be as easy to gain the upper hand.

The countryside whizzed by the windows. There were more patches of woods, more open fields, fewer houses. London recognized the large white barn on the right side of the blacktop road, with its small herd of white-face cattle. A white-washed two-story house with a double gallery was just visible beyond it—a style that had risen in popularity among mid-Atlantic and Piedmont farm families during the Civil War. This particular house had a rope swing hanging from the oak tree out front—she'd only been to Adam's farm twice, but London remembered it.

A few minutes later, she parked the Humvee in the drive. "How convenient," Julia said, glancing around. "No one's home. Let's get settled in, shall we?"

London opened the door and stepped out, her attention focused on the weapon in Julia's hand. She didn't carry it for self-defense, or even for the intimidation factor. She carried it for its killing power, and because she intended to use it. If Julia were unarmed, London might have a chance against her, despite her size and strength. Against the sheer stopping power of the weapon, she had no chance. But how could she get possession of the weapon? London was no match for her physically. Julia had spent hours in the gym. London's free time had revolved around a carafe of coffee and a meatball sub to stave away starvation while she searched for her brother's killer. The only advantage she had over Adam's ex-wife was a psychological one.

Julia was a psycho.

"What's wrong with him?" London asked, suppressing a shudder as she glanced back over her shoulder at the doll still strapped into the car seat. "Does he always cry like that?"

For an instant, Julia seemed confused, torn between her desire to get London inside and concern for her phantom child. London pushed the point, looking for just the right balance, hoping she didn't go too far and arouse Julia's suspicions. "Maybe something's wrong. I don't know much about babies, but don't they cry when something's wrong?"

Caught somewhere in the dark limbo of her psychosis, Julia turned back to the Humvee, her expression softening as she opened the door that accessed the rear seat. "Michael? Don't cry, darling. Mama's here. Mama's right here." She laid the weapon on the seat and reached in to unfasten the safety harness, but she couldn't get it to open. A few seconds' struggle, and she started to tear at the straps, then at the doll itself. "Don't cry, Michael. For God's sake, don't cry!" She yanked it hard, pulling an arm from a small socket. . . . The battered head fell off and rolled into the drive.

Immersed in her fantasy, she forgot about London, who slammed the vehicle door. The door frame hit the back of Julia's head, knocking her onto the floorboard, pinning her legs until London released it, spun, and ran for the house.

She took the steps two at a time, skidding across the porch, grappling for the doorknob. Her fingers closed over the cool metal. If she could just get inside and lock the doors, it would buy her enough time to locate a weapon . . . some way to slow down her adversary and even the odds.

A few yards to the rear, Julia squeezed off a shot. The bullet ripped through the door frame a few inches from London. Splinters flew, embedding themselves in London's sleeve. She twisted the knob, threw open the door, and Julia caught her. "Bitch!" she screamed, hitting London with an open-handed slap. There was power behind the strike, and it turned London's head completely aside. Her cheek numbed, then started to throb, but she wouldn't let the wariness that filled her show. "Do you think it matters to me when you die? I should kill you now and get it over with!"

London raised her gaze to her adversary's. "You won't do that. Adam isn't here, and that's what this is about, isn't it? You need Adam to be here so that you can inflict as much pain as possible. You want him to suffer, to feel the same sense of confusion and loss you feel. You want him to pay for Michael's death, even though he didn't cause it." Julia was breathing hard, her emotions barely contained in her five-feet-eight-inch, one-hundred-fifty-pound frame. London's voice went soft. She had the woman's attention now. The light of fury in her brown eyes had dulled slightly, replaced by the reflection of the emptiness that devastated her. "Adam didn't cause Michael's death, did he, Julia? And Wyeth would never have injected a pregnant woman with mind-altering drugs, especially not a woman carrying his child. That leaves one person—"

"If he had died in that fall, it would have ended there, but he came back, and he wouldn't let it go!" With each word, her voice rose in volume and pitch until it was little more than a hysterical, fury-filled scream. "He wouldn't let it go! I had to do something. He was going to destroy Wyeth! Adam was going to destroy the man I loved!"

"So you destroyed Wyeth's child instead, is that right? You faked the kidnapping and shot yourself full of drugs, and the baby didn't survive because of it."

She raised her head, drawing herself up even as the pain in her eyes intensified. "Great love requires great sacrifice," she said, her voice a mere watery whisper. "But you've never loved anyone the way I loved Wyeth, so I wouldn't expect you to understand."

"I hope to God I never find out," London said, sickened by Julia's admission.

Then Julia opened the door and pushed London inside.

Adam went from Llewellyn's duplex to the apartment on Water Street. Water Street was on the north side of town. Though it was once a fountain of commerce and industry, many of the businesses located there had closed down during the last recession. For a few years they'd sat neglected and empty before being snatched up by an enterprising young architect and his silent, very wealthy partner and turned into condominiums and high-rent apartment complexes. Julia's place was in the Waterson Building, one of the first to be renovated a decade before. The apartments were high-end, but not as posh or stylish as the latest renovations. Still, Adam thought as he picked the lock to apartment 3B, the place would have cost a hell of a lot more than a government employee in the lower echelon could afford.

"Seems like somebody would keep track of these

things. A government grunt living well beyond her means. Where did the money come from?"

But Pinchot would have covered for her. He had no proof the affair had been ongoing, but he had no proof it had ended, either. It wouldn't have mattered anyway. Pinchot had had a sliver more conscience than Julia. He would have felt responsible for her no matter how difficult she was to manage, no matter how insane her behavior became. Pinchot would have felt responsible for Julia because of Michael.

Pinchot, he had no doubt, had arranged for the operation at a clinic abroad to change her appearance. Pinchot had paid for the surgery, and Pinchot had arranged her clearance. If not for Pinchot's position at the Agency, someone would have caught up to the fact that Cidney Blankenship didn't really exist. Pinchot had been her handler in a profound sense of the word, and the poor bastard had paid with his life. Now Adam had to make sure that London didn't follow in Pinchot's unlucky footsteps.

The apartment was a long shot, and it didn't pay off. No one answered his knock, and when he picked the lock and opened the door, he felt as if he'd stepped into a war zone. The place had been thoroughly trashed. Glass was scattered over the rug in such a way that it appeared to have exploded. The door on an antique china cupboard hung nearly off its hinges, the uppermost screws torn from the wood. A bizarre collection of dolls lay scattered at his feet, each missing a head, a limb, the eyes gouged from plastic sockets. Adam's stomach knotted as he moved to the other rooms, just to be sure she hadn't slit her wrists in the tub.

He reached for the shower curtain, pushing it back, prepared for anything . . . But the tub was empty . . . like the apartment. Then, as he turned to leave, he caught a snail's track of crazy, slanting red lipstick across the mirror, and his soul shriveled.

Adam—she's with me.

Chapter Eighteen

If the house itself had all the charm of a mausoleum, the root cellar was more than a little tomblike—a great place for someone with an aversion to dark, dingy places, home to a dozen or so species of spiders and smelling like damp, moldy earth. Julia held the ancient wooden door open, a door that led directly into the manmade bunker. "You're kidding, right?" London said. "You don't really expect me to go in there."

"Don't worry, Lon. It's only for a little while—until Adam gets here. Then I'll come get you and we'll have a nice chat, just the three of us. Sounds cozy, doesn't it?"

"Look, if it's all the same to you, I'd rather wait out here—" London began; then Julia pushed her into the darkness.

The door slammed, and a trickle of dirt sifted down from overhead, raining on the exposed skin of her face and throat. She tried not to let her imagination run rampant, tried not to think about the wriggling creatures that preferred places like this to living in the light. She knew they were here; she just hoped they weren't hungry.

Lovely. Just lovely. How did she know I have an aversion to being buried alive? Is she intuitive, or just a sadistic freak who hit it lucky as far as the creep factor goes? She took a step and almost fell. The floor was earth as well, and uneven. It felt a little wet and slippery underfoot. Maybe if she could find the door, she could force it open. She lifted her hands, still bound in front of her, and felt for the knob. As she touched cool, painted wood, something scrambled over her skin. London screamed and stumbled back, heart thudding violently in her chest.

Somewhere in the near distance, she heard Julia's laughter. "Don't worry, Lon. It'll all be over soon."

Don't worry.

How the hell could she not worry?

There was no way of knowing what Julia had planned, but she had a pretty good idea that whatever she had in mind for Adam, it would be lethal. If he returned to the farmhouse, he'd be walking into a trap, and there was no way to warn him about what was happening, no way to prevent Julia from ending Adam's life just as she'd ended Wyeth's.

Oh, God, what about Patrick? He'd been deeply affected by Benji's death, and he'd only just started to recover. How would he survive losing her, too? Would he even know what had happened? Or would she be sealed in this dank hole forever, a savory smorgasbord for the rats, mice, and spiders, while that insane bitch Julia got away with destroying her family and went off somewhere to reinvent herself yet again.

The thought really got her steamed. "Oh, no," she said. "It's not going to be that easy. Not this time. There has to be a way out of here, and when I find it she is so gonna pay for all of this."

Ruthlessly pushing aside her fear of what lurked in the lightless recesses of the underground storage area, she forced her mind back to the moment when Julia first opened the door. "Damn it, London, think!" She pictured the gaping dark hole with its shelves, boxes, and bins along the right side. Boxes and bins . . . and several wooden handles protruding from the wooden crate nearest the door. She faced away from the door and moved to the right, stopping when the toe of her right sneaker collided with something long and low and mobile. She dropped to a crouch, extending her bound hands in that direction and groping the air until she found the worn handle of a garden rake. Broken at some time in the past, the handle had a spearlike point. Far too fragile to break through the door, but it would make a versatile weapon and just might help to tilt the odds a fraction in her favor. It wasn't her .38, but it was something.

With thoughts of Benji, Patrick, and Adam running through her head, she sat on her heels in the gloom of the root cellar, anticipating Julia's return.

London had no way of knowing how long she sat there, crouched in the blackness, praying for one chance to disarm her enemy, but the lightless atmosphere of the root cellar intensified. The oppressive chilly silence grew slowly more profound. Just when she feared she would be stuck in the darkness all night, the latch scraped, the door creaked open slowly, and London launched her assault.

Adam had been prepared for anything but a lethal thrust from a broken rake handle, and Llewellyn trying to punch him a new navel. As she lunged, he had just enough presence of mind to move to the right, the splintered wood passing harmlessly along his side and getting tangled in his shirt. Then she was throwing herself into his arms while Honz streaked ever-tightening circles around them, then dashed off in pursuit of a gray squirrel.

Adam held her for a breath, then let her go, peeling the heavy tape from her wrists. "Blimey, Llewellyn, you gave me a scare. Are you all right?"

"It's Cid," she said, her fingers digging into the flesh of his forearms. "She's—"

Before she could finish the thought, Julia's pistol butt came crashing down on Adam's head, and he crumpled at her feet like a sack full of stones.

"Adam?" London dropped to her knees beside him. She touched the back of his head where Julia had hit him, and her hand came away sticky and wet.

"Take his other arm," Julia told her. "We'll get him into the house."

"Why should I?"

"Come on, Lon. Play along. I've got a surprise for you . . . or would you rather I finish him right here? It wouldn't be as interesting, but it would save me a lot of trouble." The pistol's bore kissed the back of his skull, and Julia smiled.

"All right," London said quickly. "I'll do anything you want. Just don't kill him."

"Adam?" Llewellyn's iron-pumping girlfriend peered at him with Julia's eyes, spoke to him with Julia's voice. "Adam? Can you hear me?"

He could hear her, though her voice had an echo, and there was a bright halo above her platinum-blond head. The hanging workbench light. He tried to move, and searing pain shot through his skull. "I'm glad to see you, Adam. It's good to know you've finally let go of the past and are getting on with your life."

Then he remembered . . . not Cid . . . Julia. She'd killed Pinchot and nearly killed Patrick . . . and Llewellyn . . .

He rolled his head and saw her through a haze of red, her hands bound with duct tape and attached to a pipe near the low ceiling. She was standing on her toes to keep from putting too much strain on the fragile pipe, a pipe filled with the scalding water and steam that had provided a tropical environment for Julia's orchids. Her hands were nearly lost in the vapor cloud near the ceiling; her face and red hair streamed water.

The room was like a sauna. It must have been a hundred humid degrees, and the temperature kept climbing.

"The boiler . . . you have to turn it down." The unit was old, and the pressure release valve had often malfunctioned. It hadn't been used in years—not since Julia had abandoned her orchids. If the pressure built beyond a certain level, it could blow, sending enough shrapnel and scalding steam into the room to cook the flesh from their bones.

"Come on, Adam. I thought you might appreciate some steam," Julia said, cocking her head. "You've certainly had enough of it since Lon found you. And now you'll have a little more."

She had Adam's right wrist tied, but not his left. What the hell was she thinking? He came up in one fluid motion, grabbing a fist full of her T-shirt, pulling her down to his level. "You fucking, insane bitch! Turn it down, or you'll blow this whole place into the goddamned Beltway!"

She jammed the pistol into Adam and squeezed off a shot, then wrenched herself away, straightening her shirt with a jerk as he lay there, dazed and bleeding. She didn't even seem to notice. "Do you think you can intimidate me?" she asked shakily.

At first, it felt like the sting of a very large hornet. A solid, stinging sensation that immediately became something much more potent. Searing pain radiated outward, sickening waves of it, running down his arms and shooting out a foot from his fingertips, exploding in his chest. Adam forced air into his lungs, fighting down the nausea that rose in waves with the radiating pain. The weird echo he'd noticed upon first regaining consciousness was growing more pronounced, underscored by the drone of a thousand angry bees.

He glanced down at the wound, a neat round hole a hundredth of an inch from blue spaghettilike tubing. She'd barely missed an artery. Adam gritted his teeth, rolling his gaze up to hers. "He's here in this house, Julia—your son, and Wyeth's. I've heard him crying in the dead of night, when the house is still."

"Liar. You'll say anything to try and push me over the edge."

Adam groaned. Behind him, Llewellyn gasped for breath. She was closer to the steam than he was, more vulnerable to the suffocating heat. "You can hear it for yourself . . . hear the poor lost little boy crying for the mother who killed him."

"You bastard. Do you have any idea how much I hate you?" Julia's eyes were dry as she brought the weapon up, aiming it at the broadest part of Adam's chest.

Somewhere in the haze of pain, Adam heard a woman scream and knew it was Llewellyn. He rose up on one elbow, turning to look just as she cried out—a guttural cry so filled with anger, it barely sounded human. He started to tell her that it was all right, but her gaze was fixed on Julia. Then she leaped off her feet, jerking her arms down at the same moment with all her might. The slim pipe burst as London dropped and scrambled for Adam, and they huddled under the shelter of the worktable ledge as a blast of scalding water and steam hit the other woman in the face and chest.

Julia screamed and kept on screaming. The pistol flew from her fingers as she clawed at her face, the skin sloughing off on her hands.

Tears mingled with Llewellyn's sweat, dripping off

her chin. Adam tried for a deep breath but failed. He couldn't lift his arm to hold her. All he could do was capture her gaze with his, holding it there until he was sure he had her attention. "Go around the other way and turn off the valve, and then call Viagra. Tell him to send a couple of ambulances. Can you do that?"

London moved away to turn off the steam, and as she went for the phone, Adam quietly lost his tenuous hold on consciousness. By the time London made the call and found her way back to Adam, Julia was gone.

Outside the farmhouse, it was gathering dusk. As shadows lengthened, a small motorbike crawled along a country road. One man was pedaling frantically. "Are you sure he came down this road?" Sal asked, winded from miles of exertion. "It seems like we should have been there by now."

"Shut the fuck up and pedal," Freddie shouted, "or I'll leave your fat ass by the side of the road!"

"I'm pedalin' already," Sal told him, "but the polite thing would be to take turns. You know, share and share alike. I think I pulled a hamstring."

Freddie turned to glare at Sal and almost crossed into the path of an oncoming vehicle. The Humvee slowed to a crawl, weaving erratically before righting itself. The apparition stared at them as they went past. Its lips were moving, but only a thin inhuman cry came through the open window.

Freddie cursed, whipping the handle bars a hard right, steering off the road and into a field. The earth was soft, recently plowed; the moped fell, dumping both men onto their asses. Freddie was up and running before Sal turned to look at the apparition stretching a hand toward them that was hideously deformed. "Help me," it whispered, but the running men didn't slow until they reached the tree line, and then the Humvee drove slowly on into the encroaching night.

Freddie collapsed on the soft pine needles. His face had lost its ruddy color, and there was a large dark spot on the front of his wrinkled gray trousers. "Jesus . . ." he said. "Oh, Jesus, what was that?"

"I don't know," Sal said. "I don't know." He collapsed beside Freddie, panting. "Now what do we do? Is the house around here, do you think?"

Freddie looked at Sal long and hard. "Fuck the house," he said suddenly. "And fuck that goddamned orchid. Joey can come after me if he wants. I'm not goin' back there, no way, and I'm not goin' back to Jersey! What about you?"

Sal shook his head. "Me, neither. I've had enough of Joey's abuse. Just because the man lost a few fingers doesn't give him the right to manipulate others."

"For once I agree with you, pal. C'mon. Let's get the hell out of here."

Fat Tuesday
The French Quarter, New Orleans

She'd managed to track down Adam's old landlord, Eddie Whitefish, but Eddie hadn't seen Adam in almost six months. No one had, and London felt like a fool for coming here. For a while that afternoon, she'd wandered the streets of the French Quarter, lingering in Jackson Square to peruse the paintings and sketches lining the black wrought-iron fence, and to listen to the musicians while keeping an eye out for that telltale mouse-colored hound. When it started to rain, she caught the streetcar and rode most of the way along St. Charles Avenue, neglecting her stop, walking back in the rain.

It had taken all her savings and some fast talking to get her hands on the Maltese mansion a second time. When she broke the news of her vacation, Patrick had looked at her as if she'd grown another head. "New Orleans? What the hell's down there except for a lot of drunken New Yorkers? What do you want to go away for anyhow? I got a feeling Adam'll be back soon. What'll I tell him when he gets here and you're not home?"

It had been on the tip of her tongue to say, "Tell him I love him." But she bit back the words, covering her angst with a smile. "He said he needed some alone time, Dad. That was six months ago. I'm not so sure he's coming back."

"Of course he's coming back. De Wulf's a man of his word."

Yes, but the shoulder wound he'd sustained at the farm had cost him. Even with two surgeries and a long course of physical therapy, the use of his right arm wasn't 100 percent . . . and then, there was Julia.

The ambulances and the police car had come screaming to the farm that fateful evening, but the Humvee wasn't found until the next morning, abandoned on a well-traveled road. Burned too badly to avoid notice, Julia should have been found, recognized, hospitalized—if indeed she had survived her devastating injuries.

Viagra had consulted with the local sheriff, organizing search parties that combed the woods and fields, but only a moped lying on its side in a cornfield was found; and the mystery of what happened to Adam's murderous ex-wife remained unsolved.

London was convinced that given a little time, everything would have worked out, if only Adam's restlessness hadn't gotten the better of him. He wouldn't say where he was headed or what he intended to do, and for once, she'd resisted pressing him. She'd even driven him and Honz to the airport, leaving him with a farewell kiss she hoped he wouldn't forget, and the Weimaraner with a pat on the muzzle through the grate of his carrier.

She'd been uncharacteristically patient while she waited, and waited, and waited. Not so much as a phone call had she gotten from him, and just when she was ready to label him a callous, black-hearted prick, the envelope appeared in her mailbox. A plain brown envelope with a one-way ticket to New Orleans International Airport and a string of green plastic beads.

She caught her flight that same afternoon, not hesitating for even a heartbeat. Not that it had solved anything, and now time was running out. She had to be back at work on Monday. Her stay in New Orleans was nearing an end, and she was no closer to locating Adam than she had been the night she stepped off the plane.

Giving in to her mood, London towel-dried her hair, put on a terry-cloth robe, and went upstairs to watch the parade pass from the comfort of the shadowy bedroom. There was nowhere in the world quite like New Orleans, she thought as the bright lights faded, the noise grew distant and muted, and the last of the revelers straggled toward home. "I'm gonna miss this place," London said with a sigh.

She turned from the window, and at the same time something scraped across the roof, raising the fine hair at her nape. Instinctively she stepped back, and a black-clothed figure pulled itself up and onto the roof. London's breath caught as he tapped on the window pane, then slid the window open. "Flash as a rat with a gold tooth is what you are. What? No 'hello, Adam' kiss?"

London laughed as she took his hand, helping him over the sill and into the room. "Hello, Adam," she said softly, unbelting the robe, letting it slip from her shoulders.

He whistled low. "Hold that thought, will you? I'm not exactly alone."

She grabbed up the robe and held it in front of her, but he only reached through the open window, retrieving a pair of linen sacks. One wriggled and whined. "Adam, what on earth?"

"Honz got himself into a bit of a scrape with a lady friend," he said, extracting a gray-brown puppy with floppy ears and the most adorable little face she had ever seen.

London took the bundle, breathing in his puppy scent, kissing the top of his head. "What about Honz?"

"Parental leave. He'll come home to Virginia at the end of the month." London laughed and kissed his lips. "Don't distract me, darling. There's something else." He reached into the second sack and produced a pure gold planter with a straggling plant and a perfect black velvet bloom. "The Lady, for my lady. Since it's how we started out, I thought it only fitting."

"Adam De Wulf! Tell me you didn't!"

"My last hurrah."

"Did you say Virginia a moment ago?"

Framing her face with his gloved hands, he took her to the one place she longed to go. "I'm hanging up my gloves, Llewellyn."

"Do you mean it?"

"You bet your life I mean it. How do you feel about sharing your bed with an aging spook who just got his old job back?"

London just smiled, holding the robe out, letting it fall.